First co...
Then ...

Before her stood a building surrounded by unbelievable disarray. It was three stories in height and constructed of old, gray brick . . . A dozen steps led to the huge front door, but they were so covered with weeds and dead vegetation she could barely find a suitable path on which to walk.

Sighing and lifting her skirts, she started climbing them, and although she stepped carefully, by the time she reached the top her satin wedding slippers were covered with grass and mud.

Brent followed her . . . He looked amazingly different from their initial meeting, and his attractiveness caught her a little off guard . . . And now, gazing at the hardness of his jaw in contrast with the smoothness of his skin sent a shiver through her body. She could feel the warmth of his large, muscular form penetrating her own, and the knowledge that he would be this close to her for an uncertain period of time truly disturbed her. He was the most masculine nobleman she had ever seen in her life . . .

My Darling Caroline

ADELE ASHWORTH

JOVE BOOKS, NEW YORK

MY DARLING CAROLINE

A Jove Book / published by arrangement with
the author

PRINTING HISTORY
Jove edition / October 1998

All rights reserved.
Copyright © 1998 by Adele Budnick.
This book may not be reproduced in whole
or in part, by mimeograph or any other means,
without permission. For information address:
The Berkley Publishing Group, a member of Penguin Putnam Inc.,
375 Hudson Street, New York, New York 10014.

The Penguin Putnam Inc. World Wide Web site address is
http://www.penguinputnam.com

ISBN: 0-515-12369-2

A JOVE BOOK®
Jove Books are published by The Berkley Publishing Group,
a member of Penguin Putnam Inc.,
375 Hudson Street, New York, New York 10014.
JOVE and the "J" design are trademarks
belonging to Jove Publications, Inc.

PRINTED IN THE UNITED STATES OF AMERICA

10 9 8 7 6 5 4 3 2 1

A sincere thanks to Marilyn Price-Larson, Ph.D.,
for her informal critique and superior
knowledge of all things English.

My Darling Caroline

One

England, 1815

Caroline Grayson gently reached in and, carefully avoiding thorns, snipped the stem from the rosebush, pulling the bud toward her with nimble fingers to have a closer look. She eyed it with the detachment of a scientist, the expertise of a scholarly botanist, turning the rose slowly in her hands, taking careful note of its structure, its delicate beauty.

It was magnificent, the loveliest and healthiest plant she'd bred so far. It would take time to find a name dignified and unique enough for such a creation, though. She needed something perfect for such a perfect rose.

The sudden rustle of skirts made her turn. Stephanie, her youngest sister, was all but running toward her through the garden, the early-morning sun playing shiny cords of light through the richness of her blond hair and off the blue silkiness of her gown.

"Come and look at this one, Stephanie," she called out, smiling with complete satisfaction, her attention again focused on her rose.

"Caroline," Stephanie said, gasping as she approached, "you'll never guess—"

"Slow down," Caroline admonished as her sister grabbed her sleeve.

Stephanie took two deep breaths and wiped stray hair from her cheeks, stained pink from the cool morning air, her eyes wide and glowing with apparently delicious news.

"The Earl of Weymerth"—she gulped for air—"is here, and Father wants you to meet him."

Caroline, however, was much more concerned with the lovely creation resting firmly between her forefinger and thumb. "Do you like it?"

Stephanie dropped her gaze to the flower and gave a squeal of delight. "Oh, this one's lovely! Two colors of purple."

Caroline grinned pridefully, placing the rose in her sister's outstretched hand. "More a lavender fading into purple, really. Now explain yourself. Who is here?"

Stephanie's eyes danced in merriment. "The Earl of Weymerth," she replied very slowly.

Caroline looked at her blankly, prompting Stephanie to sigh with exasperation. "Really, Caroline! Brent Ravenscroft, the Earl of Weymerth? Society's talked about him for years—some sort of family scandal I think, though nothing that really damaged him socially. For a time he was courting Pauline Sinclair. You know, of the Sinclairs of Harpers Row. Then she dumped him on his arse—"

"Stephanie!"

"—and everybody speculated that he was mean, or foul-tempered and ugly, and that's why she didn't want him." She dropped her voice to a mischievous whisper. "But I just got an excellent look at him, and he's not ugly at all."

Caroline smiled lightly as she dropped her clippers to the soft earth, wiping her sleeve over her perspiring forehead. In many ways Stephanie, although only seventeen, was a total innocent, for she had always felt that any

vice a man might have could be ignored if he were attractive. Evidently she thought Lord Weymerth now
above reproach.

"I don't think you should be taking such an interest,
Steph," she chided as she took the lavender rose out of
her sister's fingers, starting her way up the stone path
toward the house. "You're betrothed, if you'll remember."

Stephanie fell into step behind her. "I wasn't considering him for me, Caroline. I was considering him for
you."

"That's ridiculous," she returned through a laugh.

Stephanie groaned softly. "There are other things to
consider in this great big world besides plants and . . .
Sir Alfred Markham—"

"*Albert* Markham," she corrected.

Stephanie said no more until they neared the house.
Then smugly she disclosed, "I think Father is considering Lord Weymerth for you as well."

Without pause, Caroline opened the kitchen door and
walked into the house, placing her rose on the counter
to free her hands for washing. The thought of her marrying anyone was just so incredibly unbelievable it
wasn't even worth discussing. "I don't know where you
get these ideas—"

"From Father's mouth," Stephanie cut in sarcastically. "I heard him say he's giving you to the earl along
with some things he's selling him."

Caroline reached for a towel, gazing at her sister speculatively, quick to note the cunning grin playing across
her lips, the sparkle in her pale blue eyes. That disturbed
her a little, as Stephanie was the only living soul who
knew of her plans to leave England and study botany in
America, and she had more than once expressed her desire to have her older sister remain close to home.

Still skeptical, Caroline brushed a stray curl from her
cheek. "I'll talk to him."

"I'd bathe first," Stephanie piped up in a melodious,
mischief-filled voice.

Ignoring the comment, Caroline picked up her rosebud and headed toward the study. Brimming with confidence, she approached the closed door, but before she could knock she heard tense, male voices. Suddenly oblivious to her position, she instinctively leaned closer to listen to the argument between the two pompous oafs on the other side.

"I'll pay you whatever you're asking, but I refuse to marry for what rightfully belongs to me," she heard a stranger's voice say in a deep, husky timbre. "My property was sold unfairly, probably illegally."

"Everything was purchased legally, Weymerth, and I can prove it."

The voices lowered, and after a moment of listening to words too muffled to understand, she heard them again, this time louder in tone but softer in urgency as the man tried to reason with her father.

"This has nothing to do with you, Sytheford, but if I ever decide to marry, I'd rather she be someone of my choosing, not a daughter of yours I've never met."

"Caroline will give you a smart, sturdy son—"

"That is not the issue here!"

"A man in your position—"

"Listen to me well," she heard the earl quickly counter in a dangerously subdued voice. "I do not want to wed your daughter. I don't care how many other worthy noblemen have asked for her hand. I don't care that she is the loveliest creature this side of the Continent, that she has hair the color of sunshine or eyes the color of amethysts. I care only for my property, and by God, you're going to return it to me fairly. This conversation is finished."

A long, deadly silence ensued, then she heard her father's deep growl fill the air. "Perhaps you should take a look at this."

After precisely fifteen seconds the earl yelled, "Oh, Christ!" A fist slammed hard against the desk.

Her father said smugly, "It's a bill of sale. Come Monday, they're gone."

"You can't do this—"

"I will unless you marry my daughter."

Then . . . nothing. Silence.

Caroline's heart started pounding. For several seconds she couldn't breathe as the realization hit her like a brick in the face.

This could not be happening. She had plans, she had dreams, she had . . . thought her father understood.

Horrified and disoriented, Caroline slumped her shoulders and dragged her body across the hall and into the morning room. Sunlight streamed in through beveled glass to create a peaceful feeling in the sparsely decorated room, but it did nothing for her ever-increasing sensation of panic. She sat heavily on the yellow sofa and stared into the cold fireplace, forcing herself to take deep breaths.

She felt shocked. Enraged. Even scared. She swallowed hard to fight back tears, for if nothing else, she needed to keep her wits intact and think things through before her father came out of his study to inform her that he'd chosen her a husband.

The thought made her shiver with revulsion. In her heart Caroline knew her father's love for her was genuine, deeply felt, but she also knew that out of the five daughters he had sired, she was the disappointment.

She was the middle child and so very different from the others. Her sisters were, every one, blessed with long, graceful figures, light blond hair, light blue eyes that were so like her mother's, lovely faces, and perfect marriages. Even Stephanie was just recently betrothed to the Viscount Jameson after only one season. To their credit, they made her father quite proud, as they all fit the image of gently bred women, settling down nicely in polite society.

But Caroline took after her father with her small form and dark brown hair and eyes. Plain and unbecoming, she had heard some say. Over the years, it had grown to matter less and less to her, though, because she had found her destiny. She knew what truly mattered in her life.

She was smart, exceedingly bright in the areas of mathematics and botany. At the age of four she could calculate numbers, multiplying them two, three, even four times simply with her head, baffling most everyone who knew her, especially because she was female. Females had no business understanding mathematics, even if it came to them naturally, or so she'd often been told.

Caroline, however, without being formally taught, possessed such unspeakable knowledge. By age nine, she could calculate not only numbers, but the age and growth of each plant in her mother's garden. She would spend hours with the flowers and greenery, estimating growth patterns, determining ages and variations of color and size with such precision that before she had even reached her twelfth birthday, most people, including her loved ones, assumed her to be the strangest girl in England.

At that age she didn't care what others thought. Her family loved her despite their inability to understand her. Not even her father could keep up with her computations and explanations, and he was a man. But what infuriated her was the fact that had she been fortunate enough to be born a boy, she would have been called gifted and allowed to study in the finest institutions and with the finest instructors in the world. As a girl, she was termed odd and secluded in her home until her father, Charles Grayson, fifth Baron Sytheford, could do something with her, which for years had been a problem without an answer as she was now nearly twenty-six years of age.

For as long as she could remember, Caroline had wanted to study botanical science with Sir Albert Markham at Oxford University, but trying to gain acceptance as a scholar had been the most difficult thing she'd ever attempted in her life. She'd known from an early age that being female was a hindrance, but she'd never expected Sir Albert, the greatest man she had ever read, had ever studied, to deny her entrance to Oxford's Society of Botany strictly because she was female. Only two years ago she'd sent him a comprehensive letter detailing her work, her complete analysis of breeding techniques to create the precious lavender rose, and still he'd rejected her, his condescending letter of response implying she should stay home, marry, and grow flowers for her husband and neighbors to admire.

But from that crushing blow she learned her greatest life lesson—being female got you nothing in the scientific world, but being male gave you a chance. And she would succeed as a scientist, at Columbia University in New York, because she'd been accepted to study there by one of the best, Professor Walter Jenson. She'd been accepted to study there because this time, when sending her scientific data, computations, and information regarding herself and her experience as a self-taught botanist, she'd wisely presented herself as a man, Mr. C. S. Grayson. Being a woman would never stop her again.

Or so it seemed until now.

Everyone expected her to die a spinster, and that was exactly how she wanted it. She didn't have time for an overbearing husband. She had her work, her plants and flowers, her dreams of study. Now it appeared they would all be tossed aside, for her father had suddenly, without warning, found her a husband in the Earl of Weymerth. A husband to whom he could, and would, gladly bequeath his most unusual daughter.

Caroline slowly stood and walked with wooden legs to the window, crossing her arms over her chest as she stared at the garden where her dreams lay, her flowers bloomed into pinpoints of brightness and brilliant color in the cool, sunny morning. Until only fifteen minutes ago, her world had been joyous, her life rich with beauty. Now her choices, her desires, were melting away like the wax of a burning candle.

She had all but finalized her plans of travel to America, although she had yet to tell her father of them. She still wasn't completely prepared, having notebooks and documents to update and organize, her emeralds to sell for money to book passage. Until today, her two biggest problems had been finding lodging once she arrived in New York, and persuading Professor Jenson to allow her to study with him and his colleagues when he discovered she was a woman. Because of these and other considerations, she hadn't had the time or energy to deal with her father. Now she would have to deal with him on the issue of marriage, of all the blessed things.

Caroline knew she had to think quickly. Now more than ever she would need to call upon her superior intellect if she expected to get herself out of this mess, and if she considered her actions thoroughly, perhaps she could turn the situation around to her advantage.

First of all, Lord Weymerth was a gentleman. She could assume he would see logic since he, no doubt, didn't want to marry her either. He had certainly said as much.

Second, it was already July. She wasn't ready to pack her bags, in more ways than one, and she still lacked the courage to talk to her father, to sully his impeccable reputation by running off unwed and unchaperoned to study a man's science in another country. She'd written Professor Jenson just last week to inform him she would be arriving no sooner than January, so she still had several months to plan, to think, to decide how to handle such a fragile situation.

She looked to the delicate rose still clasped in her hand, twirling it slowly between her finger and thumb. It was so awfully fine, so marvelously beautiful, soft and silky to the touch. What a joy it would be to create such flowers as these and be recognized for the talent, the skill.

She raised her eyes to look back out the window, sighing as she lowered her forehead to the glass.

Disgracing her father was truly what plagued her. She loved him deeply for the caring he'd always shown her and her sisters. Where any other father would have washed his hands of his girls and tossed them to servants and governesses to raise, hers was always there for them—listening, concerned, advising them and fulfilling their individual needs with great love—and he had taken every effort to indulge them with great affection, especially since they were motherless, as theirs had died of fever not twelve years before.

But this was a turn she didn't understand. The Baron Sytheford was cunning, and he usually planned fully and thought with great care before acting. This sudden idea of marriage seemed rash, and to her knowledge, her father had never been rash in his life.

So what was she supposed to do now? Marry Weymerth? And why him of all the eligible gentlemen in society?

Caroline's heart suddenly ached with longing of desires now seemingly more out of reach than ever. Damn, but men stunk to heaven when they used their larger muscles and tiny, narrow minds to control the smaller sex. She wanted nothing more than to overcome that convention. But perhaps the idea was indeed as futile and stupid as her sisters told her from time to time. Women were put on this earth to marry and allow their husbands the generous use of their bodies for the sole purposes of creating heirs and gratifying male sexual needs—unconditionally. At that moment, she despised them all.

She stared out to her huge bed of roses, her sweet-smelling daffodils, her tulips that she prized because they were so difficult to grow and even more difficult to breed. God in heaven, what should she do now? It all seemed so dismal, so hopeless . . .

Then suddenly, as with any sharp intellect, a small, very tiny image began to emerge from the deepest recesses of her mind. Slowly it began to take shape, to build, and without warning it grew so that even the color before her faded from the dazzle of brilliance filling her senses.

If she married him . . .

Caroline grinned and jumped back from the window to look down at her hands, now shaking with a sudden burst of energy. What if she married him? She didn't want a husband, but so what! If she married the earl, she would be fulfilling her father's wish and then she could, after that time, put all of her talents and intelligence to good use by creating a way of leaving the man to study her science. He wouldn't want her anyway, for she had all but concluded he was being coerced into taking her as a wife as well, and she certainly didn't have anything wifely to offer him. She was an unbecoming, set-in-her-ways spinster.

But if he was smart, and she hoped to God he was, perhaps she could strike a deal with him, and they could both go their separate ways as did many married couples. If the marriage were annulled in say . . . four months, she would be able to leave her husband to a life of his own, catch a ship to New York, and be free from society's demanding, irritating mores to do as she wanted—needed—to do.

This was the way out. And it was falling into her lap.

Caroline fairly twirled around in glee over her genius. Then, suddenly, she heard shouting again from the study, then scuffling, then her father's chair being pushed across the wooden floor, then shouting again.

She rolled her eyes. Idiot men.

"Caroline!" her father roared seconds later.

She tried to hide her triumphant smile as she replied smoothly, "In here, Father."

He walked briskly into the morning room, seemingly surprised that she was only across the hall; then his eyes grew angry as he looked her up and down.

"Are you never clean, girl?"

Sighing, she noticed the upturned collar and wrinkles on his usually pristine shirt, his mussed hair, the twitch in his cheek as it made the curls in his gray-brown side whiskers flair. Obviously he and the earl had exchanged more than words.

Men. Pompous fools.

Lifting her rosebud to his view, she returned lightly,

"I've been breeding African lilies and pruning roses—"

"Yes, yes, yes," he cut in impatiently. "The Earl of Weymerth . . ."

Suddenly he seemed lost. Drawing a deep breath, either from nervousness or as some sort of stall tactic, he finally finished by adding nothing more than, "The earl wants a word with you."

Caroline placed her hands on her hips and glared at him. "You want me to marry him, don't you?"

He was plainly taken aback by her keen perception, but he said nothing, giving her a look of what she considered to be complete guilt coupled with controlled fury.

"Why, Father?" she quietly asked.

Sytheford tried but truthfully failed in composing himself, standing erect as a statue and folding his hands behind his back. "You need someone to care for your needs, since I won't be around forever, and you need a husband to give you children—"

"I don't particularly want children. You know that," she interjected fiercely.

He ignored her outburst. "Lord Weymerth is a strong, decent man who would give his life for king and country—"

"I'm sure the earl is a fine and noble subject—"

"And he will no doubt provide for you. But most importantly"—he took another deep breath and exhaled loudly—"I won't allow you to go against my wishes, Caroline."

After several strained seconds, she whispered, "I won't go against your wishes."

"You will marry him or—"

"I will marry him."

He gaped at her with apparent disbelief, then his eyes narrowed to tiny slits. "If you think to undermine—"

"I agree to the marriage, Father."

For the first time in his life, Charles Grayson looked as if he would faint. His skin became pasty white, and his expansive forehead beaded immediately with perspiration.

"I want you to know, Caroline," he croaked out, tapping his cuff against his cheek, "that I've done this for your future. I want nothing more than your happiness."

Caroline slowly moved toward him. She'd never before seen her father so . . . disoriented, and the picture he presented unnerved her a little.

"Why do you want this union, Father?" she slowly asked. "Have you something to gain from it?"

He instantly became guarded. "It's best for you." Turning to the door, and with one last glance in her direction, he murmured, "The earl is waiting for you in my study. Don't disappoint me, Caroline."

Before she could summon a reply, he strode into the hall and disappeared from view.

Caroline could have dealt with his threats, his coldness or anger, but never in her life could she have dealt with disappointing him more than she already had. Fighting tears, she looked to the rose in her hand, the only piece of joy in her miserable life. This was God's creation. This small, delicate marvel of life was hers to manipulate into a bounty of beauty. It calmed her to know that she had been given such a gift, and she refused to let anything or anybody take it from her. Ever.

With biting determination, she turned, lifted her chin defiantly, and walked across the hall. It appeared her future husband wanted to meet her alone, and that was fine with her. She prided herself on being independent and self-assured, and she knew that if nothing else, she would be able to handle the man with her superior intelligence. That thought in mind, she put her hand on the knob and marched into her father's study.

She was surprised to find the earl staring out a window rather than watching for her, and although he had to have heard her enter, he didn't turn but stayed instead with his back to her, legs spread apart, hands on hips as he regarded the grassy meadow outside with apparent interest.

She waited for him to speak first, knowing that the man was probably trying to decide how he should gently ask her to marry him without prior introduction. Then he cut into her thoughts of growing annoyance with a frigid baritone voice.

"I'll assume you're a virgin?"

Caroline was so completely caught off guard by his bold, harsh words, that for the first time in her adult life she didn't know how to respond. Cheeks flushing, she mumbled, "I beg your pardon?"

"You heard me," he replied evenly, still looking out the window.

His audacity sparked her anger. Closing her arms over her chest and gathering her wits she returned boldly, "I heard you, Lord Weymerth. I was simply unsure whether you were asking a question or posing a statement."

Slowly, he turned to look at her. She kept her eyes locked on his features with complete determination, noticing first his hollow cheeks, his almost haunted expression. His eyes were hazel but more green than brown, his jaw hard and square, and his hair a very dark blond and longer than the current fashion as it curled behind his ears to fall to his collar. He wore dark riding breeches and a light cotton shirt, opened in front just enough to indecently expose a scattering of curls on his broad chest, and he looked somehow as if he'd been riding for days. His attire and appearance were most unbecoming and far too casual for a gentleman caller, especially one calling at such an unseemly hour. No manners, apparently.

He was tall, probably six feet, and far too slender, although really not at all bad to look at, as Stephanie had so bluntly stated. With a little added weight and proper clothing, he would probably be quite handsome in a rather unconventional way. Now he simply appeared tired and just as wary as she.

His gaze slowly, inappropriately, traveled down, then up the length of her body, until his eyes met hers once again, his expression completely unreadable. "I wasn't expecting someone quite so old."

Never in her life had Caroline been treated so by a man gently bred, and the strangeness of his manner almost startled her. Almost. With a deep exhalation, she held his gaze and retorted sarcastically, "I wasn't expecting someone quite so skinny."

She noticed the immediate sign of anger as his jaw tightened considerably, although her eyes never wavered from his. Then his mouth abruptly changed to a knowing smirk. "Your father said you have a saucy tongue."

"And did my father also say I have a life of my own and no wish to be married?"

His smile vanished. "That's irrelevant—"

"Irrelevant to whom?"

He regarded her for a moment, then carried on as if her words were completely insignificant.

"Banns will be posted tomorrow, and we'll be married in three weeks' time. I would, of course, prefer you to be a virgin. Since I have no choice in the matter, I will take you ruined, with the condition that any child you're now carrying be disposed of properly at its birth."

Caroline could not believe her ears and was suddenly filled with outrage. Clenching her fists tightly at her sides, she slowly began to move toward him. "Shall I hang the poor child by his toenails and leave him for the wolves to maul, perhaps?"

That truly seemed to startle him. "You know that's not what I meant," he responded quietly, defensively.

"Then maybe," she continued with absolute intolerance, "if I'm not requesting too much, you'll ask me to marry you in a gentlemanly fashion instead of coining phrases such as 'I'll assume you're a virgin,' and 'I'll take you ruined with conditions.' "

His cheek twitched, his lids narrowed, but he didn't budge or move his gaze from her face.

"I haven't the vaguest idea of how to fill a scatter-brained female with words of sweetness, so let me say only this, Miss Grayson." His voice was low, hard. "I despise the notion of marriage to someone about whom I know nothing. I have very specific situations in my life that require my full concentration, and I don't need that concentration interrupted by a weeping female clinging to my arm and begging for attention. I cannot afford trinkets, or fancy clothing, or endless parties. I cannot afford imported Spanish tapestries, or Bavarian chocolates—"

"I don't need chocolates," she cut in defensively.

He took a step toward her, and she instinctively took one back.

Suddenly his face lost all expression as he once again studied her appearance. "Actually, I'm rather surprised you're not jumping at this opportunity, Miss Grayson. I'm sure you'll not be getting any other offers."

She was so shocked by his manner that she simply gaped at him, finding it unbelievable that a nobleman would speak to a lady the way he had. Usually men at least pretended to find her charming, although truthfully she saw almost no men at all except those married to her sisters.

But after a moment's hesitation on her part, her eyes still locked with his, she decided he was simply another idiot man who undoubtedly thought himself smarter than she. She would eventually prove him incorrect in his assumptions, and that thought alone made her smile to herself.

Sighing heavily, anger subsiding, she dropped her gaze and abruptly turned her back to him, moving to sit in a large leather chair across from the desk. She leaned her head back against the soft cushion, placed her rose in her lap (hadn't she been going to put it in water about three years ago?), and closed her eyes.

"What's that?" he asked seconds later.

She peeked out cautiously through lowered lashes, noticing proudly that he had placed his curious gaze on her flower. She smiled in satisfaction and raised the rose to study it in front of her face.

"This, my lord, is a five-parted, usually fragrant flower, characteristically having alternate compound leaves and prickly stems. In Latin it's called a *rosa*, in Greek it's akin to *rhodon,* and in English—"

"A rose . . . by any other name?"

She found his mocking tone abrasive and demeaning. Since he would no doubt be utterly confused by the complexities of botany and plant breeding, she instead gave him what she hoped was a glare to remember and tried to change the subject.

"May I ask why you're willing to marry me if you believe I'm ruined?"

He was quiet for a moment, then expelled a long breath and slowly walked toward her, all thoughts of the flower in her hand apparently forgotten.

"I learned only two days ago that your father purchased some of my property and I want it back, whatever the cost," he replied arrogantly as he sat in the chair across from hers. "It now looks as if I'll have to marry you to get it, ruined or chaste."

Trying her best not to be shocked by the distaste in his words, Caroline finally wanted to give sauce to the goose. The man was unbelievable. "Do all the ladies find you as charming as I do, Weymerth?"

He had the good graces to at least look surprised.

"You find me charming, Miss Grayson? I wasn't trying to be charming."

She stifled a laugh. For a second she thought he might be teasing her. Then, before she could remark on his ridiculous words, he cocked his head and looked at her with the first hint of actual interest.

"I'd never met your father before today, but I have heard of him and his most talked-about daughters. Frankly, I expected you to be blond."

She stared into his eyes, thinking, quite certain she'd never heard of him. He couldn't be that well known among the *ton* either. Her sisters would have mentioned him if he were, since he was of marriageable age and undeniably attractive. Obviously the man had little money or was indeed foul-tempered, else more ladies than she could name would be eagerly begging for his attentions. No wonder he'd agreed to marry her. He needed her dowry, which happened to include his former possessions. Quite convenient, actually.

Understanding the situation at last, she smiled and asked rather lightly, "Does it matter that my hair is not the color of sunshine and my eyes not the color of amethysts, my lord?"

He almost laughed. She could see it in the dark greenness of his eyes. Then he seemed to catch himself.

"Do you make a habit of sticking your pert little nose into the conversations of others, Caroline?"

She dropped her gaze to her rose, suddenly unnerved by the smooth, deep, almost intimate way her given name quite naturally rolled off his tongue.

Forcing herself to be bold, she retorted, "I truly don't think I was sticking my pert little nose into a conversation undoubtedly heard at the Fairfield estate six miles away."

"Touché, little one," he all but drawled.

She looked at him again. He was watching her closely, sort of . . . amused, she guessed, which in turn made her feel even more uncomfortable, for the man wasn't three feet from her. Close enough to touch. She stopped herself. He needed a shave—or perhaps just a blade to his neck.

"To answer your question," he confessed blandly, straightening, once again reserved, "what matters to me is that I get my property, which was wrongfully sold to your father, back into my possession. If I have to marry to do that, then so be it. Your father strikes a very steep bargain, Miss Grayson, but if you must know, I care more than you can imagine about my home and belongings, and absolutely nothing about the color of your hair."

He was just so utterly blunt. Caroline had never met a man like him, for most gentlemen of quality liked to caress a lady with flowery words aimed at seducing. This man was simply unusual, or he found her so unbearably unattractive that he refused to speak with even a semblance of charm. She needed to remember that she really didn't care. She had a life of her own, with or without a husband.

Caroline gazed at the man indifferently. "Then since we are both being forced into this, I have only one request from you, my lord."

His lips twitched. "And what might that be?"

The way he spoke to her, watched her, made her nervousness grow to the point where she found herself lowering her lashes to look to her lap. "I work with plants and would like to continue—"

"Many ladies garden," he cut in impatiently, standing abruptly, his manner and voice, without provocation, becoming cold and severe. "And from the look of that wilted thing in your hand, I certainly appreciate your need of practice if you intend to make gardening a pastime. You'll never impress anyone with a rose so badly grown it comes out two shades of purple."

"It's lavender *fading* to purple," she seethed. "I did this on purpose—"

"In any case," he continued, ignoring her indignation as he reached for his overcoat, "I really don't care what you do with your spare time, although I am expecting you to comply with your wifely duties. Both my house and body demand a woman's touch immediately, and after you've seen to those needs, you may do as you like. I'm sure at your age, virgin or not, you understand my meaning."

She looked at him in astonishment, eyes wide with disbelief, cheeks flaming from his sheer boldness. The man was despicably rude and indecent, and if it weren't for the fact that he was her passage to Columbia University, she would slap the earl's face, turn her back on him, and walk out of his life with good riddance. She couldn't, however, and that knowledge made her nearly shake with fury as she watched him turn and walk swiftly to the door. Once again, as with all things in a lady's life, the men won.

Finding nothing better to say, and with every intent to shock him, she blurted, "I'll have you know that I am not a virgin."

He turned to look at her again, and once more his eyes slowly traveled down, then up her body and back to her face. After a moment he whispered thickly, "After meeting you, Caroline, I really don't care."

That statement made, he turned and walked out of the room, leaving her to stare at his departing back in pure shock while she slowly, without awareness, crushed her beautiful rose to a pulp in the palm of her hand.

For the first time in his life, Brent Ravenscroft, ninth Earl of Weymerth, felt completely and craftily defeated. Only five days ago he'd returned home from war, after months of living hell, expecting to be welcomed by waiting servants, to eat platters full of delectable foods, to take his horses for long rides of peaceful enjoyment over his land, to sleep again in his large, plush bed.

Instead, he'd found the shock of his life. His treasured home, Miramont, had been utterly neglected to the point of ruin, its interior possessions sold so that his house was nothing but a hollow shell, his servants gone, the stables in shambles. But the most devastating of all was the discovery that his prized beauties, his cherished Arabians, had been peddled off like swine to Charles Grayson, the cunning Baron Sytheford, who would actually force a marriage to his brassy, spinster daughter for their return.

He would kill Reggie for that, assuming that his cousin hadn't already fled the country.

Brent mounted the only horse he now owned and began the long ride back to what remained of Miramont. He was anxious and exhausted, and the sky was turning gray. It would be raining before he arrived—pouring fiercely, with his luck. The perfect weather to fit his mood.

With Napoleon's most recent threat in Europe, Brent had quickly left for France, placing his home in the care of his cousin Reginald Kent. He knew he'd be gone only a few months, and all he'd wanted was a man to look after the property while he was off fighting for his beloved country. Obviously he'd made a grave error in his judgment of character. Reggie was lazy and impulsive and had enormous debts, which were now probably paid in full with the money he'd received for the horses alone.

God, he'd sold even his *horses*.

It seemed every time Brent turned around, something he cherished was gone from him. He understood how it felt to be trapped behind enemy lines, to be so near death and to have to deal instead with the numbness of living and the agony of loss, and he truly didn't think he could take much more. Now, after waking this morning with nothing to consider but putting the devastation behind him and beginning his life again, he faced the challenge of marriage to Miss Caroline Grayson.

Life was one long journey of unfairness, and suddenly he had the irresistible urge to choke that journey out of Charles Grayson. The man was clever, and naturally he would have to be, with five girls. But this was a means to an end Brent couldn't understand. Why would he want to rid himself of his spinster daughter? She couldn't be that much trouble, for she was rather ordinary in looks and manner, except, of course, for her impudent mouth.

On a personal level, Brent found women fairly unimportant to him except during those rare occasions when he found himself fortunate enough to be bedding one. Like all intelligent men of his day and generation, he didn't trust the lot of them, from the lowly woman of the street to the gently bred lady of society. Not due to the usual reason, the painful rejection of a past love, but because he clearly and intimately understood the female mode of thinking, the female mind, through keen perception, careful evaluation, and years of experience.

He'd weathered decades of vanity, selfishness, coldness, and deceit from the women in his life, and had risen above it.

But Caroline was different, and that bothered him. She was unusual and far too assertive for a lady of quality. At first glance he'd thought her plain, even severe in looks, with dark-brown hair pulled tightly from her face, and desperate for a bath, as she'd been nearly covered in dirt. But after looking through some of the muck, he'd come to realize that she was probably attractive enough when she was clean. In fact, to his complete annoyance, the moment she started speaking in that husky, sexy voice of hers, his body had sprung to life, and he couldn't remember the last time that had happened. It was then that he realized, virgin or not, he wanted her in his bed, for although he hadn't thought of it in ages, he suddenly, desperately, needed to lose himself inside of a woman.

And she would do nicely. He hadn't been able to see much of her figure in the simple gray muslin gown she'd worn, but her breasts appeared to be of adequate size, and she was small, with extremely delicate features. With her hair flowing loosely about her shoulders, she would probably very nearly pass for pretty.

Above everything else, however, was the fact that she would be his wife, and providing for him sexually would be her duty. And with Caroline taking care of his physical needs, he could start to forget the war, restore his home to its former magnificence, and move on with his life, as he was in desperate want of doing. Other than that, he would consent to her doing as she pleased, for she truly meant nothing more to him than the means to retrieve his cherished horses. In that regard, he supposed she was now technically purchased, and in three weeks' time she would become his property.

Brent nearly laughed as he realized he'd much rather own Bonaparte's horse. It was probably smarter and definitely better looking.

Two

Caroline's wedding to the Earl of Weymerth, during one of the wettest, coldest days so far that summer, proved to be an unspectacular, incredibly dreary event for all of them, especially for her. But now, only two hours later, as she stepped from his coach into a sprinkling twilight rain, facing Miramont, her new home on the Weymerth estate, Caroline knew she was living a nightmare.

Before her stood a massive building surrounded by unbelievable disarray. It was three stories in height and constructed out of old, gray brick. Trees had been planted around the house to frame the approach from the road, but there were no flowers or plants, much less landscaping. A dozen stone steps led to the huge front door, but they were so covered with weeds and dead vegetation she could barely find a suitable path on which to walk.

Sighing and lifting her skirts, she started climbing them, and although she stepped carefully, by the time she reached the top her satin wedding slippers were covered with grass and mud.

Brent followed her, speaking hesitantly. "I've been working on the stables and the inside for the last three weeks so you wouldn't be so completely shocked when you arrived, Caroline. I'll soon begin out here.''

She smiled reassuringly. "I'm sure it's fine." Then she walked through the tall oaken door and knew she had never made a more erroneous statement in her life. The inside was much worse—stripped bare, deserted, and smelling as if it hadn't been cleaned in centuries.

Caroline looked around, feeling awkward and unsure in only her husband's presence. He must have noticed it, for he relaxed a little as he moved to stand beside her.

"I'll walk you around so you'll become more comfortable with your surroundings," he said quietly. "Then we'll talk."

She nodded and glanced up to his face. Wisps of dark blond hair curled around his ears, lightly touching his collar, and his mouth, soft and full, slowly turned up in a smile.

He looked amazingly different from their initial meeting, and his attractiveness caught her a little off guard. His hair had been trimmed, his skin had become bronzed from days in the sun, and his body had filled out as he'd apparently decided to eat.

He'd surprised her, too, when he appeared at their wedding dressed in navy superfine. She was almost afraid he would be casually clothed, bored to tears, for she certainly wasn't ignorant of her husband's regard for her and their marriage. She hadn't seen the earl since the day they'd met, as he was apparently more concerned with returning his home to its former magnificence than visiting his betrothed, and truthfully, she couldn't have cared any less. She knew he'd been away for several months, and his home had been neglected, so spending his free time restoring Miramont gave him an excellent excuse to stay away, she supposed.

But to his credit, he had been a gentleman throughout their wedding ceremony, and for that she was relieved. With her sisters all present, she had been certain he would spend the entire time gawking at them, unaware of her existence. But he hadn't really appeared to notice them, at least not as beautiful women, and had kept his attention focused solely on her from the time she walked down the aisle to the time he solidified the agreement by kissing her gently on the lips at the end of the ceremony.

And now, gazing at the hardness of his jaw in contrast with the smoothness of his skin sent a shiver through her body. She could feel the warmth of his large, muscular form penetrating her own, and the knowledge that he would be this close to her for an uncertain period of time truly disturbed her. He was the most . . . masculine nobleman she had ever seen in her life, and in looks alone, he put all of her sisters' husbands to shame.

Caroline drew a determined breath, gave him a shaky smile, and lowered her gaze from the penetrating directness of his to finally take in her surroundings.

Slowly she walked across the entrance hall, concluding that she indeed had her work cut out for her, for it was a filthy, dust-covered mess. The ceiling extended upward as high as the building itself, and the floor, made of a pale peach marble, spread out before her as the only lovely thing to remain inside. She also knew it had to be imported, and fairly old, for she could see markings where rugs had lain for a very long time.

To each side of her were staircases leading to the second floor, rounding the hall and meeting at the top directly in front of her. She gingerly made her way forward, her husband following in silence as she peeked into each room on the first floor. She could picture a once laughter-filled home, like the one in which she was raised, with a morning room, library, drawing room, music room, dining room, and a big, elegant ballroom. Sadly, it was obvious that Miramont had once been a beautiful home. Now all that remained was the shell of a memory.

"The only room I really spend much time in right now is my study," her husband said at last as they stood once again in the entryway. He pointed to his left, then reached down and took hold of her hand.

She flinched from the contact.

"It's all right, Caroline," he soothed lightly. "I won't bite."

Smiling hesitantly, she bravely clasped his fingers with her palm and walked by his side into the study.

It was fairly large, depicting at least a feeling of life on the premises, being cozy and smelling faintly of tobacco. On opposing sides of a large oak desk sat two black leather chairs, and in front of the fireplace sat a new, dark-green velveteen settee. The desk was piled high with paperwork, and suddenly she found herself curious as to what her new husband did with his time.

"Are there any servants, my lord?" she asked casually.

"My name is Brent, Caroline," he returned flatly, dropping her hand. "Since we're now married, you may call me that."

She was silent for an uncomfortable moment, mystified as to how he wanted her to respond, then she replied just as blandly, "Of course, Brent."

He turned to face her fully. "The only servant I have right now is Nedda Albright, my housekeeper, who returned yesterday from staying with the Vicar Drakemond and his wife while I was away. She's been working on the second floor, preparing it for you. There's also Davis, my trainer, and three additional grooms who run what used to be my stables." He glanced away from her to remove his topcoat, placing it over the back of the settee. "I'll be leaving in a few days to attend to some personal business; then I'll look for others or the ones who were here before."

She grinned. "You have four people running your stables and only one running your household?"

He turned back to her, folding his arms across his chest. "As you can see, I have no household, and Davis and Nedda are horrible cooks. That means, I'm afraid, it will be bread, cheese, and fruit for both of us until I can find someone else to do it."

"Does Davis have a first name?"

He smiled beautifully. "I'm sure he does, but for thirty years I've known him only as Davis as has everyone else. If you asked him, he'd tell you he's forgotten his given name as well."

He walked to stand in front of her.

"I'd stay away from him, though," he added most mischievously. "Davis is cranky, loud, and, although he doesn't meet many, calls all ladies by the respectful name of 'filly.' "

She laughed softly, grateful for the ease in tension. "I'll remember that."

Her eyes melded with his, then her heart began to race as he leaned so close her senses could detect the faint traces of soap and something . . . musky. Masculine. For a second she was terrified he would kiss her.

His voice deepened. "Can you ride, Caroline?"

"Of course I can ride," she admitted, surprised, "although I haven't in some time." She clasped her elbows with her palms, instinctively protecting herself from his unbearable closeness.

"I don't suppose you can cook, though, can you, little bride?" he almost whispered, slowly raising his hand to run his thumb across her exposed collarbone.

The brazen action made her jump. "No."

"No?" His voice grew deeper and thicker as he continued to caress her skin. "Then what else can you do?"

She shrugged, lowering her lashes to stare at the center of his chest. "I . . . plant things."

"Hmm . . . gardening again." He raised both hands to rest them atop her shoulders, starting a slow massage of her bare skin.

Caroline caught her breath, entranced by his boldness. The touch wasn't all that intimate for a married couple in the privacy of their home, but it made her nervous nonetheless. What bothered her was that he probably noticed it, too.

"Do you like this?" he whispered roughly.

She nodded slightly as the warmth of his palms seeped through her skin.

"So tell me about your sisters. What are their names?"

She blinked, confused at the turn in conversation. "My sisters?"

He shrugged negligibly. "I'd like to know more about your family."

She wondered for a moment why on earth he could possibly care, but he just looked at her innocently, curiously, gently caressing the tops of her arms.

Relaxing forcefully, she murmured, "Jane is the oldest at thirty, and Mary Anne is twenty-seven. I, as you know, will be twenty-six in eighty-six days."

"Eighty-six days, Caroline?" he repeated with a grin.

She faltered, then simply ignored that. "Next is Charlotte—"

"Charlotte?" His hands stopped moving, his brows furrowed. "You have a sister named Charlotte?"

She pulled back slightly. "What's wrong with the name Charlotte?"

He stared hard, then began massaging her again. "Go on."

She took a deep breath. "Charlotte is twenty-two, and Stephanie is the youngest at seventeen. They're all married except Stephanie. She'll be married next spring."

"Mmm . . ."

An uneasy moment ticked by, until she finally sighed and asked, "Have you any close relations?"

"None."

"Oh . . ." She waited. "And how old are you, Brent?"

"I'll be thirty-four on the eighteenth of March." Smugly he smiled into her eyes. "How many days is that, Caroline?"

She wanted to laugh at his arrogant question. Instead, she beamed, leaned her face toward him, and whispered huskily, "Exactly two hundred and twenty-four, my lord husband."

Brent gaped at her, amazed, and at first quite certain she'd made up a number to throw back at him. But something compelled him to quickly add the months and days together, and although it took him several moments to do so, he knew her figure was probably accurate. She would have to be fairly bright to make such summations in seconds, or more likely *extremely* bright, and suddenly, to his surprise, he found his once plain and unattractive wife incredibly appealing. Grinning at him with eyes the color of dark chocolate, revealing the dimple in her cheek and a beautiful white smile, made her almost irresistible. She was teasing him, probably without awareness, and he found himself thoroughly enjoying it.

"Remarkable . . ." he said lightly with a gentle lift of his brow.

She continued to smile proudly, relaxing to the pressure of his hands, her arms falling loosely to her sides. Smoothly he continued to massage her shoulders, growing anxious to touch her more suggestively. He had to conclude that his sudden desire for his new wife was strictly due to his prolonged state of celibacy, and that he finally had a woman to lawfully bed at his leisure. To be fair, however, he also had to admit he now thought her attractive, even striking to look at.

Her wedding gown was made of ice-blue silk flowing loosely to her ankles, but the bodice fit low and snugly across her deliciously, now noticeably ample breasts. With her hair loosely wrapped in pearls and pinned on top of her head, soft curls framing her face, he could hardly keep himself from freeing the dark, silky tresses to fall down her back.

She belonged to him now, and with that thought in mind, he decided to help himself to his new acquisition. Quickly, expertly, he turned one of his hands so that his knuckles brushed back and forth just inside the top of her gown against the fullness of her bosom.

That startled her, as he knew it would, but she didn't pull away. If anything, she became captivated, her eyes bigger, cheeks pinker, breathing labored.

"Do you get this flushed when you tend to your flowers, little one?"

She didn't say anything, just kept her gaze locked with his.

Seconds later he stopped stroking her with his knuckles and boldly, completely, closed his palm over her breast.

She drew a sharp breath. "Please . . ."

He grasped her upper arm with his left hand as the thumb on his right started brushing back and forth across her nipple, forcing it to quickly harden beneath the thin fabric.

"Please what?" he whispered.

She swallowed. ". . . Please stop."

It took everything in him to straighten and drop his arms.

And with that, she nearly fell over, catching herself on the back of the settee, then moving at once to sit in one of the leather chairs across from his desk.

Brent regarded her carefully, so ready for her that his body ached against the tightness of his breeches. After a minute of strained stillness, he inhaled deeply and began to walk toward her.

"There's passion between us, Caroline, and it might be best just to quench it by bedding you now rather than waiting for tonight."

She turned her face up to his.

He smiled reassuringly. "I'll admit it's been a long time since I've been with a woman, but I think I'll remember how to perform well enough to satisfy you."

Instead of calming from the comfort of his words, she gasped audibly, stood abruptly, and fairly raced to the other side of the room.

Brent groaned, folded his arms across his chest, and leaned his hip on his desk.

Once again, as he did so often with women, he had spoken without thinking how his words would be taken.

And once again, things weren't going in his favor. He'd frightened her, he could tell, as she looked at him through big, ambivalent eyes, fidgeting nervously with her skirt, and strangely he wanted to soothe her, to be delicate with her feelings.

"Caroline," he started again, standing erect and sauntering toward her, "I'm simply trying to help you relax before we become intimate—"

"I cannot be intimate with you, sir," she interjected with newfound strength.

He stopped abruptly and stared at her. "Of course we will be intimate."

She backed up as far as she could, her bottom pressing against a bookshelf. "I'm sure we will eventually, but not for a while."

He grinned. She looked so adorably terrified. Moving toward her once again, he reached up to untie and remove his cravat, dropping it onto the settee as he passed it.

"I want you in my bed, Caroline, and primly bred or not, I think you want it, too." He stopped in front of her as he began to loosen the buttons on his shirt. "I promise to make our couplings as gentle—"

"I'm bleeding."

He looked at her, confused. Then he noticed the faint traces of color gracing her fine, delicate features, and he was suddenly shocked to the depths of his being.

He was fully aware of women and their monthlies, but in all of his life no woman had ever mentioned or discussed the topic with him. It was just one of those little issues that men knew about but discreetly ignored, and until exactly this moment he'd never given it a thought. It wasn't something that mattered to him, though, when all he could think about was spreading her thighs, entering her heated softness, and finding the release his body so desperately craved.

Brent gave her what he thought was his most charming, comforting smile and reached up to tug at the pins and pearls holding her hair in place. That caused her to stiffen, but she couldn't budge because he moved quickly forward, trapping her firmly between his body and the bookshelf.

"I know, little one, that most men would gracefully step aside to let that particular force of nature run its course. I, however, am not like other men."

She gaped at him, deeply mortified.

He continued to free the pearls, laying them on the bookshelf behind her, allowing her dark, shiny locks to tumble loosely down her back. Then he drew his fingers over her scalp to intertwine with her hair, placed both palms on her cheeks, and gently lifted her face to within inches of his.

"I want you, Caroline," he whispered, "and you want me."

"No," she countered in a tone so low and sexy it made his blood race through his veins.

He closed his eyes and slowly lowered his head to brush her lips with his.

Since Caroline had no experience in the art of kissing, she truly wasn't sure how to react to the insistence of his mouth on hers. She pushed against his chest, but that didn't seem to deter him in the least. If anything, it made him all the more aggressive as he started applying full pressure of his mouth in such a demanding action that it made her heart speed up and her legs turn to liquid heat.

Dazed, she began to wonder if it was really so bad. She knew she would need to assuage his male appetite to some extent, so with that rational thought, she closed her eyes and relaxed against him, allowing him better access.

He moved his lips in rhythm with hers, a rhythm gradually becoming as natural to her as breathing. He felt so warm beneath her palms, his broad chest hard and strong. She moved her fingers in a slow circular pattern against his muscles, granting herself this one opportunity to drink in his very maleness with every sense she possessed.

He coaxed, teased, toyed with her mouth until at last her resistance gave way to his gentle urging, and as he flicked his tongue back and forth across her tightly closed lips, she slowly started to open to him.

He groaned when she finally closed her palms around his neck, pulling him close, and the sound of his deep, husky voice, the feel of him, the touch of every part of him made her come alive with something she couldn't understand, something marvelous. Where his massive frame came in contact with hers she tingled, and when he finally raked his strong fingers through the loose strands of her hair to grasp her head and hold her even tighter to him, she found herself actually moaning softly against the force of his urgent, unrelenting mouth.

That lovely, womanly sound of pleasure, of unashamed arousal, caught Brent completely by surprise because he hadn't really even touched her yet. He found himself desperate almost, and with the feeling came the ardent need to caress, to taste, to please as his tongue came into intimate contact with hers, flicking back and forth, up and around inside her mouth.

Oh, God, she was so soft, so dainty and feminine, smelling vaguely of violet water and cool afternoon rain. Having her so near and inviting him with her actions made it unbearably difficult for him to hold back. She was responding to him with more of herself than he could have hoped, and with the feel of her silky hair intertwined with his fingers and her supple warm body against his, he knew he had been blessed at last.

With that thought he lost his reason. He embraced her fully, clasped her lower back to free her from the bookshelf, placed his palm on her bottom, and pulled her against his fully engorged member, the feel of her hips against his sending an explosion of fine, erotic sensations through his body.

"You're going to be so good," he whispered raggedly against her mouth. "You're so hot already—"

Suddenly she was wiggling against him. "Don't move like that, sweetheart. I won't last until we get upstairs."

Brent immediately knew something was wrong when she not only kept wiggling, but started pushing with all her strength against his chest. She was moving her head as well, pulling away from him and attempting to brush his face aside.

"No—" she choked out, her voice pained, frightened.

Suddenly he couldn't breathe. His chest tightened as he opened his eyes and looked down to his new bride, her cheeks flushed a lovely shade of pink, eyes glowing, hair shiny, framing her face as it fell to her waist. And she was very definitely trying to break free of him.

"Please—let go of me."

He gradually released her, feeling at once like a poor actor in a badly played Shakespearean tragedy. She moved with amazing speed to the other side of the room, next to the fireplace, to stand rigidly, eyes closed, chest heaving, breath coming in rasps. He wiped the back of his hand over his perspiring forehead, attempting to control himself long enough to understand what had just happened.

And what the hell *did* just happen? One minute she was responding, the next she couldn't get far enough away. He might have moved a bit too fast, but she had to have known what was happening between them.

He took a reluctant step toward her, which she obviously heard, for her eyes flew open to look into his with nothing short of fear in their dark depths.

He wasn't sure how to handle such a delicate situation, but he knew he had to say something. Composing himself, he straightened and placed his palms on his hips.

"Caroline, would you mind telling me what you're thinking?"

She inhaled sharply and looked him straight in the eye. "I don't want to consummate our marriage, my lord," she said very quickly, "and I respectfully request that you placate your sexual needs elsewhere."

He had never been more astounded by a statement in his life, but what infuriated him suddenly was the insensitive manner in which she brushed him aside. He would have placed a generous wager on the fact that Caroline desired him as much as he did her, so how could she, a newly married lady, and after the passionate moment they'd just shared, tell him to go find himself a mistress? It made no sense, and as he struggled to understand it, his frustration fueled his anger.

Slowly he began to walk toward her. "You are my wife, Caroline, and you are rightfully mine to bed," he cautiously, icily challenged.

She stood her ground, holding his gaze defiantly. "And you would seduce me in your study in the middle of the afternoon, while your housekeeper wanders about—"

"I wouldn't have taken you here!" he shouted, noticing a stricken look slicing through her eyes.

He stopped and rubbed the back of his neck with his palm. As calmly as he could, he said, "I'm sorry, Caroline, but please understand that as a man I have ... certain needs."

"And I am now giving you permission to satisfy those needs elsewhere," she rebutted quickly, matter-of-factly.

Brent couldn't believe what he was hearing. Taking a mistress would have been, he surmised, an expectation of his class. But being given permission to do so from his bride of less than three hours, who liquified in his arms with one little kiss, seemed uniquely absurd, and it almost made him laugh.

"Do I understand, madam," he finally remarked, "that you want me to take a mistress?"

She nodded.

He grunted and gave her a puzzled smile. "May I ask why?"

She stared at him, brows creased in thought. Then she crossed her arms over her breasts and looked down to her blue, mud-stained slippers.

"You have no love for me," she stated nonchalantly.

Of course he didn't, and she knew that, which made her words even more unusual. And suspect. It was a rather slippery excuse, too, but alas, she was a woman, and he couldn't begin to imagine where her little female mind was roaming with it. He decided just to take the logical approach. "Caroline, we've only known each other for one day—"

"I don't love you either, so please don't ask me to come to your bed," she cut in sharply as her eyes shot back to his.

His countenance became dark with the fine line between aching passion and burning rage. "I don't think I'll need to ask, little one. You melted in my arms, and love had nothing to do with it."

She said not a word in reply, but her cheeks became rosy, which gave him encouragement as he began to saunter toward her.

"I had you moaning with one innocent kiss," he added in a husky timbre, "so think how I'll make you feel when you're lying naked beneath me."

She gasped, took a step back, and blurted, "I refuse to allow you liberties with my body. If I am forced, the result will be nothing short of rape, regardless of whether I'm your wife."

Her statement stopped him dead. He couldn't believe she would say that to him with such coldness, such disregard for his husbandly rights and his feelings as a man. Never in his life had he been so insulted by a woman, and his entire body suddenly shook with tightly contained fury. He clenched his jaw, tightly fisted his hands, and took two great breaths to keep his anger in check before he unleashed it in the only room in his home that carried anything of value.

And still she stood there, defensively, eyes blazing, waiting and saying nothing. Then reality took hold, and he understood at last.

Once again it was him. His words weren't sweet; he didn't know the first thing about flirting, or seducing, or creating an atmosphere of slow burning passion. And as he stood only ten feet from his bride, who had stressed her fear that he might actually rape her, it all finally hit him with shocking clarity.

For most of his life, Brent had seen very little admiration or respect between the few married couples he'd known, and certainly nothing akin to love. Love was a physical sensation, which had been proven to him conclusively one dark, rainy afternoon three years ago when he'd found Pauline, a woman who had claimed to love him beyond life, in her stables and intimately engaged with the boy who cared for her father's innumerable hunting dogs. At that moment he knew that love was nothing more than a word said to manipulate others, which was exactly what he'd seen between his parents. They carried no affection for each other, just the acquired skill of manipulation for personal gratification. He could accept it in his marriage as well, for realistically, he should feel nothing special for Caroline.

But now, as the idea engulfed him with a burning desire he didn't fully understand, he wanted a son. If he and Caroline went their separate ways emotionally, it mattered naught to him as long as she gave him a son who would respect him, perhaps grow to admire him, to whom he could leave his title, his estate with a restored Miramont, and a stable full of prized Arabians. If nothing else, she owed him that. And wasn't that what her father had said? Caroline would indeed give him a strong, sturdy son, and he knew she wanted him with sufficient desire to succumb to his lovemaking long enough to get her pregnant.

Now that his mind had cleared, Brent stood fully erect and masked his face with indifference.

"I have only two things to say to you, Lady Caroline," he fairly whispered, his voice hard as granite. "The first is that I would never, under any conditions, force a woman to have sex with me."

He paused to watch her face turn as white as winter snowfall.

"The second is that although you may take a liberal view of married life, I don't. I fully intend to consummate this marriage, and I do not, at any time, expect to have a mistress in my bed. Under the circumstances, I wouldn't be able to afford both of you, with what little time and money I actually have.''

He turned and walked swiftly toward the door. ''And one more thing, Caroline,'' he added, looking back in her direction, his expression darkly angered, sarcastic. ''If I ever find you in the arms of another man, or learn that you've taken a lover during the course of this marriage, I shall damage him where it counts—and you, my lovely little wife, will never look at a flower quite the same way again.''

He opened the door.

''Nedda can show you to your room. I have more engaging things to do.''

Three

Caroline sat at the kitchen table, a mug of strong tea in her hands and a bowl of sliced apples in front of her. It wasn't yet seven, and already she'd spent two hours in her new garden.

This was now her routine at Miramont, as it had been at home. She would work while the ground was moist and soft, then take a break for breakfast, then move to the greenhouse during the day. The trouble, however, was that Miramont had no greenhouse, which was something she needed to discuss with her husband.

Caroline took a long swallow of the hot brew, then plopped a slice of apple into her mouth. She, Nedda, and Davis had been meeting in the kitchen for breakfast for the last four mornings. She'd been at Miramont for less than a week and she'd seen more of them than she had her husband, for he, it seemed, wanted nothing to do with her. And that was fine with her.

After the row they'd had the day of their wedding, she'd felt a bit hesitant about being near him. She'd said some cruel things that afternoon, but they were words that had to be said, and better to get them said quickly and without pretense. He apparently now understood, for her husband of five days had spoken fewer than as many words to her.

But their private quarters were separated by only one wall and a small, nonlocking door. Not even a dressing area sat between them, and that made her anxious. It didn't surprise her, though. All married couples had adjoining bedchambers, and naturally hers and Brent's wouldn't be any different.

Actually, although modest in furnishings, her room was also lovely with bright yellow lace curtains, two yellow reading chairs across from each other and next to the fireplace, a small dressing table, and a comfortable bed covered with a quilt of peach lace. The floor was noticeably bare, needing rugs for warmth and atmosphere, and those she wanted to add as soon as possible.

Perhaps requesting them from her ever-distant husband would crack the ice barrier between them, for he had rugs on the floor of his bedchamber, as she'd briefly seen. She probably shouldn't have, but to satisfy her curiosity, she'd sneaked into his room just yesterday to take in the surroundings, finding furnishings as simple and sparse as hers although decorated with the masculine flavor of rich mahogany and deep royal blue. He also had a much bigger bed, but she refused to consider something that was none of her concern.

Caroline sighed, resting her elbows on the table, watching Davis pick at his dirty nails and Nedda scurry about the kitchen, her frizzy hair flying around her chubby, wrinkled face as she hunted for suitable foodstuffs.

"Eggs for you this morning, my lady?" Nedda asked with a smile.

Caroline glanced at Davis, who sat across from her at the small oak table, then took a quick drink of her tea to hide her choked expression. Their housekeeper was, by all accounts, the worst cook in England.

Straightening, she answered pleasantly, "I don't think so, Nedda. Perhaps just toast."

"Toast it is."

Nedda turned her back on them to slice the bread.

"I dunno, ma'am..." Davis drawled, teasing. "Seems a fine lady like yourself needs some meat on her bones. You're too skinny as it is."

Caroline gave him a hard stare, for she was hardly skinny.

"My thoughts exactly," Nedda agreed, searching for butter. "I think I'll scramble a few anyway, in case his lordship is hungry this morn."

Caroline grunted. If his lordship actually ever awakened before noon, he certainly never made his presence known.

Davis took a sip of tea, sitting back to regard her. "So how are you settlin' in at Miramont, Lady Caroline?"

She smiled to his dark, weathered face, but instead of answering his question, she asked another. "Where exactly are you from, Davis?"

"Kentucky."

"Ken what?"

He chuckled gruffly. "Kentucky. One of the United States of America. Born and raised there, before it was a state, of course."

"I see..." She casually took another bite of apple. "Have you ever been to New York?"

He frowned in contemplation. "Well . . . I shipped out from there thirty-two years ago, but don't remember much. Came here and the former countess offered me a good payin' job, so I stayed. Taught his lordship all he knows."

Caroline looked at him stupidly. "All he knows about what?"

That flustered him. "All he knows about horses."

"My husband is a horseman?"

Davis laughed outright. "Ain't love grand."

She felt her cheeks color.

"What exactly do you know about your husband, Lady Caroline?" he asked seconds later.

Warily, she replied, "Very little, really."

"Why don't you ask 'im?"

"Ask him?"

Davis snickered. "Ask your husband about his past, his motives and ambitions. I think you'll find it interestin'."

"So this is what I miss each morning."

Caroline abruptly turned to the door. Her husband stood casually against it, hair mussed, his wrinkled linen shirt half-tucked into extremely tight breeches. He was watching her as well, scrutinizing her strangely, making her pulse race.

"You're just in time for breakfast," Nedda said in motherly sternness. "Come sit."

Caroline thought he might make excuses to escape either her or the unpalatable meal. But he surprised her by rubbing his eyes and slowly walking toward them, taking the seat to her right at the table.

"Tea?" Caroline asked a bit too sweetly. The only time they spoke to each other was at meals, although until just now the only meal they had taken together was dinner each night. Conversation then left a lot to be desired, and she was, quite honestly, tired of the stupid game of avoidance they played with each other.

"Tea would be wonderful," he returned too politely.

She gave him a long, level look. Then, with what could only be considered a sarcastic smile, she slowly rose from her chair and walked to the counter.

"You look like you been tossed from hell to breakfast, my boy," Davis said, amused.

Brent leaned back in his chair. "I didn't get to bed until nearly two, but I have things to take care of today. I'll be seeing Vicar Drakemond this afternoon."

Both Nedda and Davis looked up sharply. Caroline placed his tea on the table and sat again.

"Tomorrow," he continued without interruption, "I'll start looking for servants and taking care of personal business. I won't be gone long."

"You're leaving?" Caroline blurted.

He turned to her and grinned. "Miss me, Caroline?"

She huffed. The man must dramatically overestimate his importance in her life.

Casually he took a sip of his tea and changed the subject. "So what have you been doing with your time?"

She quickly glanced to her mug, tracing a pattern around the rim with her finger. "I've been working in the garden."

"Ahh . . . of course."

"A good job she's done, too," Davis added.

Caroline beamed.

"Really? Did you plant a flower for me, little one?"

"No," she said curtly.

"It's a good thing," he replied softly, "because I'm quite sure it would wilt away and die."

Caroline shrugged lightly. "Only from lack of care." She had meant it as a very dark joke, hoping he'd catch the meaning. And perhaps he did, for he was quiet for a moment, then his eyes narrowed.

"Everything dies eventually, Caroline."

His voice was so low she barely heard the words. Leaning toward him, and with every ounce of determination she possessed, she placed her nose within inches of his.

"Nothing in my care ever dies from neglect, husband," she confided in a husky whisper. "My plants will be the loveliest you'll ever see as they grow and become strong. Within weeks, every room at Miramont will be filled with God's beautiful creations that I nurture and bring to life."

"Including our children?"

She sat back abruptly, her eyes widening as he turned her serious, passionate words to something intimate.

"My plants are my children," she bravely retorted.

He grinned devilishly. "But I guarantee that our son will be much more fun to create."

Her heart raced, but she refused to back down from his insolent male innuendos. "How would you know, husband? Have you created a son from another entanglement?''

Nedda drew a sharp breath.

Davis chuckled. ''This oughta be grand.''

Caroline kept her eyes locked with her husband's, waiting for his rebuttal.

Finally Brent laughed softly. ''An entanglement, Caroline? Is that what you'd call our relationship?''

She fidgeted. ''One could call a marriage of convenience an entanglement, I suppose.''

He spoke again cheerfully. ''Then I'm quite certain I have no child from a former entanglement, Caroline.''

''Breakfast?'' Nedda interrupted sweetly, placing a plate of mush and burned bread before each of them.

Brent stared at his food. They needed a cook right away.

They all sat together to eat, and he found it amusing to note that when his mother was alive, they would never have taken meals with any of the help. Doing such a thing was unthinkable in their station. And yet the war had humbled him, for when he was at battle he found himself eating with men from all walks of life. When one fought side by side with another, some things just truly didn't seem to matter, which was exactly how it was in his massive, empty home. With only the four of them, it seemed rather stupid for him and Caroline to eat separately—and if they weren't sitting here, they'd be sitting on the floor.

It didn't seem to bother Caroline either, which surprised him. If he'd married any other woman of quality, he felt certain she would have fainted at the thought of eating what was supposed to be breakfast at a small wooden table with the housekeeper and the man who took care of the horses. In many different ways, he was slowly finding, she was refreshingly unique.

Ignoring her for the last week had been unbelievably difficult. He'd tried to escape her presence by working, riding, poring over his books, repairing some of the damage to his property, and still he couldn't free himself of his frustration.

He had a wife. He had a wife who desired him physically but wouldn't allow herself to be touched. He was now convinced that a former lover had given her a bad time of things in bed, which would explain her reluctance, even fear of what was to prove to be the only truly enjoyable aspect of married life. Because of his newfound understanding, Brent admonished himself to take things slowly, for Caroline was bright enough to understand his motives if he pushed too quickly or too hard.

He also now knew, after considerable thought on the matter, that this was probably the reason her father had wanted her out of his house. Naturally, as a man in exemplary social standing, having a ruined daughter unmarried and living in his home could blacken his name almost overnight if it became known. And what if she took another lover? Society would cut him to pieces.

But with her at Miramont, under his husbandly influence, that would never happen again. He wouldn't allow it, and he'd made that perfectly clear to Caroline. He would be the only man in her bed from now on, and if the gods were smiling, it would happen soon.

He glanced at her from the corner of his eye, watching her toy with her food. She was once again clothed in the dowdy gown she wore the day they'd met, but now he saw her differently. Although she had a smudge of mud across her cheek and her dark, thick hair tied into the tightest knot he had ever seen at the base of her neck, she looked incredibly appealing. Her gown made her that way, he reasoned, for although it was exceptionally ugly in color and style, with its high neckline and long sleeves, it molded tightly to her bosom and waist, outlining her lovely, sexy, untouchable shape . . .

Brent suddenly attacked his food. "I'll be leaving at sunup tomorrow," he said coolly between bites. "I should be home within the week, but I'd like you to sleep in the house, Davis. I don't want the women alone.''

Davis nodded.

''And Caroline,'' he said after taking a swallow of tea, ''I have work to do now but I'd like us to talk before I leave.''

Without waiting for a reply, he stood abruptly, walked with dishes in hand to the sink, then turned to her.

''From now on you'll wear your hair down around the house,'' he ordered casually. ''No wife of mine will look frumpy at twenty-five years of age.''

''Frumpy!''

Davis snickered.

Nedda smiled.

Caroline's eyes narrowed to tiny slits. ''I cannot fathom why it matters to you how I wear my hair.'' She slowly stood to match the level of his gaze. ''I prefer it this way because if it is not pulled tightly from my face, it gets into my eyes.''

''I betcha Nedda could find a ribbon or two to hold it back,'' Davis offered with a wide grin.

She stared hard at him. ''What on earth would you know about hair ribbons—''

''I have several I'd be happy to give you, Lady Caroline,'' Nedda cut in sweetly.

She sighed, exasperated. ''Thank you, but it's my hair, and I like it just fine the way it is.''

''I do not,'' Brent articulated slowly, looking directly into her eyes, ''and I'm your husband and the master of the house.''

''Oh, you're the master of—''

''You do have pretty hair, Lady Caroline,'' Davis interjected smoothly. ''It's a shame you wrap it all up like that.''

Brent could see her anger building. In some odd, probably not too honorable way, he enjoyed unnerving her. It was a marvelous game.

''I suppose you'll tell me next I should garden in

something more feminine, maybe pearls and silk evening wear?''

He almost laughed, thinking that nothing at all could be more feminine than the garment she wore clinging to every curve of her body. She glared at him, her expression fuming, cheeks bright and pink. It took everything in him to keep his features neutral, for she looked positively adorable when she was mad at him.

''I cannot afford pearls and silk evening wear, I'm afraid,'' he countered indifferently. His eyes lingered momentarily on her figure, then he gestured toward her gown with his hands. ''You do have more than one of those, do you not?''

She pulled back from the suggestiveness of his stare, boldly lifted her skirts, and turned her back to him.

''I have plenty,'' she called over her shoulder as she walked to the door. Looking to their housekeeper, she smiled faintly. ''Breakfast was quite . . . Thank you for breakfast, Nedda.'' With that, she marched out into the open air.

Davis chuckled. Nedda grinned. Brent ignored them both and strode to the door through which he'd entered earlier.

''I'm going riding,'' he said wearily as he turned and left the room.

''I thought he intended to work,'' Nedda remarked nonchalantly.

Davis beamed. ''My boy is smitten.''

''Indeed he is,'' Nedda agreed, ''and so is she.''

''You think so?''

She nodded, then leaned toward him to say impishly, ''And I'm going to enjoy every single minute of watching them fight it.''

Davis laughed and raised his cup in a mock toast. ''And so the fun begins.''

Four

He couldn't believe he was actually going to do it. He was an earl, properly raised, more educated than most, and never in his life had he felt so uncomfortable about making a request. No other man alive would even consider what he was about to ask of his new wife.

Brent sat at his desk, arms resting on each side of his ledger as he slowly thumbed through the pages, waiting for Caroline, who had said she'd meet him shortly. It had taken him several days of work to understand clearly what Reggie had done with the money and wealth he'd had before leaving for the Continent. After working through the numbers several times, he wanted to be sure of what he'd found.

"I'm sorry I took so long but I needed to . . . um . . . find a hair ribbon."

At the sound of her deep, sultry voice, he quickly raised his eyes to the doorway. Caroline stood against it, wearing a silk lime-green day gown with a low rounded neckline, which more than adequately revealed her abundant cleavage. Her dark hair was loosely tied at her nape while soft curls framed her cheeks, now flushed and dewy soft from the warmth of a bath. It stirred his blood to see her so, for every time he looked at her she was lovelier than the last. And seemingly further out of reach.

He quickly looked back to his ledger. "You'll wear your hair like that from this moment on."

"So you've demanded," she said rather loudly, slowly moving toward him. After a long, still moment, she asked sheepishly, "Do you think you could tell me what happened here, Brent?"

He glanced at her, puzzled.

She looked around and opened her arms wide. "I mean Miramont. What happened?"

He drew a full breath and sat back heavily in his chair. "I thought Davis or Nedda would have told you."

She shrugged. "They've told me nothing."

He kept his eyes locked with hers, his features neutral. "I left for the Continent several months ago to do some work for the Crown, leaving Miramont in the care of my cousin, Reginald Kent. I had every intention of returning last spring, but without warning I was forced to stay in France. When I returned last month, I discovered that my cousin had sold everything I owned, without my knowledge or approval, to pay his gambling debts."

"Why were you in France?" she mildly asked.

Almost impatiently, he replied, "I was with the Duke of Wellington fighting Napoleon Bonaparte at Waterloo."

Caroline's eyes opened wide with surprise. He'd said the words so matter-of-factly, with so little feeling, that if she hadn't been watching she would have missed how his expression betrayed his composure. It had changed just enough for her to notice the slightest trace of well-hidden pain, and he tightened his jaw to keep that emotion in check.

Now she understood why he'd appeared so thin and haunted when they'd first met, his underlying anger, why his manner was so direct. Her new husband had been at war, and she could think of nothing to say in response to his statement.

Quickly he straightened and stood, lowering his gaze to his desk, once again casual, composed. "I need you to look at this."

"Of course," she murmured without thinking, slowly walking to stand beside him.

"I'd like you to glance over these numbers to see if I've made any mistakes in my calculations, Caroline."

She blinked quickly several times. "I beg your pardon?"

He smiled faintly. "I'd appreciate a level head other than my own to check these figures once more, since I need to know the exact status of my accounts before I leave. Not only do we need servants, but I'd like to start refurnishing Miramont as well."

She was stunned. "You—you're asking me to look through your finances?"

He lowered his voice and leaned very close to her. "Technically I suppose they're your finances, too."

Caroline absolutely could not believe that he was asking this of her, and were it not for the fact that he was practically thrusting the ledger into her hands, she would have never believed his request.

"Are you sure?" She glanced to his face, now only inches from hers, hoping to God he wasn't toying with her, for a joke like this would crush her spirit.

He stepped aside and ushered her to his desk.

"Go ahead, Caroline," he insisted, gently pushing her into his chair. He took a pen from the inkwell, placed it in her hands, then swiftly moved to take the seat across from her to watch through narrowed eyes.

Suddenly Caroline knew this was a huge, complicated, chance-of-a-lifetime test of her abilities, and strangely, she wanted to impress. Slowly she lowered her eyes to the paper in front of her.

Brent observed her closely as she hesitantly started to work. She turned the pages quickly, moving through the ledger with such incredible speed that for a while he was convinced she wasn't taking him seriously. But as he watched her chew her bottom lip, her face contorting with furious thinking, he realized this was something she actually enjoyed doing, and she hadn't used the pen even once. She was calculating mathematical equations and multiplying several large numbers using nothing but her mind. It was truly unbelievable.

Finally she looked up, eyes sparkling. "You've made a ghastly mistake, Brent," she whispered. Then she started to giggle.

That irritated him. "If it's such a ghastly mistake, why are you laughing?"

She sobered a little. "Look what you've done here."

She motioned for him to move closer, and he slowly stood and walked around to her side of the desk.

"See right here? You multiplied by three instead of three hundred. You didn't carry your zeros, silly man." She met his eyes, her lips curled up in delight. "I think we have quite a bit more money than you first thought."

He looked at her sharply. "You discovered this using only your head?"

The smile died on her face. "It just comes naturally to me," she said cautiously.

He was quiet for a moment, then sighed. "It has never come naturally to me. I don't trust bailiffs, and taking care of the books has always been my least favorite chore. From this moment on, I'd like you to see to it. Naturally, I'll need to continue dealing with my banker regarding payments made on my accounts, but I'd like you to keep track of the money. You've a marvelous talent, Caroline. It should be used."

She blinked, incredulous. "You mean permanently? Month to month?"

"Of course I mean permanently, and I'll need you to start right away. I've almost completed repairs on the stables, but some of the weather damage inside was greater than anticipated. I'll need to know the exact amount I can spend to get things running smoothly, since I'd like to start breeding again next season."

She shook her head, dazed. "Breeding . . . horses?"

He looked at her strangely. "It's what I do, Caroline.

I breed, show, and sell Arabian horses. I don't have the time or patience to keep my finances in line, so I'd like it to be one of your duties.'' He paused. ''Do you mind?''

Slowly she smiled in wonder. ''You trust me with this?''

He touched the back of his hand to her cheek and grinned devilishly. ''If I didn't think you could do it, I wouldn't have asked. And besides, if you did try to abscond with all the money, I'd find you sidetracked at my neighbor's house pruning his petunias, which are now to the point of overrunning the property.''

Caroline thought she might explode from elation. He believed in and trusted her abilities. No one, not even her father, had ever done that before.

''I'd be delighted to take this tedious chore off your hands,'' she finally acknowledged in a voice filled with joy.

''Good.''

He turned, but before he could move, she grabbed his arm, pulled herself up, and with only the briefest hesitation, wrapped her arms around him, hugging him tightly.

''Thank you,'' she whispered against his chest.

He reached up with his palm to stroke the silkiness of her hair, but before he could even think to embrace her, and without looking at him, she quickly pushed herself away and returned to the chair.

He stood silently, watching the side of her face for another minute, then turned and walked to the door.

''I'll see you at dinner,'' he softly said.

Caroline, however, was oblivious to everything but the financial computations in front of her.

Five

Caroline dressed in a pale peach evening gown, tied her dark-brown locks loosely at her nape with a small white ribbon, and purposefully strode to the kitchen for dinner, expecting to find Nedda, Davis, and Brent waiting patiently inside. Instead, she saw only her husband standing by the small window overlooking wet grasslands and hills blurred by the thickness of evening rainfall.

Sitting on the table before her sat a platter of cold roast beef, cheeses, bread, a bowl of plums, a bottle of wine, and only two place settings.

"Aren't Davis and Nedda joining us?" she hesitantly asked.

"They're busy," he replied casually, turning. He briefly took in her appearance then moved to help her sit, lighting three candles on the table before taking the seat next to her. "It'll just be us."

"Fine," she said quickly, glancing at him nervously as he poured the wine. Tonight he'd dressed for dinner as well, wearing a white silk shirt, dove-gray breeches and cravat, and a charcoal-gray dinner jacket. His clothes fit him impeccably, and naturally he looked perfect. The thought made her laugh.

"Something funny?" he asked, lightly amused.

"We look ridiculous sitting at the kitchen table dressed like this," she answered with a broad smile.

He grinned and raised his glass to his lips, taking a large swallow. Then he slowly lowered it, apparently to contemplate the clear, pale liquid inside.

"Caroline," he started in a deepened voice, "I have to admit you're not the loveliest woman I've ever known. But without a doubt, if one considers the whole package, regardless of what you're wearing you are by far the sexiest."

She was taken aback by his words and suddenly felt hot color rise in her cheeks. Why his outspoken nature continued to surprise her she couldn't guess, for during the past several days, she'd come to understand that speaking in such a manner was simply his way. Still, perhaps he'd given her the opening she needed to make her future desires clear.

Reaching for her glass, she put it to her lips, swallowed a mouthful, and, gathering her nerves, bluntly confessed, "I think you have a right to know I don't ever intend to carry a child."

The room became still as death. Even the rain stopped splattering against the window.

Caroline continued to look at her glass, waiting for her husband to yell at her or slap her soundly, as was his right. After several moments of unbearable silence, he shocked her completely when he instead reached for her plate and began filling it with food from the platter in front of them.

"May I ask why you changed the subject from our attire to children?"

She fidgeted from the coolness in his voice. "I just thought you should know how I feel before—"

"Before we become intimate, Caroline?"

He was twisting her words to his advantage, and that made her mad. "I want you to understand."

"I want a son and I need an heir."

Once again his voice was calm, controlled, as if he'd

made a final, irrevocable decision on the matter.

Bravely she retorted, "I don't want a baby. Please respect that decision."

After regarding her for a moment, he reached for his plate and began piling it high as well.

"All women want babies, Caroline, including properly bred ladies. I cannot believe you'd be any different, and that leads me to think you're either frightened of childbirth or frightened of sex. I'd like to know which and I'd like to know why."

She inhaled deeply. She couldn't argue with him and she couldn't tell him a thing about her plans without raising his suspicions. So, she reasoned, her only hope was to appeal to his logic, his intellect.

After taking another large sip of wine, she picked up her fork and started toying with her food. "I know exactly how you're feeling, Brent."

His cocked a brow. "You do?"

She smiled. "Of course I do. I understand your need for an heir and I also understand the male libido. I know that most men bed their wives over and over because they cannot control themselves. It's perfectly natural and probably instinctive."

He slowly leaned toward her, his elbow on the table, chin in palm, now seemingly engrossed in her words.

"Really? You know all of this?"

She nodded with absolute assurance.

"How learned you are, Caroline."

"I am." She gave him a light, confident smile. "I realize you need a woman in your bed to satisfy the urges you feel. I'm very practical about these things and won't be a bit jealous if you show any favors toward another."

"That's very reasonable and generous of you, Caroline," he slowly maintained. "But, to inherit, my son needs to be born legitimately."

Flushing, she ignored that issue and quickly looked back to her plate. "I just want you to know that I respect the fact that your desire for me is nothing more than lust you would feel for any woman.''

He was quiet for a moment, watching her closely, for she could positively feel the warmth of his gaze, and after an awkward minute of silence she glanced at him again. He spoke when their eyes met.

''You sound remarkably experienced, Caroline.''

''I'm both experienced and knowledgeable,'' she bravely contended. ''I've seen many animals mate and I assure you that rutting isn't all that pleasant for the female.''

He dropped his arm to rest it beside the other atop the table and leaned very close to her—so close that she could see candlelight reflecting in his eyes.

''Caroline, I'm going to promise you some things.''

She stared at him, unblinking.

''I promise,'' he slowly began, ''that I will never hurt you in any way. I promise I won't ever take a mistress, or embarrass you in public or private by flirting with another woman, gently bred or common. I promise I will take you to my bed, and even if it takes three full days to arouse you to a frenzied peak, you will enjoy it. I promise you will carry and bear my legitimate child. I promise you will never have another lover in this lifetime. And finally, I promise, to the depths of my soul, I will never rut on you like a common bull.''

With that he turned to his food.

Caroline didn't know whether she should lunge at him in rage or politely thank him for saying what were probably, to him, beautiful and honest words. Instead, she let the matter drop.

They ate together in silence for a while, Caroline finding her food tasteless, he practically licking his plate clean. When finally he reached for seconds, he cut the tension in the air by blandly changing the subject.

''So why didn't you marry and settle down at a young age like your sisters?''

She brushed over that and boldly asked, ''Why didn't you marry Pauline Sinclair?''

He looked up sharply, momentarily startled, then grinned sardonically. "I thought Pauline would have made an adequate wife and a decent mother, and those were the only reasons I wanted to marry her. She, however, did not want me."

"Did you love her?"

He snorted. "No." With a sigh, he sat back and took a sip of his wine. "Now answer my question, little one."

Suddenly her curiosity about his life with Miss Sinclair was overshadowed by the nervousness she felt at revealing her deepest desires to her husband. But after the briefest hesitation, his attention fixed exclusively on her, waiting for a reply, she felt honesty was in order.

"I long ago gave up my girlish dreams of romance and replaced them instead with dreams of being one of the world's leading authorities on plant breeding."

His brows furrowed, and his expression grew cautious.

Caroline lifted her chin, holding his gaze, certain that at any moment he would burst into laughter. She had nothing to lose now.

"At one point my greatest desire was to study at Oxford under the direction of Sir Albert Markham."

That intrigued him immediately as he slowly leaned toward her.

"I sent him some samples of my experiments, along with computations for the exact breeding of lavender roses to create the unique hue of those grown only in climes where temperatures rarely vary. As far as I know, no one thus far has been able to create such roses, for they are extremely delicate by nature and can only be grown with exact specifications and the greatest of care."

Caroline caught herself. She was delving into great and unnecessary detail. "In any case, the man wouldn't meet with me, even with proof of my experience and knowledge, and had the audacity to presume someone else had done the work." She threw her napkin on the table, trying to control herself before tears of frustration filled her eyes.

"I don't understand, since I know the man to be smart and methodical, why he wouldn't at least see you," he maintained softly, seriously, seemingly a bit perplexed.

She looked at him as if he were stupid. "I'm a woman, Brent."

He sat back at once. "Yes, you are." After a moment of silence, he added, "And now you're stuck with me and an overgrown garden instead of the famous Sir Albert and his years of expertise."

She relaxed and attempted a smile. He was trying to be delicate with her feelings. "It hasn't been so bad."

He grinned in return. "You enjoy pulling weeds?"

Her smile widened. Perhaps this was the perfect opportunity to broach the subject of a greenhouse.

Feeling almost immortally brave, she leaned her chest toward him in what she hoped was a seductive fashion. He, being a man, naturally dropped his gaze to her breasts, and for the first time since they'd met, it made her flush with delight and anticipation. She felt powerful as a woman for the first time in her life.

Lowering her voice, she placed her hand on his arm and whispered huskily, "I have a favor to ask of you, Brent."

His eyes moved back to her face, but his expression never changed. "Indeed."

"I would like to continue my work, but I've found Miramont lacking the one necessary item I need."

He arched a brow cynically. "And you'd like me to supply it for you?"

"Yes."

"Am I to assume it's a very small, inexpensive item?"

"It's . . . bigger than that," she murmured innocently, starting to feel unsure.

He cleared his throat. "Bigger than what?"

"Bigger than a small, inexpensive item." She sat up, removing her hand from his arm.

"So what you'd like, Caroline, is for me to buy you a big, expensive item?"

She nodded just slightly.

He leaned back in his chair, regarding her.

She was so incredibly nervous now that her hands were trembling, and she kept them well hidden in the folds of her gown. She felt ridiculous. She never should have brought it up.

"I'll buy it for you on one condition."

She caught her breath. He was very serious and, as she considered it, also very smug.

"Don't you even want to know what it is?" she asked, now fully frustrated with him sitting so close to her, staring at her as he was.

He shook his head lightly and stood. Before she could utter a protest, he clasped her arm and forced her to stand as well, beside him, almost touching.

"I don't care what it is," he whispered, placing his palm beneath her chin and tilting her head so she couldn't help but look at him.

He studied every inch of her face with a cunning grin on his mouth. "But I would think you'd like to know what the condition is."

She tried to back away, but in one quick movement he grabbed her around the waist and lifted her up forcefully against his chest.

That infuriated her. With her face steaming, blood boiling, she boldly stated, "I need a greenhouse—"

"I need a son."

She stared at him, horrified. "You cannot think—"

He leaned over and nuzzled her neck, making her heart start to pound. Pushing softly against him, she demanded furiously, "I need a greenhouse—"

"And I need you, Caroline," he whispered. "I believe that would be a fair exchange. We'll both plant seeds."

With that, he released her.

She stumbled back against her chair, breathing erratically, shaking.

"This is absurd," she choked out, moving quickly out of his way, refusing to look at him.

"Think about it, Caroline," he advised, now allowing the slightest traces of anger and disgust to seep into his voice.

Why he should be angry or disgusted, she couldn't fathom. She was the one who was being coerced.

Seething, she straightened, smoothed her hair, and looked across the table at him, her eyes shooting arrows of fire.

"Isn't it so like a man to use his wiles for his advantage, giving necessities to his wife only in return for sexual favors," she boldly, icily exclaimed.

His eyes turned black with deep anger as he started to move toward her. She stood her ground, though, refusing to back down.

"And isn't it just like a woman to tease her husband, then withhold sexual favors from him until he agrees to buy her necessities, which I would call niceties, actually, since greenhouses are about as useful as diamonds."

She gasped, retreating, as he now stood only inches from her.

"I'm not withholding anything and I certainly wasn't teasing you. My request had nothing to do with sex!"

"No?" His jaw tensed noticeably, and his voice became deadly soft. "If I recall, when you coyly asked for the little item you think you need, you snuggled so close your breasts nearly fell out of your gown and into my arms."

Her mouth and eyes opened wide in shock.

"Did you think I wouldn't notice or understand what you were trying to accomplish?"

"How dare you!"

"Tell me, my darling wife," he asked as his palm went up to stroke her cleavage, "are your nipples soft and rosy like your lips, or dark brown and sensuous like your eyes? I'll buy you five new rosebushes for a peek, ten for a taste."

She slapped him. Hard.

He clenched his jaw but didn't move. Even his eyes stayed locked with hers, daring her, as he ever so slowly slid his hand down to cover her left breast. Then, with an expertise she couldn't have anticipated, he lowered the top of her gown, exposing her completely.

Caroline shivered, and for the first time in her life, felt totally helpless. Her hands were at her sides, and she knew she should do something with them defensively, but she couldn't bring herself to break free of his penetrating stare. He hadn't looked down yet, hadn't moved his eyes from hers, but the fingers of his hands were gently moving over and teasing her nipples, causing them to harden and send fine points of delicious sensations through her body.

Suddenly he was breathing as heavily as she, and without notice or hesitation, he glanced down her body.

"Brent . . ." She felt weak, trembling against him.

Slowly, meticulously, he studied her by candlelight, as if marveling in a prized piece of art, a cherished possession, rotating his palms over her nipples, brushing them with the pads of his thumbs, running his fingers back and forth underneath her fullness, then gently cupping her, massaging her, squeezing her.

And finally, when she thought she might actually collapse against him, he raised his eyes and looked deeply into hers.

"I think the color is striking, Caroline," he said in a husky whisper. "Dark burgundy on smooth, pale champagne. The colors of fine French wine. When you're ready to let me taste, I will savor such a delicacy . . ." He cupped her fully with firm, warm hands.

She whimpered softly but said nothing as a fine liquid heat spread through her body and converged between her legs.

He leaned over and brushed his lips against her cheek. "They're perfect, and I'm so glad they're mine now."

Without warning, he pulled her gown up to cover her decently as he ran his tongue along her ear. That action made her nearly cry out.

"Sweet dreams, little one," he whispered.

And then he was gone.

It was the dream that awakened her. No, not a dream . . .

A wail.

Caroline abruptly sat up, her heart pounding, fear enveloping her. She heard it again. A noise. A whimper, now faint, coming from her husband's bedchamber.

Quickly she got out of bed and with cautious silence walked softly to the door dividing their rooms. She waited next to it, listening, her bare feet cold against the floor, moonglow giving her only a trace of light. But all was quiet on the other side.

After a minute or two, her body shivering, the only sound in the room coming from the faint crackling of the slowly dying fire, Caroline decided her imagination had truly caught up with her.

Then she heard it again. No mistake. A sharp wail came from the other side of the wall, then silence, then her husband's deep voice shouting, "No!"

Caroline didn't know what to do. It was possible he needed her. Yet surely he was alone inside and not in any real danger. A dream, perhaps?

She was on the verge of entering, her palm on the knob, when the silence fell once again. She waited at the door until she was so unbearably cold she could stand it no longer, then finally returned to her bed.

Probably just a bad dream, and for that she could do nothing.

She snuggled down into the recesses of her blankets and after several long minutes drifted off to sleep. When she woke again at dawn, her husband had already left Miramont.

Six

He would simply have to seduce her.

After six long days of vividly remembering the fullness of her pale, creamy breasts sitting ripe and aroused in the palms of his hands, Brent was sure there was no other way. It was only this morning, as he hitched his horses to his phaeton for the journey home, that he realized how the seduction of a woman with as much determination and intelligence as Caroline could be accomplished. Wine and charm didn't work, and he had never been very charming anyway. Instead, he would do it the same way he'd made her succumb to him the night before he'd left, the same way he'd made her moan for him, melt in his hands, become powerless to him, and truthfully the only way he could think of to do it.

He would do it with words.

Brent steered his horses along the muddy path, the going slow for the final two miles to Miramont. He had the cover raised so the light rain wasn't actually hitting him, but the dampness still managed to seep through his clothing. He was cold, hungry, and wanted nothing more than to be home for a hot meal and a hot bath.

His little travel adventure had been well worth the

trouble. He'd needed only three days to take care of estate matters, hire the rest of the essential help including two decorators who would begin refurnishing the property next week, and speak with his banker regarding his financial situation. Considering how long he'd been gone, his books were quite sound, more sound than he'd thought possible with Reggie ignoring the property and selling almost all of his possessions.

It was really quite the mystery. Why did Reggie sell everything movable and yet leave so much money in his accounts? How was he able to sell everything so quickly? And most important, where was the man?

But the part of his stay in London that troubled him most was his visit to the War Department, his first since returning from France. He talked for hours with his associates and their superiors, and the information he'd learned from that tiring day both confused and worried him.

As of yet, there was no conclusive evidence coming from their contacts on the Continent that Philip Rouselle, France's most evil son, the killer who haunted Brent's nights with striking memories of sickness and death, of lingering pain and horrifying destruction, was dead or exiled. And if he wasn't dead, Brent knew as surely as the sun would rise tomorrow that the man would come for him. Philip despised England, but his feelings for the Raven, the name given Brent by the French who knew him well, went far deeper, wounding not only his pride, but even his soul. Brent was hopeful that following Waterloo Philip had acknowledged his death, but he could never be sure. That disturbed him, and until there was word of the Frenchman's whereabouts, he would need to take precautions at home.

He just didn't know how much, if anything, he should tell Caroline. In his experience, it was preferable to know one's adversary and to understand the thinking process of one's opponent, so that in the end one could strike weak spots with some degree of efficiency. Sometimes, though, ignorance not only made you blind but saved your life, and it was just better to be kept in the dark. After two days of considerable thought he was fairly certain that with regard to Philip and Caroline, the latter idea was better than the former. If she knew who and what he was and their paths crossed, Caroline would be dead before she knew what hit her. She was safer in the dark.

So, resolved not to share the information, he set out for Miramont with the understanding that if Philip was indeed alive and was likewise aware that he still lived, it would be up to him to protect them all.

Slowly the estate came into view. He always relished in the knowledge that all of this belonged to him. His father had been dead for twenty-five years, and since that time and until her death five years ago, his mother had ruled Miramont like a queen on her throne. Sometimes he missed her presence, but then he would stop and remember the way she had ruled not only her own little subjects of servants and employees, but how she had ruled her family as well. The Lady Maude had, within the course of thirty years, pushed everyone who loved her out of her life.

But she'd left him Miramont, and it was only at times like this, when he rounded the last bend in the road, watching as tall lilac bushes gave way to the view of his home, that he thought about her—about his arrogant, self-centered mother who loved nobody but herself and managed to estrange her entire family irreversibly. Sometimes, especially on chilly, rainy days like this, the memories made him feel tired and old.

Quickly he steered his horses toward the stables. It was then that he saw Caroline running through the small meadow in the direction he was heading, wet hair flying behind her in wild disarray, her soaking dress clinging to her small form.

That's when he knew trouble had begun.

He had only been gone from Miramont for two days when she began to take count of the strange occurrences.

Caroline hardly noticed her personal things missing at first, assuming instead that she'd misplaced them—a hairbrush here, a shoe there, even some of her plants pulled from the ground for no reason. But after learning from her new lady's maid, Miss Gwendolyn Smith-Mayers, that one of the new servants had a child running loose on Miramont's property and had been seen less than an hour before carrying books as she headed in the direction of the stables, Caroline's mild curiosity turned to apprehension, and she had to check her things.

What she discovered enraged her. Although her comprehensive notes for breeding her lavender roses remained in place, among her trunks yet to be unpacked she found two items missing—a small book describing the first French botanical gardens established at the University of Montpellier, and her most cherished possession—her notes from Albert Markham's classroom lectures, which she'd collected with great care over several years and had bound into book form only last May to take with her to America. Someone had stolen them, toying with her for a reason she couldn't imagine, and Caroline was furious. Without second thought, she found herself racing to the stables.

By the time she reached the restored structure, her chiffon gown was nearly ruined, soaked through with splattered water and mud, but she couldn't have cared any less. She threw the door open and stomped inside. All was quiet except the pattering of steady rainfall on the roof and one or two rustling horses. Apparently those who cared for the animals had taken shelter elsewhere to await the storm's end. She'd never been inside Miramont's stables and she allowed herself a second or two for her eyes to adjust to the dimness.

It was then that she saw the girl.

Curled up in a corner lay the figure of a sleeping child on a bed of hay. She was a filthy little thing no more than four years of age, dressed in a worn, wrinkled cotton dress. Matted, light-brown hair surrounded what appeared to be a pale but dirty face, and long, dark lashes shaped like half-crescents shadowed the tops of her cheeks.

Beneath the grime, the face of an angel, Caroline thought, until she noticed the paper surrounding the tiny body.

Her books . . . torn to shreds.

Her breath quickened, and her heart began to pound from pure, focused rage.

Suddenly, as if sensing danger, the girl's eyes opened, and she scrambled to her feet.

"You little—"

Caroline lunged for her but missed as the slip of a child darted past her with the speed and agility of a fox, racing through the door to freedom.

She righted herself, turning toward the entrance with the determination of a bloodhound on the hunt. But before she put her palm to the wood, it opened wide and in walked her husband with the girl, wiggling fiercely, tucked under his arm like a sack of grain.

Caroline was so shocked to see him that she stopped dead in her tracks, and were it not for the fact that the child clawed at his stomach, she might have forgotten all about her.

They stared at each other, his face drawn and hard, his body wet from rain, his eyes locked with hers in silent communication. She was breathing heavily and definitely looked a sight, but she didn't care. All the work she had so meticulously compiled during the last five years into her personal book of study was destroyed.

She slumped her shoulders and started to cry.

"What did she do?" he softly asked, lowering the girl to the ground, holding her little arm as she continued to fight him.

Caroline put her face in her hands. "She—she ruined my books, destroyed my notes . . ." Abruptly she looked up to him in rage. "Get rid of her!"

He took a deep breath. "I can't do that."

She just stared at him, incredulous.

"She's my daughter, Caroline."

It took several seconds for the words to sink in. Then she was sure she was going to faint for the first time in her life.

"Wh . . . what?" She grabbed a thick wooden post to keep from falling.

He took another long breath and hugged the girl against his thigh as she slowly calmed beside him. "Her name is Rosalyn. She's my daughter."

Caroline sank down on a pile of loose hay, gaping at him, astonished to the core. "I don't believe you," she choked in whisper.

"Just look at her, Caroline," he beseeched.

Slowly she dropped her gaze to the girl. Big, dark-lashed hazel eyes stared straight at her, watching her curiously. She was slightly darker in coloring and her face more oval than square, softer in line. But maybe, in the right lighting . . .

Then she smiled, and with it came the stunning image of her husband. No two smiles were ever so alike.

Suddenly the child was gone, sprinting through the door like a rabbit on the run.

Caroline felt lost. Her head fell back against the stall behind her as she stared blankly ahead.

For several minutes neither spoke. Even the rain had quieted so that the silence between them was deafening.

Brent knew he needed to say something. She looked so forlorn, so bewildered. Calmly he crouched down beside her.

"She's not normal, Caroline."

She turned her head sharply to glare at him, eyes big and shiny black against wet lashes. Her dark, damp hair fell loosely and clung against the pinkness of her cheeks and the creaminess of her neck. Amazingly, with her gown sticking to her body, she looked sexy. Enticing. He'd never known a woman to look enticing when she cried.

"What's wrong with her?" she finally asked in a thick, broken voice.

He sat on the hay beside her, drawing his legs up to

rest his elbows on his knees, lacing a piece of straw through his fingers in front of him.

"She's . . . wild. Uncontrollable."

Caroline scoffed and turned her head. "And illegitimate, I suppose."

He expelled a long sigh, forgiving her rudeness because he understood exactly what she was feeling. "Her mother is a French courtesan—"

"You're joking," she interjected with unbelieving cynicism.

"No, I'm not joking, Caroline," he returned quietly. "Her name is Christine Dumont, a beautiful, exotic woman from Lyons who made her way through the wealthy inner circles of Napoleon's court."

From the corner of his eye he saw her turn to look at him pathetically.

"She first appeared on my doorstep a little over four years ago, by courier if you can believe that, with a note from her mother attached to her blanket. When she arrived in England she was burning with fever, and were it not for Nedda, she surely would have died."

Caroline lowered her head. "I can't talk about this now . . ."

He shifted slightly and turned to her. She stared at the ground again, eyes unblinking, unnaturally still. He knew this would be difficult, and it probably wasn't the time to delve so deeply into his past, but she had to understand the child and what she was like.

Brent threw the little piece of hay to his side, leaned back, and stared straight ahead. Gravely he whispered, "Rosalyn is sick in the mind, Caroline. She cannot learn and stays with Nedda most of the time. She's wild, unmanageable, and nothing can ever be done about it."

Caroline said nothing. She couldn't find her voice or clear her mind, and truthfully she didn't care about the girl right now, or her husband's tainted past. The only image clearly distinguishable through the fog in her head was that of the dream that had almost been hers, now torn to shreds on the floor of the stables by the horribly undisciplined, dirty child who was now her daughter by marriage.

Tears streamed freely down her cheeks once again, and she started to shiver from coldness and shock. He apparently noticed, for he quickly removed his overcoat and placed it around her shoulders.

"Why?" she asked, tormented.

"It's . . . complicated—"

"I'm not talking about you!" she shouted, turning to face him. "I'm talking about every man on earth making it so incredibly difficult for a woman to succeed!"

He looked at her as if she were insane. She stood quickly, throwing off his coat. He stood just as fast and grabbed her arm.

"Don't touch me," she said with deadly calmness.

He dropped his hand from the sleeve of her gown, his jaw tightening with building anger.

"My life was perfect until I met you, Lord Weymerth. Now everything I've ever wanted is gone."

Sternly he replied, "I think you're overreacting—"

"Overreacting?" She took a step back, staring at him as if he were diseased. "Do you know what it's like for a woman who wants to learn? We can't enroll in classes for an education like a man. The only thing we're allowed to do, if we come from a decent background, is study grammar and music from governesses so that when we become ladies, we can entertain the men in our lives by writing ridiculous poetry or sitting at the pianoforte for hours at a time."

She took a step toward him, pointing a finger at her chest. "Well, I was born with a gift, except I also had the little problem of being female. And do you know how women with gifts for unspeakable things like science and mathematics are allowed to learn? We have to sneak the information. Did you know that? We have to *sneak* it."

He just looked at her, so she straightened, placed her hands on her hips, and continued in a very subdued voice. "Several years ago, I began attending classes at Oxford University."

He was noticeably shocked, and that made her laugh.

"That's right, my darling husband," she expounded sarcastically. "I began attending classes with the few other daring women who wanted to learn, and do you know where we sat?" She crossed her arms over her chest and waited for his reply.

After a moment, he softly admitted, "I've no idea."

She chuckled bitterly. "We didn't! We weren't actually allowed *in* the classrooms, Brent. If we weren't a distraction to those who were there to truly learn—meaning men, of course—we were allowed to stand in the hallway and listen. Isn't that thoughtful of all the men who make the rules? We couldn't ask questions of the tutors; couldn't take the tests administered to the men, who were allowed to sit comfortably in chairs; we were allowed only to listen and be invisible."

She stopped her tirade and wiped her cheeks with her fingers. But the motion was futile, for at that moment she glanced back to the shredded paper, and her eyes filled with water again. Within seconds she was sobbing.

"And it's all right there," she choked out, pointing to what was left of her work. "Five years of notes I took crouching in the hallways at Oxford University while I tried to learn from the greatest botanist in the world. All right there. All destroyed by a filthy, ill-bred little girl."

"Caroline—"

"No!" He reached for her, and she backed away, moving to the door. When she opened it she turned to him.

He looked stricken.

"Your sick daughter has destroyed the only thing that has ever mattered to me." Her voice dropped to a low, dangerous whisper. "And you have ruined my life."

"Caroline. . . ."

He reached out in comfort, but she ignored him, running furiously to the safety of the house.

Seven

Caroline sat on the settee in her husband's study, in front of the fire, waiting for him. She'd been avoiding him for three days, working from dawn till dusk in her flourishing flower garden, her sanctuary, where she invariably turned to escape from the troubles of the world outside.

After three days of despondency, however, she knew it was time for a practical discussion. It was useless to dwell on what she'd lost. Her cherished collection of notes was gone, and she could do nothing about it. But she'd gained a daughter almost overnight, and it was time to address the situation. She was now the mother of a disturbed little girl whose father had created her from an affair with a beautiful French courtesan.

Caroline closed her eyes and leaned her head back against plush green velvet.

The thought of Brent engaged in a heated, passionate encounter with another woman made her blood boil and her skin flush. How could he have been so irresponsible with his desires? And if he had done it once he had probably done it countless other times, with other women. Most men did, and that thought, to her utter confusion, made her desperately sick at heart.

But even after this shocking revelation, Caroline had to melt a little inside when she thought of Rosalyn, the innocent child, found lying on his doorstep with a raging fever and her husband taking her into his home. She knew of no other nobleman who would dare keep his illegitimate, abnormal, half-French, female child. It was unthinkable. Scandalous. And her husband had done this scandalous thing because Rosalyn was his responsibility, his baby.

She'd also been giving Rosalyn some careful thought during the last three days and had come to several conclusions she wanted to discuss with her husband. The girl was certainly wild and uncontrollable, but there was something else . . .

Caroline raised her lashes and straightened as she heard him open the door.

"Well, little one, are you ready to discuss my indiscretion?"

She held her tongue from a caustic reply to his overly casual question, her pulse racing from nervousness as she watched him approach. He'd just come from a bath, for his hair was still damp and his cotton shirt and breeches were clean and fresh, and fit him far too snugly.

She looked back toward the fire, noticeably blushing and certain he saw it. Then in the blink of an eye he was squeezing his large frame in beside her, and she settled for the closeness, knowing any attempt to move would be futile.

They sat for several minutes like that, both quiet, both watching the flames flicker in the grate in front of them, both acutely aware of the other's presence.

Finally she was the one to break the silence. "Why do you call me little one?"

After a momentary pause, she forced herself to glance back to him, immediately caught off guard by his intense, piercing gaze as it bore into hers. He had the most marvelous eyes, so expressive, almost brown when he was angry and more dark, vivid green when he was passionate.

"Because it's so like you, Caroline," he revealed at last, taking in every feature of her face. "You're such a delicate creature, softly alluring, petite. Incredibly feminine." Caressingly, he added, "It suits you."

The gently spoken words flooded her with a warmth she didn't understand exactly. Never in her life had she been described in such an appealing way.

"Were you in love with her?" she whispered quietly.

The silence that followed was almost unbearable. Then he sighed and brushed her hair aside with his hand. "I had a relationship with Christine off and on for several years. Generally I enjoyed her company, but where I was concerned she was only doing her job. It was her job to please a man sexually, and she had remarkable ability."

Her shoulders tightened with those words, and he slowly started to rub her neck with his fingers. She pretended not to notice.

"I've never become emotionally involved with a woman, Caroline, for two reasons." His forehead creased in thought. "The first is that I have difficulty believing that true love actually exists, since everyone I've ever known has used the concept to manipulate others. I would rather never hear or say the words 'I love you,' because to me it really means 'I want something,' and is generally confused with lust. I lusted after Christine, and she felt the same toward me. Our relationship was strictly one of mutual gratification."

Caroline was more amazed by his negativity than shocked by his candor. "I think that's a horrible way to look at life and relationships. You're making love some sort of . . . raw need rather than a feeling—"

"I felt the raw need to have sex with Christine, and that's all," he interjected brusquely.

She would not be undone. "But you could feel the need to have sex with any woman."

"That's correct."

She sighed. "And I suppose that's how you feel about me."

The words had come out of her mouth before she'd truly thought upon them, and now, as she stared at the grim line of his lips, she regretted them.

"Caroline," he began thoughtfully, gazing at her intently, "I want you in my bed and I've made that perfectly clear. Beyond that, I don't feel anything more for you than any husband would feel for his wife."

"But many husbands love their wives," she stated defensively.

He shook his head. "I don't think so and I don't love mine."

She stared at him, and he just sat there, looking straight at her, as if they were only discussing practical dinner arrangements. His words weren't cold or bitter, just . . . matter-of-fact. But with that knowledge came a certain understanding that seeped through her skin and into her bones like hot summer sunshine. Brent had never been in love. For a reason she didn't at all comprehend, that thrilled her.

Caroline smiled playfully. "Well, husband, I don't love you either, and I promise, just so there will be no confusion where I am concerned, you will never hear the words come from my mouth." She smoothed her skirt. "Now, you said there were two reasons, and I'd like to hear the other one."

Brent slowly let out a long breath. From the moment he'd walked into his study to see her looking fresh and lovely in pale pink silk, her hair brushed shiny and secured with a white satin ribbon, his stomach had been tied in knots. Now, as she boldly confessed that she would never love him either, his nerves were unraveling. He should be grateful that she felt nothing more for him than he felt for her, so why all the agitation running through his mind? Since Caroline had been in his life, he understood himself less and less, and that made him angry.

Adjusting himself on the settee, he forced himself to blandly move on.

"I believe any emotional involvement between a man and a woman grows over the years to more of what I would call a . . . feeling of mutual attachment. I don't for a moment believe it slaps a person in the face—one day you're not in love, the next day you are. People who say they've felt that are feeling it between their legs."

He watched her cheeks pinken, proving his next point.

"I've never felt any attachment to a woman because no woman has ever wanted to be close enough to me for the length of time it would take for this kind of attachment to grow. Women generally find me abrasive and tactless and not to their liking." His expression clouded ever so slightly, his voice softening.

"In any case, I never loved Christine, and when Rosalyn appeared on my doorstep, alone and unwanted, I felt an indifference toward the woman I'd never felt before, although her decision in returning the child to me was, naturally, very practical. She's a courtesan, not a mother, so Rosalyn is probably better off here."

Softly she mumbled, "Would you ever go back to her?"

He relaxed, a smirk growing on his mouth. "Now why would I want to do that when I have you to fulfill all my needs, my darling Caroline?" Leaning very close, he asked playfully, "Would it bother you if I did?"

"I don't care what you do, my darling husband," she countered with thick sarcasm. "Just as long as you leave me out of your torrid affairs."

He reached up and clasped her chin, eyes blazing as he whispered, "*You* are my next torrid affair, sweetheart."

Caroline shook her face free of his grasp, stood swiftly, and walked forward three feet to the grate. She couldn't continue to look at him or be so close, now quite certain that her thoughts would betray her, that her pounding heart would be heard above the soft, cool summer wind outside and the crackling fire at her feet. And she couldn't deal with this kind of intimacy between them right now. She needed to change the subject.

"Why didn't you tell me about Rosalyn, Brent?"

He sat quietly for a long moment before he answered. "I don't know. At the time of our rather rushed marriage it didn't seem important—"

"Didn't seem important?" she cut in loudly. "You have a sordid affair with a French prostitute, creating an illegitimate daughter who lives with you, and you didn't think it important enough to tell your wife?" She shook her head, dumbfounded. "Didn't it occur to you that you were being a bit deceptive?"

His jaw clenched, she could actually see it, but he didn't move his gaze from the directness of hers.

"I didn't mention my daughter's existence," he disclosed, "because I understood your reluctance to be here, with me, and I felt I should give you time before I mentioned you were now the mother of an abnormal little girl who spends her days running wild and causing trouble."

She waited, then softened her voice a little. "Why didn't you tell me during breakfast the morning before you left? I asked you frankly if you had any children—"

His curt laugh cut her off. "Caroline, you were teasing me—"

"That's absurd. I am not a woman who teases a man she hardly knows."

He eyed her speculatively. "You specifically said children from another entanglement, meaning marriage, and since I'd never been married before, I believe I was truthful in my answer that morning."

She scoffed. "I hardly think so. You evaded the question purposely and craftily, and I'm certain I looked the fool in front of Nedda and Davis."

He ran his fingers through his hair and casually sat back. "Neither Nedda nor Davis thinks you're anything of the kind, and I know they both thought I was unfair in keeping this from you. They like you very much."

She braced herself. "Are there any more?"

"Any more what?"

"Children," she nearly shouted in frustration.

"No," was his smooth reply. "But I intend to change that situation soon."

She peeked out at him from the corner of her eye. "Are you sure?"

He smiled faintly. "Absolutely. On both counts."

She could think of no solid retort to effectively counter his brash innuendos, and after a moment she turned to regard the small clock on the mantel with keen interest, mesmerized by the swinging pendulum in front of her.

"I care about my daughter more than you can imagine, Caroline," he professed quietly. "She's part of me and in many ways, even with her unfocused mind, she's very like me. I hope that over time, you'll grow to care for her as well."

She couldn't think about that. She didn't want to care for any of them enough to give her heartache when she finally had to leave for America. So, pushing that from her mind, she realized this was her opportunity to move on and discuss the problem at hand.

"I've had some thoughts about Rosalyn, Brent," she said with forced confidence.

He expelled a long breath. "I'm anxious to hear them."

Caroline turned to look him squarely in the eye. "Is she trained?"

His eyes narrowed. "Trained to do what? She's not a dog, Caroline."

"Of course she's not a dog." Her cheeks flushed. "I mean, is she trained to relieve herself properly or does she need to be changed?"

He showed surprise at her question, but not embarrassment. "She can generally take care of her own needs. Why do you ask?"

Caroline became serious, pausing to gather her thoughts. Her assumptions about her new daughter were becoming clearer.

Dauntlessly she said, "It seems to me that a four-year-old child who can take care of her own private needs, manipulate an adult by moving her possessions from one room to another, be cunning enough to purposely hide my shoes in the blue room—"

"She hid your shoes in the blue room?" he asked through a small, almost prideful laugh.

She looked up sharply. "You're not listening to what I'm saying, Brent."

He sobered a little. "Then what exactly are you saying?"

Quickly she blurted, "That I don't think she's all that sick in the mind."

He was decidedly unimpressed. "Caroline, I'm her father—"

"A child who can think ahead, plan her actions, and manipulate an adult is rational," she interjected with newfound strength. "She has a rational mind, and causing trouble is the only way she can think of to get attention."

"You're implying she hid your shoes and tore your books to get your attention?"

"No," she stated firmly. "I think she did those things to get *your* attention."

He shook his head. "I don't think so, Caroline. If she were rational she wouldn't cause me grief. Your theory doesn't make any sense."

"It makes perfect sense if you consider that she's a typical little girl who hasn't seen her beloved papa in a very long time, and when he does return for her he has taken a wife. Now suddenly she has to share the one person she loves the most with someone else."

She watched him lean forward and place his elbows on his knees, clasping his hands in front of him. He looked more than skeptical, which in turn made her almost fierce in her attempt to convince him. Bravely, standing directly in front of him, she forced him to look up to her. He would see reason.

"Brent," she slowly began, "has it never occurred to

you that Rosalyn's only problem is that she cannot hear?''

He sneered. ''Of course she can hear.''

She smiled faintly. ''I think you should consider that she can't.''

She expected him to laugh, or dismiss her notions completely, but instead he lowered his gaze, thoughtfully pondering the statement she had posed.

''What makes you think such a thing?'' he finally asked.

Caroline wiped the back of her hand across her brow. ''Well, she never utters a word, and three days ago, when I found her in the stables, she didn't hear me come in. I think she was sleeping, but even someone in a very deep sleep would have heard me, or the horses, or the wind and rain when I opened the door. She heard nothing.''

He shook his head skeptically.

''If you think about it, it's not implausible,'' she persisted. ''If she is a perfectly balanced little girl, she should be able to speak. I've concluded she's perfectly balanced and yet she does not speak. In nearly all cases where people do not speak, they also cannot hear.''

After a moment of staring at the rug beneath his feet, he admitted quietly, ''I don't think it's ever occurred to me.'' He looked at her again. ''Don't you think Nedda would have noticed, though? She's the one who's practically raised her.''

Caroline shook her head. ''I think Nedda probably did more taking care of her needs than raising her. I'm sure she fed her, changed her, cuddled with her, but she isn't her mother—and you were gone much of the time, were you not?''

He nodded negligibly.

''I think, under those conditions, the only person who would have likely noticed she was deaf would have been her mother, someone keenly aware of a problem from the beginning. You and Nedda probably noticed she was different when she matured and didn't learn to communicate with speech. By then she was communicating the only way she knew how, and the two of you accepted it as a problem with her mind.''

She lowered her body onto the settee. ''I think she either was born deaf or lost her hearing with the fever she had when she arrived here. I know that fevers in children sometimes do that.''

He stood quickly and began to pace the room. ''Children who cannot hear are usually placed in institutions, are they not?''

She refused to look away. ''Sometimes. I would say nearly always, in the case of the underprivileged. Where the nobility are concerned, that decision would be strictly up to the parents.''

''I see.''

He stopped and faced her squarely, arms crossed over his chest, legs spread apart like a soldier ready for battle. He looked formidable and intimidating. She knew what was coming.

''Well, I absolutely refuse to have my daughter placed in an institution. It would tear us both apart. I'd rather she stay here for the remainder of her life and live as she is now, in my care.''

Caroline melted. ''I was hoping you'd say that.''

His brows shot up. ''Indeed.''

She rubbed her hands together in her lap, choosing her words cautiously. ''Brent, Rosalyn is not stupid or insane, she is deaf. I would like your permission to teach her to communicate.''

He was taken aback by that. She could see it in his eyes. Then his lids narrowed as he began sauntering toward her.

''If she can't talk or hear, Caroline,'' he asked suspiciously, ''how do you expect to accomplish this?''

Her expression became grim. ''She can learn associations between objects, to move her lips to form words, to use gestures for meaning, to write. The possibilities are endless, I should think.''

He said nothing for a moment. Then Caroline raised

herself until she stood only inches away, taking his warm, large hand in hers and squeezing it gently.

"I think Rosalyn is as quick-minded as any child her age," she said passionately. "And if you allow her behavior to continue as it is now, if you only feed her and clothe her and let her run wild, you'll be cheating her. She's a beautiful girl and she deserves a better life than that."

He stared at her for a long moment, taking in every feature of her face. Then slowly he raised her hand to his lips, kissing the inside of her wrist, lingeringly, making her knees weaken and her breath quicken. She tried to pull away, but he held tightly, the corners of his mouth turning up to form a lazy grin.

"You'd do this for us, little one?" he asked softly.

The intimacy entranced her. "I'll do it for Rosalyn."

He continued to watch her, clasping her hand, eyes darkening with intensity. Then without warning, he leaned in to brush his lips against her temple, and the suddenness coupled with the gentleness of the action made her powerless to his touch.

"If your ideas work," he intimated with a feathery kiss to her cheek, "I'll have to thank you"—kiss—"personally"—kiss—"and completely." He ran his tongue from her jaw to her ear, gently sucking the lobe.

Caroline shuddered and instinctively leaned toward him, oblivious to all but his mouth on her skin.

Then he brought his lips to hers, kissing her fully, with no hint of passion, just pure tenderness and warmth. After several seconds he raised his head to peer into her eyes.

"One more thing, Caroline," he whispered.

She blinked, dazed.

He grinned and cupped her face with his palms. "Rosalyn is not a flower. No experimenting on her without my approval, understood?"

She nodded and closed her eyes, waiting for his mouth to touch hers once again. But the action was fruitless, for at that moment he released her burning cheeks and swiftly walked to the study door.

"I'll see you at dinner, Caroline, and wear something else," he ordered casually, frankly. "Pink is for blondes."

She reached for something—anything—to throw at his face, but her insufferable husband had already quit the room.

Eight

For two weeks she worked diligently, only to find defeat at even the smallest attempt at getting her newly acquired daughter to just sit still in her presence.

Rosalyn spent most of her time with Nedda or running wild, even sleeping in the servants' quarters, where she felt more comfortable. Caroline wanted to change that habit, though, for the girl was the daughter of an earl, regardless of her legitimacy, and she deserved her own room in the main house.

But that, along with everything else, would come with time. She acknowledged the difficulty of her task, feeling certain she would eventually see results, and finally, on the seventeenth day of her struggle, she made contact.

She and Nedda were sitting at the newly purchased dining-room table, sipping tea and discussing trivial household matters, when in came the girl, pouncing onto their housekeeper's lap, eager for her usual afternoon snack, the fare of the day being raspberry cream tarts and lemon cakes. Still unsure of her stepmother, the child clung to Nedda and nervously watched her through piercing, hazel-green eyes.

Caroline had been avoiding the sweets, but this was

a prime opportunity to attempt communication, and what better way to communicate with the child than on her level. That thought in mind, she reached for a tart, leaned her elbows on the table, and began to eat. Rosalyn did the same, and that made her grin in satisfaction.

"She looks a great deal like my husband, doesn't she?"

Nedda smiled and wiped a stray hair from Rosalyn's face. "She really looks more like his lordship's late mother. The Lady Maude was beautiful, the rage of society in her day."

Caroline, so engrossed in her own thoughts and work since her arrival, hadn't given much consideration to Brent's family. That was probably selfish, too, for she'd never asked him a thing about his childhood, his relationships with his friends, and now she was curious.

"Tell me about Lord Weymerth, Nedda. What was he like growing up?"

Nedda sighed. "Well, his childhood was the same as most men of his class, I suppose, except he was always so serious, so focused. He didn't get on well with his mother; they were just too different, and he resented her involvement with the family."

Caroline was confused. "What family?" She took a bite of her tart and studied her housekeeper, who now frowned in deep thought.

"Lady Maude was a bit . . . demanding," Nedda continued carefully. "She had the ability to push people in whatever direction she chose for them, regardless of what they wanted."

She picked up a napkin to wipe Rosalyn's mouth, but the girl knocked her hand away and reached for a second tart.

"In any event, she was the reason his lordship began working for the government, why he was in France so much of the time."

"But what about friends and"—she swallowed dryly—"the women in his life?"

Nedda regarded her, thinking. "Truthfully, Master

Brent didn't have many friends. He was always so . . . shy, so quiet as a child, preferring the company of Davis and his Arabians. Then when he left to study at university he became compulsively driven, absorbed in his work like a poor man hunting for gold, with no time to spare for anyone but himself.''

Caroline was shocked. "I didn't know he was a scholar.''

Nedda looked at her strangely. "He has advanced degrees in both foreign government and French studies. He didn't tell you?''

"I—I never asked." She shook her head thoughtfully. "French studies? Is that the language or the people?''

Nedda smiled and placed her chin on Rosalyn's head. "Both, I think. He studied the culture and the language. He speaks fluent French, my lady, and he does it so well you'd never know he was English.''

She gaped at her housekeeper. "I had no idea he was formally educated.''

"He's more than educated," Nedda divulged with wide eyes. "I think he's just this side of brilliant, although I am quite prejudiced where Lord Weymerth is concerned.''

She watched the woman stuff her mouth with half a tart—her fifth in that sitting, Caroline mused. After swallowing hard and licking her lips, Nedda continued her tale.

"Your husband was a bit different as a child. Some even thought him unusual, but those who thought that didn't really know him. He was clever but quiet, and he took to horses sure enough, although people didn't seem to understand or like him much. Girls and then women especially.''

Caroline frowned and asked hesitantly, "What about Pauline Sinclair?''

Nedda puckered her face so tightly that Caroline almost broke out laughing.

"Miss Sinclair is brainless," she said with complete distaste. "I only met her twice, and both times she con-

cerned herself with nothing but her hair and fashions.''
She shook her head and wiped crumbs off Rosalyn's
cheek. ''I don't know this for fact, but I think when she
learned his lordship had an illegitimate child she conveniently changed her mind about marrying him. He
hadn't yet formally talked to her father, but he was about
to, and everyone knew it.'' She softened her voice. ''I
think it hurt him, too, but only because of his pride. To
this day I'm not sure why he wanted to marry her.''

''Is she pretty?'' she casually asked.

Nedda nodded. ''Quite. Although Lord Weymerth
would never marry a woman strictly for her appearance
or social graces. Personally, I believe he was more concerned with getting an heir and a mother for Rosalyn,
and she happened to be the first woman who really paid
attention to him.'' She exhaled a deep sigh. ''I also think
he was lonely.''

Caroline felt her first ever pang of deep-felt sympathy
for her husband at that moment. She understood how it
felt to be termed unusual and have few friends, what it
was like to feel completely alone. In many ways her life
paralleled her husband's, and where she'd found comfort
in her plants, he'd found it in his horses, his work.

But where women were concerned, she was quite sure
he'd pushed prospective wives away as soon as he
opened his mouth and discussed what was wrong with
their appearance. Or perhaps he sat down with them and
frankly explained how the bedding would take place on
their wedding night. There was no way around his forth-
right nature, for it was simply the way he was.

Still, she couldn't be the only woman alive who found
him unbearably attractive. And having an illegitimate
child was certainly undesirable in a prospective husband,
but it could be overlooked if other conditions in the betrothal agreement were adequate and the bride's family
was compensated for the indiscretion. Many noblemen
had bastard children, although truthfully, very few of
them had them living under their roofs.

Nedda adjusted Rosalyn so that the child sat straighter

on her lap and went on with her disclosure. "After the fiasco with Miss Sinclair, he turned his attention away from the ladies, away from finding a wife, and focused on his work and then the war. Until you came along, I was certain he'd never meet a woman who complemented his intense nature, who was perfect for him in so many ways."

Caroline reached for her tea to hide her choked expression.

Nedda smiled again, hugged Rosalyn against her ample bosom, and leaned toward her. "Honestly, Lady Caroline, I've known Lord Weymerth almost all of his life and I've never seen him so confounded by a woman. You've certainly shaken him up, and for the better, I think. I know it's none of my business, but I believe you've completely enchanted him."

"We don't even really know each other," she whispered shakily, knowing it was a ridiculous thing to say to defend her position.

Nedda relaxed against the back of her chair, her expression growing serious. "The man you married is kind, understanding, and fiercely loyal. He's confused by you, yes, and enthralled and uncertain, and even with his blunt nature, very shy. But he's also a man—stubborn, demanding, and just as quick to show his temper as he is to hide his tender emotions."

She tapped a thick finger on the table for emphasis. "He's never cared deeply for any woman in his life, that I know. But I think if he knows you return the feeling, he will fall in love with you, deeply and passionately, and with a devotion even you probably won't ever understand. It's already happening. I can see it in his eyes when he looks at you, and quite honestly, I think that through all his efforts to deny it, he knows it, too. That's why he's scared."

Caroline sat very still, her eyes wide open in absolute horror. If Nedda thought any affection between them was scary for Brent, she couldn't possibly imagine how terrified it made her. Suddenly, urgently, she needed to get away.

Rosalyn stopped eating and looked at her strangely, sensing a change in mood. Caroline slowly stood and wiped her hands with a napkin, trying to control the trembling inside of her by forcing a smile.

"I just remembered something I have to do, Nedda." She started for the door, and just as quickly Rosalyn was at her feet, pulling at her legs, squirming wildly.

Caroline abruptly stopped moving and stared down at her, stunned. Rosalyn clung to her tightly, a shrill, wailing noise emanating from her throat as she tugged at the hem of her gown in an attempt to keep her from leaving the room.

All other thoughts vanished as Caroline knelt beside the child, grasping her arms and pulling her up to stand in front of her, eye to eye. Rosalyn continued to struggle for several seconds, then gradually stilled and blew scraggly hair from her face to see better.

They looked at each other, Rosalyn red-faced and panting, Caroline determined but uncertain of what to do next. She'd never been so close and didn't want to lose a chance like this. Nedda understood, it seemed, for the woman, bless her heart, sat silently, watching from her chair.

Caroline steadied herself and slowly released the girl, allowing her to stand on her own, praying she wouldn't run. Then with the care and instinct that should have belonged to the woman who bore the beautiful child in front of her, she reached up with her right hand, tapped her chest three times with her palm and opened her arms.

Rosalyn blinked, unsure. Then, as if the sun had suddenly burst through the window to shine brilliantly into the room, it all became perfectly clear. Her mouth turned up slowly into a lovely, sweeping grin, and in one quick movement she threw her tiny body against her mother's bosom, wrapping her arms around her neck to hug her fiercely.

"Oh, good heavens, I've never seen her do such a thing," Nedda whispered, astonished.

Caroline held tightly, afraid to let go, and almost certain she was going to cry. "She's hugging me, Nedda."

Nedda shook her head. "I never thought I'd see the day when that child would respond instead of react. It's almost as if she can think like a normal little girl."

Caroline grinned joyously. "She is a normal little girl."

And so the teaching began. It was a good two days before Caroline saw her pupil again for a long enough period to attempt any communication, but by the end of the week the child had attached herself permanently to her side, following her everywhere.

Rosalyn had always been difficult to keep clean because she was wild and allowed to behave that way, so Caroline took it upon herself to instill a few basic manners and introduce the girl to several daily necessities she'd sorely lacked in the first four years of her life.

She bathed the child herself every morning, Rosalyn fighting her ferociously the first three days. She then realized if she put cups and bubbles in the bathtub, they would distract the child long enough to get her clean.

She brushed and braided the girl's unruly hair, kept her clothes presentable, and ordered Gwendolyn to have them cleaned and mended as needed. Only three weeks after their first hug in the dining room, everyone at Miramont saw a completely different child, and all were astounded at the transformation.

And Caroline pursued her efforts to make contact with the girl, pointing at things as she created words with her hands and arms for meaning. She started with small items—a bowl, a hairbrush, a bird, even a flower—gesturing over and over again. The only two things that truly exhausted her were the tantrums Rosalyn threw, born from frustration, and constantly saying no to the child by shaking her head and holding up her index finger in protest. She was forever saying the word, and after a month of constant work, she knew that Rosalyn understood there were things she could not do, places she could not go, and behaviors that were simply not allowed. Rosalyn was starting to learn, and through it all, her daughter by marriage trusted her implicitly.

So did her husband.

From the beginning he'd been dubious. Even the day she'd told him his daughter had hugged her in response to a gesture, he wasn't convinced. Then he tried it himself, and when Rosalyn walked into his arms, Caroline was sure she had never seen a man so positively speechless.

From that point on he was her champion, allowing her freedom to work with the girl as she chose, watching her closely from time to time, though always keeping his distance. He'd curbed his male appetites as well, and for that she was both relieved and troubled. He talked to her only of Rosalyn or estate matters, never of their relationship, and Caroline wasn't sure what to think of that, could not understand her feelings on the matter. Every once in a while he would kiss her, but the action was brief and affectionate, not filled with desire, and certainly not filled with love. If he felt anything akin to love, he hid it flawlessly. What bothered her deeply was not knowing whether her husband just didn't want her as a woman anymore, or had taken her advice and was now pursuing the company of a mistress.

She was incensed at herself for caring either way.

Caroline knew she was losing perspective. The dream of her lifetime was only months away, and her impatience was getting the best of her. She'd done her part by initiating contact with those in America, and her plans were essentially set; now all she had to do was wait for a reply to be sure of the dates, to know when she could finally push her husband, his home, and his family from her mind to truly begin the life she'd envisioned since she was twelve years old. She just needed to hold on for another few weeks, which would undoubtedly be the longest of her life.

That was the problem. The longer the wait, the greater the internal struggle. She was beginning to adore Rosalyn, and after the discussion with Nedda regarding Brent's past and his innermost feelings, she knew she could grow to want him for herself. If that happened, she would never realize her destiny, and not realizing her destiny would destroy her.

Nine

The flowers bloomed brilliantly.

Brent hadn't ventured into the garden since the first week of his marriage, but now his curiosity got the better of him. He wanted to see what miracle Caroline had achieved during the last two months, and a miracle it was.

Circling the garden on the stone path, he allowed the calm of the surroundings to touch him, the fragrance to envelop him, the sunshine to melt the early-morning chill in his bones.

It had been a week since he'd shared an eventful talk with Davis, his closest confidant, and during that time he'd given the old man's advice a great deal of consideration.

Davis thought rather highly of his new wife but was deeply suspicious of her motives. He felt she was hiding something and that her reasons for not wanting to consummate their marriage were detailed and involved, maybe because she was saving herself for an annulment or another man. Brent, however, as highly as he regarded Davis and his opinions, didn't believe this at all. Caroline wasn't a virgin—of that he was convinced—and an annulment was simply out of the question. But what bothered him most was the old man's awareness that he and his wife weren't yet lovers. If Davis knew this, then probably everybody else at Miramont did as well.

It was embarrassing, really, the wealthy and powerful Lord Weymerth unable to bed his wife without force. Many men would have used it by now, but he wasn't forceful. He wanted his wife to come to him because she wanted him.

But he and Davis agreed on one thing—Caroline wasn't going to climb into his bed and seduce him of her own free will. Not, at least, as things stood now. She desired him beyond any doubt, but she was also strong-willed and wanted to stay out of his bed for reasons he still questioned. What made him smile, though, was knowing that women, when given the choice between logic and want, almost always chose the latter. All he needed to do was speed things along, putting his original plan into action by seducing her with words.

At last he saw her, down on all fours, working quickly and efficiently as she planted in the far west corner of the garden. She again wore her ugly, snug dress, which, with her back to him, leaning over as she was, presented a wonderfully delicious view of her bottom.

"I think I'll wander out and enjoy this view more often," he finally announced, sitting across from her on the hard stone bench.

The intrusion made her jump.

"I didn't hear you," she said breathlessly, turning to him, wiping the back of her gloved hand over her forehead.

She raised herself, pulling off her gloves and brushing her skirt with her palms. As she walked over to sit beside him on the bench, he stared with undeniable appreciation at her small, shapely waist, the curve of her hips, her full, rounded breasts. At that moment he knew he would gladly give the horses he'd purchased for her back to her father in exchange for just one night. If she was anything undressed like he imagined her to be, with her hair flowing dark and shiny to her waist, eyes stormy with desire for him alone, she would look absolutely beautiful lying naked in his bed.

Brent shifted uncomfortably and glanced back to the garden. "Tell me what you're doing here, Caroline. What are you planting?"

"Well," she started, placing her gloves on the bench beside her, "these are morning glories. By next summer the vines will spread from here to the south wall."

"And the roses?"

She gave him a devastating grin. "They're my favorite. I've been breeding the whites with the yellows, and I expect to see buds in about twenty-seven to twenty-eight days. If they fail to produce or if the color isn't right, I—" Abruptly, she stopped. "I'm sure you don't want to hear this."

"Yes, I do," he admitted honestly. "Tell me how it's done."

"You mean breeding?"

Brent nodded as his eyes grazed over her face. Her cheeks blushed with hot color and her dark eyes shone brightly, filled with surprise and a tinge of embarrassment. That made him smile. "You do know how breeding works, don't you, little one?"

"Of course," she expelled in a defensive breath. Then she relaxed. "Well, nobody knows how it works, really. We plant seeds, or usually bushes in the case of roses, mixing certain colors with others, certain plants with others, in the hope of creating a desired color or breed."

"And what color do you expect to get from these?" he questioned mildly, pointing to those on which she'd been working.

"I hope they will be a pale, almost translucent yellow, but that won't be known until they bloom."

"But how do you know with any certainty you'll get a pale yellow from a bright yellow and a white mix?"

She sighed. "I don't, and neither would any other scientist. It's like mixing two colors on a canvas, although mixing paint is much more exact. If you mixed equal amounts of bright yellow with white, you'd get a very soft, pale yellow. Plants are different because the science can never be exact with things that are alive. It's believed that plants mix like two parents do when creating a child, with the flowers having traits from both plants. For instance''—she cleared her throat and looked to her lap—''is Rosalyn's mother dark or lighter in coloring? What does she look like?''

That sure as hell came out of nowhere. He smiled and leaned back casually against the wall. ''She's blond and beautiful.''

''Of course,'' she acknowledged with a degree of irritation, looking once again to her garden.

Her remark made his grin widen. ''Does that bother you?''

''No,'' she retorted. ''It's quite obvious that someone as worldly and . . . attractive as you would couple with beautiful women. Naturally, like most men, you would choose blondes.''

''Naturally.'' He was suddenly having a wonderful time. ''You find me attractive, Caroline?''

''And I'm sure there were others,'' she added firmly, ignoring his question.

''Other what?''

Her jaw tightened. ''Other beautiful blondes in your life.''

''You are?''

''Weren't there?'' Her tone was rising.

He chuckled softly. ''I thought you didn't want to concern yourself with my torrid affairs, Caroline. If you're suddenly curious, I'd be happy to prepare a list—''

''Absolutely not! Your past is none of my business.''

He adored provoking her, and she was definitely irritated now. He could see it clearly in her ramrod-stiff posture, the grim line of her mouth. He truly didn't think he'd ever found so much enjoyment in teasing a woman.

After an awkward moment of silence, she put her

hands over the hair hanging in her face and smoothed it back into place.

"As far as breeding is concerned," she continued casually, "I was only drawing a conclusion for your benefit. Usually two people create a child who is a mixture of both parents. Personally, I think Rosalyn looks very much like you except she has slightly darker hair. Because of this, I assumed her mother would be darker."

He expelled a deep breath. "Actually her mother's coloring is similar to mine. Her hair is very dark blond, although her eyes are blue."

"I see." She looked back to him, her voice and features controlled and unreadable. "Science is rarely exact with flowers or children, so one cannot predict coloring in offspring with much accuracy except in the cases of two very dark or two very blond people, or two red roses from the same type of bush. For a reason nobody understands, sometimes a violet and a white rose will combine to create not a lavender mix as it would with paint, but something akin to yellow or peach. It makes no sense and it's rare, but it does happen."

She lowered her gaze to study the dirt at her feet. "As for Rosalyn, her hair is a mixture, but her eyes are yours. There's no mixture there." Her voice became deep and serious, silky to his ears. "She's so like you, Brent, in her expressions, her mannerisms, her face. She's your daughter through and through, a sweet and loving child. When she's grown, I'm sure she'll be stunning to look at, very beautiful. If her mother is indeed lovely, then she received that attribute from both of you. Her physical beauty is the mix you and her mother created together."

The breeze picked up to carry her softly spoken words. She was still looking at the ground, avoiding his gaze, but he was entranced nonetheless. Of all the women he'd ever known, not one of them had expressed such deep thoughts and feelings about him, for him, as Caroline did. In that instant he felt the most uncontrollable urge to grab her around the waist, mold her body against his and kiss her fully, passionately, putting a cease to the longing he knew they both felt for each other. She was probably unaware of her desires, but he could see them in her eyes, her body, her work. She was like the most unique of flowers, blooming in dazzling light before his eyes, and to his sheer disbelief, he found himself almost in awe of her, drawn to her honesty, her hunger for the beauty in life and all things good.

He reached up to cup her chin with his hand. "Do you know what I think about, day and night, Caroline?" he softly asked.

She looked up, eyes wide with uneasiness. "I'm sure I don't."

He smiled, his lids narrowing as he stared at her intently. "I think about you."

She was noticeably shocked but didn't pull away.

Slowly, eyes locked with hers, he started caressing her jaw with his thumb. "I think about your pale, creamy skin, your lovely face so filled with expressions of shocking secrets and hidden desires for me yet to discover. I think about your eyes, like dark, polished jewels, shining with hurt and joy, beauty and intelligence. I think about your small, voluptuous body, desperately needing to be touched, aching to be one with mine, to be ignited into a flame of desire so intense—"

She jerked her face away from his hand and abruptly stood. "I—I need to leave."

Brent wouldn't allow it, not when he finally had the advantage. He grabbed her wrist and was standing in front of her before she could move.

"Don't, Caroline," he pleaded in a whisper, encircling her waist, pulling her tightly against him. "Not yet . . ." He reached up and tugged at the ribbon in her hair, freeing the shiny locks to fall over her shoulders and down her back.

He could feel her trembling against him as he buried his face in her hair, breathing the scent of violet water and sunshine. He lightly ran his lips along her ear, his fingers interlocked with the silkiness of her hair, feeling her breasts flattened against his chest.

"Please . . ." she whispered. It was an urgent whisper, but she didn't push against him for release. She was breathing as hard as he, as fast as he, and he knew he held her powerless by more than just strength.

"Every night I lie awake in my bed and think about you, Caroline. I wonder if you're asleep or if you're lying awake thinking about me, wanting me." He started running kisses along her cheek and jaw, then her neck, his gentle touches making her shudder against him. He reached down and grasped her bottom with his palm, caressing it softly in slow circles. Then he pulled her into him, forcing her to feel his need for her.

She molded against him, succumbing to the feel, wrapping her arms around his neck, fingers weaving through his hair. He continued to kiss a pattern along the sensitive line of her neck, her jaw, and back to her ear, his hand on her head holding her tightly to him.

"Sometimes, my darling Caroline, when I can't take the want any longer, I go and look at you. Did you know that? I stand by your bedside and watch you sleeping by moonlight, your angelic face draped in shadows, so lovely, so peaceful, and I wonder if you're dreaming about me."

He heard her gasp faintly—in surprise or desire, he didn't know. But he held to her firmly.

"I need so badly to hold you, to feel you," he whispered huskily. "But more than anything, I need to be inside of you. I need to feel you surround me, wet and hot and excited. I swear to you, that will be the greatest pleasure yet to come, for both of us. I can't wait to make you moan for me, little one." He took a deep breath and squeezed his eyes shut. "I need to hear you cry out for me, Caroline. Only me."

"No . . ." She tried to pull away. He wouldn't let her go.

In a fast, sweeping movement, his lips were upon

hers, kissing her with a passion both rough and tender, hot, vibrant, and filled with desire.

She pushed against him for several seconds then fell to the need, succumbing to his urgency. He opened her mouth with his tongue, searching, and when he found hers, he grasped it and began to gently suck.

Her knees buckled, but he held her against him firmly, possessively, listening to each moan of raw pleasure escape her throat. She was suddenly on fire for him, as he was for her. They melded to each other in a blinding, frenzied rage of blissful torment. He sucked her tongue, caressed her head with his palm, and pushed her soft, luscious body against the hardness of his. She fell into step with him, kissing him back in a fever of need, rubbing her hips and breasts against him in an instinctive wild abandon as old as time.

The yearning was there. The craving, the longing, the delicious forbidden fruits, all there for the picking. The urge he felt at that moment, to make her his forevermore, was nothing less than torturous. She needed him just as badly, felt as deeply as he that becoming one with each other was unavoidable. He could feel it in her response to his touch.

But this wasn't what he'd planned. Now was not the time. Patience would be his watchword until she came to him.

Gently, with a control he didn't know he possessed, he gradually relaxed his body and released her mouth, running his tongue across her lips then along her jaw to her ear. He heard her whimper again softly, felt her cling to him in desperation.

"We need each other more than you can imagine, my sweet wife," he said thickly. "When the time is right, you will come to me, and together we will create the most beautiful child of all."

Slowly he released her, watching her until she opened her eyes, providing him a view of dark, smoky orbs glazed with passion. She was breathing rapidly, her body shaking, expression stunned, confused, her face flushed beautifully with color.

He smiled knowingly and brushed her cheek with the back of his hand. ''When you are ready, Caroline.''

With that, he turned and walked out of the garden.

Ten

Sleep was impossible. Cold wind and rain had been building in strength throughout the day, now blustering against her bedroom windows in torrential waves. It was going to be a long and dreary night.

Caroline sighed restlessly and turned onto her back. Her room was in almost total darkness, the fire banked hours ago. From time to time she glanced at the door—the only barrier, useless as it apparently was, between her and the man she'd married—watching carefully for signs of his intrusion.

Since he'd left her standing in the garden early that morning, flustered and shocked at her own behavior, she hadn't been able to concentrate on anything but him—his words, his caressing voice, hands, mouth.

Oh, God, he had sucked her tongue. He had actually sucked her tongue, and she'd brazenly allowed him to do it. She would never, in a hundred years, consider sucking a man's tongue for the pleasure it would give him. Yet each time she thought of what they'd shared that morning, swirls of charged heat started from her belly and radiated through her body, converging in a fire between her legs.

She covered her eyes with her hands, snuggling down deep beneath her blankets, mortified and wanting to remain there for the rest of her life.

Yes, of course she wanted him in a base, physical sense. She was a woman, and he was a man. Perfectly natural. It was also a given that nothing in her life had ever felt so perfectly marvelous. But to know he crept into her room to watch her at night made her so ill at ease she could hardly think straight. All day she'd tried to digest the meaning of why he would do such a thing, and in the end she couldn't fathom a reason beyond his physical needs. That left her panic-stricken.

She turned her face to the window, watching as thick rain pelted against the glass, listening to the ferocious gusts of wind. And it was because of the clamor of the outside storm that she almost missed the noise.

Caroline sat up quickly. She waited for a moment, then heard it again—the same sound coming from her husband's bedchamber that she'd heard her fifth night at Miramont.

Throwing back the covers, she stepped onto the cold floor, the contact drawing a shiver from her body. She rapidly donned her robe and slippers, then walked to the adjoining door.

For a long moment she heard nothing but silence. Then the thrashing began again, disturbed and unnatural. Her first thought was fever, although that seemed unlikely. Brent had been in perfect health just that morning. No, more than that, he'd been a prime example of pure, hard, aroused masculinity, and with such a vivid image flashing through her mind, it took everything in her to bravely place her hand on the knob, turn it gently, and slowly open the door.

His room appeared lighter than hers, his fire not yet completely extinguished, and when she looked to the bed she saw his large form outlined in shadow. For a minute she only stared, shocked as she watched him thrash so violently under his blankets, his head jerking from side to side.

It was a nightmare. He was having a savage nightmare, so controlling, so deep, he thrashed around in his bed without waking.

He's afraid of something.

Concerned, fascinated, she tiptoed to the side of his bed. His blankets were pushed down to his waist, exposing bare chest and arms, fists clutching the sheets to his sides, muscles in his neck and stomach fiercely knotted, skin damp and gleaming with perspiration . . .

Suddenly he was speaking in French.

Caroline jumped back and stifled a gasp. He moved wildly, his voice gravelly as he spoke in a language of which she had limited knowledge and little understanding. He arched his body, straining against the sheets, and at that point she knew she needed to do something.

She took a deep breath and reached out to touch his arm.

His skin felt tight and clammy to the touch. With an attempt to stop his head from shaking, she stretched across his chest and placed her palm on his cheek.

That's when he grabbed her wrist.

She nearly screamed. He did it for her.

"Caroline!"

He sat up, his eyes opened wide with horror and fear, his breathing erratic and fast.

Her mouth went dry, and suddenly she was shaking uncontrollably from the cold building inside of her.

"Caroline," he mumbled again, pulling her toward him.

She allowed herself to be led, her mind confused, her body now freezing. She swallowed in an attempt to regain her voice, her composure.

"I think you were dreaming," she whispered roughly.

He clutched at her in desperation, drawing himself against her as she stood next to him, shaking as he buried his head in her breasts. "Oh, God, Caroline, don't leave. Don't leave."

The pleading, the raw and unmistakable fear in his voice, persuaded her to do the irrational.

"It's all right," she soothed, sitting beside him, cupping his head with her palm. "I'll stay."

She felt him begin to breathe easier, his arms relax behind her. She kicked off her slippers and crawled in beside him, holding him as she snuggled down under his blankets.

She cradled his head against her chest, gently combing her fingers through his hair, giving comfort through her touch, enjoying the warmth of his large body against her smaller one. He hadn't said another word but he wouldn't release her, wouldn't let go, and finally, as his breathing slowed and deepened, and the wind and rain quieted to nothing more than sprinkling against glass on a cold autumn night, she closed her eyes to the serenity of sleep.

Caroline stirred and slowly opened heavy, sluggish lids to the dimness of the room and the sight of deep hazel eyes watching her from only a foot away.

She was in his bed.

He smiled, resting his elbow on his pillow, his head in his palm as he took a lock of her hair to lace through his fingers.

"Do you know what my greatest desire is, Caroline?" he asked in a low voice.

She couldn't speak.

His gaze brushed over her face slowly, caressingly, before it once again locked with hers.

Deepening his smile, he whispered, "My greatest desire is to wake up every morning for the rest of my life with you beside me as you are now, to see your hair flowing over my pillows in dark waves and your face looking soft and beautifully sensual."

"I should leave. It's already getting light," she heard herself saying, feeling strangely detached.

"Don't." His features turned serious as he reached up to place his palm on her cheek. "You belong here."

He'd pushed the sheets and blankets down to his waist once again, and the sight of his muscled chest only inches away did nothing to sedate or reassure her. She looked down her body, uncertain of her position and grateful she still wore her robe and nightdress.

With a calmness she didn't realize she possessed, she slowly sat up. "I really have to go. The servants—"

"—can go to hell," he finished for her, grabbing her around the waist and pulling her back down beside him.

That made her nervous. "Brent—"

He put his finger to her lips to silence her. "We need to talk, little one."

His words were gentle but firm, crisp but arousing to her ears. She had the incredible urge to touch him as her eyes once again strayed to his chest, to the bronzed and down-covered muscles and cords of strength only inches away. He must have noticed where she fixed her gaze, for at that moment he took her hand in his and placed it between his exposed nipples.

Her eyes shot back to his face. He was watching her closely, but his lids had narrowed. She felt stunned and unsure of what to do, knowing she should pull away. But with all her logical reasons for avoiding physical intimacy, she couldn't bring to an end the emotional responses overwhelming her.

"It's all right Caroline," he comforted in a deeply smooth voice. "I want you to touch me, and you can stop when you like."

Green orbs pierced her mind and soul, mesmerizing her. She was reacting rather than thinking, but at that moment she daringly wanted to feel.

Slowly, her head resting on his pillows, her body once again warm beneath his blankets, she began to run her fingers through the curls on his chest, her eyes never leaving his. His jaw tightened, and his breathing became shallow, but he didn't move to touch her in return. He lay perfectly still, content in simply watching her. And finally, when she drew her thumb across his nipple and circled it slowly, he succumbed to the feeling and groaned softly, closing his eyes.

The intimacy entranced her. Her body ignited from

one simple touch, from only looking at him and feeling his response to her fingers on his solid, male form. She felt both powerful and delicate, in control and yet swirling into a maelstrom of delight she didn't at all comprehend.

Bravely she lowered her palm to his stomach, stroking the smooth, taut lines, her hand now beneath the blankets. He was so firm, so strong, everything she'd imagined. And when at last her fingers found his navel, she knew without any doubt that he was completely naked beside her and had undoubtedly been so all night. If she lowered her hand any further she would be touching him as intimately as wives touched their husbands. The thought both scared and thrilled her, and she nearly yielded to the desire.

She stopped the movement of her palm, and he opened his eyes. For a long moment they stared at each other, oblivious to the outside world, dark velvet brown melding with blazing vivid green. He said nothing, just gazed at her with stark desire, untamed arousal, his head only inches from hers.

Through it all she was captivated, her mind telling her to run, her body unable to move. The ache was so great, so overpowering, she could think of nothing but the promises of passion to come, of what he would feel like towering over her, taking her, embedding himself inside of her.

As if sensing her thoughts, he slowly reached for her palm, raising it to his lips, softly kissing the tender skin on her fingers, her wrist. Then without hesitation, he once again lowered it and gently placed her hand on the most intimate part of him.

She heard his sharp intake of breath, but beyond that he didn't move; his eyes never wavered from hers. She was in another world, her heartbeat staggering, breathing shallow, mind unfocused yet clear with newfound wants. He felt like hot, satin-covered marble to her fingertips, and with desires she didn't know she could ever feel, she closed her eyes and touched him, picturing in her mind the perfection of that which she could only see with her hand.

Slowly she began to move her palm, her fingers, up then down the front of him in slow form. She licked her lips and leaned her head back, marveling at the strength he possessed in just this one area of his body. He was long and thick, wonderful to touch. She grasped him firmly, her knuckles brushing against coarse, springy curls as she continued to explore the length of him. Gently she placed the pad of her thumb on the tip, circling it once, and that's when he touched her arm.

"Caroline . . ."

She opened her eyes. His expression was grim, eyes glazed.

"No more." He breathed deeply. "I need you to stop unless you're ready for me to touch you."

His voice was strained and barely audible.

Her chest ached with emotion, her body for completion, wanting to feel his hands touching her, caressing her, his mouth on hers, kissing her as he'd done before. She stared at him for what seemed like hours, her hand still resting firmly on him, until she found the courage to speak her mind instead of what was in her heart. "I can't . . ."

He closed his eyes to her softly spoken words, drawing her hand back to the safety of his chest, trying to regain control.

Caroline closed her eyes as well, allowing reason to force its way into her mind, feeling his heart beating hard beneath her hand, his warmth seeping through her fingertips. Part of her wanted to break down and cry, so touched as she was from his gentleness, from the honorable way he held himself back for her. He deserved so much better, so much more than she could ever give. Suddenly she recognized within herself the first flicker of danger in truly losing herself to the power of a man.

She opened her eyes again to find him watching her, fighting tears until they overwhelmed her.

"Don't cry, Caroline," he soothed, wiping his thumb

across the wetness on her cheek. "It will happen when the time is right."

She shook her head but couldn't reply.

He smiled, grabbed her around the waist, and hugged her against him, her head tucked under his chin, hands and breasts flattened against his chest, her toes rubbing the coarse hairs on his legs.

Timidly she whispered, "Sometimes you can be wonderful."

He lifted her face to his. "Only sometimes?" Brows pinching thoughtfully, he added, "Come to think of it, that's quite a compliment. Women have called me many things, but I don't think even one has ever called me wonderful."

She wiped her eyes and grinned bashfully. "Good. I'd like to think I'm the first for something in your life."

Smiling, he said, "You could start by sleeping with me like this every night. That would be a first for both of us."

"I cannot imagine why you would want that, my lord. Many a nobleman would sell his wife to the lowest bidder for the comfort of sleeping alone—"

He stifled her words with a firm kiss to her lips. "Perhaps if I found you a nag, I would feel the same way," he said gruffly, seconds later. "But I find you adorably sexy and I despise being alone in such a large bed while my sexy wife sleeps in the next room."

Her heart fluttered again. "Nobody would ever use that word to describe me."

He grunted. "Caroline, the day we met in your father's house my first impression of you was not that you were plain, or old, or . . . unattractive. I found you incredibly alluring. From the moment you opened your mouth and spoke in that sultry voice of yours, you've had me erotically entranced, and you keep me in that uncomfortable state just by speaking to me daily. You are the sexiest woman I have ever known in my life."

She stared at him, stunned, and that made him chuckle.

"Believe it or not," he teased, "I even find you sexy clothed like a nun as you are now."

"I'm not clothed like a nun, this is a *nightdress—*"

"It's ugly and leaves everything to my imagination."

"As well it should," she scolded.

"My imagination is not that good, Caroline."

"I'm certain it's adequate."

"Take it off and let me have a look," he suggested devilishly.

She gaped at him and blushed furiously. "Don't be absurd."

Suddenly he shifted his body to climb onto her, grinning wickedly, pinning her beneath him while his palm slowly moved under her gown and up her leg to rest on her thigh.

She looked at him as if he were a naughty child. "Brent . . ."

He stroked the smooth skin of her leg and leaned in to nuzzle her neck. "Maybe you can just provide me with a tantalizing peek of your legs, then?"

"No," she asserted in a teasing voice that startled even her.

Slowly he raised his head in contemplation. "In fact, I don't think I've seen any part of you below your two rather large, shapely—"

"That's enough," she interjected through an amazed laugh. "If you continue to carry on so indecently, I shall never show you any part of me above my ankles."

"Then you would consent to letting me suck your toes?"

She didn't know whether to be shocked or break into laughter. "You would do that?" she asked in wonder.

He grinned again. "Of course."

She glanced at him skeptically. "It sounds disgusting."

"But it feels marvelous." He sat up a little and wrapped a lock of her hair around his fingers. "There are lots of places on your body I will suck and kiss and caress, Caroline, and it will all feel marvelous. I promise you that.''

Had he not been speaking so lightly, she might have jumped off the bed. But he was teasing her unashamedly, and she found herself enjoying it immensely.

Mouth twisting slyly, she sat up as well, leaning toward him to whisper huskily, ''And I suppose you'll tell me next there are places on your body you'd like me to suck. Am I right, Brent?''

She giggled at the sight of his reaction, his suddenly bewildered expression.

He groaned, rolled his eyes, and fell back hard against the sheets. ''Go on, before I lose what control I have left. We need to talk, but we'll do it later.''

She stared at him, unsure and not entirely ready to leave the comfort of his company.

He gave her a mischievous smile. ''You'd better leave now, Caroline. I'm about to stand up, and you know *exactly* what I'm wearing.''

Before the words had completely left his mouth, she scrambled to her feet, grabbed her slippers, and raced from the room.

Eleven

Brent had suggested they go for a walk, the two of them and Rosalyn, and Caroline couldn't argue that. The sun had shone all morning, and what dampness remained from the previous night's showers had finally given way to a lovely autumn afternoon, beckoning even the most reclusive souls to stray outside and take in the freshness, the sweetness of wild roses and heather.

After bathing and spending an hour in attempted communication with Rosalyn, Caroline had sat at her writing desk in the parlor for the better part of the morning, preparing a list of suitable foodstuffs for tea. Her sisters Jane, Charlotte, and Stephanie would be visiting Miramont for the first time that afternoon, and she wanted everything to be perfect. Mary Anne, poor thing, was in the last stages of pregnancy and couldn't make the trip, which was fine with Caroline. She didn't need Brent so obviously reminded of his need for an heir.

The day was beautiful and warm, and the two adults strolled side by side in silence, Brent carrying a blanket under one arm, Rosalyn running in circles around them. They reached the top of a grassy hill overlooking the house, where he spread the blanket, sat heavily upon it, and pulled Caroline down beside him.

For a long while they sat peacefully and quietly together, watching the child jump and play and pick flowers.

"You've done the impossible with her," Brent acknowledged at last. "I never thought I'd see the day when she would be clean and beautiful and play like a normal child."

Caroline smiled, drew her legs up under her peach day gown, and wrapped her arms around her knees. "She's a smart little girl. She just needed a little push in the right direction."

He turned to her, watching the side of her face. "She didn't learn to calm down and play normally all on her own, Caroline. Because of you, Rosalyn hugs me now, holds my hand, waves to me. For the rest of my life I will be grateful for the wonderful thing you've done for us." He lowered his voice. "How do you feel about her?"

That caught her off guard. "Feel about her?"

He regarded her thoughtfully. "I want to know what your feelings are for Rosalyn. It couldn't have been easy to learn your husband had an illegitimate daughter, and frankly I'm surprised you handled the situation so easily."

Caroline shrugged, stalling. How could she explain that her feelings didn't matter when she would be leaving them soon to pursue her dream?

Finally she said softly, carefully, "Because she's an innocent child, I care about her a great deal. But since there's nothing I can do about her illegitimate birth, it doesn't bother me. Your past is your own, Brent."

He shook his head, amazed. "I've never known a woman like you, Caroline. You're so different with regard to me and my past affairs, not caring at all that I had sexual relations with someone before you. Most wives would complain endlessly, or bitterly, or snivel foolishly for days." He paused and lowered his voice.

"I don't know whether to be thankful or bothered by the fact that you're so incredibly unruffled by it all."

Slowly she pulled her gaze from his and looked out over the meadow. It annoyed her to know that his former relationship with the courtesan did bother her a little, but she wanted to keep that hidden from his penetrating stare. "I suppose if ours were a love match it would matter a great deal, and I would indeed be upset by such an indiscreet liaison. Since ours was a marriage of convenience, I must accept you as you are, knowing that my feelings for you and your daughter must remain rational and unencumbered by your complicated past."

She turned to him then, noticing how quickly his jaw had tightened, how his eyes had thinned to hazel slits. She faltered a little but continued anyway. "I simply meant that if we loved each other, my feelings would be different from what they are now. I would probably be very jealous of Rosalyn's mother."

"You're implying that jealousy and love go hand in hand," he stated sardonically.

She gave him what she thought was a comforting smile. "Yes, usually. Probably always."

He grunted and glanced back to Rosalyn, watching her pick wildflowers and gather them into her arms. "Well, Caroline," he said blandly, "regardless of some elusive feeling women choose to call love, I intend to keep a sharp eye on your whereabouts from this moment on. Not only will I not permit another man to lay claim to any part of you, I don't know what Rosalyn and I would do without you in our lives."

Although he had said it lightly, his words, oddly enough, made her feel both joyful and discomfited. She tried to smile as she wiped a stray piece of hair from her cheek.

"I'm sure you'd manage. You managed before."

He drew his leg up once again and rested his arm across his knee. After a quiet moment he turned his head back to her and gazed into her eyes. "We didn't manage before you, little one, we barely existed. Rosalyn was lost in her private inner world, and I was lost in mine."

She noticed at once how his features betrayed his emotions. He looked troubled, intense in his thoughts, his expression scarred with pain from a past unknown to her.

Without thought, she raised her hand and brushed a lock of hair off his forehead. "This is about last night, isn't it?"

He expelled a deep breath, his eyes turning solemn. "There are some things I need to tell you, Caroline, most of which aren't pleasant. As my wife, however, you have the right to be informed about them."

She nodded.

He wiped his palm over his face, then said bluntly, "For the last six years I've been employed by British intelligence."

She gaped at him, nonplussed, but he didn't seem to notice.

"During the first nineteen months, I worked my way deep inside the French government until I moved in top circles as a different person from the one you married, appearing sophisticated, cunning, arrogant. Quite French. Those who knew me never suspected what I was because I went through years of intense training before I left for the Continent, becoming all things French, speaking the language perfectly, acting the part impeccably, knowing the history and culture as if they were my very own. I was sent to France expressly for the purpose of infiltrating Napoleon's military, to become one of them, which I managed to do flawlessly."

He grasped her hand, intertwined her fingers with his and squeezed gently, waiting for her to look him in the eye. When she did, he gave her a comforting smile. "I worked in France on and off for six long years, moving from here to there, depending on the political climate." He paused, unsure, then whispered, "You married a British spy, Caroline."

She stared at him wide-eyed and utterly incredulous, for nothing in her life had ever shocked her so. He held her gaze, watching her intently as if waiting for response or reaction, but she couldn't think of a suitable reply.

The breeze picked up, blowing loose hair across her face. Gently he lifted his hand and brushed it aside, taking the time to run his fingers down her cheek.

"You could have died," she murmured at last.

He pursed his lips. "True enough. It's a dangerous occupation, and had I been discovered in France I would have been hanged." He shrugged and lightened his tone. "Or more likely guillotined."

"Oh, God . . ." She felt sick, her head suddenly reeling.

"Try not to concern yourself with it, Caroline," he soothed. "That part of my life is over." He glanced back to his daughter. "Nobody in the world has needed me as Rosalyn does, and it took the fighting at Waterloo and a horrible three days of hell for me to understand exactly how much." He dropped his voice to a faint whisper. "And how much I need her."

Instinctively Caroline clasped his hand tightly, shock giving way to intrigue. "Tell me what happened."

Brent felt fear well up inside of him again, as vivid as the day it had begun. Until now, the only person who knew of his battle in the pit of death was Davis, and although uncontrollable feelings of panic and hopelessness filled him, he still had the overwhelming urge to confide in his wife.

Rosalyn played more than ten feet away. She couldn't hear him, but he wouldn't have spoken of Waterloo with her any closer. There was no one else around, and Caroline, looking innocent and lovely just as she was, sat patiently holding his hand. He pulled himself up to sit straight and began at the beginning.

"I'd been in France for nearly two years when I met a man called Philip Rouselle, a low-ranking officer in the French military. I immediately disliked him because of his nature—always suspicious, shrewd, greedy, doing whatever was necessary for personal advancement.

"Philip followed my every move, and my guard was

always up when he was around. What made him resent me, though, was my affair with Christine. She didn't want him, she wanted me, and his ego was grand, Caroline.''

He watched her closely but saw nothing except the slightest trace of tightness cross her mouth. In some very obscure manner, knowing that his wife held a dislike for his former mistress pleased him enormously.

He rubbed her knuckles with his thumb. "For nearly three years Philip and I played a game of cat and mouse with each other, and finally, about a year ago, I discovered exactly what he was.''

"What he was?'' she whispered.

He paused, looking out over the hills. "You have to know that much of my reason for seeing Christine over the years was personal. But although she seldom discussed government or political issues, she moved in those crowds and from time to time was an unsuspecting and knowledgeable informant.''

"How convenient for you.''

Brent glanced at her quickly then back to the meadow, deciding it best to ignore the biting comment and move on.

"One . . . evening together, she accidentally said something that led me to believe that Philip might actually be my counterpart, a French intelligence agent and a hired killer. I checked the facts, and indeed, the man was everything I feared. He was handsome, highly intelligent, and trained to move in circles above his class or below it, speaking English as if it were his mother language. During all the years I worked for British intelligence, that man is the only one who ever suspected me of being something other than what I appeared, and it all came to a head last June during the fierce fighting at the Battle of Waterloo.''

He needed to stop for a moment, allowing the calmness of the early afternoon to seep inside of him, the sunshine to soothe him. His wife said nothing but held his hand tightly as if afraid to let go, fully engrossed in his words.

"Philip grew to hate me, Caroline," he said bleakly, quietly, "because of Christine, because of Napoleon's defeat and exile to Elba as if that were my doing, because I was English, because I refused to kill without honor, which he considered the gravest human weakness. He would kill ruthlessly and without feeling, striking those in his path regardless of age or sex, even those unable to defend themselves."

"Are—are you telling me you've killed people?" she asked shakily, shocked.

There was no easy way to confess. He squeezed her hand, raised it to his lips, and kissed her wrist gently. Gazing intently into large, dark orbs full of uncertainty, he boldly admitted what he knew she feared.

"I am trained to kill with skill and efficiency, Caroline, and over the years I have done so." He felt her try to pull away but he wouldn't let go. With his free hand he firmly grasped her chin, forcing her to keep her eyes locked with his. "I have killed in defense and only those who have in some way jeopardized my life, my country, or my king. I would also, without question, kill to protect my family."

His tone became fierce, his gaze piercing. "But I swear to you, Caroline, on the life of my daughter, I would never kill, nor have I ever killed, randomly, unjustly, or without feeling as Philip has done. He would kill even Rosalyn without blinking an eye, without feeling anything, and certainly without honor, which is precisely where we differed."

She continued to look at him, and gradually he released her chin, stroking her cheek with his thumb. Then he dropped his hand from the softness of her face, raked his fingers through his hair, and turned his head to stare hard at the grass-covered ground before him.

"During the battle at Waterloo I stayed deep in French territory, my cover intact, and worked on gaining a foothold for our forces. The Prussians had moved in from the east, and Napoleon's troops, strong and heroic as they were, were divided. The English probably won the war because of this advantage.'' He exhaled loudly. ''The French went to work, their cavalry charging the English center, and I was caught in the middle of it.''

He swallowed with difficulty, fighting the raging conflict inside. The pain was obviously evident, for at that moment Caroline scooted closer and placed his hand in her lap. He felt softness and warmth, smelled wild roses and the violet water only she wore, and still the remembrance clouded his mind, choking him.

''Caroline—''

She slowly stroked his hand with hers. ''It's all right.''

He shook his head and continued to look at the ground in front of him. ''It was a field of mass suffering, of men slowly dying in unbearable pain. I'd experienced war and certainly death before, knew what it looked like, and for that I was prepared. But I wasn't prepared for what happened to me.'' He drew a deep, shaky breath. ''I saw Philip coming for me through the smoke and haze, attacking with vengeance, charging at me from the side before I could defend myself. He knocked me off my horse, hitting me in the temple with the butt of his pistol, stunning me, the pain shooting through my head as if a dagger had pierced my skull.''

Bitterly he chuckled. ''Hell came upon the French cavalry in the most peculiar way that day, Caroline. Because of the thick fog of gunpowder and dust surrounding us, nobody saw the trench until too late—a trench large and deep, virtually hidden in the brush. Suddenly men and horses began falling into it, some wounded, most of them dead. After several hours of fighting, the French began using the filling trench as a human bridge to encroach on the enemy.''

''No . . .'' she whispered.

He looked back to see her beautiful eyes so expressive, wide with horror, her face white, wisps of dark brown hair stark against her skin and flying loosely in the breeze.

Boldly he kept his eyes locked with hers. "Philip fought me, hitting me in the head with his pistol, over and over, until I fell into the trench, Caroline. Until I fell into a hole of dead and dying humans and horses, where I was covered with blood, with burned and torn flesh, with vomit and human waste. Where I heard the moans of the dying, the battle above, the screams, the terror. Where the smell was obscene, the weight of the dead and bleeding on top of me excruciating . . ."

His nostrils flared, and he squeezed her hand. "I remained there, weak and dazed, for three full days and nights until I was certain the fighting had subsided and the French had retreated. Men lay beside me, on top of me, below me, moaning, bleeding, gaping at me through the stare of death.

"And through it all I couldn't move, could barely breathe. I drifted in and out of consciousness from lack of air, from the weight on top of me, nauseated from the pain in my head, from the smell of sickness and blood."

She shook her head, tears filling her eyes, now clear, round pools of shock. He rubbed the back of his neck, feeling the tension beneath his fingers, breathing deeply of the scent of the meadow to help erase the lingering smell of death. He never intended to be so graphic in his detail, but his wife needed to understand, and he wanted her to know everything, know the deepest part of him.

"When I was finally able to break free," he continued at last, quietly, brokenly, "I was so ill, so weak in mind and body, I could barely move. During the course of several hours I tried to lift myself, stumbling over the remains of good and honest men as I attempted to climb out of the trench. At one point my arm seared right through a man's body as if it were pudding, his rotting gut just . . . open and spilling out over my hand and through my fingers." He shivered and looked down to the blanket. "Cold blood filled my eyes, and I couldn't wipe it away. I couldn't wipe it from my skin, my clothes, the smell and feel of it from my mind.

"I fled by walking for miles, blindly and numbly during a cold and moonless night, but I didn't know who'd won the battle or where to go. Eventually I came upon a farmer and his wife who let me stay with them for several days, recovering. When finally I felt physically ready to move on, I'd learned Wellington was decisively victorious and I joined the British camp. After two weeks of intense discussions and sleepless nights, I left France to return to England, to the safe haven of my home, my family."

He wiped his shaking hand over his face, fighting to stay in control, watching his wife as she tried to come to terms with what he was saying.

He lowered his voice to a husky whisper. "Something inside of me snapped that day, as I lay motionless in the grave, and the only thing keeping me together and alive while I waited for the battle to end was remembering Rosalyn. I centered my thoughts on the little girl who needed me, and lying under a massacre of waste and blood and death, I realized how much I needed her. I suddenly felt important to someone, little and fragile as she was, and never again will I lose sight of that."

He squeezed her hand, his voice fervent. "She is the only thing precious in my life, Caroline, and she depends on me. Nobody except my daughter has ever depended on me for anything, and because of her I will never work like that again. My existence now has a purpose I clearly understand. Government policies, social order, and the fighting can all go to hell when it comes to what truly matters in my life, and Rosalyn is my life."

He stilled completely after that, his voice, his body, even his breathing, and Caroline found herself so moved by his words that for a moment she could do nothing but look into his eyes as tears spilled onto her cheeks. Only the strongest of men could withstand such inhumanity and live to tell about it, and at that moment she knew her husband was the strongest man she had ever known.

"You're so brave," she whispered hoarsely, still unable to move her gaze or her body. She sat with a rigid back, throat closed tightly; then her hand reached up of its own accord and stroked his cheek. He just watched her for several seconds, then covered her hand with his and moved it to his mouth, lightly kissing her palm.

"Now you understand why I need you so, Caroline," he said huskily, passionately, her palm lightly resting against his lips. "You and my daughter will help me forget and move on. You and Rosalyn have given me beauty to behold, and true beauty will always outshine and envelop the fear within."

His words touched her deeply, his love for Rosalyn greater than she could have ever imagined. He was baring his soul to her at that moment as she read pain and honesty in the dark green depths of his eyes, and never in her life had she felt such a rush of tenderness toward another human being.

As if reading her thoughts, he reached out and pulled her against his chest. She allowed herself to be led, moving into his arms, resting her palms on the softness of his shirt, kissing his cheek and neck without shame or second thought.

He kissed her in return then, his lips brushing away the tears from her cheeks. Slowly she moved her head down to rest it on his lap, her body and thoughts calming as she stared out to the meadow and his beautiful little girl.

They watched the child together in silence, her head resting on his thighs, his hand lightly stroking her neck. With the smell of flowers in the air and sunshine on her back, Caroline was certain she'd never felt so emotionally close to anyone in her life. With each passing week, she knew she was losing herself to her husband, and even with her mind centered, her thoughts controlled, for the first time ever she didn't care.

Suddenly, as if sensing the quietness of the moment,

Rosalyn looked up and grinned. Then quickly she grabbed at something on the ground and ran to them, standing before them, hand held out.

Caroline sat up and looked at the outstretched palm. In it sat a wild, red rose. Smiling, she closed her fists tightly in front of her chest and held them together, then released her fingers in an upward and outward motion— her gesture for a flower.

Rosalyn watched her closely, then giggled and turned in a full circle. When she stopped she looked back into her eyes, held out her hand, and once more pointed to the rose.

Caroline was cautious, not at all used to such concentration from the girl. After only a brief pause she again, deliberately, used her hands to form the flower gesture she'd created for Rosalyn's benefit. And once again the girl pointed to the rose, more directly and forcefully, her face contorting with the beginnings of frustration.

Now she was clearly dumbfounded. So apparently was her husband.

"What does she want?" he quietly asked.

"I'm not sure," she whispered. Then her eyes brightened. "I want to try something, so don't do anything to distract her."

That said, she raised herself on her knees so they could see eye to eye, and made little movements from the alphabet she had painstakingly created with her fingers, one for each letter, to spell the word *rose*.

Rosalyn looked from her fingers to her father, then back to the flower in her palm. Then she pointed to herself.

Caroline felt the first real flood of excitement. Quickly she placed her hand in the child's line of sight again and spelled *Rosalyn* with the same finger movements, one for each letter.

"What are you doing?"

"I'm spelling her name."

"What?"

"Shh . . ."

After seconds of getting nothing but a puzzled look from the girl, she spelled it again, slowly, with more emphasis on each letter.

The silence became deafening—even the breeze had stopped all movement—and Caroline, waiting for a reaction, had trouble forcing herself to remain still and breathe. Time ceased to exist until Rosalyn's face suddenly illuminated brilliantly with comprehension. Her little mouth broke out into an enchanting grin as she pointed to her chest, then followed it with the gesture for flower.

The two of them stared. Then Caroline nodded vehemently and fell back hard against the ground.

Brent noticed instantly the change in his wife. Within seconds she'd become ashen and speechless as she gazed upon his daughter, and with that he swiftly pulled himself to his feet.

"What is it, Caroline? What did she do?"

She blinked hard and whispered, "She talked to me . . ."

"What!"

"Oh, God, Brent, she talked to me," she repeated, dazed, still looking at Rosalyn, who stood in front of them, clutching her little blue dress, smiling coyly.

He glanced from his wife to his daughter. "You're sure?"

"Yes."

"What did she say?" he asked slowly, skeptically.

Caroline started giggling and crying at the same time, shaking her head in wonder. "She said 'I'm a flower.' "

His pulse began to race, and he could only bring himself to mumble, " 'I'm a flower?' "

She clasped her hands together in glee, raised her eyes heavenward, then grabbed Rosalyn and hugged her fiercely. "She pointed to herself to say 'I' then made the gesture I showed her for flower."

Brent fell to his knees in front of them, no longer able to stand on his weak and trembling legs. "I don't understand."

Caroline laughed and cried as she held his daughter against her chest. "She associated *rose* with *Rosalyn,* similar in spelling and both exquisitely beautiful." She looked back to him with water-filled eyes, her husky voice rich and ecstatic. "I didn't know if it would ever be clear for her, Brent, but it is. She used a gesture to communicate with me, to talk to me, and if she said this, she can learn to say anything. She finally understands."

Wiping her tears with her fingers, Caroline stood and took Rosalyn's hands. Then together they began jumping, laughing, and spinning around in the meadow.

Brent covered his mouth with his palm, too choked to speak, and for the first time in his miserable life he felt tears fill his eyes—hot and stinging and blurring his vision. He blinked them away as fast as he could, staring at his incredible wife and beautiful daughter as they embraced each other and danced among the wildflowers.

In all of his life, he'd never experienced a feeling like this, a surge of joy so powerful, so intense, it took his breath and melted his heart, bathing him in warmth. Only now, as he watched them in the meadow, did he fully realize exactly what his wife had done for him. He was alive today because of Rosalyn, because he loved her so deeply, and one day he would be able to tell her that because of Caroline.

Suddenly he was on his feet, chasing after them, pouncing on them as he circled their waists with his arms to pull them to the ground, the three of them laughing, tumbling and clinging to each other as they rolled across the grass.

"My girls," he said in a voice rich with happiness. "My girls . . ." He nuzzled their necks, one at a time, both of them giggling and squirming beneath him.

Caroline was the first to stop laughing, to stop moving as she rolled on top of him, hair flying, loose from its ribbon, one arm pinned under her husband, the other under Rosalyn, who was now at her side. She grinned, breathing rapidly, releasing her daughter then wiping her hair from her eyes to see his face.

The look he gave her was beautiful, warm, and filled with pleasure. He was breathing fast, holding her tightly, but his eyes were what grabbed her attention. They were bright and charged with emotion, dark green orbs of longing and thankfulness.

Rosalyn scrambled to her feet and raced toward the house. Caroline didn't notice, and neither did Brent.

He loosened his arms and placed his palms on her cheeks. "My darling Caroline," he whispered in the wind.

Then he kissed her deeply, passionately, embracing her fully, his mouth locked with hers in a private communication only they shared.

She ran her fingers through his hair, inhaling the scent that was only her husband's, relishing in his strength, the hardness of his body beneath hers. She would have given almost anything to allow the moment to last an eternity, to be lost in his touch forever.

She moaned softly, aching with needs untouched when he finally pushed her lips from his. He ran his fingers over her swollen mouth and flaming cheeks, then back through her hair.

"Caroline . . ." he said softly, gently cupping her head. "Thank you."

She stared into a sea of vivid hazel-green, blinking back her tears of warmth and joy. Then Rosalyn was kneeling beside her once more, tugging on her gown for attention.

She looked up, in the direction of the house, and to her complete mortification, all three of her sisters stood no more than thirty feet away, staring at her in stunned disbelief.

"Oh, God, they're early," she murmured, coming to her senses quickly as she pushed against her husband. He held her firmly and chuckled.

"Brent, let me go," she said frantically. "They'll think—"

"They'll think what?"

He was grinning unashamedly, and that made her mad. "Let me go!"

"Kiss me again."

She gaped at him. "They'll see us."

"They've already seen us, Caroline. Kiss me . . ."

"No!"

He grinned rakishly. "Kiss me, or I'll give them something to really talk about."

She rolled her eyes and lowered her head to give him a peck on the cheek. Instead, he pulled her head forcefully against his once more and smothered her mouth until she became breathless.

At last he released her. "Do you know what I think, Caroline?"

"I don't care," she countered, pushing herself up.

He smiled. "I think your sisters will think you're happy."

She stared at him, feeling strangely defeated. "I *am* happy."

Quickly turning her face away, she smoothed her hair behind her head with trembling hands and stood, brushing grass from her skirt.

Not only that, my sweet, brave husband, she allowed herself to admit with a sinking heart. *They'll think I'm falling in love with you.*

Twelve

He preferred thick, strong coffee in the morning, but alas, when one was on a mission, one had to bow to the customs of the region. Unfortunately he hated tea almost as much as he hated England.

Philip René Rouselle stirred a trace amount of sugar into his cup, smiling pleasantly at the fat, pock-faced man in front of him.

"I do say, Sir Stanley, the bed felt marvelous, and the breakfast and tea are superb." He forced a small laugh and took a sip. "It's amazing what comforts one fails to recognize until one goes to war, hmm?"

Sir Stanley Grotton, suffering from a chill, sat beside him at the polished oak table, his plate of sausages, eggs, and toast sitting untouched in front of him while he repeatedly pinched his red nose with a handkerchief. "Honestly, I don't see how you boys survived all that nonsense with Bonaparte. Good to have so many of you back alive after such a dreadful circumstance."

Philip tightly grasped the handle of his cup and took another sip to calm his building anger. He didn't come to this stinking country to hear some old, fat bastard talk about a person and situation of which he knew absolutely nothing except gossip spread by dirty English pigs. And a circumstance? How could the man call a great and magnificent battle a circumstance? He dreaded the necessity of staying in this ill-decorated home, eating bland food, while he listened to an old pig talk of nothing but nonsense for perhaps weeks. His glorious mission required such a sacrifice, however, and he refused to leave until he completed it. It would all be worth the effort anyway when he finally cornered his mark.

The Raven evidently thought Philip presumed him dead—murdered at Waterloo—or he wouldn't have been so careless in returning home. Stupid English bastard. But even as Philip now made his way on the freezing, filthy, rat-infested island, he knew it would soon be worth the effort. Surprise would be his weapon this time, and he would finish his job with pleasure. The Raven would be his, on English soil, and Philip would have the last laugh, would be the one to triumph in their long and arduous personal war.

Smiling, he purposely relaxed in his chair. "I hear your neighbor, the Earl of . . ."

"Weymerth," Grotton offered.

"Ah, yes, Lord Weymerth. I hear he's recently returned from the war himself, eh?"

Grotton sneezed loudly. "Brave boy. Came back skinny as a rail and hungry as a horse. Never seen him look so weak in the twenty years I've known him, but he's filling out nicely from what I hear. Probably due to having a wife now—"

Philip choked on his tea, and for the first time in nine years, the time he'd been working for the government, he nearly lost his composure. Coughing gently for distraction, he laid his cup back on the table, wiped the corners of his mouth delicately with his white lace napkin, and turned his attention to his eggs.

A wife? A *wife*? That seemed so unlikely and bizarre. Incredible. Why would someone so keen on deception, so focused on his work, want to marry? Not the Raven. He got plenty of sex from Christine, the stupid bitch always spreading her legs for his convenience whenever he snapped his fingers. And there were certainly others here he could use just as casually.

"So the earl took a wife after returning from battle, eh?" he asked evenly.

Grotton nodded and blew loudly into his handkerchief. "Baron Sytheford's daughter. Haven't met her, but I hear they're all handsome, blond ladies."

"How very fortunate for the earl," he conceded lightly, seething inside. The Raven mocked him even from afar, first stealing his woman then abandoning her for a beautiful but witless English wench. If he didn't know his own capabilities, he might be tempted to believe there was truly no justice in the world.

"Quite fortunate," Grotton maintained, becoming interested in his food at last as he picked at his sausage. "Perhaps you'd like to meet them, Mr. Whitsworth. I could invite them for dinner during your stay."

Philip hid his surge of panic well. "That would be lovely, I'm sure." He sighed deeply, casually lifting his cup to his lips and draining it of the pale, tasteless liquid only English weaklings would enjoy.

"However," he continued, delicately dabbing at his mouth with his napkin, "it might be better if you invite them for a visit after I've taken care of straightening your stables. Does the earl ride, perchance?"

Grotton swallowed a mouthful of tea and nodded. "The man's a magnificent horseman."

"Well, there, you see?" Philip gently swiped his palm across the table, smiling, his voice jovial. "If the man can ride, why not show him your new horses after they've been properly conditioned and trained? A good horseman will always appreciate a decent mount, and the stallion and mare your cousin gave you are fine steeds indeed."

Grotton grunted and stuffed his mouth with eggs. "What I don't understand," he said while he chewed, "is why Marjorie would think of giving me horses.

What the devil am I supposed to do with them? I haven't ridden in years.''

Philip shook his head patiently and answered the question in an extremely condescending tone. "Who can understand a woman? The whole lot of them tend to be scatterbrained at least most of the time.''

Grotton nodded in agreement.

"I'm sure she must have felt you could do something with them or benefit from them in some way,'' he went on. "And if you think about it, what would a spinster do with two horses she inherited from an old reclusive grouch like my former employer? The man died and left her the horses along with my services until they are trained, but she doesn't even own a stable.''

"So why leave them to her? That hardly makes sense.''

Philip shrugged nonchalantly. "She'd been caring for him as a good Christian neighbor while he was bedridden, and I think that was the only way he knew to repay her for her kindness when he passed on.'' He leaned forward in his chair and lowered his voice. "I'll admit that after his death I was ready to return to the city, but Mr. Perkins paid me well, and I suppose training these two horses that now belong to you won't be much trouble.

"Frankly,'' he stammered with forced embarrassment, "these horses, Sir Stanley, are of the finest stock. You will be able to show or breed them, or perhaps even sell one of the offspring to the regent himself if my talents are used fully.'' He sat back in his chair. "Just think about that.''

Grotton eyed him speculatively as he freely ate at last, devouring his breakfast with such speed that Philip thought he might actually choke on underchewed meat. English animal. He knew the man inside and out, had taken the time to learn his weaknesses, two of which were money and pride—and, he considered with disgust, the third was probably food if his table manners were any indication. But if the fat man thought for a moment that the prince regent might want to buy the horses his cousin had freely given him, his arrogance and desire for an elegant lifestyle would surely be his undoing.

Since his arrival only yesterday, Philip had used his charm and good graces to weave his way into the man's home, gently applying the right amount of persuasion in offering to stay and care for the two Arabians he'd supposedly brought with him from poor cousin Marjorie, the fat man's spinster cousin he hadn't seen in years, who now lay dead at the bottom of a lake.

He'd introduced himself as a down-at-the-heels gentleman, an authority on horses, doing a favor for a friend, only just hinting at payment for services rendered. He discussed the war and English heroism at length with Grotton, so the man, for the sake of his company both knowledgeable and patriotic, would want him to remain in the house instead of the servants' quarters. Indeed, he'd presented himself as an equestrian scholar, far above the station of a simple trainer or groom, and naturally he spoke, looked, and acted like the perfect gentleman. He deserved the comforts of a soft bed and warm surroundings for the trouble of being in such a filthy land, and if the idiot fat man adored the talk of battle, he would endure it.

He now stayed only miles from the Raven, allowed to roam the property at will for an indefinite period of time, and training two horses would be his only trouble for the opportunity. Simple. Only the French could be so cunning and gifted, and patience was his gift.

"I suppose I'll have to write Marjorie and thank her for her thoughtfulness," Grotton remarked at last as he sat back in the creaking chair, his plate nearly licked clean.

Philip smiled. "I think that's a marvelous suggestion. I'm sure the lady would appreciate your gratitude." Slowly, deliberately, he creased his brows. "I do believe, however, that your cousin mentioned she'd be in Lincoln for the winter visiting an old lady friend who suffers." His voice brightened. "But you could write her all the same. She'll eventually receive the letter.''

Grotton nodded and blew his nose again. ''Good heavens, it's been . . . five years now since I've seen Marjorie. The last time was a Christmas celebration with my aunt Helena.'' He rolled his eyes. ''Now *she* was a character, let me tell you . . .''

Philip sat back casually and smiled with feigned interest, knowing that by the end of the month, he would suffer as well.

Thirteen

On her twenty-sixth birthday, exactly eighty-six days after her arrival at Miramont, Caroline found the greenhouse. She came upon the structure so suddenly that she nearly tumbled into dirty, ivy-covered glass. But as she stopped and stared in acute surprise, she realized she'd accidently discovered the greatest birthday gift imaginable.

Only two hours after a luncheon with Rosalyn and her husband to celebrate the event, she'd decided to walk the grounds thoroughly for the first time, all alone, to contemplate the changes in her life. The afternoon was lovely, the sun shining warmly through the tree branches, and the relaxing atmosphere gave her the distraction she needed to think.

It had been nearly four weeks since Rosalyn had first spoken to them with her hands, and in that time she'd practiced patiently with the child each day to teach her new words, the meanings of which she was slowly beginning to grasp. Rosalyn made gestures for feelings now and knew several words, an accomplishment that continued to amaze everyone. Even Brent finally took the effort to learn to communicate, stopping his daughter frequently to gesture or motion for this or that. Caroline taught him the alphabet she'd created as well, so eventually they could all spell words and talk to each other with their hands and fingers, easily and efficiently. Over time it would all come together, but time was not on her side.

She would be leaving for America soon. She'd made her plans, persuading her sister Stephanie to sell her emeralds and book passage for her aboard ship. It took a great deal of persuasion, actually, since Stephanie, young and romantic, couldn't understand why she was still inclined to leave England, and especially her husband, for a lifetime of study and research. She'd vocalized her irritation and disapproval, nearly scolding Caroline outright for her determination and continued intentions. And the pressure was starting to take its toll.

For the first time in her life Caroline was uncertain of her path. She had never been torn between two things as she was now. Logically she wanted only her flowers, her plants and precious lavender roses, her breeding calculations, and the recognition of being a learned botanist. But emotionally she wanted the little girl she'd taught to communicate to grow up to know her as her mother, and she had to admit she ached for Brent to want her for more than her ability to bear and care for children.

He already respected her, which was more than most wives could ever expect from a husband. He never demanded that she sleep with him, although he discussed it frequently and teased her shamefully with suggestions. Only two nights before, he'd awakened again with a nightmare and she had gone to him.

He kissed her, sometimes sweetly, sometimes passionately, but never did he touch her with more intimacy than she was willing to accept. And she was fully aware that the passion they shared could only be held in check for so long. Eventually, if she stayed at Miramont, she would push reason aside, honor the marriage vows, and succumb to his lovemaking. Acknowledging that need in her was tearing her apart.

So, confused and alone, she'd left them all to think, to walk without direction through the thick forest, and suddenly it stood before her. A greenhouse, old and covered with ivy and weeds from years of neglect, but a greenhouse nonetheless.

Slowly, excitement overtaking the initial shock, she walked around the rectangular building, finding it to be of average size and sound of structure, the door on the far end tightly shut and covered with wild greenery.

Carefully she tried the rusted handle, but it wouldn't give, and she didn't have the adequate tools with her to pry it open. But, as she considered all the options for breeding, with a greenhouse now available to her, her mind immediately began to race with possibilities.

And she was instantly filled with questions.

Did it belong to him? It had to, for she was only a mile from the house, in deep woods, and it certainly hadn't been used in years, maybe decades. So why had he never mentioned it when he knew how desperate she was to acquire such a structure?

Did he even know it existed? He had to, Caroline surmised after careful consideration, for the man owned the property surrounding the house for miles and rode his horses daily over his land. Yes, he would have to be aware of a greenhouse on his property, so why the secrecy? The only conclusion she could draw was that he wanted to keep the use of it from her for personal reasons.

That made her angry. She'd asked for a greenhouse, and he had spitefully denied her one he already owned, although truthfully she had been overly flirtatious in bringing up the subject. But this would cost him nothing, not even his time. He needn't be concerned with it at all.

The more she thought about it, the angrier she became, and with it came the awareness that she wouldn't be able to acknowledge the find. If he learned of her discovery, he could reasonably deny her access, and that she refused to allow.

So, determined and annoyed, she turned and marched back toward the house. If he could keep his greenhouse a secret, she could keep the use of it a secret. He obviously didn't go near it often, and if she was careful, she could work in it during those times she knew he'd be otherwise occupied. Keeping the greenhouse a secret would be something they could both share.

Quickly she made her way through the trees and across the meadow, feeling the urgency to start exerting her efforts on the structure immediately. She stepped through the back door, passed the dining room, and was so engrossed in thoughts of planting that she nearly ran into Nedda, who in turn raced into the hallway from the drawing room.

Nedda took a step back, breathing fast. "We have guests," she blurted anxiously.

Caroline smiled. Obviously whoever had arrived had startled her housekeeper by calling without notice. And since she wore only a plain white blouse and cotton work skirt, she would have to change before receiving.

"Why don't you serve tea while I dress, Nedda. I'll be there shortly."

Her housekeeper faltered slightly, her eyes shifting to the drawing-room door. "I think it would be best if you saw them now," she mumbled before darting past and racing away.

Caroline gazed after her, curious, having never seen Nedda so pink-cheeked and flustered. Deciding she didn't need to be announced, and forgetting completely her inappropriate attire, she walked to the door of the drawing room and swiftly stepped inside.

She saw the woman first, a lovely blond woman, sitting primly on the blue velveteen sofa, staring at her gloved hands while she nervously rubbed her fingers together. She wore a pale-pink day gown and her hair was fashionably pinned to frame her creamy, pale face. For just an instant, Caroline feared this was Pauline Sinclair, here to announce she'd given birth to her husband's second child.

The woman looked up and smiled faintly, her eyes vibrantly blue and filled with trepidation. "Hello," she said softly, hesitantly. "We're here to see Lord Weymerth."

She shifted her attention to the fireplace. Caroline followed her gaze, and that's when she noticed her companion, a man, huge of stature, dark and exceptionally handsome with thick, jet-black hair, and eyes as blue as the woman's. He stared at her hard, his expression unreadable but not at all pleasant. He had also dressed impeccably for the occasion, and suddenly Caroline felt embarrassed and out of place.

"I beg your pardon," she replied as evenly as she could, "but your business with Lord Weymerth is?"

The woman glanced once again to the man, then quickly back to Caroline, her body shifting uncomfortably on the soft cushion.

"I'm Mrs. Charlotte Becker, and this is my husband, Carl. I apologize for calling without notice, but we only arrived yesterday." She fidgeted slightly. "Are you a servant perchance?"

Caroline was taken aback by the impertinent question, but she quickly recovered her composure, standing erect and walking as gracefully as any queen into the room to sit casually on the sofa next to the woman.

"I am the Countess of Weymerth," she informed rather coolly. "May I ask how you are acquainted with my husband?"

The woman paled and gawked at her, then looked again to her husband who was now rudely facing the fireplace with his back to both of them. "I—I didn't know," she mumbled.

After an awkward pause, Caroline had had enough. "I'm terribly sorry, but you've missed Lord Weymerth." She stood abruptly. "Perhaps if you would like to call another—"

The woman grabbed her arm. "No, please. I'm sorry."

She looked so forlorn. Caroline watched her for a second or two then slowly sat again, deciding she should at least allow the woman to explain her position.

"This is just such a . . . shock," Mrs. Becker finally admitted diffidently, releasing her arm and looking once again to her lap. "I would have liked to think Brent would have told you about me." She laughed bitterly and shook her head. "And I can't believe he didn't let me know he'd married."

Caroline's puzzlement suddenly gave way to such an incredible rush of jealousy that she felt less angry at the woman and Brent for their romantic affair than she did at herself for reacting so. No wonder this woman's husband appeared annoyed, acted so discourteously. He was undoubtedly enraged and had forced his wife to confront the earl in his presence, not knowing at all that the earl had a wife of his own. Brent obviously felt he needed to keep such a trivial matter a secret as well when he took a mistress, which was now proving to be an embarrassment for all of them. All the more reason to clear the air without delay.

"Are you pregnant with my husband's child?" she calmly asked, desperate to keep her poise intact.

Mr. Becker flipped around to stare at her so quickly that she thought his head might fly off his neck. Charlotte, poor thing, had at least the dignity to become ghastly white and look so incredibly appalled that Caroline feared she might actually faint.

For a moment nobody said anything, then Carl Becker addressed her directly. "I believe, madam, that my wife has given you the wrong impression."

Caroline, heart pounding, shifted her gaze to his face, her expression as slack as she could keep it. The man was American, judging by his accent.

He cleared his throat and lowered his deep, baritone voice. "This is Charlotte Ravenscroft Becker. Lord Weymerth is her brother."

Caroline did nothing, said nothing, just stared blankly at the man for several moments. Then slowly she forced herself to look once again at the woman sitting next to her.

The resemblance was there, in the square jaw, the full mouth, even in coloring, although her complexion was slightly fairer. But the eyes were exactly the same, save for the fact that hers were blue, so brilliant, so expressive, and Caroline couldn't believe she hadn't noticed the similarities at once.

He had a sister. The damned, insufferable man had a sister about whom he'd told her nothing, and what infuriated her was that she had embarrassed herself to such an extent in front of this woman and her husband, she truly wondered if she would recover or be able to rectify the situation.

Slowly she stood, cheeks flaming, chin high. "I would be deeply grateful, Mrs. Becker, if you would forgive my atrocious behavior. I had no idea my husband had any close relations."

The woman smiled. "The misunderstanding was partly mine. You needn't apologize."

"Please, call me Caroline, both of you." She swallowed to repress a scream. "I'd like you to remain here and I'll have Nedda bring refreshments. In the meantime, I think I'll personally announce your arrival to your brother."

Fourteen

Caroline fairly ran to the stables, intensely angered, stopping for breath only when she reached the front gate. She paused, listening and seeing nobody, then heard pounding from the other side of the building.

With a grim set to her jaw, back ramrod-straight, she smoothed her hair, collected herself, and marched around the structure to the north end.

He was leaning over a post, nailing something to a fence, and she stopped short when she saw him, gaping, for the man was half-naked, wearing nothing but tight black breeches and work boots.

Dark golden hair flew wildly in the breeze, falling loosely over his forehead and face, now strained with effort. Light-brown curls softly matted against sun-bronzed skin, and the muscles on his chest and arms gleamed with sweat created by pure, hard labor as he pounded large nails into the wood.

The man had an absolutely beautiful physique, firm and strong and taut. His hips were lean and narrow, and his breeches had scooted so low she couldn't stop her imagination from blooming brightly with ideas, or keep her eyes from following the trail of light-brown hair as it gradually grew thicker and wider from his navel down to his—

"Well, if it isn't my sweet, dirty wife, back from her walk in the woods."

Quickly she covered her hot, flushed cheeks with her palms. Her heart sped up from nervousness, and she hoped to heaven he hadn't noticed on which part of his rather impressive anatomy she'd fixed her line of sight.

"Have you nothing decent to wear?" she blurted. Then, because she didn't want to give him the wrong idea about where her thoughts were leading, she quickly added, "You'll catch your death dressed like that."

He chuckled softly, climbed over the fence, and started to move toward her. Without thinking, she took two steps back and crossed her arms over her chest.

The smile died on his lips. "Are you afraid I'll ravish you right here, Caroline, or do you just find sweaty men repulsive?"

His tone didn't imply anger, just . . . indifference, as if he weren't certain if he'd offended her. That bothered her.

"Nothing about you repulses me, Brent, I've just never seen a man look so"—she nervously flicked her wrist—"like that . . . before."

Eyeing her suspiciously, he reached for a towel and wiped his face. "Like what?"

She sighed and attempted to change the subject. "I'm here to discuss something else—"

"Answer me, Caroline." He glanced up suggestively, the side of his mouth turning up slightly. "Did you mean . . . strong?"

She fidgeted, suddenly uncomfortable. "Of course."

"I see . . ." He threw the towel on the post to his left and slowly walked toward her. "Maybe you were thinking about my masculinity as well, hmm? I am a man, after all—"

"Of course you're a man," she said, exasperated.

"Or maybe you find me . . . sexy?"

She blinked, blushing furiously, and sternly stated

once more, "I'm here to discuss something else."

"I think," he countered softly, "I'd rather discuss the two of us while we're all alone, while you're standing here staring at me like a woman in need of a man, while your face is flushed from desires you don't even fully recognize."

He towered over her now, powerfully arrogant, eyes mesmerizing and boldly locked with hers.

"Do you find me sexy, little one?" he whispered.

"No," she replied firmly, suddenly hot, breathless, and completely unable to move.

"Liar," he returned thickly, positively, lifting his fingers to stroke her collarbone lightly through her blouse. "You are so sexy to me, Caroline, so bewitching. Your eyes are like dark, rich chocolate, your hair like priceless Japanese silk, and your body . . ." He smiled softly. "Your body is something most men can only dream of possessing. Every day I find you lovelier than the one before, and you can't imagine how crazy that makes me."

She couldn't breathe, and within seconds she was trembling. "You humiliate me."

His eyes narrowed, his body stilled. "I would never humiliate you, Caroline."

The tenderness in his voice warmed her heart, and every part of her wanted to surrender to the moment. In seconds he'd be kissing her mouth, she knew it, and from that point on there would be no escape.

He leaned over and brushed his lips to her cheek, and gathering strength, she boldly moved to the moment of truth. "Why didn't you tell me you have a sister?"

It took time for the words to sink in. Lots of time, really, as he stood motionless, his cheek to hers. Then, slowly, he pulled his head back and stared down at her, his jaw like granite, eyes blank and unreadable.

"I had a sister, Caroline. She's dead now."

She stood unruffled. "Well, then, she must have risen from the grave, because right this very minute, sipping tea in our drawing room, is a lovely woman who claims to be the former Lady Charlotte.''

The blood drained from his face.

That reaction satisfied her immensely. ''And she evidently has exceptional taste in men. Her husband, Carl, is with her as well, and had I realized such dark, robust, exotically attractive men existed in America, I surely would have gone there years ago to find a husband of my own.''

His expression suddenly contorted in rage, his eyes becoming tiny slits of dark fury, his color now returning in full form except for his lips, which were bloodless and thinned. She had never seen him like this, and for a moment she wasn't certain whether it was because his sister had returned or because she had spoken so presumptuously about the lady's husband. In either case, she didn't care, remembering how she'd managed to disgrace herself completely in front of members of his family because he'd never bothered to mention he had any.

Calmly she continued. ''I'm sure you'll find this rather amusing, Brent, but because we didn't know about each other, Charlotte thought I was a servant, and I thought she was your mistress.''

''Oh, Jesus . . .'' He faltered, his gaze shifting quickly to the house.

Caroline laughed derisively. ''I actually asked her if she carried your child, can you believe that?''

He looked at her sharply again. ''You asked her what!''

She took a defensive step away from him. ''I thought as beautiful and nervous as she was, she had to be your mistress. Here with her husband, I assumed she was pregnant with your child.'' She sighed loudly and stated matter-of-factly, ''She's also blond.''

''Goddamn it, Caroline!'' He raked the fingers of both hands through his hair in complete irritation. ''Let's get something straight before we deal with that woman and her husband.''

''That woman? That's what you call your sister? And

lower your voice,'' she demanded, now fully angry as well. "Davis and the grooms will hear you shouting."

"I don't give a damn who hears me!" He glared into her eyes, face hard as steel. "I don't have a mistress—I don't want one. You're too much trouble for that kind of complication."

She bit her lip and glared in return.

"And furthermore, not every man desires blondes. Some of us actually prefer women who look like you. Why have you never considered that with that calculating little mind of yours?"

Color bloomed in her cheeks. "You don't have to take your anger out on me."

He snickered. "Why not? You're the one who makes me angry!"

Her mouth dropped open, and at that point she truly lost every ounce of control she possessed.

"I make *you* angry? You're the one who's made a habit of chasing blond, beautiful women. What was I supposed to think when I walked into the drawing room looking like the plain, dirt-covered spinster you married, to find a lovely blond woman, wearing pink chiffon—hich is, naturally, the color you prefer your blondes to wear while they're clothed—nervously rubbing her hands together and telling me she wished we all knew about each other?"

Her voice grew in strength, and her eyes blazed wildly, but she no longer cared.

"Do you know what I thought when I first saw her, Brent? I thought she was the beautiful Pauline Sinclair here to discuss the child you and she had bestowed upon the world together." She raised her palms and looked at him in feigned wonder. "How grateful I was that I hadn't embarrassed myself to such an extreme in front of one of your lovers, but in front of your sister. A sister I didn't even know existed!"

She'd been so engrossed in her tirade, she hadn't noticed the change on his face. Suddenly she blinked hard and took a step or two away from him, unsure, and knowing she'd said too much, for the man practically gaped at her now with an expression she could only term as wide-eyed amazement.

Then his mouth broke out in a smile until he grinned vibrantly, the pleasure he conveyed reaching even his eyes.

"I never bedded Pauline, Caroline," he said easily, arrogantly.

She didn't expect that. She wanted to discuss his sister, not some flirtatious little wench he'd almost married. Gritting her teeth, she fairly seethed, "That is not the issue. I don't give a damn who you've bedded—"

"Yes, you do."

She stared at him hard, shaking her head in awe of his stupidity. "That's the most ludicrous statement you've ever made."

He laughed at that. "Do you know what I think, little one?"

"I'm tired of hearing what you think, you pompous, good-for-nothing little toad—"

He cut her off by grabbing her around the waist and pulling her hard against him. Instinctively she placed her palms on his chest to push herself away, but within seconds she knew that was a mistake. Just the feel of his bare skin and tight muscles beneath her fingers made her tingle, and the pure, musky scent of him clouded her mind so suddenly that she forgot what she'd intended to say anyway. The only thing she could bring herself to do was hold completely still and try to ignore him until he saw fit to release her.

Then he nuzzled her neck. "I adore the fact that you aren't afraid to say anything."

"Go to hell."

He laughed again and lifted his head, peering into her eyes with smug enjoyment.

"I think, Caroline, that not only are you lovelier with each passing day, you are positively stunning to behold in a fit of jealousy."

Her eyes opened wide with horror. "I've never been jealous of anyone in my life."

He raised a brow cynically. "Really? Then I'm glad to know I'm the first for something."

She pushed against him with every bit of strength she possessed. "Let me go, you asinine, arrogant—"

"Toad?"

She stopped the struggle, scowling at him, nostrils flaring.

He smiled wryly and whispered, "You're so delightfully unconventional, I'll bet you adore little creatures, don't you, Caroline? Spiders, snakes, even little toads like me."

What on earth did he expect her to say to that? He was an idiot if he thought she would simply give way to his male prowess, his enormous ego.

She closed her eyes and quietly muttered, "I don't love you, Brent, if that's what you're thinking."

She expected him to laugh sarcastically, outrageously, or even release her without incident, but nothing happened. After several agonizing seconds, she opened her eyes to his once more, and the intensity of his gaze unnerved her. He grasped her chin, lifting it to take in every feature, every soft contour of her face, and she couldn't for the life of her pull herself away. Then, without a sound in response, he lowered his lips, gently brushing them back and forth against hers.

Caroline knew she needed to temper the magic immediately, before it consumed her. If he kissed her fully, embraced by his strength, she would crumble and he would win.

"I don't love you," she insisted urgently, turning purposely from the touch of his mouth.

He paused, released her chin, and slowly raised his head.

She dropped hers, unable to look him in the eye, and hoped he would take her withdrawal from his kiss as an affirmation of her words instead of cowardice and confusion, which, she had to admit, was really what it was.

For a moment or two he said nothing, then he sliced the tension in the air with a voice both pensive and reserved.

"I wasn't suggesting you do, Caroline, but I think you want to believe it so badly you're trying to convince yourself."

She gave an acrid laugh. "Don't worry, Brent. I'm not the kind of brainless female who would ever present you with the awkward moment of confessing my love and expecting you to respond in kind. I'm not romantic by nature, and you've made your position perfectly clear."

She felt his body become tense, then rigid, and slowly he released her. She backed away, and when she finally drew the courage to look at him again, she found him watching her with a face completely void of expression.

Coldly he said, "As far as the guests are concerned, you may treat them as you like. I have no intention of acknowledging them, but I will permit them to stay at Miramont for the time they need to find lodging elsewhere."

Turning and walking to pick up his tools, he added over his shoulder, "I need to get dressed. There's a sudden chill in the air."

Without a second glance in her direction, he disappeared behind the stables.

Fifteen

It took Caroline nearly thirty minutes to gather the strength to face Charlotte again, and nearly as much time to persuade the lady and her husband to stay at Miramont as her guests. They were reluctant, naturally, and Charlotte, though she had expected that her brother wouldn't see her, couldn't begin to hide the disappointment in her eyes. That made Caroline all the more adamant. These Americans were her relations now, and she had every right to know them.

The three of them met for dinner in the large dining room, dressed for the occasion and carrying on as if it were a state function. Brent was noticeably absent, taking dinner with Rosalyn in the nursery, but Caroline put her best face on in an attempt to feign disinterest. She refused to allow the man to ruin the evening simply because he wasn't there.

The talk was trivial during the first course, but by the time they'd completed half the main course, she began to feel annoyed at the superficial chatter and took it upon herself to get to the heart of the matter.

Patting her lips with her napkin, she sat back and

asked, "Would you mind telling me why Brent won't speak of you, Charlotte?"

The woman glanced up quickly, eyes widening as she swallowed dryly. "It's . . . complicated."

"I'd really like to know," Caroline returned matter-of-factly.

Charlotte gazed at her for a long moment, unsure and obviously considering her words, then threw a quick look to her husband, who had stopped eating and was watching her speculatively as well. Finally she sighed in concession, placed her fork on her plate, and folded her hands in her lap.

"Brent and I have always been different from each other, Caroline. He's six years my senior, quiet and reserved where I am talkative, a brooder where I am a socializer. As there were only the two of us growing up, he became my silent protector around our mother, who had her nose into everyone's business, especially mine. He resented the way she attacked me for little things— my hair, dress, speech. Brent loved me as I was and wanted me to be happy. Mother wanted me to be a perfect model of social grace, to become everything she never was."

Charlotte rubbed her hands together nervously and looked blankly at her unfinished plate of pheasant and wild rice.

"Seven years ago, my brother and mother found a man for me to marry." She laughed caustically. "I think it was probably the only thing the two of them had ever agreed on in their lives. The man was a viscount, likable, powerful and well respected. But he was also forty-two years old, homely, widowed with three young children, and plainly after a respectable woman who could become an instant mother."

Caroline had to interrupt. "I cannot believe my husband would force you to marry someone so obviously inappropriate, could be so insensitive to your wishes."

Charlotte shook her head. "You don't understand. To Brent, the man wasn't inappropriate. He represented stability, companionship, respectability. To him, the match was legitimate and proper, and provided me with the means to leave Miramont. He truly believed he was securing my future while helping me escape my mother the witch.''

Caroline's eyes opened wide.

Charlotte smiled faintly. ''Brent hasn't told you much about her, has he?''

She frowned. ''Nothing actually, although Nedda mentioned she was lovely.''

Charlotte rolled her eyes and shook her head with pure disgust. ''She was exquisite to look at, but on the inside she was cruel, conceited, demanding, and treated Brent and me as if we had the plague. Her social life meant everything, so socially we were expected to be perfect, always on display, supporting her position as a beautiful woman with perfect children. Publicly, she petted and complimented us; privately, she threatened, belittled, and beat us with a riding whip whenever we managed to displease her, which was frequently. When my brother was finally able to physically defend us against her, the beatings stopped, and that's when she became verbally abusive, calling us names, telling us what horrid, inept people we were, how we'd ruined her life.''

She looked up through vivid blue eyes, sparkling from candlelight and filled with sadness. ''I think that's why Brent is so quiet, why he mistrusts people as he does, especially women. Growing up was a miserable experience for both of us, but probably more so for him because he felt such responsibility for me. The weight on his shoulders, I realize now, had to have been extraordinary.''

Caroline swallowed with difficulty, thoroughly shaken. Of course Nedda wouldn't have told her such intimate details about her husband's childhood and family, for that would surely have been overstepping the boundaries of propriety. But an abusive mother? Sadly, it explained so much about Brent's nature, why he spoke so bluntly, wanting to get everything out in the open as if waiting for a negative reply. It explained why he chose such a dangerous profession of isolation, why he spent his free time in the quiet companionship of his horses, his disbelief in romantic love, and his deeply felt, unconditional love for Rosalyn.

Gradually she was beginning to understand the man, and with that she felt profoundly moved as she thought of the sad, lonely boy who grew up with a sister he felt bound to protect and a mother who humiliated him.

Caroline took a sip of wine in an attempt to contain her emotions. "If he cared for you so much, why does he now treat you as if you don't exist?" she softly asked seconds later.

"She married me," Carl bluntly revealed, sitting back in his chair.

She looked from one to the other. "I don't understand."

Charlotte gave her husband a small, loving smile. "I refused to marry the man chosen for me. Brent and I had several rows over it actually, but in the end I won, though not without devastating consequences. My brother had agreed to the marriage; betrothal papers were signed and a wedding date set. Two weeks before I was to walk down the aisle, I packed my bags and I left. Just like that." She snapped her fingers. "I knew I needed to go as far away as possible, and in my own naïve way the only place I could think of was America. So I sold some expensive jewelry in London and booked passage. Three days after we sailed, I met Carl, who happens to be one of the owners of the company that builds the wretched ships." Her face puckered and she shivered. "To my complete mortification, he saw me heaving over the side, and because he felt sorry—"

"Desperate, sweetheart," he muttered with a satisfied smile.

Charlotte blushed, fully grinning at him. "Because he felt *sorry* for me he took me . . . uh . . . under his wing, and three months after arriving in Rhode Island we were married.''

Caroline picked up her fork and thoughtlessly toyed with her food. "I suppose my husband felt awkward explaining your disappearance to the viscount."

Charlotte scoffed. "I don't think Brent would ever feel awkward about saying anything to anyone."

She paused for a moment then leaned toward her to continue, sorrow coloring her voice. "My brother will not acknowledge me to this day, has returned every letter I've ever sent him unopened—and I've written him once a month without fail for the last six years—simply because he'd found me a respectable, socially adequate English husband, and instead, I ran off and married an American. That's it. To him I'm dead."

Caroline was incredulous. "That's ridiculous," she mumbled, looking from the woman to her husband, who now stared at his wineglass, twisting it with his fingers.

Charlotte smiled and shook her head. "Not really. Brent is above everything else an Englishman, Caroline. He adores his country, his heritage, and would give his life for the Crown. The man he'd chosen for me was an English viscount who met my needs socially and financially; therefore, I should have been happy. In his very practical mind, my brother now views me as the daughter of an earl who threw everything away when she left and married, not someone she deeply loved, but someone whose family had rebelled against his king."

Of course her husband would see only the practical reasons for marriage and not the emotional ones, Caroline mused. To Brent, marrying for love would be silly, illogical, and completely beside the point.

"How long will you be in England?" she asked after a quiet moment of contemplation.

Carl sat back and pursed his lips. "A little more than two months. I need to attend to some business in the city." He shook his head firmly. "But as much as my wife wants to see her brother, we won't stay here unless his high and mighty lord of ignorance decides to acknowledge us and grace us with his presence—"

"Carl!"

Caroline burst out laughing.

"What?" the man blurted, intolerant. "Calling him that in front of his wife shows no more disrespect than he's shown in turning from the only family he has."

"He has his wife and daughter, darling, and he's done without me in his life for six years."

"You know about Rosalyn?" Caroline asked, surprised.

Charlotte smiled, her lovely blue eyes soft with understanding. "Nedda writes me several times a year to keep me informed. I know about his beautiful child and her problems, what Reggie did to Miramont while Brent was at war. I'm sure she even wrote me about you, but we'd probably sailed before the letter had a chance to reach me." She leaned forward and lowered her voice to a whisper. "Please don't tell Brent, Caroline. He would forbid Nedda to write, and I'd like to keep what little correspondence I have between us intact."

Caroline glanced from the woman to her husband, then back again as she nodded, sobering a little, thinking. Quietly she announced, "I think we should have a dinner party."

Charlotte's expression was dubious, but Caroline would not be discouraged.

"We'll invite my sisters and their husbands, and friends of yours if you'd like. It doesn't need to be an enormous occasion, just a comfortable gathering." She breathed deeply, adding confidently, "He can hardly ignore you at a party he'll be forced to attend."

"Can you talk him into it?" Charlotte whispered.

She shrugged. "I'll certainly try."

As exhausted as she was, Caroline wanted to talk to her husband, and as disturbed as it made her feel, she also felt the confusing need to simply see him, be with him.

She stood at their adjoining door and knocked twice, feeling suddenly foolish and certain he was asleep, since it was just after midnight. To her surprise, though, he spoke almost immediately.

"You don't need to knock, Caroline."

His quiet arrogance convinced her to straighten her shoulders and enter with her chin in the air. But the tension and anger drained from her at once when she saw him, all the feelings of compassion filling her as she tried to imagine the complications of his past.

The room was dark save for a blazing fire in the grate. He sat on the small settee in front of it, staring into the flames. His shirt was unbuttoned, sleeves rolled up, and he held a half-filled snifter of brandy in his hands. As he heard the rustle of her skirts upon entering, he raised the glass to his lips, took a full swallow, then glanced in her direction.

"I see you dressed for dinner."

He sounded sullen, tired, and slowly she walked toward him, doing her best to answer him lightly. "Is yellow a color you prefer only on ladies with red hair? Pretty soon, Brent, you'll tell me you prefer dark-haired women to wear nothing at all."

He chuckled softly and looked into the amber liquid, twirling the glass in his hand. "I've considered that." He moved to his right slightly. "Come and sit with me."

That was all she needed to hear. Walking quietly to his side, she gazed down at him for a moment, then sat beside him on the soft cushion, slipping her shoes off, and pulling her legs up and under her gown.

For several minutes they watched the fire in silence, Caroline feeling warm, relaxed, even peaceful in his presence.

"You've had a long and interesting birthday, haven't you, little one?"

"Mmm . . . More than you can imagine."

He took her hand in his and lightly caressed her fingers, back and forth, with the pad of his thumb. "Would you like a brandy?"

Smiling, she gently captured his hand and raised it to her lips, kissing his palm delicately just once. That action seemed to surprise him, which made her smile widen.

"I had two glasses of wine with dinner," she replied softly. "And it's late."

He looked back to his glass and took another sip. "Wine will make your head ache, but brandy will help you sleep."

She cocked a brow. "That sounds like a statement made by a man who would know."

He smiled and leaned his head back against the settee, still holding her hand but staring once again into the flames. "I have brandy every night, sitting here in front of the fire, Caroline," he said quietly. "It helps me relax so I sleep better. It's one of the many things about me you still don't know."

She turned her gaze back to the hearth as well, watching the flickering blue and orange light, listening to each crackle and hiss as the heat of it filled the room. He was right about that, at least. There were many things about the man she'd married that she didn't know and probably never would until she became completely intimate with him. And being with him intimately, she had to admit, was becoming more and more difficult to avoid as time passed.

The thought made her shiver. He evidently felt it, for at that moment he pulled his hand from hers, reached over, and drew her up against his chest.

"Have a sip, Caroline. It will warm you on the inside."

She hesitated, then took the glass from his hand and swallowed a mouthful of the burning liquid, rich and full-bodied. Licking her lips, she handed the snifter back to him, watching as he drained the contents and placed the glass on the side table. That done, he pulled her closer against him, both arms circling her waist, and she willingly rested her head on his chest.

"This should become a habit," he suggested thoughtfully, staring once again into the flames. "We should take brandy together every night like this, just the two of us." He lowered his voice. "I'm tired of being alone, Caroline."

It was an admission he didn't make lightly, and with it she felt her heart warm as she sighed contentedly and snuggled into him.

For a long while she lay against him in quiet companionship, listening to his heart beating, his slow, even breathing. Finally, from the closeness, she drew the courage to discuss the topic they'd been avoiding.

"Your sister is lovely, Brent."

He stiffened just slightly but offered nothing in response, so she bravely continued, turning her head to glance up to his face. "I have a favor to ask."

He looked into her eyes.

She took a deep breath to encourage confidence she didn't feel at all. "I'd like to have a dinner party for Charlotte and Carl. Please don't say no—"

He cut her off with a finger to her lips.

For several seconds she watched the deep hazel-green of his eyes as they gleamed in the firelight and grazed over every inch of her face.

"Rosalyn and I had a nice dinner together, Caroline," he said at last, the deep, rich quality of his voice filling the room.

She continued to hold his gaze, curious and unsure because the words he spoke implied a casual change in topic, and yet his tone was somber, denoting something more.

He inhaled deeply and lightly ran his finger along her lips and jaw until he cupped her face in his hand. Then amazement and wonder crept into his voice as he whispered, "And when we finished eating she came to me, Caroline. She stood directly in front of me, pointed to herself, and spelled *Papa* with her fingers. She called me her papa then grabbed me around the neck and hugged me, voluntarily."

Caroline beamed. "I thought it should be the first word she learned to spell."

"I know." He tenderly stroked her neck. "She knows

who I am in her life because of you. She responds and talks to me because of you. One day she might even marry and give me grandchildren because of you. All the things I never thought could happen are suddenly possible.''

Gently he leaned over and kissed her, his lips soft and warm and tasting faintly of brandy as they brushed against hers, not passionately, but with aching sweetness, with deep, heartfelt gratitude.

Gradually, reluctantly, he pulled back, lifting his head, his eyes conveying what words could not. ''You have given me the greatest gift, Caroline,'' he whispered huskily, fervidly, ''and I don't think I'll ever be able to deny you anything.''

She drew a shaky breath, her gaze never shifting from the intensity of his as she lifted a hand to run her fingers through his hair. In all of her life, she knew she would never forget this moment.

''I'm certain Rosalyn knew, even before I gave her the words, that you loved her. And I'm just as sure that someday she'll tell you how much your caring has meant to her, how deeply she loves you.'' She ran her palm down his cheek and neck, resting it over his heart. ''You, my darling husband, are the most fortunate one of all.''

He swallowed hard with emotion. ''Yes, I am, Caroline,'' he admitted in a thick, caressing voice, ''because I married you.''

She stilled. Even her breathing seemed to stop in that instant as she stared into eyes of calm, vibrant green expressing the feelings his mind wouldn't admit and his heart couldn't convey. She blinked several times to fight tears of joy from having him as her very own, tears of anguish from the confusion he presented in her life by his very being, but mostly tears of sorrow because she realized in that instant that her destiny was changing. At that precise moment, she understood what losing him would mean to her, and never again would she be able to go on as she had before, content with only the solitude of her plants. She was beginning to love him.

He placed his palm on her cheek. "Come to bed with me, Caroline."

She absolutely knew to the depths of her soul that denying him this would be the greatest, most difficult decision she would ever make in her life. She needed him, but the confusion still existed. If she gave in now, her dream of a lifetime would end.

Tears she could no longer control filled her eyes. "You just don't understand what I'm going through, Brent."

His jaw hardened, and he gripped her chin tightly. "Tell me what it is, Caroline. What are you afraid of?"

She closed her eyes and shook her head, unable to answer. After a long moment of knowing that he stared at her with desire, confused and frustrated, he dropped his hand from her face, wrapped his arm around her head, and pulled her against his chest.

"I'm sorry," she whispered, wiping her eyes with the back of her hand.

Brent sighed heavily, saying nothing as he pulled the ribbon from her hair. He held her tightly for a long while, running his fingers through the thick, silky tresses, until he felt her relax, heard her breathing slow and deepen as sleep overcame her.

Finally, as the fire died to glowing embers, he gently lifted her in his arms and carried her to her bed. The exhaustion of the day had seeped into her bones, for she didn't stir or utter a sound when he laid her on the sheets. He turned her to her side, unbuttoned her gown and slowly pulled it down the length of her, lifting her legs to ease it from her body.

By the glow of moonlight he studied her figure, dressed in only a white chemise as it clung to every soft contour of her small and delicate form. Her dark hair cascaded in long, shiny waves over her pillow. The skin on her face, neck, and arms glowed with the sheen of ivory satin, and her black lashes fell across pale cheeks as if painted by a skilled artist in long, soft, sensuous strokes.

"You're so beautiful . . ." he whispered as he slowly began to run the tips of his fingers along her body. Her breasts were full and round, and through the thinness of the material covering them he could see the darkness of her nipples, inviting him to touch. Gradually, with reverence, he grazed his palm along the curve of her waist, the flatness of her stomach, his throat closing tightly, constricting his breathing as he looked down to notice at once how the thin barrier of pale linen could not completely hide the dark triangle between her legs. Slowly, very slowly, he ran the back of his hand across her hips to feel the cushion of curls covering the most intimate part of her, which she continued to keep from him.

"Why won't you let me in, Caroline?" he whispered into the darkened, quiet room, to her silent, peaceful form.

An ache squeezed his chest, gripping him as it grew in strength. He ran his palm down the length of her leg, then pulled the quilt over her body and turned away.

He looked back to her as he stood at the door, knowing the wait couldn't last, the ache to have her as his own couldn't go on much longer. She made him laugh, she made him crazy, she made him proud, but more than anything, she made him happy, and in all of his nearly thirty-four years, he'd never imagined a woman would make him happy.

Sixteen

The guests were beginning to arrive, taking sherry and hors d'oeuvres in the drawing room as they awaited dinner. Besides the four of them, only ten others would be present—Caroline's sisters Jane and Charlotte and their husbands, her father and her sister Stephanie, and two friends of Charlotte Becker's whom the lady hadn't seen in years, and their respective husbands. Mary Anne would be absent, as she'd just given birth, and for that Caroline was almost grateful. Fourteen to entertain would be enough.

Her hands shook as she stepped into her evening gown, turning so Gwendolyn could button the back. She'd borrowed it from Charlotte and had it altered to fit her form during the last three weeks since she didn't own any gowns quite so grand. This one was beautiful.

"Good gracious, you look lovely," Gwendolyn exclaimed.

Caroline turned and walked to the full-length mirror to study her reflection. The final picture amazed her indeed, for she looked like a completely different woman.

The gown was a deep wine color, elegant in style with an extremely low, rounded neckline and high waist. The bodice was straight and simple, the skirt flowing to her ankles in a smooth cascade of dark silk, and the short sleeves puffed high and full. On her left arm, just above the elbow, she wore a simple band of diamonds to match the two dangling from her earlobes, and to complete the picture she wore long, wine-colored silk gloves. She couldn't remember the last time she'd dressed so formally, and never in her life had she looked so appealing.

And it was all because she'd given Charlotte permission to cut her hair not three hours before.

Caroline wasn't sure what had overcome her to allow such a thing, for she'd never in her life given hairstyle any thought. But her sister-in-law had pleaded with her, wanting to slice the front off just enough to cover her "rather expansive, cumbersome forehead," as she'd put it. So, tense and reluctant, Caroline had surrendered to the woman's decree, allowing Charlotte to cut enough of her hair to completely cover her forehead. That done, she'd curled the rest of it with a hot iron and piled it on top of her head, pinning it loosely, giving her not only height, but an aura of elegance and grace.

Staring at herself in the mirror, Caroline felt a rush of pure pleasure from knowing that she had never in her life looked lovelier than she did now. It had taken twenty-six years and a sister-in-law of only three weeks to discover that if she styled her hair by covering her forehead, she was almost beautiful to look at. Her reflection truly stunned her.

"Wish me luck, Gwendolyn," she said nervously, turning to the door.

"You won't need any, Lady Caroline. Have a wonderful time."

She took a deep breath, smiled to her maid, and stepped into the hallway.

She hadn't seen much of Brent during the three weeks his sister had been at Miramont. He woke early, took breakfast in the kitchen, and was usually gone from the house before she'd even dressed. But alas, the man, even with his consent to attend the party, wanted nothing to do with the preparation and even less to do with Charlotte and Carl. As far as she was aware, he'd only briefly set eyes on the two of them, nodding curtly and saying not a word in acknowledgment. She knew that Charlotte felt stung by his avoidance, but Carl was angered by it and refused to acknowledge Brent in return. Tonight's dinner party would be the first time they would be thrust together for a length of time. She hoped the event would be heated enough to thaw the ice barrier between them. If this didn't work, the Beckers would most certainly leave Miramont posthaste.

Brent's avoidance, however, couldn't have come at a better time for Caroline. Because of his disappearance each day, sometimes for hours, she'd been able to work in the greenhouse. It had initially taken two hours to break the lock, but once the door had been pried open and she'd stepped over the threshold, her heart had raced with anticipation. The interior was immaculate. Although no live plants existed and the soil had dried years before, it had evidently been cleaned and scrubbed before being sealed. That's the only way she could describe it, as there were few bugs and even fewer spiders with webs to clear away. The inside had been stripped, cleaned, and sealed, as if it would never be used again.

Realistically she'd expected conditions inside to reflect the abandonment of the structure, but because the opposite was true, it had taken only a week to get it ready for planting. She'd taken two full days just to clear the surrounding area of brush so the building could receive several hours of sunlight each day; then she concentrated her efforts on the inside, filling the trays with rich soil. The hinges to open the top had been rusty and stiff, but she oiled them repeatedly until they eventually gave way, allowing fresh air and sunshine to filter through the opened glass windows. She now had a working greenhouse at her disposal, and few things since arriving at Miramont had excited her so.

The only time she saw her husband regularly was late at night when she entered his room in her nightgown and robe to have brandy with him on his settee. At first she'd been nervous, but after three or four nights it became an eagerly anticipated ritual, the most pleasant time of her day. Since the night of her birthday, though, he hadn't asked her to stay, and deep down she knew he was hurting because she wouldn't come to him voluntarily. She could see the longing, the confusion his eyes betrayed each evening when she left him to another night of sleeping alone.

But she would be sailing in just sixteen days. All arrangements were finalized. Instead of excitement, though, she felt profoundly sad because she knew leaving would mean a decisive, irrevocable choosing between the two passions in her life—her studies and her husband. Somewhere deep within her she wanted to stay; she wanted to love him, completely and forever. She realized that now, just as fully as she'd always known she would never be completely whole and happy as a wife and mother if she allowed botany, the greatest part of her, to wither away to nothing but a hobby. If she stayed at Miramont, always would she know regret.

And now, complicating everything and worrying her into a desperate panic, was the thought of telling Brent of her plans. She was certainly stalling, but she just didn't know how to broach the subject, and time was running short. He cared for her, even depended on her where Rosalyn was concerned, and her scientific desires were completely foreign to him. It would be difficult, if not impossible, to explain, and she was positively sure he would never just passively grant her an annulment by request. An intense argument was bound to ensue.

In all of her life, Caroline had never felt so frustrated, so emotionally shattered and unsure what to do. But in sixteen days, the decision would be final, and all would be clear again. She had to believe that.

Brushing her turbulent thoughts and nervousness aside, she entered the drawing room. Everyone was present, and one after another, those who knew her each stopped talking in midsentence to stare at her with varying expressions of bewilderment.

All except her husband. He stood near the closed French doors, alone, staring outside and sipping a glass of whiskey. Naturally he looked handsome and perfect in dark, charcoal-gray trousers and topcoat, dove-gray waistcoat and cravat, and a white, impeccably tailored shirt. He'd combed his hair from his face, exposing the tautness of his features, the expressiveness of his eyes, and truthfully, as uncomfortable as she knew he was, he looked marvelously calm.

Slowly he turned to look in her direction as the chatter in the room slowly ceased with her entrance, and although he was in the process of taking a sip of his drink, his hand froze halfway to his lips as his gaze fell upon her at last.

She flushed deeply when he stared at her openly, raking her body up and down with a completely unreadable expression. Then he drained the contents of his glass in one gulp and set it on a side table.

Quickly, her nervousness returning as her confidence faded, she moved to make unavoidable introductions. She mingled with her guests for several minutes, stopping finally to converse with Jane and her husband, Robert Waxton. Suddenly Brent stood next to her, taking her elbow with his hand.

"I need to discuss something with you, Caroline," he said in a deep, smooth voice.

She looked up at him, surprised and irritated that he could be so rude in the presence of company, but before she could utter a response, he'd made small excuses and practically pulled her from the drawing room and across the foyer to his study.

Once inside, he softly closed the door and turned to stare.

Her heart pounded, but she refused to drop her gaze from his. After a brief moment of silence, her impatience grew to intolerance.

"That was impolite and tactless, even for you," she

contended, hoping to sound braver than she felt.

He smirked, leaned back against the door, and crossed his arms over his chest. "What did you do to your hair?"

She rubbed her gloved hands together nervously. "Your sister made me cut it."

He cocked a cynical brow. "Really? Did she hold a pistol to your head to force you to do it, Caroline, or did she sit on top of you to keep you still while she sliced it herself?"

That made her fume. "I don't particularly like it either, but Charlotte thought, in her own sweet, naïve way, it might make me look a bit more appealing. Obviously she was wrong—"

He grabbed her wrist and yanked her against him before she could blink, holding her tightly, possessively.

"Do you know what I thought when I first saw you tonight, little one?"

She gave him a most sarcastic glare. "I can't imagine that a man with a mind the size of a worm's would have any thoughts whatsoever."

He grinned rakishly, his eyes narrowing to dark green slits as he pulled her so close to him that her breasts flattened against his waistcoat.

Before she could consider his intentions, his lips were upon hers, firmly, eagerly, his embrace hot as fire as he kissed her deeply. As always, she opened for him, allowing his tongue to invade her warmth in search of hers, wrapping her arms around his neck, running her fingers through his hair, pulling his head as close as she could. He ran one hand up and down her back, and the other he placed against her bottom, caressing her in small, slow circles, until the blood raged through her veins and her breathing became raspy.

Seconds later he released her, gently, lifting his head slowly to gaze into her eyes once more.

"I suppose you must be right, Caroline," he admitted huskily. "I must have the mind of a worm since I've been married to you for nearly four months, and not until tonight, when you walked into the drawing room, did I realize I'd married a voluptuous, ravishing beauty. I don't think I've ever been so astounded in my life.''

She stared at him, incredulous.

''And just in case you're wondering, sweetheart,'' he added, placing his fingers inside the top of her gown and running his knuckles back and forth, ''I think this color is stunning on you.''

''It's Charlotte's,'' she mumbled, wide-eyed and knowing it was an incredibly stupid thing to say.

His smile broadened. ''Being blond, I'm sure burgundy makes her look pale and sickly.'' He glanced down to her bosom. ''And I'm sure she never filled it out quite so nicely.''

That made her blush. ''What a presumptuous thing to say about your sister.''

He grinned wickedly and pulled the material as high as he could to cover her breasts. ''It's also too low.''

She looked at him bravely, defiantly. ''Well, I'm wearing it now and I refuse to change.''

''Just don't fall out of it, Caroline.''

She stared into his eyes for a moment then said shakily, ''I think we should return to our guests.''

He exhaled deeply, his expression becoming serious as he reached up to cup her hot, pinkened cheeks. Quietly he said, ''I just wanted to clear the air about who exactly you belong to, Caroline, so there wouldn't be any confusion this evening. Not every man takes the marriage vows as literally as I do, and since several of them will be ogling you tonight, I wanted to take a minute to remind you that you're mine. That's all.''

He dropped his hands, grasped her elbow, and opened the door. ''And now that I've put color in your cheeks, my lovely wife,'' he added blandly, ''let's go and eat. I'm starving.''

For nearly two hours they ate, course after course. Her husband sat at the opposite end of the table from her, which, although keeping him at a distance, allowed him

a straight view and the ability to stare at her throughout
the meal. Caroline talked mostly to Stephanie, who sat
next to her, discussing trivial things like her upcoming
nuptials to the Viscount Jameson. Then suddenly the
room quieted as her father cleared his throat and addressed her husband.

"You've done an excellent job with the estate, Weymerth," he commended smoothly.

Brent looked squarely at the older man. "Indeed,
thanks to your daughter."

"And what a marvelous job you've done decorating,
Caroline," Jane offered sweetly, buttering more bread.
"Miramont is lovely from room to room."

"Anyone can decorate a house," Brent carried on casually, leaning back in his chair to study his wineglass.
Then he glanced across the table at her again, twirling
the stem with his fingers as he softened his voice. "I
was talking about the finances."

With that, everyone stopped eating at once, turned
their heads, and stared at him—including Caroline, who
now couldn't breathe as a huge bite of plum stuffing
lodged itself in her throat.

The room seemed still as death until Gavin, her sister
Charlotte's husband, shook his head and found his voice
before the others managed to do so. "What on earth
would any woman know about finances, Weymerth?"

Brent smiled. "I wouldn't know about other women.
I do, however, know that my wife has a firm grasp of
numbers, and because she's better at keeping the books,
I asked her to do it. She's done a perfect job so far and
in fact found several thousand pounds I'd managed to
lose on paper simply because my mastery of mathematics doesn't compare with hers. What takes me hours, she
can do in minutes."

He took a sip of wine, savoring it, giving his audience
the chance to absorb his shocking words.

"If it weren't for Caroline," he finished slowly, honestly, "we'd be having this dinner on the floor with
wooden spoons."

They all stared at him in astonishment. For a split second not a sound could be heard; then Charlotte Becker pierced the silence by bubbling over with giggles.

"Bravo, Brent," she blurted, quickly covering her laughing mouth with her hand as she gazed at her brother through vivid blue eyes filled with admiration.

Caroline slowly lowered her lashes, her face pink with embarrassment, her mind enraged at her husband's audacity, and her heart so full of joy she could hardly contain the feeling. With a shaky hand, she reached for her wineglass and took three large swallows.

Then her father broke in. "Good for you, my boy," he mumbled as he returned to his food. "Good for you."

Caroline's eyes shot up to stare at him.

Robert grunted. "This is a farce, Weymerth. You cannot possibly expect us to believe your wife takes care of your books."

Jane looked at her husband with hard, angered features. "I've told you for years about Caroline's ability, Robert. Why must you be so stubborn in your belief?"

He gazed at her as if she were completely dense. "Because, darling, women are never clearheaded about such things. It's difficult enough to concern yourselves with poetry and babies and charitable causes." He patted her hand. "You know as well as anyone that a lady of breeding has no business learning mathematics. Doing so isn't normal or proper."

That statement made Caroline so angry she nearly picked up her full plate of food and flung it in his face.

"I don't know if I entirely hold that belief, Waxton," Carl drawled, speaking at last as he stared at his wineglass in deep contemplation. "If Charlotte, my wife, were talented in a field of study reserved for men only because of convention and nothing more, I think I would encourage her to use her knowledge in any way she could." He looked up and shrugged. "What could it hurt?"

Robert's face turned completely red; Gavin's mouth

opened wide in speechlessness; Brent looked at her father, who did nothing but eat ferociously; Charlotte Becker fairly beamed at her husband with complete adoration; the other ladies and their respective husbands looked increasingly uncomfortable; and her sisters, bless their hearts, sat back and simply appeared lost.

Caroline wanted to laugh at the absurdity of the entire conversation.

"What could it hurt?" Gavin finally bellowed, slamming his hand on the table for emphasis. "I could lose every penny I earn if I let a woman keep my books!" He lowered his voice a little. "No offense, Weymerth, but I simply don't believe Caroline really knows as much as a man when it comes to numbers. This is not a matter reserved for men because it's a convention. As a woman, mathematics is completely against her nature."

Brent's eyes narrowed. "Really?" He leaned forward in his chair. "Can you multiply three hundred and twelve by oh . . . say . . . ninety-seven, Gavin?"

The man looked baffled for a second or two, then quickly composed himself and sat straight up in his seat. "Of course. Give me a pen—"

"That's not what I mean." He turned his head and looked to the end of the table, smiling. "Caroline?"

She swallowed hard, attempting to push that ever-present piece of stuffing down her throat. "Pardon?"

They all looked at her except her father who continued to stare at his food.

"Can you multiply three hundred and twelve by ninety-seven?"

"Of course she can," Stephanie admitted for her. "Tell them, Caroline."

She tensed her body, eyeing her husband nervously. "I don't think—"

"Caroline . . ." Brent cut in, daring her not to answer, "can you multiply three hundred and twelve by ninety-seven?"

"Yes," she finally muttered.

"This is preposterous," Robert exclaimed, throwing his napkin on the table. "If given a moment to think, I'll come up with the answer in my head." Then he turned to her and smiled arrogantly. The smile of a man without a brain, in her opinion. "Can you multiply four hundred seventy-six by one hundred thirty-two, Caroline dear?"

Intense fury bubbled inside of her. She despised men who treated women in such a manner, who chose to humiliate them in the company of others. Instead of trying to understate her abilities as she would have done at any other time, at that moment she wanted to shout her talent to the world, to show the pompous fool just what an idiot he was.

Her face broke out into a brilliant smile to sweetly reply, "Sixty-two thousand, eight hundred thirty-two, Robert dear." With that, she filled her mouth with more stuffing.

"She made that up," Gavin asserted, turning once again to his food and slicing his duck as if it were leather.

Carl slowly stood. "Let's see if she did."

"You'll find a pen in my study," Brent said quite casually, the first words he'd ever actually spoken to the man, although he did manage to avoid looking at him by reaching for his wine.

The minutes Carl was gone from the room were the longest in Caroline's life. The silence was deafening as everyone pretended to be involved in eating. When he finally returned, tension filled the air so thickly, she knew she couldn't begin to cut it with a sword if she had one.

Then she glanced at Carl's face. He smiled at her and winked as he placed a piece of paper on the table. "It took me a bit longer to multiply four hundred seventy-six by one hundred thirty-two, but I believe she's right, gentlemen." He looked back to her. "What number did you arrive at, Caroline?"

She cleared her throat. "Sixty-two thousand, eight hundred thirty-two."

"Well," Carl said flatly, sitting once again in his chair, "I'd trust her with my books."

Caroline grinned delightedly at him, then drew the courage to gaze once again at her husband. The soft look he gave her was filled with admiration and pride. In that instant she had the incredible urge to stand and walk to him, take his face in her palms, and kiss his mouth with all the deep-felt passion she possessed for him alone.

"Goodness me, is it ten already?" Jane asked too loudly. "I believe I'm ready for dessert."

They all started talking at once.

Charlotte knew what she had to do. Just watching her brother stare at his wife across the dinner table, his face betraying such depth of feeling for the woman he'd married, filled her with compassion and understanding.

By all accounts, Brent and Caroline had not yet been intimate with each other. She was almost certain of that, although she'd never speak of it to anyone. She could see it in the way they looked at each other during dinner with such longing between them, both trying to hide the fact that they were doing so, could sense it in the detached, matter-of-fact way Caroline spoke about her brother. There was something holding back the closeness, and in her own loving, irritating, sisterly manner, she felt it her duty to force each of them to acknowledge what their stubbornness wouldn't allow to come forward.

Everyone had left the estate or retired for the evening, including Carl, who willingly left her side so she could talk to Brent alone. It took her only minutes to find him. He stood just outside the French doors overlooking the garden below, in the frosty, late-November air, hands resting on the railing as he stared at the clear, star-filled sky.

Wrapping her shawl tightly around her shoulders, she walked out onto the terrace, moving quietly to stand by his side. He drew a slow breath as he realized who was beside him but he didn't move, didn't speak, didn't acknowledge her in any way.

"It was an interesting affair, Brent."

"Madam," was his rather curt reply.

She turned her body to face his stiffened side. "I'm certain you remember my name."

He said nothing, just continued to stare blankly at the stars.

Finally, her patience wearing thin, she murmured, "Caroline is a lovely woman. You did a wonderful thing for her tonight."

He exhaled loudly and slowly as he lowered his gaze to the darkened garden. "Her family needs to recognize that I married an intelligent, elegant lady instead of a plain spinster who can do no more with her time than plant flowers."

Charlotte looked out over the garden as well. "She's certainly done a tremendous job with that. It's as beautiful as I've ever seen it." Dropping her eyes to study her blue satin slippers, she added, "I think she probably has more talent than Mother—"

"Of course she has," he interjected with sudden distaste. "That's plainly obvious."

She gave him a calculating look and softened her voice. "You care for her very much, don't you?"

He said nothing, and it took everything in her not to clobber him over the head for being so obstinate. He probably hadn't even admitted as much to himself. Folding her arms across her chest, she decided to get directly to the point.

"Do you have any idea where she goes each morning?"

She nearly smiled when, just for a second, he seemed startled by the question as he turned his head to look directly at her for the first time since she'd returned to Miramont. Not wanting to ruin the moment, she just watched him by the glow of the dining-room light, holding his gaze and forcing him to speak before she said another word.

He drew himself up to stand erect. "Caroline attends to Rosalyn and gardens each morning."

"Well," she responded nonchalantly, looking back to her slippers, "perhaps she did that before Carl and I arrived, but lately she's been leaving after breakfast each day, secretly, without telling a soul where she's going, and usually I don't see her again until well after luncheon."

She glanced up cautiously, noticing how his face had hardened while he tried to keep his features masked.

"What exactly are you implying?" he asked in a dark, dangerous voice.

Men could be so positively predictable. "Truly, Brent, I wasn't implying anything. Several of us have noticed that she leaves. I simply wondered if you knew where she spent those six or seven hours each and every day all by herself."

Slowly he turned, clutching the railing with both hands as he once again stared into the night. "If you know something, you should tell me instead of dallying around the facts."

She shrugged lightly. "I don't know anything." Which was a lie, because she was fairly certain that Caroline, being the botanist she proclaimed to be and the expert with flowers everyone at Miramont proudly admitted, had found the greenhouse, and for whatever reason hadn't told a soul about the discovery.

Brent could just find out about it later this evening when he accused her of being unfaithful, which, she hoped, would make them unlock the honesty, then the passion brewing between them.

She placed a gloved hand on his arm. He flinched but didn't pull away, and although she felt saddened at what she considered an old and ridiculous argument between them, part of her knew it wouldn't last. They were talking, she was touching him, and that was a beginning.

"I'm sure she's still awake, Brent. Just ask her where

she goes each day.'' She pulled her hand from his sleeve and turned to leave. ''I don't want to see you hurting.''

Charlotte stared at the side of his darkened face, and when she realized he didn't intend to reply, she lifted her skirts and walked back into the house.

Seventeen

Gwendolyn finally made her nightly departure, leaving Caroline alone at her dressing table, her body clothed in only a purple silk wrap as she brushed her hair in contemplation.

The evening had been the strangest, most awkward she'd ever experienced. She'd never realized just how unhappy her sisters Jane and Charlotte appeared to be with their husbands, how condescending the men they'd married were, how they humiliated the women even in small ways. As gently bred men of polite society, however, they probably didn't know how to behave any differently.

But it was her father's quiet acceptance of her handling the finances at Miramont that had surprised her the most. He hadn't seemed startled by the revelation, hadn't lectured, hadn't even really spoken, and keeping opinions to himself was completely against his nature.

During the last several hours, she'd gained a clear understanding of just how fortunate she was to have a man who defended her, who treated her as if she had a mind, who understood her as an individual, who made her shiver with desire from a look, a simple touch.

Placing her hairbrush on the dressing table, Caroline slowly stood and moved to the bed, where her night-gown and robe lay waiting. Reaching down to loosen the sash at her waist, she heard him open the door. No knock, just an entrance, as if she'd been expecting him.

She opened her mouth to tease him, but something in his eyes unnerved her.

"What a fool I've been, Caroline," he said quietly, leaning back against their adjoining door, now closed behind him.

He'd removed his waistcoat, unbuttoned his shirt just enough to expose the top of his chest, and rolled up his cuffs. She stared at him, unsure and growing more nervous with each breath.

"What is it?" she asked. "What are you talking about?"

He just watched her for a moment, then the corner of his mouth curved up in a cynical smile, his eyes narrowing as he slowly began to move toward her.

"I just came from a nice talk with Charlotte."

That stunned her. "The two of you spoke?"

He remained silent until he stood directly in front of her, and were it not for the fact that his statement had surprised her so, she surely would have taken a step back from his formidable stance.

He shook his head disdainfully. "The conversation was unwanted but truly enlightening, sweetheart."

He grabbed her chin, forcing her to look into eyes now cold, daring, and utterly spilling over with rage.

He dropped his tone to a whisper. "She insulted both of us by asking me exactly where you go each morning, and to my complete, husbandly ignorance, I couldn't respond because I didn't know."

"Brent—"

"But she didn't have to splash water in my face with the answer, Caroline. Obviously since you don't want to have sex with the man you married, you need to get it elsewhere."

The expression of astonishment that graced her features evidently forced him to falter; she could see it on his face. Then he dropped his hand abruptly.

With a very deep breath, he closed his eyes and placed his hands on his hips. "Who is your lover?"

She gaped at him, the shock of his words finally giving way to indignation as she fairly shouted, "I don't have a lover!"

"Don't lie to me, Caroline. I know you've had them before, you've made that clear, so your virginity is not the issue. I couldn't care less who took it from you." He raised his lids to gaze at her sardonically. "According to Charlotte, everyone knows you leave the house for hours each day, and now, since your absences have come to my attention, I demand to know if you're spreading your legs for someone I know, someone you've met at Miramont, or are you doing it for someone you've been sleeping with for years?"

She simply stood there, looking at him, cheeks burning, heart pounding, wanting to slap him but unable to do so because her mind was working fiercely to determine where and why he would suddenly acquire such wild, fatuous notions. But she was also relieved that his anger brewed simply and only because Charlotte had seen her leave for the greenhouse and had inadvertently mentioned it to him. It pulled at her inside, too, for if she told him about it now, he could very well take away the only part of her dream she'd managed to preserve. She needed to confess, but she would also need to be careful in defending herself.

Relaxing, she gave him a pleasant, reassuring smile. "It's true, I leave, but you don't understand—"

He chuckled softly to cut her off, shaking his head in disgust. "I understand, Caroline, because I've seen it before. Women are coy, deceitful, self-absorbed, and cruel. I've never known a faithful woman in my life, and you certainly fit the image of the perfect woman since you have the ability to kiss me as if you actually desire me, rub yourself against my body with the expertise of a paid tramp, then turn to another man for

release." He clenched his jaw. "I only wish I hadn't
been so ignorant of why you avoided me for so long.
How ironic that it took another woman to point out what
has been staring me in the face for months."

Her anger grew with each word from his lips, building
to an intense boil as the insufferable man in front of her
spoke to her so heartlessly, wronging her terribly, without allowing her to explain what was obviously a misunderstanding.

Eyes shining defiantly, her voice filled with a rage
now equal to his, she retorted, "I absolutely refuse to
discuss anything while you're standing here shouting instead of listening to what I have to say. You are being
illogical and ridiculous, and I want you to leave."

With that she turned away, excusing him rudely, but
he grabbed her instead, jerking her around to face him
once more. She opened her mouth to call him the name
he deserved, but sudden apprehension compelled her to
hold her words in check. His features had hardened to
granite, and his eyes had darkened and thinned as he
stared at her, tightly clasping her arm with his hand.

"Yes, I suppose I've been illogical and ridiculous for
believing in us, Caroline. I believed we could have
something between us because you were different and
smart and fit me like a glove in so many ways. I even
thought you were beginning to like me, to enjoy my
company, to want me as a man."

He dropped his hand, and she took a step away,
amazed at such a disclosure from someone who kept his
personal thoughts so tightly locked within.

He looked her straight in the eye, his voice harsh,
strengthening with each word as rage emanated from his
entire body.

"I wanted you, Caroline. I've wanted you since the
day we married. I'm a human being just like you, with
wants and needs, with emotions that can be bruised, with
hopes and dreams that can be crushed. I have feelings
deep inside of me that I've learned to protect because
they're the only part of me remaining that hasn't been

picked apart and destroyed by someone else. And I'll bet you've never once thought about that, have you? You've never thought about what I want, or about my feelings, my desires.''

She couldn't bring herself to respond, or even breathe for that matter, stunned as she was. Whether it was from her continued silence or the look on her face, his dark, dangerous hazel eyes suddenly came alive with fire as he pointed to his chest and began shouting in pure, uninhibited fury.

''Well, *this* is what *I* want, Caroline! *I* want to make love to you! *I* want to touch you and make you feel passion you've never felt with anyone else! *I* want to hold you and go to sleep with you in my arms every night! *I* want to open up and let you know what I feel deep inside, the part of me nobody has ever known! *I* want you to need me as much as I need you! And suddenly, slapping me in the face tonight, I realize that in the four months we've been married, you've never considered *my* desires, *my* needs, because the greatest talent you possess, Caroline, is thinking only of yourself!''

She stared at him, speechless, mouth dry, pulse racing. After a moment of watching him battle the conflicts within himself, now unmasked and visible to her eyes, he slowly stood back, wiped a shaking palm over his face, and turned to the door.

Pausing in front of it, he looked back at her, his expression pained, his voice filled with deep sorrow.

''I lived with a woman for twenty-five years who berated me, despised me, who left me thankful for the times when she only ignored me. But never, until now, have I felt useless and unwanted. Thank you for giving me something new to experience, Caroline.'' Dropping his gaze, he added, ''Go to your lover. I'm tired of trying.''

He walked through the door and slammed it in her face.

Caroline stood where she was, unmoving for minutes, until finally she started shaking uncontrollably. Slowly, her palm covering her mouth to keep from crying out, she moved her leaden legs to sit on the bed.

She'd never meant to hurt him, and now it was clear that since the moment they'd met, that was all she'd done. Yes, she'd helped his daughter communicate, had listened with profound understanding as he spoke of the war, even felt that with her help, he and his sister would put their troubles behind them. But through it all, on a deeply personal level, she'd done nothing but hurt him, and realizing that for the first time made her eyes fill with water.

He was right. She'd been selfish and unfair from the beginning, marrying him for an annulment she knew, even on their wedding day, he would never give her, ignoring him as if he didn't exist, speaking to him arrogantly, even rudely. He deserved so much better, but he'd married only her.

Staring at the floor, Caroline dropped her hand as it slowly dawned on her that this was the moment for which she'd been waiting, hoping, since arriving at Miramont. She had two choices tearing at her heart, but right now, as things stood with Brent, an annulment was feasible, the worry of approaching him suddenly gone. Since he believed she had a lover, and because their marriage had not been consummated, he had grounds for letting her go. The path before her was illuminated, leading the way toward her lifelong dream. This was the time to tell him she was leaving. Botany was and always had been the truest part of her, and she would honor it.

Standing, knowing what she had to do and forcefully telling herself that her life, her destiny, was in another world entirely, she moved quietly to the adjoining door, put her hand on the cold, hard knob, and walked into his room.

She melted when she saw him. He sat on the settee, exactly as he'd looked the night of her birthday, staring into a blazing fire, a brandy snifter half full in his hands. And although he had to have heard her enter, he didn't move his gaze or utter a word.

She stood there for a long, quiet moment, watching the glow of firelight dance across smooth, bronze skin, catching each soft, shiny curve of his hair with every flicker. She felt his anger, his grief, his loneliness, and finally something new—a blooming comprehension of what had been staring her in the face for months, what she'd been blindly refusing to recognize. All she'd ever wanted from the time she could remember was the beauty of her flowers, her garden, and instead, as a gift from God, she'd been graced with a man more intricately designed, more brilliantly woven, more intensely beautiful than any flower or any one thing she could ever imagine. At last, after months of uncertainty and conflicting desires, it all became perfectly clear. This was where she belonged. He was her destiny.

"I go to the greenhouse."

The words came out raspy and low, just a whisper above the sound of the crackling fire. For a second, as she watched him slowly grasp the meaning of the confession, his breathing seemed to stop, his body stilled, and she knew then that that statement was the most honest she'd ever made in her life.

"I didn't want to tell you because I was afraid you would take it from me," she admitted in a gentle, unsure voice, "and until just now, I thought it was the one thing in my life that made me complete."

Slowly she began to move toward him.

"But I was wrong because I realize now I could never be complete without the one man who has become my champion, who respects me as none have before, who is braver and smarter and more compassionate than any I've ever known. I should have trusted you," she whispered with aching sweetness as she finally stood beside him. "I'm sorry."

After a moment of silence, he drew an unsteady breath and looked down to the snifter in his hands. "I cannot be anything more than I am, Caroline," he said hoarsely. "I just don't know what you want from me."

She swallowed, her eyes glittering with unshed tears,

and in a soft, passion-choked voice, she replied, "I want you to make me your wife."

For seconds or minutes or even hours, she couldn't be certain, time seemed to stop. Then he raised his head, his eyes piercing hers, sparkling in the firelight like dark emeralds.

"You deserve a husband who wants you, Caroline, just as you are, and you know I do. But as much as I need you, I don't want you if you're here right now from a feeling of guilt, or pity, or some odd sense of self-righteousness or duty." He abruptly glanced down once again to his brandy. "Because I also believe, even with my numerous faults, that I deserve a wife who wants me in return, just as I am. Anything less isn't worth the pain."

She blinked hard for strength, to clear the blur in her vision as she grasped the meaning behind his words. Then ever so slowly, with a braveness she didn't really feel, she reached out, gently pulled the brandy snifter from his hold, took one full swallow for confidence, and placed it on the side table.

She looked at his face, his beautiful, masculine face, as she stretched her hand out to softly glide her fingertips along each firm point, each fine etch of perfection, vitality, and uncommon grace. Then, resolute in her decision, breathing deeply, she took his hand in hers, rubbed her thumb against his palm, and opened her silk wrap just wide enough to place it directly on her breast.

He sucked in a clear, rapid breath the instant his skin came into contact with hers, lifting his eyes again in surprise or confusion, she wasn't sure which, but he didn't move or speak, just watched her.

Boldly she held his gaze in a timeless grasp until finally she whispered in a deep, husky, impassioned voice, "You were wrong about one thing, Brent. Your feelings mean everything to me, and I promise never to hurt you again."

With gentle acceptance in her heart, and knowing with peace and finality that the time had come for them, she slowly closed her eyes, tilted her head back, and pulled at the sash around her waist until it opened for him, exposing to all of him—his eyes, his touch, his soul—the only remaining part of herself he had yet to know.

Brent could not recall a time from his past when he had felt such a surge of raw, tumultuous emotions consuming him from the inside and making him weak. Never in his life had he laid eyes on anything as beautiful as the vision in front of him.

She stood no more than a foot away, her left side to the fire, her lovely face innocent and soft, hair falling to her waist in luminescent waves. As the deep-purple silk fell away from her, the flickering glow from the hearth played delicately on the pearlescent sheen of her skin, the crested nipple exposed not to his palm but to his eyes, and on the few dark, shiny curls escaping the shadows between her legs to reflect the firelight.

Slowly he began to trace her nipple with the tips of his fingers, moving from her breast down the length of her body, skimming her waist, her stomach, moving gradually to her hip and down the outside of her thigh. He felt her shiver, felt gooseflesh rise to his fingertips, and with that he softly moved in until his knuckles grazed the inside of her leg.

"Caroline . . ."

"I'm scared," she whispered.

That admission made his heart swell with tenderness. Dropping his hand, he slowly stood to face her. She still hadn't opened her eyes, hadn't moved, but he felt her trembling. He cupped her face with his palms and leaned in to brush his lips against hers.

"Trust me now," he pleaded quietly.

She nodded imperceptibly and whispered, "I do."

In that instant, he knew he belonged to her as he had never belonged to another. He ran his thumb along her jaw, placed his hand behind her neck, and covered her mouth with his.

The initial contact was both shocking and sweet, familiar and awkward. They had certainly kissed before, but not with the mutual understanding of what was about to happen between them. He toyed with her lips almost timidly at first, giving her time to adjust, then increased the pressure, running his tongue back and forth until she opened for him.

Slowly she relaxed, kissing him back with growing need, raising her hands to run her fingers through his hair. She tasted of brandy, smelled of violets, and felt as delicate and smooth as a rose petal.

He ran his hands down her neck to grasp her shoulders just inside her silk wrap. He moved his mouth, his tongue, in gentle rhythm against hers, and she followed his lead, allowing the magic to consume her. He caressed her skin with his fingertips then carefully, gradually, lowered her dressing gown over her upper arms and pulled his lips from hers.

She opened her eyes and looked at him, uncertain. "I . . . I'm not sure what to do."

That melted his heart. With a comforting smile he raised one hand and placed it on her cheek, the other he rested on her chest, his fingers stroking her collarbone in tiny, wispy movements.

"Tonight I'll do everything," he reassured in a husky timbre. Then before she realized what was happening, he pulled at the purple silk until it slid from her body and onto the cold floor.

He felt a shiver escape her, and she instantly dropped her lashes. With that he grasped her chin and raised her head, forcing her to look at him.

"Don't be ashamed," he beseeched, his gaze piercing hers. "I'm the only one who matters now and I think you're beautiful."

Caroline knew, when the shock of those words seeped in, the tears would begin to flow, and that was the last thing she wanted to happen on what she now considered to be her wedding night.

"You're the first man ever to call me beautiful," she disclosed in a thick, choked voice.

He grinned. "I knew I'd be the first for something."

She smiled in return and cautiously reached for the buttons on his shirt.

Immediately he covered her hand. "I'll do it."

She dropped her arm and stood before him unmoving, watching until he'd removed his shirt and tossed it on the settee.

They stood only a foot apart, he undressed to his waist, she completely naked and feeling more vulnerable than she'd ever felt in her life.

Gently he reached out and lightly stroked the tops of her breasts with the fingers of both hands, inciting a gasp from her lips and a sudden weakening of her legs. His eyes melded with hers in silent communication as his face became serious once more, intense. He stroked her then cupped her fully, his palms rotating to make her nipples tingle and stand out against his hands. Within seconds she was breathless, shivering from new sensations beginning to burn inside of her, and flushing not from the warmth of the fire, but from a rising inner heat now slowly starting to replace the apprehension.

Instinctively she reached for him, and understanding her growing desire and need to feel, he released her, moving his hands to take off his boots. Those discarded, he unbuttoned his trousers and removed the remainder of his clothing to stand before her as naked as she.

She closed her eyes, partly because she couldn't bring herself to look down and partly because she suddenly felt so nervous she wanted to bolt from his bedchamber.

He must have felt her uncertainty, for within seconds he wrapped one palm around her neck, grasped her around the waist with the other, pulled her toward him, and lowered his mouth.

The kissing began slowly, allowing the passion to increase at its own pace. He caressed her back and neck, ran his fingers through her hair, all the while keeping a distance between them, for they still hadn't fully embraced. He teased her lips apart, forcing her to open for him. Then he invaded her warmth, searching, and when he found it, grasped her tongue and began sucking it as he'd done so perfectly the day in the garden.

As with that day, a sudden bolt of lightning passed through her body, causing fire to erupt between her legs. Anticipating her response, he pulled her tightly against him, holding her firmly so she couldn't help but feel every muscle, every cord of strength, every point of hardness he possessed.

She whimpered softly and wrapped her arms around his neck, relishing in his size, his body, so firm and warm against her. The curls on his chest teased her nipples. His erection, hard and hot, caressed her belly as if begging for attention.

She held his head with her hands and kissed him back fervently, possessively. He groaned deeply when he felt her response to his touch, her eagerness, and finally he reluctantly released her mouth and looked into her eyes.

She stood against him, panting, flushed. His lids had narrowed, his breathing was labored, and after what seemed like an eternity to her, he reached down, grasped her around the knees, lifted her into his arms, and carried her to his bed.

She nestled her face in his neck, clinging to him, filling her mind with his feel, his scent, until he gently laid her on the sheet. She stretched out willingly, expecting him to lie beside her, but instead, he stood back to view her body unclothed.

"Brent—"

"Shh . . ." His gaze traveled down the length of her. "I've wanted this for months, Caroline. Let me look at you."

Boldly she allowed herself to look at him as well, to see a man completely for the first time, and the man before her looked like a god, exactly as he'd felt beneath her hands and fingers—hard, firm, beautiful of face and form. And as she placed her gaze on the part of him she'd never seen, she wasn't overcome with bland curiosity or repulsion, but instead felt a surge of desperation to know the unknown, to touch him as she'd never done before, to stroke him, to feel him enter her. Suddenly passion filled her senses, and she was no longer afraid.

For Brent, to see her body bathed in firelight, nipples exposed and aroused to hard peaks, her slim, tapered waist leading to softly curved hips and smooth, silky legs, was not so much a viewing as it was an unveiling for his eyes of what his mind had been trying to imagine for weeks. She was perfect, voluptuous yet slender, enticing and seductive, and more than he'd ever thought she could be.

He lowered himself onto the bed beside her, leaning against her as he crossed one leg over hers. He placed his left palm on her head, his thumb stroking her brow, and with the right he began to caress her stomach lightly in small, slow circles.

"Do you know what I think, Caroline?" he asked thickly, almost thoughtfully.

She bit her lip nervously and tried to smile. "That you wish you'd married someone with longer legs?"

He chuckled softly and leaned in to kiss her cheek. "No, that isn't it," he murmured, moving his lips to the crook of her neck. "I think dreams, for most people, are perfection." He ran his tongue along her jaw, feeling her respond to the touch. Then slowly he raised his eyes to hers once more, dropping his voice to a husky whisper. "But my dreams of you, Caroline, were nothing compared to the real thing. You are lovelier than anything I've ever dreamed before."

She stared at him for several seconds, then her eyes filled with tears, and that was his undoing. He cupped her face in his hands and lowered his mouth, kissing her not sweetly or softly, but fully, hungrily, passionately, wiping away her teardrops with his thumbs.

She wrapped her arms around his neck to hold him close, and finally, as if waiting any longer would be simply unbearable, he moved his hand to cup her breast, kneading the fullness, gently squeezing her nipple, rolling it with his forefinger and thumb until she moaned.

He released her mouth and began a trail of kisses

down her jaw, neck, and chest. She breathed rapidly, hands on his shoulders, eyes closed, and when at last he covered her free nipple with his mouth, she jumped and clutched at him, pulling him closer.

And closer he moved, sucking, tasting, caressing as he'd wanted to do for so long, increasing the pace, groaning with the touch, feeling the blood rush through his veins as his heart pounded in his chest. She responded in kind by coming alive beneath him, allowing the passion to engulf her. He ran his hand from her breast slowly down her waist to caress her hip, desperately wanting to touch her intimately, to stroke her between her legs, to feel just how ready she was for him.

"You feel so good," he whispered, his voice strained with desire. "I've wanted so long to touch you."

Caroline had never felt more out of control and so filled with cravings and desperate needs she didn't understand. He was so gentle with her, so giving, and she wanted him now more than anything she'd ever wanted in her life.

That thought in mind, she took his hand in hers, raised it to her lips, kissed his palm just once, and lightly placed it between her legs.

She shivered from the intimacy. He groaned as if he hadn't touched anything so delicate or precious in his life. Then he was kissing her again, covering her mouth with his in a sudden fever of need. He wrapped his free arm around her neck to hold her close as he began to move his hand, his fingers, slowly at first, then more and more intimately with each stroke until she instinctively raised her hips for more.

She couldn't breathe, couldn't think as her mind emptied of all but thoughts of him and the magic he created with his hands and mouth. She whimpered softly as his tongue clasped hers once again in a now familiar embrace. Her heart thundered in her breast, and her body ached with need for something else, something moving closer. She ran her fingers through the curls on his chest, lightly rubbing the pads of her thumbs across his nipples.

He drew a sharp breath at that and slowly released her mouth, lifting his head to look at her. His face was hard, strained, his eyes narrowed and glazed, his breathing raspy and short. He watched her, focusing intently on her face, and then she realized why as he gently pushed his finger inside of her.

She gasped and arched her back slightly, closing her eyes to the exquisite sensations, and after several marvelous seconds of savoring the feel of that one small part of him invading her warmth, he started moving his finger in and out while he returned to stroking his thumb up and down along her cleft, slower now but with the same intensity.

"You're so wet," he said in a rough, shaky voice. "You were made for lovemaking, Caroline."

Her heart filled with emotion as she returned in a whisper, "I was made for loving you."

He stilled completely, his hand, his body, his breathing, and for a second or two she was afraid she might have said something wrong. She opened her eyes to his once more, nearly certain she'd quelled the passion by disclosing such an intimate part of herself, but with one look, she knew she'd only poured oil on the blaze. Her words had touched him deeply; she could see it in his expression as firelight danced upon his face. Then, as if reading her thoughts, he pulled his hand from her, shifted his body, and moved to cover her completely.

Leaning over and adjusting his weight above her, he kissed her breasts almost in reverence, delicately, lightly running the tip of his tongue across each nipple, then slowly moving upward to place little kisses on her neck, her cheek, her lips and lashes.

She relished in the feel of a man, her husband, on top of her and ready to make her his wife. Instinctively she spread her legs even wider to allow him better access, intertwined her fingers through his thick, silky hair, and began to kiss him back just as tenderly as he was kissing her.

He lifted just enough to place his hand between them once more, finding her, stroking her, making her moan from excitement, anticipation, and pleasure. Then, when she was as ready as he, he took her mouth with his, steadied his body, and began to push himself inside of her.

Immediately she tensed from the pressure, and he stopped the movement. His free hand cupped her breast, his thumb stroking her nipple, and after a moment he tried again, only to find the same resistance.

Brushing his lips against hers, he pulled back a little, fighting the strain, one hand on her forehead, the other gently kneading her, holding her.

Caroline remained oblivious to everything but the desire to feel him. She rotated her hips to better touch him, aching for completion, moving her legs up and back so the inside of her thighs rubbed against the outside of his. That drove him wild, for he gritted his teeth and squeezed his eyes tightly shut, breathing heavily and hard as he willed himself to stay in control.

She placed her palm on his chest, feeling the strong, quick pounding of his heart. He waited a second longer, then adjusted his hips and tried once more to enter her, a third time, forcing himself slightly deeper, and finally it hurt too much.

"Brent—"

She cringed as her body automatically became rigid, and with that, something seemed to happen to him. Slowly he raised himself to look down at her face. His eyes hid in shadows, but his features had softened, and after several seconds of unsureness, she almost feared he'd changed his mind about taking her because she was such a tight fit.

"Please don't stop," she begged in a whisper. "I don't care if it hurts a little."

Deathly silence filled the air, until full comprehension pervaded his mind.

"Oh, Caroline . . ." he whispered through a sigh both

staggered and pained with softness. "You've never done this, have you?"

She couldn't believe he'd ask her something like that as they lay in bed together, nearly joined, that he wouldn't know from her obvious inexperience and apprehension, and her stunned expression must have told him so.

"Oh, Jesus," he mumbled, his voice and face conveying a mixture of disbelief and wonder.

She gazed at the confusion on his brow, watched his face as he struggled inside from the revelation. She put her fingers to his mouth, tracing his lips with the tips, and he started kissing them, slowly at first, then earnestly, taking one into his mouth to gently suck, causing her to cry out from sharp pleasure.

His hand began caressing her breast again as well, and within seconds desire returned in full force. He kissed her palm, then lowered his head to kiss her forehead and lashes, her cheeks and neck.

Something had changed in him, she could sense it, but a short moment later she was beyond caring. He moved his hand between her legs once more, stroking her gently until she could feel nothing else, until her hips arched, her heart pounded in her chest, her breathing became erratic. Then he raised himself once again, placed his free hand on her cheek, and rested his forehead against hers.

"Hold me," he urged softly, his hard form towering over her, his shaft poised once again at the entrance between her legs.

She nodded and grasped his shoulders. Then as quickly as he fully covered her mouth with his, he tensed his body and drove himself inside of her, filling her deeply, completely.

Her nails dug into his skin, her back arched, and she gasped sharply against his lips. Her eyes filled with tears, trickling down the side of her face, and he kissed her tenderly, sweetly, running his thumb along her cheek to wipe them away.

He kept himself quite still, except for the gentle prod-
ding of his kiss, and after only seconds the pain inside
and between her legs began to dissipate. She inhaled as
deeply as she could to relax, and as he felt the anxiety
drain from her, he moved his hand to her breast, lightly
stroking the tip with his thumb, squeezing her nipple,
running the back of his hand underneath her fullness,
kneading softly, cupping her and caressing her with his
palm. She squirmed a little, almost restlessly as the pleasure began to build, wondering what she was supposed
to do, and that's when she felt him start to move inside
of her.

He deepened his kiss, flicking his tongue across her
lips then plunging it fully into her mouth. She wrapped
her arms around his neck, and with an inherent drive as
old as time, she began to move her hips in rhythm with
his.

He groaned, his breathing shallow once more as he
quickened the pace. She followed, allowing herself to be
led by the unknown, the magic, whimpering in response
to his touch, keeping her eyes tightly shut to his kiss, to
the marvelous and new sensations in the center of her
being as they began to expand and grow toward the light
like rose petals in morning sunshine.

Suddenly he broke his lips from hers and lowered his
mouth to her nipple, sucking, licking, kissing, teasing,
then moving to the other for more of the same. She
leaned into the pillow, wrapping her legs around his
thighs to hold him closer, weaving her fingers through
his hair.

He began circling his hips, changing the rhythm, and
slowly she felt him lift his head, his body, to hold himself directly over her.

She licked her lips, feeling drugged by desire and
more sensual than she'd ever felt in her life. With extreme difficulty, her lids sluggish and heavy, she opened
her eyes to find him studying her intently, his expression
serious, focused. He supported himself with one hand,

and with the other he caressed her chest, her neck, and then her cheek in soft, sensuous strokes.

She pushed up against him instinctively, harder, faster, forcefully, meeting each thrust with her own, aching for a release to the torment, moaning softly, holding his head with her fingers in his hair, biting her lip, staring into his grave, dark eyes, wanting desperately to unlock the secret of what he was giving her. Then in the furthest recesses of her mind, she heard his voice.

"Let it happen, my sweet wife . . ."

Suddenly she discovered the treasure. In all its splendor and beauty, the pleasure enveloped her from the inside and shattered outward in a rush of brilliance, forcing her to cry out, to clutch him, to squeeze her eyes shut to the ecstasy that filled every nerve and cascaded over every pinpoint of her body.

"You belong to me," he said softly, watching her face as he traced his thumb along her lips. Then he leaned over her, kissed her cheek, and once more whispered into her ear, "You belong to me."

With that, she cradled her head in his neck, allowing her breathing to slow as she floated back to reality, feeling the bliss subside to peacefulness, and knowing she might break down from the sweetness of his words, the tenderness in his voice.

Slowly he leaned up once more to look at her, supporting himself with one hand on the bed while he caressed her neck and breasts with the other. He reached down, straightened her hips under his, and began the rocking motion again, gradually building the heat to a fever once more.

It was his turn, she knew, and within seconds he was on fire; she could see the strain on his face, the tautness in his muscled chest. He closed his eyes tightly to relish in the feel, kneading her breast, slowing gliding in and out of her, moving faster and deeper with each penetration.

Caroline watched him, mesmerized, absorbing the warmth of his hard, masculine form, knowing he was seconds away from realizing the same wonderful gift he'd just given her. More than anything, she wanted to be part of it.

Reaching for his hand, she pulled it from her breast, kissed his palm, and held it against her cheek. With the other she touched his face.

"You're so beautiful . . ." she sensually whispered.

At the sound of her voice, he slowed his actions, prolonging the fulfillment, pulling back gently so the tip of him rested just inside of her. He held himself still for several long seconds, straining, breathing heavily, teeth clenched, grasping for control, then he opened his eyes.

The look on her face shattered him.

"Oh, God . . ." he murmured tenderly, brokenly, his expression slowly becoming one of enlightenment and awe. "Caroline—"

She placed her fingertips on his lips to silence him, her throat tightening with emotion as she held his fervent gaze, a witness to the feelings that matched her own.

She took his hand from her cheek and tightly intertwined their fingers. "I know. It's wonderful."

He drew a shaky breath, then once again entered her, gently, watching her face closely, fully embedding himself inside her and holding completely still.

She looked deeply into his eyes for what seemed an eternity; then she wrapped her legs even tighter around his and started moving her hips beneath him, slowly and deliberately.

"Caroline . . ."

"Give yourself to me," she whispered urgently, passionately, quickening her movements. "Give yourself to me."

Suddenly his expression changed, and his eyes widened. "Oh, God, oh God—"

And then he was there, plunging into her forcefully, over and over, his eyes squeezing shut, head falling back, hand clinging to hers as if it were a lifeline. She met every thrust with her hips, clutching his thighs with her own, unsure but wanting desperately to prolong the ecstasy he was finding with her, because of her, inside of her.

His breathing remained hard and shallow as he dropped his head, collapsing on top of her, then wrapping his arms around her and hugging her close. Never in her life had she expected such contentment, such incomparable warmth from the intimacy of a marital union, and she cherished it with more reverence than she did even her fine lavender roses. Her husband meant more to her now than all of that.

Snuggling into him, she wrapped her arms around his neck. "You belong to me, too," she whispered into his ear.

He kissed her cheek and jaw, ran his fingers through her long hair flowing over the pillows.

For a long time they did nothing but listen to the crackle of the dying fire, caressing each other. Finally he moved, sliding out of her carefully. But instead of adjusting himself to hold her as she expected him to do, he turned to the edge of the bed and sat up.

"Why are you leaving?" she timidly asked.

He looked back to her, surprised, then smiled in understanding. "I'm not leaving you, Caroline. I'm going to stoke the fire, light some candles so I can have a decent look at my new wife lying naked in my bed, and then I'm going to wash you where I hurt you."

That satisfied her until the meaning of his words seeped in. "I can wash myself, I'm sure," she countered softly, starting to rise.

He leaned back and grabbed her ankle. "You're not going anywhere, and you cannot continue to be embarrassed or afraid for me to see or touch you." He released her and stood. "I'll be doing both for years to come."

She forced herself to relax, watching her husband move about the room, adding logs to the fire and lighting candles by the bedside. Then he poured water from a pitcher into a bowl, placed a face cloth inside and walked back to her.

She stared at his naked form, marveling at his physique.

"What are you thinking?" he quietly asked, pulling the quilt from her body and sitting beside her.

She shivered from the sudden chill, but sat up a little and leaned back on a pillow, supporting herself against the large mahogany headboard, never taking her eyes from his face. "I was wondering why God gave you to me."

That startled him for the smallest second, then he smiled, placed the bowl on the table next to the bed, and wrung out the cloth. "To satisfy you perhaps?"

She giggled adorably, face flushing as she boldly disclosed, "And what a marvelous job you did of that."

She could positively see the prideful grin of male arrogance on his face as he leaned over to touch her, carefully spreading her thighs with his hand.

Reluctantly she widened her legs and glanced down. "You made me bleed."

He held the cloth in his hand for a moment to warm it, then began cleaning her gently. "Most virgins do, Caroline. I only wish you'd told me first."

"I shouldn't have had to," she quickly retorted.

His eyes shot up to lock with hers. "I would have never considered otherwise, little wife, but you purposely led me to believe—"

"As you did about having a child," she interjected smoothly. "We're even."

He evidently had nothing to say to that, and after a minute of staring at her speculatively, he returned to washing her.

"Why didn't you want to become my wife?"

That caught her off guard, stinging her deeply. She'd hurt him already with her secrets, but revealing this truth would be devastating. So instead, with a suddenly dry mouth, she acknowledged the obvious. "I did, but I was scared. And even as attractive as you are, you're hardly the type to romantically seduce a terrified virgin."

He raised his eyes to her face once more, cautiously,

considering her words. "If there is a God, Caroline, I'm certain he gave you to me to fill my life with aggravation." In a rich, teasing voice, he added, "And tremendous physical discomfort from waiting to make you mine."

She huffed and leaned toward him. "I hope the wait was worth the pain."

He dropped his head and kissed her thigh. Once. Then several times, up and down, until he came so close to the part he was cleaning that she lightly tapped his head. "I'm sure you shouldn't be kissing me there."

Slowly he looked up and grinned lasciviously. "You won't say that after the first time I do, Caroline. You'll beg me for it so often my mouth and tongue will constantly ache from exhaustion."

She gaped at him, blushing furiously, and that made him smile broadly, almost pompously as he returned to cleaning her gently.

"Now I know," she said blandly.

"Know what?"

"God gave you to me by mistake."

He chuckled at that, then after a moment raised a brow and looked at her quizzically. "You believe in God, Caroline?"

Who didn't believe in God? "Of course I do." She hesitated. "Don't you?"

His features went slack as he placed the cloth once again in the bowl and leaned casually back on the bed at her feet to regard her. Sighing softly, he replied, "If God exists, I've never seen him."

Her forehead crinkled into tiny lines of confusion. "How could you not see God? He saved your life in the war, he gave you Rosalyn—"

"*I* saved my life," he cut in, "and Rosalyn sprang from my loins. The world would be a simpler, happier place if each individual took actions for himself rather than blaming them on an unseen God who heaves his wrath upon the people of the earth."

She stared at him in contemplation. Then, lowering

her voice and peering into his eyes, she said huskily, passionately, "I *know* there is a God because I see his beauty every day, in a rainbow, in Rosalyn, and even in you, you idiot man. But regardless of that, I could never doubt God's existence because I know that nothing but God could create something as beautiful as a peach-colored rose."

He inhaled deeply, watching her closely, lying on his side across the foot of the bed.

"You are so unique," he said at last, lifting her foot to massage her toes. "A perfect picture of unmatched intelligence, sensual beauty, and keen philosophic thought."

That made her pulse race. With the back of her hand, she wiped stray hair from her forehead. "Have you always talked so romantically to your ladies, Brent?"

He frowned. "Romantic to my ladies?"

She snickered and wiggled her toes in his fingers. "All the ladies you've bedded before me."

He stared at her blankly, then shook his head incredulously. "Only you would mention such a thing at a time like this."

Extreme curiosity overcame her. "Well?"

"Well what?"

She could see he was amused, and with frustration filling her in a rush, she knew he planned to tease her, avoiding the issue, until she embarrassed herself by begging for details.

She exhaled loudly, deciding to play his ridiculous game by refusing to give him the satisfaction. "Did you speak to them in French?"

"No."

She blinked. "No?"

"No."

"Not even the Frenchwoman who gave you a child?"

He watched her for a moment, then leaned over to kiss the bottom of her foot.

"That tickles," she said through a giggle.

He raised his head and said richly, "You like this, don't you?"

She pulled her foot from his grasp. "You didn't answer my question."

"What question was that?"

She rolled her eyes and slammed the backs of her hands on the bed. "I'm sure you know what I'm asking, Brent."

"Why?"

"What do you mean, 'why?' " she fairly blurted.

"Why do you want to know?" His gaze became intense. "Do you care that much about me and my past?"

"Of course I care," she admitted quietly, timidly, crossing her arms over her chest. He grinned in satisfaction, and she dropped her gaze. After a moment of silence, and without glancing up, she softly asked, "You'd never consider letting me leave, would you?"

"Leave to where?"

She shrugged. "Anywhere."

He took her other foot and began the same circular motions with the pad of his thumb. "If you left me for more than a week, Caroline, I think I'd be crushed."

"Crushed?" That answer pleased her enormously.

"Are you planning a holiday away from me already?"

She smiled coyly. "No." Then she looked from his fervent stare down to her nails with apparent newfound interest. "But I'll take a holiday from your bed if you continue to avoid my questions."

Suddenly he grabbed her leg and pulled her down to his level, beside him, grasping her around the waist and practically flinging her up to lie on top of him.

With playful exaggeration, she pushed her hair from her face to better view his brilliant, greenish-brown eyes, now crinkled once more in mild humor.

"I adore the way you feel on top of me, Caroline," he whispered through a groan. "You're warm and soft and fit me perfectly, making me hard and desperate to be inside of you again."

Her breath quickened from the comment, stirring sensations of recklessness and sensuality she'd never felt before. "Goodness, my lord, hard and desperate? That's not very romantic."

He gave her a rakish grin, then holding her against him, rolled them both over on the bed so she lay beneath him. "Unromantic, maybe, but directly to the point, my sweet wife."

She laughed quietly and said, "I'm sure 'hard and desperate' sounds romantic in French."

"I don't think so."

"Speak to me in French," she quietly demanded after a moment of silence.

He shook his head.

"Yes."

"No."

She scrutinized every inch of his face as she ran her fingers through his hair. "You can't remember any romantic words?"

"I can remember plenty," he boasted.

She giggled and squirmed beneath him, and with that he nuzzled her neck. "Please, Brent?"

He brushed kisses along her neck and jaw as he pulled his head up slightly, moving to his side just enough to take his weight from her.

"English is my mother tongue, Caroline. French was my job."

"But—"

He touched her mouth, his expression becoming contemplative. "The words are the same—they only sound prettier because they're different and you don't understand what they mean. It's the meaning that matters." He traced a pattern along her lips with his fingertips, then moved his hand to stroke her cheek.

Bravely she prodded for what she truly wanted to hear. "So you never spoke French to the other ladies you bedded?"

He looked down at her strangely, then slowly shook his head in disbelief. "For as long as I live, I'm sure

I'll never understand females." She did nothing but stare innocently into his eyes, and after a moment of apparent indecision, he murmured, "You really care to know?"

She nodded, wrapping her arms around his neck to keep him from escape if he chose to attempt one.

He sighed and kissed the tip of her nose. "I spoke French to Rosalyn's mother because it's the only language she knows. I did not, however, speak to her while we had sex because we had nothing much to say before, during, or after." He cupped her cheek with his palm. "I don't think I ever spent more than fifteen minutes with her in bed each time, and since you're so unbelievably curious, my darling Caroline, let me inform you that all the other ladies I've bedded have added up to only two."

She looked at him stupidly. "Only two what?"

He grinned sheepishly and lowered his voice. "Only two other ladies."

Her eyes widened in surprise. "But you're a man."

That made him laugh. "What does that have to do with it?"

She closed her arms even tighter around his neck and ran her fingers through his hair. "Nothing, I suppose, except men seem to find bedding women over and over so relevant to their masculinity. After tonight I suppose I understand the pleasure, which leads me to wonder how a man your age, unmarried, could keep himself from a lady's bed."

He lifted his leg over hers, holding her down with his thigh. "My education and work were very important to me, demanding most of my attention for several years, Caroline. Sometimes I felt lonely, even undesirable, but I had other things to do to occupy my time, and truthfully, women didn't hold that much significance in my life. Then in France I met Rosalyn's mother, and she satisfied my physical needs when I needed her to do so."

"That sounds so positively arrogant," she said with a smile, brushing a stray lock of hair from his cheek. "What about the other two ladies?"

He grinned. "What about them?"

She looked into his eyes. "Who were they?"

He reached down to cup her breast, causing a sudden flutter in her stomach. She, however, would not be undone.

"Who were they?" she asked again slowly, more firmly.

He gently flicked his thumb over her nipple, watching her succumb to his touch, as he softly replied, "The first was the daughter of one of my mother's chambermaids."

She gaped at him, and that made him grin again.

"She was nineteen, I was seventeen, and before I really knew what was happening, she seduced me in the stables one rainy afternoon. The whole affair was quite awkward, but she knew what she was doing. We managed it eight times in two days without getting caught, then she left the estate to pursue . . . other gallant men, I suppose. I haven't seen her since."

Loudly, incredulously, she said, "Eight times? You did it eight times in two days?"

"I was seventeen years old, Caroline," he explained in defense, as if that explained everything.

Her eyes remained wide with keen interest. "Could you do it that many times now?"

Slowly he started running his toes up and down her leg. "I doubt it but I'd be happy to try, little one."

Her mind suddenly turned to something more pertinent to their lives at the moment. "And what if you got her pregnant?"

"I didn't."

"How do you know?"

He gently squeezed her nipple. "Because if I had, her mother would have demanded compensation from my family, and I would have had to leave the country to escape my mother's wrath."

That statement saddened her tremendously, and she leaned up to kiss him fully. He responded in kind by wrapping his arms completely around her and holding her tightly until she released him.

"Who was the third?" she whispered against his mouth.

Without hesitation, he murmured, "The third was you."

Caroline grinned, satiated, cupping his face. "So you really never bedded the beautiful Pauline Sinclair?"

Quickly and unexpectedly, he climbed completely on top of her, twisting her hair around his fingers to firmly brace her head in his palms.

"Who told you she was beautiful?" he demanded, grinning pompously.

Since she could think of nothing to say except the truth, she finally mumbled, "Nedda . . . mentioned it."

He laughed softly, amazed. "You asked my house-keeper about the women in my past?"

She scoffed and rolled her eyes. "Of course not." Then, as he didn't look the least bit convinced, she confessed what he already knew. "I just wondered why you didn't marry her since, according to Nedda, she was the epitome of social grace and loveliness."

His features softened. "I didn't want to after I found her having sex in her stables with another man." He laughed again mildly. "Besides the bedroom, that seems to be the place for first couplings."

She stared at him, shocked. "You *found* her like that?"

"With her legs spread wide and her skirt above her waist."

Caroline felt a flood of sympathy wash over her, trying to imagine how he must have felt to see the woman he intended to marry engaged so indecently with another.

"Nedda told me she didn't want to marry you because of Rosalyn," she quietly confessed.

He lightly caressed her cheek with his knuckles. "I let others believe she didn't want me because that was the honorable thing to do. It wasn't my place to spread the news to society and ruin her life. She was managing to do it nicely all by herself.''

Caroline cupped his cheeks with her hands, holding him firmly in front of her face. "I've never known a person I've admired more than you, Brent," she whispered with absolute adoration and wonder. "I'm so proud to be your wife."

The honesty she conveyed in her tone and expression seemed to daze him for a moment as she watched confusion, then gentleness cross his brow. Then he lowered his mouth and kissed her deeply, fully, wrapping his arms around her as if they were one.

"I want to make love to you again, Caroline," he urged softly, his voice thick with emotion.

"I want you to," she whispered in complete surrender, clinging to him tightly, moving her hand to glide her fingertips along his spine, kissing his face and jaw in smooth, gentle touches. After hearing him groan and feeling his growing need rubbing against her hips, she quietly amended, "But I do have one condition in allowing you the generous use of my body."

He slowly raised his head to look at her smugly. "I'm truly frightened to ask what that might be."

Her face broke out into a smile again. "How did you acquire a greenhouse?"

He relaxed, his eyes flashing with knowing sensitivity. "It was my mother's."

"Your mother was a botanist?" she asked, surprised.

"She tried to be." He covered her breast with his palm. "She never had your talent or commitment, though."

Her gaze dropped to his chest, her heart swelling with pleasure from that statement.

"Can I keep it?" she fairly begged, knowing she sounded timid and unsure, and even in her boldness unable to look him in the eye with the question.

Suddenly, as if in answer, he moved down and covered her nipple with his mouth, rotating his tongue with expertise, sucking and kissing and making her weak. She spread her legs for his probing hand and succumbed to the need.

Words were no longer necessary.

He woke with a start, sitting abruptly, heart pounding, body bathed in sweat. His eyes tried to adjust to the darkness surrounding him as his mind worked to lift the cloud of confusion, to calm the rush of fear that enveloped him.

It was night, the dead of night since no fire burned, and as he wiped a shaking hand over his head, the disorientation slowly gave way to remembrance.

To his side lay his wife, sleeping peacefully. As his eyes slowly adjusted to the room lighted only from soft moonglow, he turned to her, watching her, his body calming, his tense muscles relaxing as he breathed deeply and purposefully.

Her beautiful hair flowed in waves across the pillow, eyes shut firmly in deep slumber as she faced him. One bare breast peeked out from the sheet, nipple hardened from the chill in the room, and without thought he reached down and covered her gently with the blankets, which in turn caused her to stir and swiftly turn onto her stomach, her arms pushed up under her pillow.

His chest tightened as he thought about her, about the night before, her loving him with such passion and beauty, giving not only her body but her soul to him as well. And because of their growing closeness, the dream filled him with disparity and urgency. With Caroline in his life, becoming everything to him, his greatest fears were ahead, disguised in the unknown.

Philip knew he was alive somewhere. That was the dream, so vivid and terrifying.

Philip was coming—he could feel it in the air, in the darkness—and his sweet, beautiful wife would be the killer's target. Rosalyn was Christine's child, and that alone would keep her safe. He knew of her already and had so for years. But Caroline was English. She belonged to him. And that knowledge, if he knew of it, would eat at the Frenchman. Until he saw Philip dead with his eyes, he could never be sure, and the nightmares would never end.

He looked back to her, moonlight filtering through the window to strike the softness of her back, and suddenly he felt the incredible urge to hold her. He lowered his body onto the bed again, covered both of them with the quilt, and snuggled against her warmth. He wrapped his arms around her, pulling her to him, holding her tightly as he grazed his palm along her arm.

In all of his life, through the loneliness, the devastation of war, the trench of death, he'd never felt so frightened of the unknown, of what was to come. Philip was probably already in England, and Caroline's very existence was now in his hands.

"I will keep you safe, my love," he whispered into the cold, quiet night, burying his face in her hair. "I will keep you safe."

Eighteen

He watched her walk toward the door of the structure, her dark hair flowing loosely behind her in the breeze, her dirty hands filled with some sort of dark vine she evidently intended to plant inside. She hadn't noticed him crouching in the brush, and in fact had seemed completely oblivious to his presence for the last five days.

Philip couldn't have been more pleased.

She was an ugly little thing, being English and dark, although to be fair he'd only laid eyes on her from a distance, and each time she'd been clothed in rags and covered with dirt. He would hardly call her handsome, and certainly she was never blond. The English pig was so stupid, and had he not checked his facts, he'd have probably killed the wrong woman.

Still, he considered, staring hard at her in growing appreciation, she had a marvelous figure, which was undoubtedly why the Raven married her, as she was full-breasted, small-waisted, and a sensual pleasure to watch, her hips swaying so erotically as she walked that she made even him grow fully erect each time he saw her. What he wouldn't give to surprise the Raven's English whore of a wife, climb on top of her, and force her to succumb to French passion before he sliced her throat.

He gazed at her until she opened the door and disappeared inside, his trained mind absorbing everything, knowing it was all falling into place at last, as he now had what he needed. He knew when she arrived each day, how long she stayed, and she was almost always alone except for the occasional company of Christine's sick, half-English little girl.

Yes, the Raven's wife was his weakness, the flaw in his armor, regardless of whether he cared for her, because haughty English scum prided themselves so much on heirs and bloodlines. He would just take it upon himself to deprive the English of one more quality heir by disposing of the broodmare before he took vengeance on the only person to arrogantly think he'd bested the great Philip Rouselle, to arrogantly think he could infiltrate the French and not pay the price.

Slowly he backed up and moved silently into the trees. It was getting late, the air unbearably chilly and growing colder, and the fat English pig was probably already missing him.

But it would be over soon, and then he'd find himself on a long holiday with several bottles of red bordeaux and a willing Frenchwoman to wrap her legs around his body of ice. He deserved such comforts after living so long in utter filth, and with each passing week he grew more restless. The time had come to strike.

In days it would all be over.

. . . I hope you'll not have any further delays in leaving England, since we've been anxiously waiting to combine your experiments with ours for more than a year now.

By the way, Mr. Grayson, we've finally been able to produce the lavender species; however, they're unstable, and the purple tips don't always breed into them. We'll certainly be thankful to have you with us on a permanent basis . . .

Caroline folded the letter and placed it next to a stack of notes on her desk. Stephanie had brought it to her only that afternoon, along with other correspondence and the innocent announcement that she'd be wearing her older sister's emeralds for various social functions throughout the holiday season. Stephanie had never once considered selling them to help her, she'd admitted bluntly, confident that her sister would see reason, admit to the growing affections she felt for her husband, and stay in England. How anyone could be so sweet and naïve, yet at the same time so calculating, Caroline couldn't fathom.

Sighing complacently, she returned to her planting.

She needed to write Professor Jenson and explain as well, but doing so, even thinking about it, saddened her tremendously. Although she'd been her husband's eager and passionate lover for nearly three weeks, the turmoil still burned within. Her mind and talent as a superior botanist would never be known and used to the fullest. Never would she realize her dream of becoming one of Europe's leading experts on plant breeding, all because she'd allowed her heart to envelop her rational thinking the night she gave herself to her husband.

How ironic that she would allow her wonderful, giving husband to unwillingly and unknowingly take away the only thing she'd ever truly cherished. She almost laughed with bitterness as she realized Sir Albert's original letter of rejection was quite literally correct. She would no doubt make her husband and family proud of her accomplishments, and in a very small way, even content as she was at Miramont with Brent, she felt hurt and frustrated that they would be the only ones to lay witness to her beautiful creations, her expertise.

What really made her angry, though, was knowing that the men in the world had won again. She just didn't live in a time when women were allowed any advancements or achievements, any personal recognition; gradually, as if maturing to fully grasp the complexities of life, she realized she should just be grateful for the things she had. Even with anguish raging inside each time she thought of the world of adventure and study she'd given up for love, she would have to accept her life as it was. There was no turning back. It would simply have to be enough.

But she did have her greenhouse, and that she adored. During the last two weeks she'd begun filling it with greenery and flowers from the estate proper, watching as they took to the soil, some of them budding almost at once. Most of the plants inside, however, were those she'd finally had transplanted from her greenhouse at her father's home, and all were different from those in the garden. During the coming months she expected the structure of glass to fill with color and brilliance, producing just as well as her creations did in the open air.

She'd been working on vines for twelve days, and although the woodbines were already taking to the soil, the scarlet runners would be difficult, for they only grew ornamentally in northern climes, and she hoped to provide them with the ability to sprout their edible beans in her greenhouse as they did in the tropics, their natural environment. Botany, as with any science, usually proved to be the greatest unknown, and she adored the challenge.

Within the week she intended to return to flowers— rhododendrons, violets, carnations. After that she'd again delve into the nightmare of breeding her cherished lavender roses. With so much work in the coming months, she hoped her mind would be too full to contemplate America and what could have been.

Thank God she had a husband who allowed her the freedom to do what she loved.

That thought made her smile as her hands dug into the soil. He'd left at sunup, quite secretive about his plans for the day, but she didn't care. Her work took her mind from everything else, and she'd just pry it out of him later.

•　•　•

He quietly opened the door, the box in his hands, trying to come to terms with his feelings as he gazed inside the structure that had, in part, torn his family to pieces more than thirty years ago.

"It's as . . . green as I've ever seen it, Caroline."

She whirled around and smiled. "Well, if it isn't Miramont's resident spy sneaking up on his wife again."

He grinned and stepped inside, taking in the surroundings.

She'd placed two large, oblong tables parallel to each other along the center, both almost completely covered with greenery. To his immediate left was a small desk piled high with papers, books, and what he assumed to be notes, and to his right along the glass wall were three small wooden benches, side by side, leading to a basin for water in the far northeast corner. Beyond that, the greenhouse was full of nothing but plants, dirt, and tools. This was where she belonged, and in a rush of guilt he wished he'd given it to her sooner.

Taking it from her again wouldn't be easy. He only hoped his little gift would lessen the blow.

"I brought something for you," he said mischievously, sauntering toward her.

"A gift for me?" she returned, grinning, and reaching for a towel to wipe her hands.

He stopped in front of one of the tables, placing the small, ribbon-tied box on the only clearing he could find. "I will, however, demand compensation for my effort," he teased, crossing his arms over his chest and leaning his hip on the wooden surface.

She gave him a sideways glance, smiling slyly in return, as she slowly started toward him, hands on hips.

"Compensation? A . . . plant for your sill perhaps?"

She stopped two feet in front of him and leaned over the table to lift a small pot containing some ugly green thing with sickly leaves.

"That's . . . not exactly what I had in mind," he murmured, watching her breasts push hard against her blouse as she strained to reach it. Seeing that was enough.

Quickly he moved to stand directly behind her, pinning her against the table, pulling the ribbon from her hair, and nuzzling his face in the long, shiny locks as they fell down her back.

"You intend to take advantage of your wife in her greenhouse?" she asked sweetly, as if she couldn't feel him against her, his rigid erection gently rubbing her backside.

"Mmmm . . ."

She sighed loudly, leaning her head back against his shoulder. "Coupling in the dirt doesn't sound all that romantic."

"It doesn't have to be romantic. It can be fast and furious."

"Fast and furious?"

"And just as gratifying," he whispered gruffly, wrapping his arms around her, caressing her stomach.

She laughed softly, attempting to turn, and with that he reached down and began to lift her skirt, holding her firmly against the table. He felt a shiver escape her as his left hand began to knead her breast, the tiny bud hardening against his palm.

"Brent—"

"Rosalyn is with Charlotte. We're all alone, little one."

"You planned this," she said sternly.

He nuzzled her neck. "Of course I did. I'm not going to walk all the way down here for nothing."

She ran her palm along his arm. "What about my gift?"

Slowly he pulled her skirt up to bunch around her bottom, and before she could protest, he started stroking the outside of her thigh with his fingertips.

"Open it," he whispered.

Her breath began to quicken, her skin flushed beautifully, but he knew, as did every man, no woman could

refuse a present when it sat directly in front of her, beckoning to be opened.

She reached for the small oblong box, gently trying
to push his hand from her breast to no avail. He clung
to her, caressing her, running his fingers along her thigh,
and then, when finally she had the satin ribbon completely untied, he quickly moved his hand to hold the
top closed.

"I thought you said open it," she exasperated with
feigned annoyance.

He softly kissed her ear. "Spread your legs for me
first."

She turned her head sharply to glare at him. "That's
obscene, you insolent man."

"I know." He grinned. "And you cannot imagine
how pleased I am that you wear nothing under your
work gowns. Had I known this little fact, I surely would
have taken advantage long ago." He lowered his voice
to repeat impishly, "Spread your legs, Caroline, or no
gift . . ."

For a long, drawn-out moment she did nothing. Then,
smiling coyly, she turned back to the box and moved
her feet just wide enough to allow him access. With her
surrender, he lightly moved his fingers forward, around
her thigh to the front of her, inside, then covered her
completely with his palm.

She drew a sharp breath as he started to move his
fingers back and forth along her cleft, already growing
wet and hot to his touch. He lifted his hand from the
top of the box and placed it back on her breast, cupping
her, kneading her through the softness of her blouse,
grazing his palm across her nipple.

"Open it now," he whispered.

"You're tormenting me," she murmured in a deep,
sexy voice.

"It's my duty as your husband."

She placed her fingers on the box.

He kissed her neck, gently squeezed her nipple, and
slowly continued stroking her.

She lifted the lid, and as comprehension enveloped her, she nearly stopped breathing, fell completely still.

"This is what you mean to me, my darling Caroline," he said in a thick, deep whisper, stroking her back and forth, teasing her breast in slow circles with the tips of his fingers.

For a moment she just stared at the box.

"Don't cry yet," he added tenderly, placing little kisses along her ear and neck. He eased his fingers between her folds, found the tiny nub hidden so intimately, and began rubbing it gently, quickly, making her gasp. "I need you first."

"How did you—"

"Shh . . ."

She leaned her head back, closing her eyes to the feel, her breath growing erratic and fast. He kept her pinned with his hips and chest, unable to move, one hand caressing her breasts, the other between her legs, under the table and her gown, pushing her against him while his fingers moved expertly, faster, harder.

She moaned softly, and he quickened his movements, ran his tongue along her ear in slow form, and he knew she was fast approaching her peak.

He nuzzled her neck, breathing her scent, rubbing his swollen member against her backside, trying to stay in control.

"We shouldn't . . ." She clutched his arm. "Brent . . ."

"I love to hear you say my name," he whispered in her ear, squeezing her nipple gently once more. "I love to watch you when you're aroused. I love to feel you in my hands, your moist heat surrounding me, making me ache to be inside of you, a part of you." He increased the pressure and speed of his fingers, making her whimper, making her hips move rhythmically, instinctively, erotically against his hands. "I love to touch you, Caroline . . ."

Suddenly her nails dug into his arm. "Brent—"

Then she cried out, clinging to him, her body quivering against his. He held her tightly, feeling the tiny spasms with his fingers as he continued to stroke her, sucking her earlobe, kissing her neck and cheek over and over until he heard her soft whimpers of pleasure, felt her slow to his touch, her body begin to relax.

She breathed hard and raspy, eyes squeezed shut, face beautifully flushed. Then slowly, shaking, she turned, and this time he allowed her to do it, pulling his hand from her and letting her skirt fall once again to the ground.

She leaned into him, her head and palms against his chest, hair flowing loosely around her face. He embraced her fully, dropping small, delicate kisses on the top of her head, holding himself still, listening to her soft breathing and the faint rustle of trees outside.

And then she moved her hand down his stomach, slowly, until she grasped him firmly against the tightness of his riding breeches. He inhaled deeply but he didn't move, didn't let her go, then seconds later she gazed up at his face.

Her expression was one of fulfillment and warmth, the pure yielding of herself to only him.

His pulse raced, his blood rushed through his veins, and she smiled as if reading his thoughts. Then within seconds she lifted her hand and started unbuttoning his shirt, moving faster as she opened each one. He raised his hands to help, but she brushed them aside, and almost immediately she had it pulled from his body and discarded, tossed on the bench behind him.

Gently, her eyes never leaving his, she ran her fingers through the curls on his chest, making him suffer with want, then teased his nipples with the pads of her thumbs.

He groaned, pulling her hard against him and closing his mouth over hers, hungrily, passionately, kissing her possessively as his tongue plunged into her mouth, searching. Suddenly, as boldly intimate as it was unexpected, she grasped his tongue exactly as he'd done to hers so many times, and began to suck gently, the shock of the touch causing his knees to weaken beneath him.

He touched her shoulders, but she pushed his arms away once more as her hands reached down to his breeches. She placed her fingers just inside, gradually drawing them back and forth across the soft curls low on his stomach. Then quickly, before his mind cleared the fog of desire to understand what she was doing, she pushed down with her finger until she touched and circled the tip of him.

"Caroline . . ." he whispered against her lips.

She pulled back, and he opened his eyes.

She was watching him intently through dark, glazed orbs, features lovely and soft, cheeks dewy pink, and clearly outlined on her face was the look of a satisfied kitten ready to pounce on a nest full of birds.

He inhaled deeply for control, keeping his eyes locked with hers. Then swiftly, as if she'd been doing such a thing for years, she unbuttoned his breeches with incredible speed, placed her hands inside, and pulled them down just enough to expose the tip of him. Before he could even consider touching her, she put her hands on his chest and began pushing his body toward the bench behind him. He moved with ease, allowing her to guide him, sitting finally on the hard wooden surface and atop the shirt she'd taken from his torso and discarded only moments before.

Coyly smiling, she lowered herself to remove his boots, one at a time, pushing them to the side, and finally, his skin on fire, the wait excruciating, she moved back to his breeches, grasping and pulling them from his body in one fast action.

Still her gaze never wavered. She stood before him, fully clothed, and he sat on the wooden bench completely naked and never feeling more sexually aroused or exposed to a woman in his life. She had absolute control, and he was captivated.

Then she was on her knees, leaning over and kissing him intimately.

He closed his eyes and leaned his head back against

the glass, weaving his fingers through her hair, fighting the urge simply to lose himself to the moment. Her lips moved up and down the length of him, kissing gently, her tongue circling the tip in slow, blissful, agonizing form. As if sensing the urgency, she raised her head slightly and began placing tiny kisses on his thighs, back and forth from one to the other, then moving up to his stomach, her lips warm and moist on his bare flesh.

She softly cupped him with her hand, making him moan when she started gently massaging him, stroking his hardness. She continued kissing his stomach, running her fingers through the curls surrounding his shaft, until finally she released him and moved her body up to his, placing her knees on the bench, straddling him and raising her skirt to bunch between their bodies.

He reached for her, and she grabbed his wrist.

"Touch me, and I'll stop," she whispered, looking deeply into his eyes.

Without allowing protest of any kind, she delicately grasped him once more and placed the tip of him against her sheath, gently moving back and forth until he slowly slipped inside of her.

She was hot, wet, tight, surrounding him with the softness of velvet, making him crazy with longing just to let go and spill himself completely.

She started moving, stroking the length of him, and he relished in the feel, watching her, trying once more to touch her as he attempted to cup her breasts over her blouse. Immediately she stopped.

"I said no."

That nearly killed him.

She must have noticed his pained expression, for at that moment she reached for his hands and placed them up under her skirt, his palms on her thighs.

Again she began to raise and lower her hips, slowly and gradually as she pushed her fingertips through the curls on his chest.

His heart pounded, his throat ached, and he desperately needed release, especially seeing her as she was now, on top of him, her long, glossy hair draping over her shoulder and down her right breast, the very thing he craved to touch, to cover with his mouth. She was so beautiful, her lips moist and rosy, eyes shiny and dark, skin luminescent and rich. He had completely lost himself to her a long time ago, and as frightening as that realization was now, he marveled in the feeling.

Suddenly she stilled her body, placed her palms on his cheeks, and eyed him suspiciously, intensely.

"How did you get copies of Sir Albert's notes?" she asked in a daring, sultry voice.

He teased her skin delicately, the tips of his fingers skimming her thighs. Cautiously he replied, "I know people."

She shook her head and raised her hips so the tip of him remained only barely inside of her. "Not good enough."

He focused his thoughts to maintain control. "I know someone who knows his secretary, Stephen Phelps. He's compiled the man's personal lecture notes for years." Glancing quickly to the fullness of her bosom, he added, "The cost of having the work done was enormous, but I think you're worth it."

She grinned and narrowed her eyes to slits of shiny skepticism. "Years of notes are in that box?"

"Most are," he said as smoothly as he could. "Some he'd lost over time or discarded, but I asked for everything he had." He began to move his fingers up her thighs, inch by inch, hoping she wouldn't notice.

"Brent . . ."

She'd evidently noticed. He'd raised his hands high enough on her legs for her to feel his thumbs lightly touching the curls at the junction of her thighs, but the sound of her voice made him pause. She wanted to dominate this love play, and he was both intrigued and immensely excited by such a bold action from a woman.

He stilled his movements and waited, whispering, "I'm at your command, my lady."

With that concession her smile broadened, and she

slowly pushed herself down onto him once more, encasing him tightly. "It must have taken weeks to copy them."

He held her gaze. "I'm certain it did."

"And they won't be the same as my notes."

"They'll be as similar as you'll ever be able to find."

She ran her fingertips across his lips. "I can't believe you did this for me."

He stared at her hard and fervently, breathing deeply to contain the powerful, confusing emotions descending on him in waves.

Then she gave in, closing her eyes, leaning in to him and kissing him fully, running her fingers through his hair.

"Touch me . . ." she pleaded against his mouth.

That was all he needed to hear. Grabbing her hips, he pulled her tightly against him, holding her still, relishing in her feel. He was close to release just from watching her, feeling the warmth of her, knowing she controlled the actions as she spread her thighs across him, pinning him to the bench.

Slowly she began to stroke the length of him once more, moving her hips against his, faster, up and down, one hand on his chest, the other splaying across his cheek, her lips brushing his, then moving to lay tiny pecks on his face. He reached up with one hand to cup her breast over her blouse; the other he placed where their bodies met, gently beginning the stroking motions with his fingers once more.

She whimpered softly, and her head fell back. He kneaded her fullness, then gently caressed her nipple to a hard tip against his fingers. He stroked her, teased her, watched her, savoring the rush of raw pleasure she gave him willingly each time she lifted her hips to plunge down on him, faster and harder and making him weak with yearning.

"I need you," he admitted hoarsely, almost inaudibly.

She clutched his shoulders and opened her eyes, her face softening with sensitivity. "You have me."

He pulled his hand from her breast, took hers, and held it firmly against his chest. Then he reached around and grasped her bottom, holding her as he moved against her, faster in rhythm, knowing she was almost there as she licked her lips and quickened her pace.

Suddenly her eyes widened, her gaze searing his.

"I need *all* of you, Caroline . . ."

And with those words she found her release, dropping her head back, crying out his name to the open air, squeezing her eyes tightly shut from the deep penetration of his, clutching his hand, her breathing hard, fast, unsteady.

Watching her reach her crest again was his undoing. He met each of her thrusts with his own, deeper, harder, holding her tightly, and only seconds later, when he knew he'd succumbed to the heat of surrender at last, he pulled her hand to his lips.

"Caroline . . . My wife . . ."

He exploded inside, a roar of completion escaping from deep in his chest as he poured his seed into her, fully, totally, grasping her, embracing her as he could.

She hugged him against her, gradually slowing her movements, allowing her weight to collapse onto his hard frame, kissing his face and neck and finally his lips, passionately, then sweetly as his breathing slowed.

He cupped her head with his hand, feeling her silky hair between his fingers, dropping tiny kisses on her temple and cheek, she doing the same on his neck and shoulders and chest.

He held to her for a long while, listening to her slow, steady breathing and the breeze from outside as it caused trees to sway against the glass. Dusk was falling around them, making the surroundings inside and out seem dark and lush, removed from civilization, reminding him exactly why he'd come to the greenhouse.

"It's getting late, sweetheart," he quietly said at last, shifting his weight to gently and completely slide out of her.

She moved her hips to accommodate him but snuggled into his body even more. "I'm not ready to leave."

He softly, soothingly, brushed his fingers through her hair. "Well, my darling, I'm certain if Rosalyn, or Charlotte, or her—how did you put it?—her robust and exotic-looking husband walked down here to see what's been keeping us, I wouldn't want to be caught in such a state of undress."

She sat up.

He grinned. "Clothed as you are on top of me, and naked as I am, it looks suspiciously as if you took advantage of your husband."

She giggled adorably, eyes sparkling impishly as she covered her mouth with the back of her hand. "I did do that, didn't I?"

He nodded, boasting, "But not without allowances on my part."

"Your word against mine." She leaned over and kissed his chin, then moved to her side and off him to sit on the bench next to his long, hard body. Suddenly she looked down at him and laughed.

"You didn't find it so amusing when it fit so snugly and enjoyably inside of you, my lady Caroline," he stated with forced gravity as he stood, towering over her, hands on hips.

She glanced up to his face, trying to hide her amusement. "It has nothing to do with your particular anatomy, Brent. I only find it funny that men can be so filled with egos, so pompous and sure of their superiority. But seeing you like this makes me realize just how vulnerable all of you really are to us."

He gave her a calculating glance and reached for his breeches, stepping into them quickly and pulling them over his hips. "I had always believed, Caroline, that women were born with the ability to manipulate the men in their lives. I now understand, after being with you, it's not manipulation on the part of the woman, but vulnerability on the part of the man."

She looked at him curiously, and he grabbed his shirt

out from under her bottom on the bench, putting it on and buttoning as he talked.

"Men innately have a vulnerability to the women they adore, but they must appear superior in mind and body because that's how they stay in control of their lives. What all men are taught to believe, through schooling or family or culture, is that by using physical or mental control they can easily manipulate women, all the while believing that sexual control, or appearing weaker, is the inherent way women fight this manipulation in return."

He sat heavily on the bench, his eyes never leaving hers as he reached for his boots. "But it's just a complicated game, Caroline. I now understand you aren't manipulating me any more than Charlotte manipulates me or her American husband, or your sisters manipulate their husbands, or Stephanie manipulates your father—"

She laughed at that.

"The point is, it's not manipulation, and it never has been. Throughout time, men and women haven't been manipulated *by* each other but vulnerable *to* each other, because they need each other on an emotional level."

He stood again in front of her, fully dressed. "Your power as a woman, Caroline, is not the power to manipulate me, but the power of being what and who you are." He grinned sheepishly. "I'm sure I'll live to regret this admission but I'm nothing but butter in your hands, little one. And I'm probably the only man in the history of time to confess that to a woman."

Smiling, she stood and reached up to cup his face. "I don't think of you as butter, husband, I think of you as . . . chocolate."

He raised a brow quizzically, protectively crossing his arms over his chest. "Chocolate?"

"Mmm . . . You melt from my touch, but you're sweeter, marvelous to taste, rarer and more cherished than any other delicacy."

"You enjoy tasting me?"

She sighed loudly, shaking her head, then dropped her

arms and turned away from him, walking quickly to the table to put the lid back on the box of notes he'd given her. "Only a man would be concerned with sex before love."

"Are you telling me you love me, Caroline?"

The quietly spoken words left his mouth before he considered them, and although part of him wanted to take them back quickly or add to them in humor, the rest of him desperately wanted to hear the answer from her lips.

Slowly she raised her head, her eyes piercing his, probing for enlightenment from his nearly blank expression. Then she grinned cunningly, lifted the box, and nonchalantly walked to her desk. "You'll never hear me say it first, Brent."

She was alluding again to the first discussion of love they'd shared, and by doing so, purposely holding back a part of herself, an admission of feelings they both knew existed. He instantly and irrationally found himself annoyed.

"I suppose you want to hear it first from me," he baldly retorted.

She shrugged but didn't look up as she began stacking books into piles. "Oh, I'm quite certain you'll never say the words, since you wouldn't know love if it slapped you in the face—"

"Don't push the issue, Caroline," he interjected quickly, matter-of-factly, his voice hard and controlled.

She was visibly startled by his response, the sudden coldness in his tone. She'd only been teasing, talking jovially, and because of the inane, confusing feelings burning inside of him, she'd sparked his anger unwittingly.

But he should have known that of all the women in the world, his wife wouldn't take his words and manner lightly.

As she pulled her body upright, back rigidly set, he watched nervousness cross her features in the flash of an instant; then she placed her hands on her hips and stared hard at him.

"Are you in love with me?" she asked in a deadly calm voice.

He wasn't prepared for the directness of the question, and until he knew how to control every complication, until he could organize his feelings and put them into words, the only possible way for him to answer was to be blunt and take the easy way out.

"No," he insisted flatly as his heart began to pound.

Her eyes wavered just slightly as the only sign that she was bothered by his reply; then she reached over and lifted the box of notes into her arms. "With that answer you're not only foolishly protecting your male pride, you're telling me I may have just conceived your child from the same type of casual, meaningless coupling you experienced with the courtesan. That thought disgusts me." She raised her chin defiantly and turned toward the door. "You're lying to both of us, Brent, and I have nothing more to say to you."

There was nothing he despised more than being dismissed by a woman at her convenience. His mother and sister had done it for years, and he absolutely refused to have Caroline start with him now.

"You'll need to stay away from the greenhouse for a while," he coldly demanded, keeping his growing fury intact.

She stopped abruptly, turning back to him in shock.

"Why?" she asked in a slow, deep whisper.

He stood stiffly, undaunted. "Because I said so."

For a second, the smallest second, she looked as if she could kill. "That's it? You give me something, then take it away at your discretion with no reasonable explanation?" When he said nothing, she steadied her voice and clenched her jaw. "Isn't that just like a man, punishing me by control because I won't give you the satisfaction of telling you I love you first."

His eyes narrowed to rocks of hard, freezing ice as he started to move in her direction. "I don't think I've ever heard you say anything so incredibly stupid, Caroline.''

He watched her hesitate, then lose her composure completely as her body sagged, her eyes widened to pools of hurt and confusion, which in turn gave him the most unusual, dishonorable sense of confidence. He didn't like the feeling much, but he was enraged by her audacity, words that if he considered them honestly hit very close to the truth. None of it mattered, however, because the fact remained that she needed protection without his illumination, and that excuse, at the very least, was rational.

''I'm telling you to stay away because I'm your husband, and my word is final. I don't need to explain anything.'' He stopped directly in front of her, gazing down to her colorless face. ''Now you may leave.''

She stared at him, fragile and lost, hugging her box of notes, letting tiny teardrops spill from her eyes onto her cheeks without notice. Then she lowered her gaze to his stomach. ''You're no husband,'' she choked in whisper, ''you're the devil.''

Her words stung him deeply, quickly turning his anger to guilt, then regret, and finally sorrow. He reached for her, but she slapped his hand aside.

Without looking at him and with remarkable ease, she lowered her body and placed the box on the floor. ''I don't want anything from you.''

Without pause, she turned and gracefully walked from the greenhouse.

Nineteen

Charlotte knew she was carrying. She'd probably conceived at Miramont, the place of her birth twenty-eight
years ago, but she would have her son in her home, in
America, where he would grow up free of the complications of class to become anything he chose, where his
future would begin with nothing more than bright op-
portunities and promise.

The thought made her smile as she looked over the
garden, the scent of flowers surrounding her, the afternoon sun warming her back as she sat on the stone
bench.

Carl should be the first to know, she decided, but she
didn't want to tell him before they sailed, for the man
would become a hopeless puppy lost without direction
from the knowledge that his wife who had such trouble
getting pregnant with his child now finally carried his
son.

She knew it would be a boy. It had to be a boy. Then
maybe, if God blessed her with a girl . . .

Charlotte sighed, hugging her dark-gray woolen pelisse even closer to her body as she dropped her gaze to
the ground.

Her only problem, and the reason she still remained at Miramont, was in smoothing relations with her obstinate brother. He spoke to her and Carl on occasion, but the talk was laughably formal and stiff. He wouldn't put his guard down, wouldn't relax and enjoy their presence for a second, and for the first time since she'd arrived seven weeks ago, she was beginning to fear the wounds might not heal between them before she left.

That troubled her so deeply that for the last two days she'd been brooding. Because of her sensitive mood, the emotional instability caused by her condition, Carl had practically demanded she take a walk to clear her head. Poor man. He would feel so horrible when he learned she'd snapped at him because she carried his child. Then he'd probably faint.

She laughed softly at the thought and glanced up. As if knowing he was the problem to address, her brother suddenly stood before her, blocking the sun with his large body and staring down at her as if she'd done something naughty. It certainly brought back memories.

"You find my wife's flower garden amusing, Charlotte?" he asked easily.

She sighed, leaning back against the wall. "No, I find it beautiful, which is why I'm here. I find men amusing which, as it happens, is also why I'm here."

"Ahh . . . Men." He sat beside her on the stone bench, feet spread wide as he leaned forward to rest his elbows on his knees. "It's a wonder any of us does anything right."

She smiled lightly. "I can think of one or two things."

He grinned; she could see it etched on the side of his face as he stared at the ground. He was trying to break the ice, she supposed, and this was probably a perfect opportunity to push a little, as no one else was around. She hadn't seen or really known her brother for more than six years, but they'd been very close before she'd left, and she wanted that closeness back. He was her only brother, and still, through all the anger and hurt, she loved him deeply.

"Is something troubling you?" she inquired innocently, knowing fully well, as did everyone at Miramont, that he was definitely troubled.

He exhaled loudly. "I just—I was thinking . . ." He paused, then sat back and stared vacantly at the roses in front of them. "You knew she went to the greenhouse, didn't you?"

It was Charlotte's turn to grin, watching him struggle uncomfortably with his thoughts. "Of course I did, and had you taken ten minutes to think about it rationally, you would have figured it out as well."

"Explain yourself," he ordered.

She shrugged. "Love is blind."

He rolled his eyes and shook his head. "Women, women, women . . ."

Charlotte almost broke out laughing from his perplexed demeanor. She'd never before seen her brother, the great Earl of Weymerth, look so confused.

"And you said those things the night of the party because you knew how I would react and what would happen between us," he maintained awkwardly.

She sobered, softening her voice. "Yes; at least I thought I would try to make it happen."

"Did it not occur to you, madam," he formally charged, "that perhaps she had a lover, or was already comfortably warming my bed, and your words would only make matters worse?"

That shocked her. "Brent, a stranger could have looked at Caroline, talked to her about you for less than five minutes, and concluded without any doubt that she was a virgin."

The lines on his face tightened, his lips thinned grimly, and she knew she was close to igniting his anger. That was the last thing she wanted to happen now.

She looked to her lap, conceding. "Perhaps that's not true. I probably noticed because I'm a woman and was once in her—"

He cut her off by taking her hand and squeezing it.

"Thank you," he whispered gruffly.

That so surprised her she instantly felt the urge to cry. "You're my brother," she quietly affirmed.

She clung to his hand, both of them silent, and after taking a minute to put a grasp on her tumultuous feelings, and knowing instinctively the man had approached her because he needed her advice as a woman, she decided just to be candid, bringing the issue front and center as delicately as she could.

"Caroline loves you as much as you love her, and I'm quite certain that somewhere inside that thick head of yours, you know that. What you need to do now is admit it to yourself, then go and tell your wife."

He stood abruptly, and slowly, stiffly, started pacing the ground in front of her. "She hasn't spoken to me in two days, Charlotte. That hardly seems a shining example of love."

She sighed, confident that Caroline avoided her brother because of a conflict over the greenhouse, since the woman hadn't gone near the structure in that same length of time. That, she reasoned, would be the only item of importance to cause such a gigantic rift between them almost overnight, but she was unwilling to pry. If he so desired, he would eventually give her the details.

"You know, Brent," she disclosed, becoming somber, quiet, "four years ago I didn't speak to Carl for twenty-two days because he shot the cat at a party one night and gambled away the ruby brooch you gave me for my sixteenth birthday."

She heard him grunt in annoyance, but she continued before he could utter a caustic reply.

"It was the only thing I carried to America that held any value or deep personal meaning, and in the blink of an eye it was gone." Grinning suddenly from the memory, she added, "He had to practically give one of his silly little ships away to get it back for me, but he did because I didn't sleep in the same bed with him for almost a month. I've never seen him so scared."

The corners of his mouth lifted in a smile once more, and that gave her encouragement. "The point is, I forgave him eventually, as I'm certain Caroline will do. And I'm just as certain Carl and I will spend our lives forgiving each other for this or that because the word *forgiveness*, as I've learned so well through the years, is just another word for *marriage*."

He stopped pacing and looked down in contemplation, pulling a petal off one of the pale yellow roses at his fingertips.

"She bred these."

"I know, they're lovely. They should be dormant now, but I suppose it's been a rather warm winter."

"It's her gift, Charlotte, not the weather," he countered firmly, proudly. "Caroline can make anything grow."

She waited a moment to see if he would add anything. When he didn't, she decided to gather her courage and be direct. "You didn't tell her about Mother, did you?"

"No," he answered in a whisper.

She leaned forward, intrigued, as she was nearly certain this was at the heart of the troubles in his mind. "Can you tell me why?"

He pivoted back to face her, actually looking into her eyes for the first time since approaching her in the garden. "You can't guess?"

She shrugged. "No. I can't imagine why you wouldn't."

He raised his arm and forcefully threw the rose petal into the wind as if skipping stones on a lake.

"Carl is a decent man, Charlotte," he quietly stated after a moment of strained silence. "He's intelligent, hardworking, honorable from what I know of him, and he seems to care for you a great deal. He's made you a good husband."

She couldn't for the life of her decide where that came from, so she simply continued to look at him, puzzled and admittedly a bit dubious.

His expression turned to one of embittered amazement. "You don't understand, do you?"

She shook her head.

He strode back to the bench and sat beside her again, looking once more to the roses. "All this time you thought I wanted nothing to do with you because you ran off and married an American, a man you assumed I despised on principle." After a quiet, hesitant moment, he said gravely, "But the truth, Charlotte, is that for six-and-a-half years I've wanted nothing to do with you, have treated you as if you never existed, not because you left me and married an American, but because you left me period."

Her mouth went dry as she gaped at the side of his face in stunned silence.

"It never occurred to you that by leaving impulsively you would be handing me to the Lady Maude on a platter. I had to bear the brunt of her criticism and enmity because you were her precious jewel, and she believed to her soul that your departure was my doing, my fault." He sat forward, elbows on knees as he gazed blankly ahead. "I could never do anything right in her eyes—you know that already—but when you left, she turned on me in the most vicious way of all by refusing to look at me or speak to me civilly from that moment on. When you left, I had nobody."

Charlotte's eyes filled with tears. "I didn't know," she mumbled.

"Well, now you know," he retorted sharply.

He paused uncomfortably, then turned to her, his gaze impassioned, voice oddly subdued.

"You were all I had, Charlotte, and when you walked out of my life, I felt as if someone had ripped my heart from my chest. You were the only person who'd ever loved me for who I was, and suddenly you were gone to the other side of the world. I don't think you'll ever be able to imagine how I felt the morning I realized you had run away."

Those words cut her to the core, forcing her to come

to terms with honesty as she stared into his pained hazel eyes. Through all the years apart, not once had she considered herself the sole reason for his bitterness, his resentment. She'd always assumed it stemmed from Carl and his parentage, his family untitled, born and raised in the colonies. But maybe, as the light of understanding embraced her now, that was simply an excuse. It had been much easier during the last six years to believe she was dead to Brent because of her husband rather than because she'd wounded him deeply just by leaving.

"I'm sorry," she said at last, shakily, hoarsely, finally failing to hold her tears in check as they fell onto her cheeks.

"Don't cry about it now," he urged through a sigh, sitting fully erect and wiping her tears aside without thought to the contrary. "I've had years to come to terms with everything, and I realize now that the man I chose for you to marry wasn't exactly appropriate for your emotional needs." He smiled and softened his voice. "I just wanted you to be happy, Charlotte, and if you think about it, you found happiness and escaped the Lady Maude in one irrational action. It took me years to do both of those things."

He was trying to be delicate with her, to keep her from feeling guilty, and that was so like him. She'd never known anyone more filled with a sense of duty than her brother, and of course she should have considered that over the years as well. Brent had always, from the day she was born, felt honor-bound to protect her from their mother, from the outside world, asking only for appreciation and love in return, and she had practically shoved that in his face one stormy night nearly seven years ago when she packed her bags and left Miramont.

She wiped her eyes with the back of her hands as understanding and then compassion gradually filled her. "This is really the problem, isn't it? You're afraid of losing Caroline."

The whispered words were barely audible in the cool

winter wind, but she knew he heard them because his features softened and he dropped his gaze.

"You're afraid she'll leave you, and that's why you never told her about Mother, why you kept the greenhouse from her. I'll bet you never . . ." She hesitated, eyes widening with growing awareness. "I cannot believe you never told her—"

"I'm going to tell you something, Charlotte," he interjected calmly, "something I've never admitted or discussed with anyone."

He drew a long, steady breath, his gaze never straying from the cold, dark ground.

"I have lived nearly thirty-four years, and most of those years have been filled with bitterness, self-doubts, disappointments, and periods of extreme loneliness. But through it all there has been one thing in front of me outshining the ugliness and filling the void, and it hasn't been my advanced education, or the intensity of my work, or the strength and beauty of my prized horses, as any one of those things would be for most men."

He turned to peer into her eyes, his voice suddenly deep and passionate with his disclosure. "The greatest joy, satisfaction, pride, and—this is the absurd part—the greatest peace I've ever known in my life, have come from three truly beautiful females—you, Rosalyn, and Caroline. You now have a life in another land, and one day Rosalyn might leave Miramont, even England as well. It's her life and it's ahead of her."

He dropped his voice to a harsh, fierce whisper. "But Caroline is mine, Charlotte. She is the one beautiful woman I intend to have by my side to adore for the remainder of my life. I'm so completely adamant about this I refuse to have you or anyone divulge things that could plant seeds of anxiousness and regret—"

"You're being selfish," she cut in directly.

He stiffened and looked back to the roses. "Maybe. But losing my wife is unthinkable to me. I will never take the chance."

Charlotte stared at him, love and sympathy melting

her heart, knowing his fear was probably irrational but understanding it nonetheless. With a very deep breath for strength, she placed her hand on his arm.

"Caroline isn't planning to leave you, and she wouldn't dream of doing so even if you told her about Mother's past." She leaned toward him to add decisively, "You are the most important thing in her life, Brent, not her flowers or her greenhouse—"

"I'm sure she never told you this."

"I *know* this," she stated without pause. "She's not twenty-one years old and running to America to escape a shrew of a mother, she is your wife. She may have married you for convenience, but when she took the vows she became yours unequivocally."

She relaxed and smiled. "Go and tell your wife you love her. And after she tells you she loves you in return, you can feel comfortable divulging all your little secrets without fearing botany is more important to her than you are."

He sat silently for a moment, brows furrowed in thought, then slowly shook his head. "It's just not that simple."

"Maybe it's not simple that first time—"

"Two days ago I told her I didn't."

She looked at him blankly. "Didn't what?"

"Didn't love her," he answered in whisper.

After a moment of utter bafflement at the stupidity of the entire male sex, she shook her head in disgust. "Was it an accident on your part?"

He turned to stare at her. "What kind of question is that?"

Shrugging, she lightly expounded. "Did the words spill out of your mouth in a moment of insanity? Were you drinking heavily, or taking revenge in a fit of jealous anger?"

His eyes darkened in annoyance. "She asked me directly if I loved her, and I said no."

"Why?"

That seemed to stump him. "What do you mean, 'why?' "

"Why did you say no when it would have been just as simple to say yes?"

He exhaled loudly and sat back hard against the stone wall. Uncomfortably he mumbled, "I refuse to say it first."

She simply gawked at him, absolutely knowing that if she lived a hundred years she would never learn to understand men. "Well," she declared sarcastically, "that certainly makes perfect sense—"

"It's a game, Charlotte," he cut in forcefully. "It's a game Caroline and I are playing with each other because I told her right after we married that I didn't believe in love and she would never hear me say the words. She said she'd never speak the words to me either, and I'm positive she said that because she thought my belief was foolish."

"It is foolish."

"Love is foolish, Charlotte. It's difficult to define, irrational, complicated . . ."

"Love most certainly is all of those things," she tenderly affirmed, taking his hand in hers, "but that doesn't mean it does not exist. If nothing else, love is *real*, Brent, and through all of the rough edges, loving my husband has been the greatest experience of my life, only made more glorious because I know he loves me in return. It can be the same for you and Caroline if you will just give it a chance."

He reached to his side with his free hand and abruptly pulled a leaf from a plant, spinning it in his fingers, staring at it in contemplation.

Charlotte watched him, fairly certain he was just having trouble coming to terms with complications that might arise from such a frank and open admission. With all his intelligence, rationality, and devotion to family, Brent had never been so close to losing this part of himself to anyone. He loved Caroline and had probably loved her for months, but for the majority of men, accepting and then confessing love was something akin to being stripped naked and forced at knifepoint to read Dryden or Pope to thirty old, fat ladies who sipped tea and nibbled on sweetmeats as they stared at you with feigned interest at the biannual meeting of the Ladies Society for Readers of Great English Poets. For many men, accepting and then confessing love was exposure at its most embarrassing and very worst.

He continued to stare at the leaf, saying nothing, and Charlotte decided to take action, as it was obvious the time had come for honesty on her part as well. Since the afternoon had grown increasingly warm in the brightness of sunshine, and because she needed time to adjust her thoughts and compile her next carefully spoken words, with grim determination she released his hand, reached up to unbutton her pelisse, and slowly removed it, laying it gently behind her on the stone bench.

She wiped the back of her hand across her brow, glancing back to view him closely. "I had a child, Brent," she quietly disclosed.

At that moment she was certain no statement had ever shocked him more. He turned his head as the words seeped in, looking at her through wide, stunned eyes.

She smiled and held his gaze. "About three years ago I realized I was carrying. I suffered through months of sickness, weight loss and then gain, despondency, elation, crying for no reason, everything a woman goes through when she's with child—"

"Charlotte—"

She grasped his arm to silence him. "Let me finish."

Trying to keep her nerves calm, she looked to her lap, moved both hands together, clutching them between the folds of her peach day gown, and continued.

"As far as the horrors of pregnancy are concerned, I was spared nothing except serious complications, and through all of the misery, Carl was wonderful. He massaged my aching back and feet, he held my head more than once as I unexpectedly started retching. He was chivalrous and adoring, and I in agony more often than not, but from beginning to end, I was also ecstatic because it had taken me years to conceive and I was finally going to be able to give my husband a child.''

The remembrance caused her to waver, but with control she kept her emotions in check.

"During the two months before the birth, I decorated the nursery, made lace window coverings, a lace quilt, sewed tiny baby gowns. Carl is an expert woodcarver, and he crafted a beautiful cradle.''

She raised her head to stare at the dark pink roses in front of her, holding tightly to her hands, now starting to shake involuntarily from a memory still so sharply vivid in her mind.

"On October second, eighteen thirteen, after two days of intense, exhausting labor, we had a daughter. A beautiful, healthy, six-pound baby with her father's hair and chin and her uncle's eyes.'' She looked back to him. "Your eyes, Brent. She had a loud wail and a strong grip, and everyone, especially her father, adored her from the moment she entered this world. We named her Margaret after Carl's mother and called her Meggie . . .''

Her voice trailed off as tears she could no longer contain began to trickle down her cheeks. But she held his gaze courageously, and he didn't move, didn't utter a sound.

"On December sixth, exactly nine weeks, two days, and eleven hours from the moment she was first swaddled and placed in my arms, I put her down for a nap in her beautiful cradle, and she never woke up. My baby was so healthy, Brent, so strong, and nobody will ever know the feelings that overtook and crushed me the moment I walked into her room and found my beautiful baby girl lying dead in her cradle. All I did was feed her and put her to sleep.''

She paused, watching the stricken look cross her brother's face as her words penetrated his mind and heart, as he slowly began comprehending deeply the very same feelings of pain and loss she'd felt and was feeling once more, as she felt every single day without fail and would feel for the rest of her life. Brent understood them because he was a father.

Shaking her head for clarity and poise, she wiped her cheeks to proceed.

"Nobody took her death harder than Carl," she continued in a whisper. "The following year was horrible for us emotionally because we didn't and still don't understand how a healthy baby with no injury or illness could just . . . suddenly die. And because it had been so difficult for me to conceive the first time, compounding our feelings of outrage and anguish was the unspoken knowledge that Meggie might be our only child."

"I'm sorry, Charlotte," he murmured.

She stood abruptly, suddenly chilled. Hugging herself for comfort and warmth, she walked across the dirt path to the roses, staring down at them, carefully considering her next words.

"I know what your feelings were for me, Brent, from the moment I left, and in many ways I believe they were justified." She turned to face him fully. "But never in my life had I felt rejection, anger, and hurt as I did when you didn't acknowledge me, when I wrote and you returned every letter unopened. I became pregnant, went through a miserable nine months of carrying, a painful birth, then experienced the death of my baby, and you didn't know. I wrote you once a month and told you everything as I experienced it, and you never knew because you didn't even bother to read my letters."

Charlotte watched him closely as he slowly began to ascertain all she was saying.

"You had a niece, Brent, as beautiful as your own daughter, and had I not insisted on coming here and staying at Miramont even when I felt completely unwelcome, you never would have known."

He slowly dropped his gaze from hers. He was certainly suffering inside, and she didn't want that. Forcing him to experience a rush of guilt or pain wasn't her reason in recounting such a horrible piece of her life.

Charlotte gracefully walked to stand in front of him,

looking down at the top of his head as she spoke in a soft, clear voice. "I'm not trying to make you hurt, Brent. I simply wanted you to see your life in a different light."

He glanced up, and quickly she sat beside him once more, bravely taking both of his hands in hers.

"My point in telling you this is not to open old wounds but to open your eyes," she quietly maintained, peering intently into hazel orbs so plainly overflowing with sympathy and remorse. "Don't waste time dwelling on past failures or things that could have been. The last thing I want is for you to feel guilty about never knowing my daughter, or about me and the six-and-a-half years you and I have lost that can never be returned to us. There's so much more life ahead, it gives us no reason to look back. Meggie's death took a part of me that will never be replaced, but it also taught me that life is precious and short, and the people we love can be taken from us instantly."

Charlotte reached up to touch his face with her fingertips, smiling tenderly as her eyes grazed over every feature.

"Seize the moment, Brent. Live for your future. I'm here with my wonderful husband whom I want you to know, you have a beautiful, healthy daughter who is learning as she never has before, and you are married to an intelligent, charming woman who isn't at all sure how much you care for her."

She lowered her voice to a fervid plea. "Go find Caroline and tell her, Brent, before there are any regrets. Swallow your pride, look into her eyes, and tell her without any reservation how much you love her. I think she'll take it from there."

For a long time he just stared at her, and she didn't move her gaze or body or even her palm from his cheek. Then he surprised her by grasping her hand, moving it to his lips and gently kissing the back of it.

"My sister is as intelligent, I think, as my wife."

She laughed softly, the tension draining in a quick,

relieving rush. "Well, since I'm suddenly so smart and filled with insight, I think I'll take my own advice and go find Carl." Her eyes twinkled. "If a chandelier falls on his head tomorrow, I wouldn't want him to go to his grave not knowing I carry his son."

His eyes brightened. "I shall be an uncle again?"

She squeezed his hand. "In August, Lord Weymerth."

"How are you feeling?"

She smiled, her eyes once again watering from the sound of his concern. This was her brother as she remembered him.

"As you can see, I'm a bit more emotional," she replied as she wiped her cheeks, "but I haven't been ill even once. I'm filled with energy and crave chocolate and tarts as I never have before. I'm certain I'll gain a hundred pounds, but I don't care. It will all be worth it the day I place this baby into my husband's arms."

He gave her a smile full of warmth. Then, as unexpected as it was sincere, he reached for her, pulling her toward him, embracing her with powerful, comforting arms as he hugged her tightly to his chest. And from that tiny brotherly gesture, she allowed years of encased resentment and grief to bubble up and spill forward at last as she broke down completely and cried openly against his shirt.

"I'm so sorry . . ." she whispered through broken sobs.

"I'm sorry, too, Charlotte," he conceded quietly, delicately, rubbing his chin along the top of her head, "and I promise to be a good uncle for this baby. The pain is unneeded because the past is over. You've opened my eyes."

She relished in the closeness she'd missed for so many long years as she calmed in his arms, experiencing quietness, contentment, and sudden, rich happiness. This was the dream she'd envisioned the day she'd returned to Miramont, hoping Brent would forgive her and accept her as his sister once more. Now she could leave for

America, and return to her home in Rhode Island, with a heart full of joy, a baby inside her, and her brother returned to her at last.

She sat up reluctantly, wiping her eyes and then his wet cotton shirt with her palms. "Now you'll need to change."

"Yes, but this will save me from disrobing completely and bathing in a tub."

Charlotte laughed through her sniffles and patted his knee. "Go and talk to your wife first."

He groaned, standing, and suddenly Rosalyn stood beside them, breathing fast and hard from running, face flushed, hair in disarray, her lavender dress covered with dirt.

As quickly as she appeared, she began urgently pulling on her father's leg.

He immediately knelt beside her, face-to-face, grasping her by the shoulder with one hand in an attempt to hold her steady while he wiped stray curls from her pinkened cheeks with the other.

Rosalyn, calming, and realizing she had their undivided attention, clutched her hands in front of her, purposefully, then opened them in one sweeping motion.

"What do you suppose that means?"

"It means *flower*," he whispered almost absentmindedly, his features contorting in quick speculation.

"Flower?"

Rosalyn panted, awaiting a response, eyes wide as saucers, then repeated the gesture, more forcefully.

Brent regarded her closely, and when he did nothing but lightly shake his head in ignorance, she once again started pulling at his shirt.

"Something's wrong," he murmured, grabbing her body and firmly holding her still. He held up his right hand and made four finger movements in front of his daughter's face.

To Charlotte's sheer astonishment, Rosalyn raised her small right hand and repeated them exactly. On occasion she'd seen her niece gesture for this or that, but never manipulate her fingers to communicate calmly.

Now fully intrigued, she knelt beside her brother on the cold ground. "Those are letters, aren't they?"

"Yes . . ."

"Spelling what?" she beseeched in wonder.

"*Mama.*"

"Flower . . . Mama?"

Brent shook his head again, and Rosalyn, her growing frustration becoming obvious in her expression, moved her fingers quickly once more, this time adding three new letters.

Suddenly his face became ashen. "She's saying 'Mama bad.'"

Charlotte's heart began to pound as she watched her brother spell *Mama* once more, then put his hands together in front of him, clench his fists, and release them outwardly in the same gesture his daughter had shown them.

Rosalyn nodded vehemently.

"Oh, Jesus."

Now she was scared. "Brent—"

He grabbed her wrist, thrust her hand against his daughter's, and looked straight into her eyes.

"Caroline is in the greenhouse, and she's in danger, Charlotte," he enunciated precisely, quietly, in a voice taut with fear. "Take Rosalyn into the house and stay there until I return."

"I should go, too—"

"Goddamn it, Charlotte, just do what I say for once in your life!"

That stunned her so thoroughly she couldn't reply. She nodded and grasped his daughter's outstretched hand as Rosalyn, with keen perception, began to squirm in protest.

He stood, instantly calm and composed. "I'll be fine. Tell no one where I've gone and don't let her out of your sight for a second because she'll follow me. Understand?"

She nodded once more, and with that he was gone.

Twenty

Instinct alone told her she'd made a devastating mistake the moment she laid eyes on the stranger.

Purposely and blatantly defying her husband's authority, Caroline had sneaked away to the greenhouse, never intending to stay and work but to simply retrieve the letter from Professor Jenson, which she'd forgotten two days before when she'd made her hasty departure. As furious as she was with the pompous idiot she'd married, she'd rather risk being caught and laying witness to his rage than have him learn of her original plan to leave for New York.

So, with resolve she stepped inside the glass structure. Just as quickly as she lifted the folded piece of paper from the desk, in walked the man, as casually and boldly as if he owned the property, catching her completely and immediately off guard not only from his surprise entrance, but also from his stunning appearance.

He had marvelous features—blond hair trimmed to his shoulders, side whiskers framing his hard, square jaw, slate-gray eyes thickly lashed, and an elegant, almost sculpted mouth. He was striking to look at, and never in her life until now had she been made speechless by a man simply because he was so physically attractive.

But at closer glance, his appearance was also odd, not that there was anything wrong with it exactly. He dressed impeccably, wearing lightweight breeches in dark rust, a pale, cotton shirt, starched, wrinkle-free, and buttoned severely to his neck, black riding boots both polished and clean as if they'd never touched a speck of mud or even a horse for that matter, and he carried a black woolen overcoat across his left arm. If she didn't know better, she'd swear he was wearing a costume, although even a costume would surely have gathered dirt or wrinkles when he rode or walked to the greenhouse. This unusually handsome man looked as if he'd stepped out of his bath and into the forest.

He started talking to her, and for no rational reason she felt tiny hairs rise on her neck. His name was Peter Whitsworth, a horse trainer who worked for their neighbor. According to him, he'd suddenly and unexpectedly come upon the greenhouse as he'd wandered north to view the area fully, had seen her enter, and had decided to introduce himself.

Still, something about him didn't seem right, and although he spoke perfect English, his manner and almost too congenial voice troubled her intuitively. He was too smooth, too pleasant, and because of the strangeness of the entire situation, her instincts told her to start working rather than try to leave, smiling casually as she quickly dropped the letter back on the desk and began moving plants from one table to the other.

For nearly ten minutes he followed her around, discussing pleasantries and the freezing English winter, which in itself seemed strange as this one had thus far seemed unusually warm. It wasn't until he dropped his overcoat onto one of the benches and started talking of her personally that his voice began to change, to deepen in intensity, his eyes turning dark as he watched her.

"I saw a little girl as I rode in," he quietly said, moving next to her as she carried a plant in each hand to the basin. "Before I could speak, she ran off." He snickered. "I don't think I look so very frightening. Do you?"

Caroline tried to smile, avoiding his gaze, and making every attempt to keep her voice affable. "She's my daughter and not very used to strangers, I'm afraid."

"Really? Your daughter?" His voice lowered. "How surprising that she didn't look at all like you."

Her head shot up immediately. He stood two feet from her, with his perfectly etched mouth turned up into a smile that never reached his eyes. Keeping her poise intact, she mumbled, "She looks more like my husband's family."

"Ahh . . ."

The urge to run crept under her skin. If she could only keep her cordial demeanor long enough, keep him talking, someone at the house would miss her, probably assume where she was, and perhaps come looking. On the other hand, nobody would have any reason to believe she'd be in danger at the greenhouse. The only person who'd likely care would be Brent, and as she hadn't spoken to him in days, she had no idea where he was right now.

It was clear she needed to delicately attempt to take her leave.

She wiped her hands on a towel beside the basin. "Well, it was certainly a pleasure, Mr. Whitsworth, but my husband—"

"Let's talk about your husband," he interjected softly as he lifted a finger to run it slowly down her arm.

She shivered, her eyes opening wide to his gray, suddenly malevolent gaze. "What do you want?" she coldly, quietly asked.

He smiled again, faintly. "You are indeed *audacieuse*, are you not, *petite dame*?"

She had only a vague idea of what he said, but she positively knew he spoke French. And as she grasped the coincidences, this man's underlying strangeness coupled with Brent's demand in staying away from the greenhouse, her mind began to clear, and that was when she realized exactly who he was.

As if reading her thoughts, or perhaps it was from the glaze of terror filling her eyes, his expression changed.

"Plain hair, plain features, but exquisite eyes and a figure . . . *tres voluptueuse et érotique.*" He moved his hand to boldly cup her breast. "The Raven chose well, I think."

"Yes, I did."

Caroline knew she was more startled than the Frenchman when she heard Brent's clear, deep voice from across the room. But she couldn't take her eyes from the man beside her, couldn't move, suddenly paralyzed from a surge of raw fear. He caressed her breast lightly through her gown, daring her to react and certainly taunting her husband; then he dropped his arm to her wrist, grasping it firmly as he turned in Brent's direction. With one look, pure and centered hatred graced his features.

"Well, *mon ami,* we meet again."

From the corner of her eye, she saw Brent nonchalantly take three steps inside so that he stood next to the oblong table closest to them, innocently push several potted plants out of his way, and jump up to sit on the table, never looking directly at her but instead to the man, waiting.

The Frenchman turned his attention back to her, lifting his finger to gently stroke her cheek. "She is little and ordinary, Raven. I wonder why you married her?"

"She's a very good fuck." He casually leaned back on the table, resting on his palms. "What are you doing here, Philip?"

Slowly, stunned, Caroline turned to stare at her husband. He was so calm, so calculating and controlled, apparently indifferent to her and the danger at hand. And the only sign of anxiety, of any emotion other than apathy he exhibited was the tiny trickle of sweat that slid from his left brow to his hardened jaw. He had run to the greenhouse, she was certain of that, and now he was composed and smooth and desperately attempting to save her life.

The man pulled her against him, her arm twisted behind her back, then cupped her breast once more with his free hand, hard and unexpectedly, making her gasp from the touch.

"I am here for you, *mon ami*," he answered pleasantly, gazing down at her, challenging. "But I think, since she is so tempting, I will also have your wife."

Her heart pounded, her eyes widened, and she swallowed forcefully to maintain control of her fear, keeping her gaze focused on her husband, who didn't appear to notice her at all as he stared at the man who caressed her so suggestively through the delicate silk of her day gown.

After a long, unbearable moment of silence, Brent gravely maintained, "I don't think so."

"*Non?* You use my woman and do not give me a taste of yours?" He grinned. "The French enjoy sharing their ladies, Raven. I thought you knew that."

"The French share their whores, Philip, as I shared yours, but the English do not share their wives." He cocked a sardonic brow. "I thought you knew that."

Philip's eyes became dark and dangerous as he dropped his hand from her breast, tightening his grip on her wrist with the other.

"And you are English, aren't you, Lord Weymerth?"

Slowly, meticulously, he confirmed, "Quite . . . English."

If the conversation had taken place at any other time, under any other circumstance, Caroline might have laughed. They sounded like children fighting over a toy or territory of play, but the pain in her hand assured her this was no small disagreement. Pure evil was present—she could feel it slicing the still, cold air—and this confrontation was real. One of them would surely die.

She started shaking, and Philip noticed in satisfaction. "You are scared of me already?"

Her eyes flashed defiantly. "Yes, I'm scared," she

hissed in a frigid, trembling voice. Bravely and without clear thought, she sneered, "You're a heathen animal. It's no wonder Christine Dumont didn't want you—"

"Caroline!"

She heard her husband's roar above the thunderous crack reverberating through the room before she ever felt the stinging pain of the madman's hand on her face. She stumbled back against the basin, attempting to catch herself with her free arm, and though she was dazed and startled into submission by his sudden action, he grabbed her by her hair and struck her a second time, violently, the force of it slamming her face into the ground.

"Touch her again, Philip," Brent threatened carefully, deliberately, his words calculated and thick with loathing, "and I'll cut off your balls, stuff them down your throat with my fist, and watch while you bleed to death."

The Frenchman chuckled once more and purposely stepped on the hem of her gown to keep her from crawling away. Shaking and breathing in gulps, she tried to push herself up on all fours, attempting to wipe tears of pain from her eyes, licking her bloodied lips. The skin on her face burned, her cheek throbbed, and her skull felt as if it had been stabbed with a dull knife; but as stunned and hurting as she was, she managed to draw the courage to glance up at Brent.

Just as before, he sat on the table, leaning back on his palms, calmly composed as if she weren't even present in the room.

Suddenly he started speaking in French, and it was the astonishment of hearing the subtle changes in his voice, his expressiveness, that kept her from breaking down into terrified whimpers, kept her staring at his face both in pride and wide-eyed disbelief. He spoke not just fluent French as Nedda had intimated, but gracefully eloquent, absolutely perfect French. If she hadn't met him until just now, she'd never suspect him to be English.

Brent felt the only way to get Philip's mind off his wife was to quickly change the subject, to find another common ground, and truthfully he wanted to switch languages because he refused to risk losing his beautiful, brave Caroline simply because she had confronted and insulted a professional killer. As smart and courageous as she was, she had no vivid understanding of what Philip could do, which in turn made her fragile and helpless, and most definitely dead without his quick action. His hope was that if she was ignorant of the exchange, she'd keep her mouth shut.

"You still haven't mentioned your reason for coming to me, Philip," he calmly remarked, trying with difficulty to keep his boiling rage and burning fear under control as he made every attempt to avoid looking at his wife. "I'm no longer your threat, and the risk of returning to England after the emperor's fall seems a bit stupid, even for you."

The Frenchman raised a palm in innocence. "Waterloo is over, my friend, but our battle will not be finished until one or both of us is dead. You know that."

He shrugged indifferently. "How did you know I didn't die in the trench?"

"Filthy place to die, Raven," Philip returned quietly, holding his gaze as he reached down to stroke Caroline's hair, making her physically cringe from his touch. "But I think the excitement I felt by finally having the chance to kill a menace to the emperor heroically while in battle was only surpassed by my joy when I learned you did not die. You lived in hell for days, did you not?" He chuckled as his eyes shone in pools of cold, silvery steel. "Living in a swamp of death is much worse than dying in one. I made you suffer in France, and now you will die in England. Only fitting."

Brent sat forward, elbows on knees, and glanced quickly at Caroline, who remained huddled next to the water basin, now staring at the ground in front of her. He didn't want to provoke the man, but he knew she was his target, and any attempt to unsettle Philip could force him to strike her again with something more dangerous and damaging than his fist. He needed him unsettled, though, because catching him off guard would be his only advantage, and unfortunately he could think of no way to do this without endangering his wife. He would simply have to do what he could and be faster and smarter than the killer who now stood only a few feet away.

"The war is over, Philip," he ridiculed in utter contempt. "The English have won, the French have fallen. You have nothing to fight for now that Bonaparte is exiled for good, the troops are disassembled, the money gone. Why did you come here to continue this game of tactical illusion when you could have stayed on the Continent and become a new person?" He grinned cynically and sneered. "Perhaps you should have given up on me and centered your time on something constructive like . . . learning to please a woman well enough to keep her in your bed for an entire night." He chuckled mildly. "Now there's a novel thought."

Cords of hard muscle in the killer's neck stood out against his starched shirt, his side whiskers flared with the tightening of his jaw, and Brent was encouraged.

"You are a fool, Raven," he spat in abhorrence. "But I should have understood your stupidity because of what you are—an English bastard who still, with all his education and deductive reasoning, cannot clearly grasp why I'm here."

For the first time since walking into the greenhouse, Brent was uncertain. Philip despised him and wanted him dead, but it was also quite true that in coming to England, to Miramont, he took an extreme risk in never returning to his homeland. They were equally skilled, but he had the advantage this time by being on his ground. Philip knew this.

As if reading confusion in his hesitation, the Frenchman laughed. "It was the woman."

For several seconds he remained unsure, then slowly the fog began to clear. "Christine."

"Christine," Philip repeated through an arrogant grin,

"the woman who spread her legs for you but whose heart belonged to France."

He reached for a lock of Caroline's hair again, intertwining it with his fingers, and it took every ounce of strength Brent possessed not to lunge at the man for touching her, frightening her, using her to enrage him. He placed his hands on the table, beside each hip, and squeezed it for control.

Suddenly and without provocation, Philip yanked her to her knees with his fist in her hair.

"Brent!"

Her scream of terror and pain consumed him, and he jumped to his feet, eyes blazing in fury, face contorted in absolute hatred.

"Leave her alone," he warned in a whisper.

Philip's eyes turned as hard as dark, gray marble, piercing his, defying him to attack, keeping his tight grip on Caroline, waiting.

But Brent refused to look at her, knowing instinctively he'd lose what self-control he still maintained, and she would die before he even reached her. She whimpered softly, her hands in her lap, eyes closed, tears streaming down her cheeks; that much he could see without dropping his gaze. He remained where he was, erect and challenging in his stance, legs spread wide, hands on hips, facing them.

Philip slowly shook his head and switched tongues once again in an attempt, he was certain, to upset and intimidate Caroline with his English words as they became rough and crass.

"You thought you were so clever fucking her, learning about me and my talents from her, but it never once entered your mind that she knew you were an English pig, that she was using you, hating you."

Brent clutched his hips with his hands as it all finally began to sink in.

"She told you of me on purpose, Raven, to win your affections, your trust—"

"She never had either," he said almost inaudibly.

A nerve in the killer's cheek twitched as he gripped Caroline's hair even tighter around his hand. "I came to this filthy island, to your home, my old friend, understanding the risks, just so I could look you in the eye when I told you it was Christine who betrayed you to the French."

Slowly Brent whispered, "I know."

Philip's eyes widened just perceptibly enough for Brent to realize he'd startled the man with that disclosure. In truth, he didn't know this at all, but it did make sense. He'd often wondered how Philip had learned he was English when not one other soul in six years had ever suspected, why Christine had not only disowned Rosalyn but despised her as well. She'd dropped their daughter on his doorstep as if she'd never existed—not in England when she was seven months old as he'd originally told Caroline to keep her unaware of his secret life in France, but days after her birth and at the only residence about which the courtesan knew—his home on the Rue de la Politique in the center of Paris.

In all the years he'd bedded the woman, she'd received her own pleasure from the couplings when she so desired, but she'd never wanted closeness, never wanted to really talk, only asking questions of him when it pertained to Napoleon, his court, his government, things that should hold very little interest for a woman of her profession. She'd been spying on him without his awareness, had probably been planted in that position purposely because Philip suspected him from the moment they'd met, and although he'd never divulged information or the fact that he was English, Christine had discerned the truth over time. She was the perfect informant, and he'd never suspected she was anything other than what she appeared.

Brent remained calm as he laughed softly, pathetically. "I knew about Christine from the beginning, Philip, my old friend," he returned pointedly, allowing just the slightest trace of sarcasm to creep into his voice, dropping his gaze to the table and brushing stray dirt off with his fingers. "I understood who you were, what game she was playing when she took me to her bed, and I was the one who laughed inside each time she spread her legs for me. I used her, and you would have saved your life by confronting me with such old information when you attacked me at Waterloo."

He looked back to the killer's face, into cutting gray circles of rancor now conveying fire instead of ice, rage instead of confidence.

Cautiously, quietly he added, "You were the one she betrayed in the end, because you are here, Philip. Christine was your weakness. She made you a fool, and your devotion to a whore has killed you."

The Frenchman's body became rigid, his eyes glassy, and in a strained voice he contended, "But I will not die until I kill yours, *mon ami*."

Stillness descended on the greenhouse, the air thick and tense, the room filled not with the scent of flowers, but with the smell of sweat and fear. Although Caroline kept her eyes tightly shut, she knew she was going to die in seconds. Her husband couldn't save her; he had no weapon, was too far away to simply attack Philip, and she was held firmly in his grasp by her hair. He would break her defenseless neck before she had time to realize it was happening.

So, with resolution and in a surge of courage and love, she raised her lids to look at her husband one last time. In the same slice of time, she felt a *whoosh* of movement, heard the madman at her side grunt heavily; then he slowly released her, stumbling back a foot or two before he fell against the back wall of glass and slid to the ground.

She gulped for air, shaking violently, heart thundering wildly as she forced herself to look back at him.

He stared at Brent with eyes wide in horror, his expression incredulous, and the slender, ivory handle of a knife sticking out from his chest. She watched him reach for it, desperately attempting to pull at it, but his strength waned as blood, thick and ruby red, quickly seeped from the wound and into his stark, pristine shirt.

Suddenly Brent was beside her, grabbing her under her arms and lifting her to hug her against his chest.

"Don't look, Caroline," he demanded in a tender whisper of sweetness, cupping her head with his palm.

She buried her face in his shirt, trying to stand on weak, shaky legs, to calm her breathing and her tears as they flowed from her tightly shut eyes of their own volition. She felt the tenseness in his arms, heard his heart pounding rapidly beneath her ear, and with the knowledge that he had been just as frightened, the shock overwhelmed her and she began to sob uncontrollably.

"He—he hurt me . . . My h-head—"

"Shh . . . I know, sweetheart," he cut in brokenly. "I have you now. I have you."

He held her tightly for minutes, allowing her to cry openly, kissing her temple, weaving his fingers through her hair, rocking her gently.

"H—how did . . . How did you—"

"Rosalyn told me," he answered soothingly, understanding her need to know and the numbness created by talking about it. "She found me, agitated, and with a little deduction I figured it out." He brushed his lips against her forehead. "I grabbed the first weapon I could find, ran here faster than I've ever run before, stopped outside to catch my breath, and when I felt it was the right moment to confront him, I tucked the knife into my breeches and moved in to rescue my beautiful wife who foolishly stood up to a killer."

Trembling again inside and shaking her head in negation, she squeezed her eyes shut and lifted her hand to lightly cover her mouth. "You saved my life," she whispered against her palm.

With those words he buried his face in her hair, tightening the strong, comforting arms encircling her waist and back. "I would never let anything happen to you, Caroline."

From the tenderness in his voice, she wanted to mold herself against him, to become a part of him and never let him go as she wrapped her arms around him, hugging him fiercely. "I'm so sorry."

Gently he raised his hands to cup her cheeks, tilting her face to his. Brushing her tears aside, he waited until she steadied herself with a long, full breath and opened black, damp lashes once more.

"Listen to me carefully. You need to return to the house quickly, find Harolds or Cressing, or even Davis for that matter, and have one of them send for the authorities. Then send Carl here alone. Nobody else."

"I don't want to leave without you—"

"You have to," he insisted. He read uncertainty in her expression and shook his head. "I need to stay here to assure that nothing is touched or moved until the magistrate arrives. There will be questions and a full inquiry, I expect, and I'm afraid I'll be in the middle."

After a moment of indecision, she nodded negligibly.

"It's all right, little one," he consoled with a grin. "You defied my authority as your husband, and now I'll have to punish you. That will give you something to think about until I return."

She stared into his softened gaze, reaching up to touch his jaw with her fingertips. "Brent—"

"I know," he whispered, kissing her palm, acknowledging each intense emotion gracing her features and radiating from deep in her eyes. "I know, Caroline, but not here. Tell me later."

Her throat ached as she nodded in understanding and reluctant agreement, and slowly he released her. She walked to the door and, with one hesitant glance back in his direction, swiftly left the greenhouse.

Brent waited, watching her until she disappeared into the thick foliage and growing darkness of late afternoon, then turned back to Philip.

The man had died in stunned awareness that he had been beaten by the Raven, by the English, on their soil. How ironic for him. Even with the shock of death on his face, he appeared cold, remote, his steel-gray eyes like a lifeless doll's as they gazed blankly into nothingness.

Brent wouldn't close them, wouldn't touch the man again, and suddenly, filling with an almost sublime sense of serenity, he realized that what had remained of his violent past of destruction, of death and blood, resentment and loneliness, was finally put to rest. The war was over, the fear was gone, and eventually, finally, the nightmares would cease to exist as well. The best of his life was only just beginning.

With such a calming thought filling his mind, and with every intention of walking to one of the benches and collapsing, allowing the lingering tenseness to drain from his body as he waited for the questions to begin, he turned and saw the small, folded sheet of paper.

He probably wouldn't have noticed it at all had it been sitting on the desk like the rest of Caroline's innumerable notes, but it had fallen, conspicuously white against the dark floor. Without thought, he lifted it and gently placed it where it belonged. This, however, was no note but a letter, lying open to his eyes, and the strangeness of it immediately grabbed his attention. Frowning, he began to read.

November 20, 1815
Dear Mr. Grayson,

We were pleased to receive your most recent letter informing us of your plans to attend Columbia this winter. Enclosed is a study schedule and a list of American botanists with whom you may wish to independently correspond. Naturally, we regret you won't be joining us sooner, as originally planned, but we also understand entanglements that must be addressed before one embarks on new studies. I hope you'll not have any further delays in leaving England, since we've been anxiously waiting to combine your experiments with ours for more than a year now.

By the way, Mr. Grayson, we've finally been able

to produce the lavender species; however, they're un-stable, and the purple tips don't always breed into them. We'll certainly be thankful to have you with us on a permanent basis.

> *Until January,*
> *Walter P. Jenson*
> *Professor of Botanical Science*
> *Columbia University*

Brent finished reading each word for a third time and slowly, meticulously, folded the letter. Then, staring vacantly ahead, mind numbed from enlightenment and acceptance, emptied of all thought and feeling, he sat heavily on the cold, hard floor of the greenhouse and leaned his head back against the glass to watch the growing darkness as it fell within the quiet jungle surrounding him.

Twenty-one

Caroline slowly opened her eyes to the light of morning, her body aching and drained, lids sluggish as her vision gradually adjusted to the brightness of day.

It was unlike her to sleep so late, for it had to be after ten. Surely Gwendolyn would have attempted to rouse her by now, but as the memory of the previous afternoon came flooding back in dismal waves of clarity, perhaps the events of the last eighteen hours had stirred the entire staff for the worst and everyone was a bit on edge.

After returning to the house late yesterday and blindly carrying out Brent's orders, she'd doused herself in a long, hot bath, calmly answered grueling questions from as many as twelve different men in authority, picked at a late supper she didn't even remember tasting, then succumbed to the softness of her pillows, awaiting the return of her husband. He'd evidently been involved until the early hours of the morning, since he hadn't gone to her bed or carried her into his, undoubtedly letting her sleep off the shock of the night before.

That was so like him, she considered with a tug to her lips as she slowly pulled herself up to sit on the edge of the bed. She'd likely received ten hours of slumber and yet she had to force herself to respond, even with a pounding headache and a gently throbbing cheek telling her otherwise.

Quickly rinsing her face with ice-cold water and running a comb through her hair, she donned a morning gown of dark-blue bombazine with long, straight sleeves and a modest neckline, tied her dark-brown locks with a white ribbon, and took one fast glance in the mirror for confidence. At least she looked presentable, although her top lip was cracked and her right cheek scratched, swollen, and dusted with blended shades of purple.

The house seemed deserted compared to the chaotic night before, but finally, as she wandered into the dining room, she came upon their housekeeper taking inventory of newly purchased crystal.

"Morning, Nedda. Have you seen Lord Weymerth?" she pleasantly asked.

Nedda turned to her, her chubby face crinkling in a smile. "I haven't seen him in hours, but before he left this morning he asked me to have you meet him in his study at noon."

"He left?"

Nedda nodded. "Rode out at sunup, alone I think, telling me nothing but to have you waiting for him when he returns."

"I see . . ."

Her housekeeper frowned in thought, starting toward her. "Actually, the house has been quiet. Davis was in for breakfast, and I know Rosalyn is playing outside. The Beckers have yet to come down this morning, so perhaps they're still sleeping. I know Mr. Becker didn't return from the greenhouse until very late." She leaned toward her, brows furrowed. "Nasty bruise, that. I could get you a cold cloth, Lady Caroline."

She touched her arm affectionately. "That won't be necessary. It doesn't hurt really. I think I'll just visit the garden."

For nearly two hours, Caroline busied herself with a little work, trying to keep her mind from confusing, even troubling thoughts. It seemed strange that Brent would leave without seeing her first. She certainly needed to see him, to be held by him, to tell him everything. Finally, as she waited on the settee in his study, absorbed in questions and staring into the roaring fire in front of her, she began to feel almost irrationally scorned by his sudden departure.

The door clicked open, and she smiled in an attempt to dismiss her irritation. But with one look at the blank, hard expression on his face, she knew something was horribly wrong. He should be smiling in return, relieved to see her, wanting to take her into his arms. But as he moved across the room toward his desk, he stared at two sheets of paper he carried in his hand, not even bothering to glance in her direction.

Slowly standing, she gazed with uncertainty to his expressionless features, his strong and imposing stance. His face looked very tired, and rightfully so since he'd probably been awake most of the night, but he walked with ease, dressed comfortably in navy trousers and a plain, cream silk shirt.

"I'm sorry I missed you earlier. I overslept, and Gwendolyn didn't—"

"I dismissed her this morning," he interjected immediately, still looking to the desk as he placed the two pieces of paper side by side on top of it.

The coldness and bluntness of his words startled her. "You dismissed her? Why?"

"I've offered to give her an exemplary reference and I believe Lord Hestershire's wife is in need of a lady's maid."

Caroline's heart began to pound. "What's wrong?" she gravely questioned, gripping the arm of the settee for comfort.

"I've made some provisions for you, Caroline," he simply replied, reaching for his pen and sitting comfortably in the large leather chair at his desk. "I've spent the morning with my solicitors discussing money and certain arrangements that need to be addressed before you leave.''

She blinked. ''What the devil are you talking about? I'm not going anywhere.''

''Divorce is out of the question,'' he proceeded mildly, without raising his eyes or head. ''Nobody in my family has ever divorced, and I see no reason to do so now as long as we have a satisfying agreement between us.''

He paused for a moment as he began writing on the paper in front of him, and that was when she felt the first spark of trepidation hitting her so quickly and effectively that her hands and legs began to shake, and she could no longer stand.

Sitting on the settee once more, she looked at him through wide, shocked eyes. With a hesitant breath, she tried to gain some rationality. ''I demand you explain yourself, Brent, because your words and abrasive attitude are beginning to scare me.''

Slowly he raised his head. She expected to see fire or coldness, some degree of misplaced anger or hurt, even disgust, but the look in his eyes frightened her more than she'd ever felt in her life. For the first time since she'd known him, she witnessed no feeling of any kind, saw absolutely nothing.

''I found your letter from Professor Jenson, Caroline. I now understand how our marriage has been a sham for you, an entanglement which, as it appears, everyone at Columbia University knows about as well. You obviously need your freedom, your . . . dirt and plants, more than you need me, Rosalyn, or Miramont, and quite frankly I don't want you living here as my wife anymore.''

He dropped his gaze back to his desk, and as the meaning of his words began to penetrate her mind, as awareness grew within to overtake and alarm her, she suddenly felt gut-punched and couldn't breathe.

''I've booked and paid for your passage on a ship to America, the same ship on which Charlotte and Carl will sail in three weeks' time," he continued brusquely. "You may stay here until then, since I will be riding into the city late this afternoon to attend to lingering government business. Rosalyn will be joining me, and we'll likely be gone until the day you sail, so there will be no conflict where the three of us are concerned."

"I—You don't understand, Brent."

"That's probably the most honest thing you've ever said to me," he retorted, with a tinge of sarcasm dripping through his words. "I don't understand how you could have possibly thought you'd be welcome at a scholastic institution once they realized you'd lied about being a man. You're a bit too curvy to hide it."

"If you'll just let me explain—"

"Now, before you leave I need to know if you've any idea if you're carrying my child. Have you any symptoms of pregnancy?"

If it weren't for the fact that she felt so terribly frightened, the absurdity of him posing such a question would likely make her laugh. But his straight-faced bluntness and the reality of what was happening instead filled her suddenly with the oddest combination of fear and boiling rage—hot, intense, and seeping from every pore in her skin.

"How dare you," she spat as she slowly stood. "How dare you carry on as if I don't exist, as if my future means nothing and I've been nothing more to you than . . . breeding stock for convenient use. I should at least be given an opportunity to explain my position."

He drew a deep breath as he sat back hard in his chair, looking directly at her with a face entirely void of expression. "To start with, Caroline, you made your position perfectly clear when you married me planning an annulment. Secondly, you mean absolutely nothing to me because our relationship was founded on lies; therefore, it does not exist and what happened between us during the last five months has been invalidated. And finally, Lady Caroline, your future no longer concerns me. You've made your bed and you may lie in it." His eyes narrowed as he dropped his voice to a gruff whisper. "Now, do you have any idea if you are pregnant with my child?"

She glared at him furiously. "I most certainly am not pregnant with your child, Lord Weymerth, and right this very moment I've never been more grateful for anything."

Without reaction of any kind, he slowly placed the pen back into the inkwell, turned the papers around to face her, then pushed both in her direction.

"I've made arrangements for an allowance to be sent to you on a monthly basis—"

"—You're only doing this to hurt me—"

"—in an amount I believe is fair," he persisted swiftly. "I've also agreed to allow you to take lovers at your leisure, as will I; however, this is the tricky part."

"This isn't tricky, it's completely unbelievable," she countered in exasperation.

He ignored her words, leaning forward to rest his elbows on the desktop. "Since I bedded you for less than a month, the chances are slim that you are pregnant. Be that as it may, any child you deliver during the next eight to ten months I will consider mine and will raise accordingly. Any child you deliver after the said ten-month period will be your responsibility entirely. Do you understand these provisions?"

Caroline couldn't find her voice as she stared at him in disgust, in bafflement, and in escalating fear and desperation of what she witnessed both in words and bearing from a man who only three days ago professed to care for her deeply.

Slowly he stood. "Since you're evidently having trouble comprehending my question, let me elaborate. In graciously allowing you to study in America as you've apparently wanted to do for some time, in 'funding your interests' as my solicitor aptly put it, in not causing scandal to your family or mine with a nasty divorce which would no doubt be costly and difficult, I have only two requests."

He leaned over, placing his fists, knuckles down, on top of the hard oak surface, looking blankly once more into her eyes. "The first is that you are never to contact me for more money. What I will send you is more than adequate for a woman who married under false pretenses. The second request, and the most critical to our arrangement, Caroline, is that if you are carrying, you will return my legitimate child to me within six months of his or her birth. I will raise him accordingly, and you will no longer be a consideration or a person of any importance in his life."

"This is insane," she murmured, clutching at her gown.

He tapped a finger on one of the pieces of paper. "I've spent the entire morning having these provisions outlined here. You must sign them both, one for you and one for me." Leaning toward her and lowering his voice to a husky challenge, he added, "If you don't sign them, Caroline, you get nothing. You have the choice of going to America as you'd planned the day we wed, with the stipulation that you stay out of my life and give me my child unconditionally if you carry him, or you may go to America with nothing to support you except your smarts and magnificent body. Is this all becoming clear at last?"

Caroline gaped at him, at the man only five feet away who so callously dismissed her as if she'd never meant anything to him at all. Rage filled and exploded from every fiber of her being, her pulse raced with disbelief and shock, and yet with a control she didn't know she possessed, she sauntered up to the desk, eyes locked with his.

"This cannot be legal," she seethed. Leaning toward him, she whispered, "I won't sign anything."

He shook his head and gazed down to her face. "This is not for me, Caroline, it's for you. I don't owe you anything, but if you want to be able to live with some shred of dignity in a foreign country, you'd better give this agreement serious consideration."

He placed his palms flat on the desk, leaning so close to her that she could feel the warmth of his skin.

"I want nothing to do with you from this moment forward, but because you will still legally be my wife, supporting you carries some responsibility—"

"I'm not your property to dispose of at your convenience!" she flung at him in a shout of fury.

His cheek twitched but he didn't move. "According to the law, you *are* my property."

Caroline knew she needed to remain calm. If he would give her an opportunity to explain, she could make him see reason.

Boldly she stood upright and affirmed, "I want to stay with you—"

"That was the greatest lie, Caroline. You *never* wanted me."

For the first time since he'd entered the room, she noticed a trace of emotion escape him with those words, spoken bitterly and almost sadly.

She softened her voice to a gentle plea. "It's true I didn't want you when we married, but you're my husband now, Brent, in every way. I don't want to leave you. I need you and Rosalyn."

His eyes grew stormy, dark. "I am not a toy to be taken out and played with at your leisure, Caroline, and Rosalyn is my daughter and none of your concern. What you want is irrelevant now."

He stunned her more with his stilted attitude than he did with his words. She, however, was ready for a fight, absolutely refusing to simply give up as she attempted a different approach by appealing to his logic.

"You seem to forget, my lord, that you wouldn't have Miramont if it weren't for me," she reminded him firmly, smoothly. "You and my father had an agreement and you cannot force me to leave my home."

His brows furrowed for a second, then his eyes widened in clarity. "Is that what you thought? Miramont was always mine, Caroline. My cousin couldn't sell it. I agreed to marry you and took you as loose baggage from your father for the privilege of buying and acquiring nine horses, darling, that's all. Absurdly enough," he disclosed, smiling cynically, "your father, the good Baron Sytheford, got the better end of the deal because he rid himself of you."

Dropping his gaze to the desk as if he hadn't noticed her stricken look, he nonchalantly added, "As for being your home, Caroline, it never has been. It's been nothing more than your place of residence while you awaited your chance to run from your unwanted entanglement. Now sign these and get out. I have work to do."

Suddenly, standing in front of the blazing fire, she was freezing, and although she tried to hold them in check, her eyes slowly filled with tears.

"I cannot believe you're doing this to us," she said in a husky, desperate whisper, wrapping her arms around her waist for warmth and comfort.

"There is no us, Caroline, there never has been." He sat again casually and pulled his ledger forward, turning through the pages and effectively ignoring her.

Rising panic overwhelmed her. "I'm not going anywhere or signing anything until you listen and allow me to explain. I'm hardly young and naïve, and I won't stand for it, Brent. You cannot dismiss me as easily as you dismissed Charlotte. I am not a disobedient sister, I am your wife."

He looked up. "There's a concept here you're not grasping, Caroline. Charlotte left me, and I pushed her out of my mind. You never existed."

"What does that mean?" she fairly shouted. "I never existed in your mind? In your bed?" She swallowed to fight stinging tears but refused to look away. "What we shared was real, and you know it. You'll never be able to convince me or yourself that what happened between us the night you made me your wife, or the beautiful intimacy we shared in the greenhouse three days ago, meant nothing. I remember everything I saw in your eyes and heard from your mouth quite vividly. It was very real, Brent, and it exists even now."

She sparked something inside of him with that. His lips thinned, his jaw tensed, and his soft silk shirt became tight across his chest as his muscles flexed. This reaction of building anger was certainly better than coldness, aloofness, and as instantaneous as the change in his demeanor occurred, she wanted everything laid bare.

Calming, she bravely contended, "I admit to you now that when we married I wanted to leave you. I wanted an annulment. You didn't want me either, so even if you don't like the thought, you should at the very least understand it. Many married couples live separate lives or receive annulments, and I rationally believed we could be one of them."

Boldly she straightened, looking him dead in the eyes. "But our feelings for each other changed everything. I didn't calculate love as being part of our relationship, but it happened, Brent, it's there between us, most assuredly, and you *know* it—"

He stood so quickly that his chair fell back hard against the floor, and for the first time since he'd entered the study, his features contorted in absolute fury.

"Love?" he whispered in rage. "You think this is love? Love is never built on lies, Caroline, and that's the only constant we've ever had between us."

Keeping her gaze locked with his, she said dauntlessly, defiantly, "Whatever you think about me, Brent, I swear I never lied to you—"

"You lied to me when you took the goddamn vows!" he exploded, his eyes erupting in blazing fire as he towered over her. "From the moment we met you lied to me, used me, and I was the fool because it never occurred to me that any woman could be so deceitfully heartless!"

She stared at him, wide-eyed and stunned at the strength of his outburst, the repulsion in his tone, no longer caring as water, hot and salty, slid freely down her cheeks.

He breathed heavily and fast, the muscles in his throat sticking out tautly against his collar. "I just don't understand how someone with any brain at all could think to get away with this kind of complex prevarication. How did you think you were going to ask me for an annulment? Were you just going to come right out and say it, explain your thoroughly organized plans after you'd booked passage and had your notes compiled? Or perhaps you wanted to wait until I was most vulnerable because you simply enjoyed pulling me along on a string like a puppet.''

"It—it was never like that—"

"It was always like that, Caroline! You teased me with your body, proficiently exploited my feelings to your advantage, hurt me, then lied to me about never hurting me again. You tactfully implied that Rosalyn and I would manage without you, cleverly remained secretive with your thoughts. You skillfully avoided the marriage bed until you needed satisfaction yourself; then, while lying there naked, you casually wondered aloud if I'd let you leave me.''

He raised his hands in absolute wonder. "Even Davis saw it coming and advised me about your scheming little mind months ago, but I refused to acknowledge it because to the depths of my soul I found it unthinkable, incomprehensible, that a wife would be so disloyal, so conniving, that she'd actually consider marrying her husband strictly because she assumed it would be easy to *leave* him.''

Caroline, dazed, placed a shaky hand on the desk to keep from reeling. "It—it was never like that," she whispered hoarsely once more. "Please—"

"Please what?" He slammed his fists on the desk. "Please what? Forgive you? Forget about it? Please . . . let's start over? Christ, you are pathetic, Caroline!''

Her body sagged, and she dropped her head, no longer able to look at him, and uncaring as wetness freely dripped from her chin and jaw, staining the neckline of her dark-blue gown.

"You wove your way into a new home, a new life,'' he slowly, calmly articulated, "taking the precious innocence of a deaf child into your hands without considering the consequences of how your departure would shatter her.''

Without warning, he reached across the desk, gripped her jaw tightly, and forced her head up.

"Look at me," he whispered.

She opened wet lashes to a blurry vision of hard, cold eyes filled with complete intolerance and pity.

"You don't love me or Rosalyn, you love yourself. You used and manipulated me when you moved into my home and my bed, lied to me when you spoke vows to honor me, planned to leave me from the moment we met, not considering for a second how I would feel to lose my wife, the woman I had vowed to protect and cherish for the rest of my life. You are the cruelest, most selfish person I have ever known, Caroline, and looking at you nauseates me even now.''

He abruptly dropped his hand from her face, pushed the pen in her direction, then turned to lift his chair. "Sign these and take one with you if you don't want to end up on the street, then get out. I never want to see you again.''

Numbly she lowered her gaze once more, staring at the rugs beneath her feet, suddenly realizing that her choice, her destiny, regardless of where it was, had been made for her the minute she'd agreed to marry the earl under what he so appropriately called false pretenses.

He was right. She had been dishonest and deceitful, and now he was giving her the opportunity to leave, the only thing she'd wanted from the beginning of their marriage. Except now she felt not elation or excitement; she instead felt as if she were drowning in a lonely sea of emptiness.

Trembling, she took the pen in one hand, wiped her eyes with the fingers of the other, steadied herself the best she could, and signed her name at the appropriate lines on the two pages in front of her. Then, with finality and the oddest sense of detachment, she slowly stood upright, lifted one of the pieces of paper, turned, and walked on leaden legs to the grate.

She stared into the fire, tears of pain and helplessness streaming down her cheeks, and quickly, without second thought, she tossed the paper into the flames.

"I don't need this kind of degradation from you, regardless of what I've done," she said huskily. "Keep your money."

He had nothing to say to that as he once again sat casually at his desk, engrossed in his ledger.

Smoothly she turned and walked to the door.

"I hope you find fulfillment breeding roses, madam," he stated formally, gruffly, never bothering to look up to her. "Your plants may require the attention and devotion we did, but they won't give you anything in return, least of all companionship. Remember that in the lonely years to come."

Quietly, anguish and frustration consuming her, she turned and left the study, closing the door softly behind her.

Twenty-two

Jane held her gloved hand out to one of the four polished footmen, then stepped from the coach. The morning was bright and clear, and the smell of spring was in the air. A lovely February day for a bout with her arrogant brother-in-law.

She ascended the steps to the front door with confidence and was immediately ushered in formally by a parlor maid who took her pelisse and told her without the slightest trace of interest that she was to wait in the drawing room for Lord Weymerth's appearance.

This she did, but as the minutes ticked by, she grew impatient and incensed. The earl was indeed as insufferable as Caroline had described without hesitation, and he was purposely making her wait as she sat primly in a chair, staring into the slow-burning fire.

"Well, finally. If it isn't number one."

She turned to the sound of his voice.

"I beg your pardon, Lord Weymerth?" she said stiffly, boldly looking him up and down.

"Number one, meaning you, Jane."

His usually expressive face appeared drawn and exhausted, as if he'd been awake into the early hours of the morning, tossing back whiskey and wallowing in pity. Good for him. She hoped he was miserable.

He dressed casually in a cotton shirt, dark-brown breeches, and black scuffed boots. Obviously he wasn't dressed for receiving but ready to ride. Too bad for that. The man would listen to what she had to say even if he had to throw her out on her heels, which appeared to be the only thing Weymerth was dexterous at accomplishing where women were concerned.

After eyeing her speculatively for a moment, he sauntered toward her. "Why did it take you so long?"

"I'm sure I don't know what you mean."

"I'm sure you do," he drawled, sitting heavily in the chair across from her. "Why are you here?"

"I'm here to discuss Caroline," she replied bluntly.

He leaned his head back against the soft leather, eyes narrowing. "Really? The rest of Baron Sytheford's daughters were here to plead for her before she left. And where *is* your father, by the way?" he added suspiciously, "He hasn't contacted me at all."

She brushed a lock of shiny blond hair off her forehead. "I am here for more important matters than to tell you Caroline feels terrible about what she did to you," she brusquely informed. "As for my father, he is under the assumption you'll take her back, so he chooses not to get involved."

He raised his brows. "Assuming I wanted her, how could I take her back when she left the country weeks ago to pursue . . . glorious dreams of flowers."

Jane ignored his statement. "I'll not play games with you, Lord Weymerth," she related, composed and daring him to counter with the determined glare she gave him. "My sisters love Caroline, as do I; however, being the oldest and most practical of them all, I'm not here to tell you she loves you more than roses, or wants you more than a greenhouse, or would give her life for you, or any other piece of nonsense. Those are romantic notions that do not concern me. I'm here to tell you, among other things, that I know without question that Caroline

had every intention of annulling your marriage the day
you wed.''

That statement surprised him, for he lifted his brows
almost imperceptibly. Jane, though, prided herself on being enormously perceptive, which was, in fact, exactly
why she'd bothered to visit the earl.

Slowly she began to remove her gloves. ''First I'm
going to explain why I came to you, sir, and then I'm
going to tell you some things about your amazing wife.''

He groaned, annoyed, and gently rubbed his tired
eyes. ''I see no use in rehashing old lies that I've tried
to erase from memory, Jane.'' Candidly looking back at
her, he added, ''There's no point in discussing any of
this.''

She set her features with grim determination. ''If you
will allow me the opportunity, I believe you'll see the
point.''

He shook his head, smiling pompously. ''Caroline
didn't want what I offered, and now she is on her own.''
He shrugged. ''I no longer care—''

''Oh, of course you care. Don't give me that rub-
bish,'' she cut in, standing abruptly. She dropped her
gloves on the chair and strode purposefully to stand at
the window.

Her eyes grazed over sunny grasslands and patches of
white velvety clouds dotting the sky beyond as she
shook her head pathetically. ''Everybody knows you
care, and that's why we're all more irritated with you
than concerned about my sister's welfare. Just one look
at you reveals it all, for heaven's sake. You're not sleeping, you've probably been drinking far too much whiskey, and the lines on your face tell a thousand tales of
worry. In fact, it's Mary Anne's opinion that you're angrier at yourself than you are at Caroline right now. I
happen to agree with her.''

She turned, facing him fully, eyes piercing his with
confidence as she stated firmly and with pure pleasure,
''Everybody knows how you feel about my sister.
You've loved her for a very long time, Weymerth, are

still in love with her now, and yet strangely enough, you are the only one left to accept this. You are undoubtedly the most stubborn and foolish man alive.''

She waited for him to rage at her audacity, watching him closely for signs of an impending verbal attack or rebuttal. Instead he stared directly into her eyes for a long moment, then slowly dropped his gaze to the cold, polished floor and leaned forward to rest his elbows on his knees.

''Why are you here to . . . scold me now, Jane?'' he asked in a gravelly whisper. ''The entire matter has become irrelevant.''

She took a deep breath and boldly replied, ''Because for the last few weeks, Caroline has been staying with me. She hasn't gone anywhere.''

His head shot up immediately.

''That is to say, she hasn't gone anywhere *yet.*''

That startled him, as she knew it would, and she watched his face display powerful emotions of shock, confusion, elation, hope, and grave uncertainty, which in turn gave her tremendous encouragement.

Suddenly he masked his features and sat back. ''Yet?''

She began walking toward him. ''Caroline has remained in this country under the hopeful assumption that you'll come to your senses, forgive her and yourself, and request her return to Miramont as your wife. However, since you haven't made inquiries regarding her intentions in America, or where she can be reached, or even if she's still in England, she's gradually come to believe you truly don't care anymore. Because of your lack of concern, in three days' time, on Friday, she will sail to New York.''

''How is she?'' he hesitantly asked, looking to his hands.

That made her smile. ''Just as you are. She's angry, worried, hurting, feeling lonely because she misses you and Rosalyn terribly.'' And quite noticeably pregnant, but that was beside the point and not something Jane intended to reveal. If the earl wanted his wife, he would take her back because he wanted her alone, not because she carried his heir.

"Does she know you're here?"

"No," she quickly returned. "That would just make her angry with me, and as I said before, I'm not here to boast of how much she cares for you or declare how wrong you were to dismiss her—"

"She lied to me," he interjected coldly, as if that explained everything.

"Oh, good heavens, married people lie to each other all the time. That's nothing new," she said, exasperated. "But it's also not the issue here. Caroline didn't really lie—she just kept her feelings from you."

"Her well-made plans, I think you mean."

He continued to look at his hands, so she took the opportunity to return to the point.

"I am here for two reasons, Lord Weymerth. The first is to tell you some very private and extraordinary things about your wife, many of which I'm quite certain you're completely unaware. The only reason I'm willing to discuss and divulge this information is because I personally think you are an exceptional man, and I'm not saying that to boost whatever ego you possess. I'm saying that because I think Caroline found a rare jewel in you."

He raised his head and stared at her sheepishly, bemused.

She sighed heavily. "I want you to know that I understand what marriage is nearly always like for ladies of our class. Mine is no exception. My husband is generally kind to me, Weymerth, but to him I am his property, his caregiver and the mother to his heir. Nothing else. He has taken lovers over the years and has one even now in the Baroness Montayne. He doesn't realize I know he beds her, because he has no idea how quick wives are in discerning such things."

She lowered her voice with intensity. "As with all ladies of our station, I've put up with my husband, using him for stability, and likewise he's put up with my usual frivolities over the years so I could give him a son. If Caroline had married a man like Robert, I would do everything I could to persuade her to leave, but she didn't. She married you.''

Jane placed both palms on the back of the chair and gently squeezed the soft leather. "Caroline married you for an annulment, and this you know. What I don't believe you know is why—''

"I know precisely why," he interrupted harshly. "She cares for roses more than life itself.''

Fiercely, eyes flashing, she murmured, "You've never been more wrong about anything.''

"Indeed," he said dubiously. "Do you know this instinctively, Jane, or did Caroline confess to such a falsehood?''

She waited for a moment to gather her thoughts, annoyed at his sarcasm. Then, watching him speculatively, she changed her approach.

"Do you remember the numbers you had her multiply the night of your dinner party, Weymerth?''

For a second he looked confused, then irritated. "I can vaguely recall the evening.''

He was purposely irritating her in return, but she decided it best just to ignore his impudence and move on.

Curtly she revealed, "Caroline did such equations in her head when she was four years old.''

Slowly, with growing comprehension, his eyes widened to gape at her, and the fact that he couldn't hide his astonishment pleased her so much she graced him with a broad grin.

"You think you married a smart, talented, sharp-mouthed woman, but that's not the half of it. Caroline is not simply a learned scientist, a woman wishing she could compete with men. She is an absolutely *brilliant* individual who was born with more intelligence than anyone I've ever known. She's never needed to learn mathematics—she was gifted with the knowledge when she entered this world twenty-six years ago.''

She paused, allowing him to grasp and absorb the significance of her disclosure, then abruptly started to pace the room.

"From the moment she was born, she was different, and my parents realized this early because Caroline was very advanced for her age in everything she did. She walked at seven months, talked intelligibly at ten, and began speaking in short sentences when she was little more than a year old." She flicked her wrist. "Some babies learn faster than others, so naturally my mother and father tried to brush these things aside as simple peculiarities. But when Caroline started to demonstrate her unusual ability with numbers, they found they could no longer do so, because it was slowly becoming apparent that their middle daughter wasn't just advanced, she was extraordinarily gifted.

"She could count to twenty on her first birthday, to a hundred at eighteen months. She started adding objects around her before she was two, saying very odd things like, 'Mary Anne got fourteen blueberries, and I only got twelve,' or 'There are nineteen cows in that pasture, and six of them are very fat.'" Jane grinned. "On Caroline's second birthday, my mother placed a pile of pebbles in front of her, and with one look Caroline told her precisely that there were sixty-seven of them. After counting them herself, my mother nearly fainted."

She stopped pacing and stared at the polished marble floor.

"Caroline began to read, without any help or tutoring, when she was three, and not simple nursery rhymes, mind you. She began reading books, Weymerth. You cannot imagine how baffled my mother and father were to see their little girl no more than a toddler, absorbed in the works of Dryden, Chaucer, Shakespeare, and perhaps not grasping the adult concepts, but reading the words and understanding the stories nonetheless."

Jane raised her head and turned to him. His face told her nothing, but his eyes, so expressive and intense, showed intrigue, admiration, and amazement. It was just as she thought. He didn't know any of this.

She continued fastidiously. "When Caroline was seven, she began working in the garden, and it immediately grabbed her attention. I think my mother purposely turned her in that direction because nobody in our family really knew how to relate to her. Suddenly she was not only planting, but growing things that shouldn't grow in our soil, planting flowers just to see if they would bloom at the wrong time of year, which, I might add, some of them did."

She shook her head, walked again to her chair, and leaned over the back of it, turning her face to the fire in tender remembrance.

"I vividly recall the day she began breeding. She was nine years old, Weymerth." She tossed him a quick glance, but he just watched her, so she carried on. "Caroline decided to cross a white rose with a deep red, all on her own, without one shred of information on how to go about doing such a thing. They bloomed in the dead of summer, and I will never forget the look of pride and absolute joy she wore on her face the moment she walked into the garden to find blended, healthy pink roses. She, in her words, had found her destiny, and her life would be spent breeding flowers."

Jane quieted for a moment and walked around her chair to sit again. She regarded the earl as he sat four feet across from her, taking note of his large stature, his chiseled facial features, and vibrant, attentive hazel eyes. Caroline was indeed fortunate, for this man was not only exceptionally attractive, but he also listened with interest when a woman had something to say. Remarkable.

Sighing softly, she creased her brows, concentrating to delve into the heart of the matter. "Two years after her first breeding, when she was nearly twelve, my sister learned of a man called Albert Markham who was attempting to breed a lavender mix from two unique and extremely fragile bushes. I think you know who this man is, so I will not embellish on his behalf."

She dropped her gaze to her lap in reflection. "Caroline became his unknown champion, and at that tender age, she began to study his work enthusiastically and passionately. For years she did nothing but follow what she could of him and his experiments, laboring in the garden and greenhouse from dawn till dusk, breeding roses, varying temperatures as she could, calculating growth patterns and color hues and various soil conditions, and above it all, taking notes on everything she did.''

She raised her lashes to look at her brother-in-law again. ''As a child and then an adolescent, roses were the center of her life, Lord Weymerth, because not only could her unusual talent with flowers be used as a means to achieve personal satisfaction from something she adored doing, but that same talent was also a means to escape from a society that had termed her odd from the moment she left the cradle.''

That confounded him. ''Caroline has never struck me as a woman who would hide from society, Jane. She's unusually clever, perhaps even intimidating to other ladies, but she's also elegant and can handle her own at any social function. I've seen her do it, and she's hardly shy.''

''That's not what I mean,'' Jane replied, shaking her head. ''Of course she knows how to behave as a lady should, but you're simply describing a well-bred, properly raised individual.'' With deep feeling, she leaned toward him and soothed her voice to an impassioned whisper. ''Caroline had no friends, Weymerth, not one. Children thought she was so strange when she would rattle off Shakespearean sonnets from memory at the age of seven and innocently announce things like . . . it would be one hundred and forty-three days until Christmas. Nobody understood her, and children can be very cruel, so in the end, after the tears had dried and she'd accepted the fact that she was different, she retreated to her garden. Caroline hid the hurt of loneliness and bitter rejection the only way she knew how, by absorbing herself in her plants.''

Slowly she sat up. He scrutinized her sharply, his narrowed eyes penetrating hers as if to discover untruths or distortions to her revelations of past events, but in an almost truculent manner, she refused to back down.

Then gradually, with a jagged, deep inhale, clarity seemed to wash through him, and he lowered his gaze to the floor, his features and his formidable posture softening as he leaned back heavily in his chair.

"Why didn't she ever tell me this, Jane?" he asked quietly.

She shrugged. "Frankly, I think it embarrassed her, but probably more than anything she didn't want you to be repulsed by her."

His head shot up. "Repulsed? How could intelligence repulse me?"

"You don't understand," she gingerly returned. "When Caroline met you, she didn't want you so she didn't care. There was no point in telling you anything. After she grew to adore you, she was afraid of losing you. It's as simple as that."

Quickly he stood and walked to the grate, staring down into the flickering flames, his back rigidly set.

She waited, and when it appeared he didn't want to voice his thoughts, she decided to just move on. "When Caroline was sixteen, she began attending Markham's classes at Oxford—"

"Sixteen?" he interjected in disbelief.

Jane smiled. "Yes, sixteen."

"And your father just allowed her to go?"

"My father has been flustered by Caroline since the day she was born. He's never been sure what to do with her, so as she gently persuaded and pushed him, he finally consented, allowing her to attend Oxford University, chaperoned, with the condition that she keep to herself and Markham's classes exclusively."

"And she went for five years," he softly said without turning.

"To my knowledge, she never missed a lecture, although by then I was married and living elsewhere."

Carefully she proceeded. "From a very young age,

Caroline was consumed with her work and then her studies. But over the years, she grew frustrated and discouraged because, I think—and this is my opinion entirely—as she matured she realized she was never going to be treated as a respected, gifted scientist, but as a woman. And as you are aware, in our world those are two distinctly different things.''

Her voice shook with compassion as she continued without pause. ''Not once, in all the years she stood outside the door of Markham's classroom, was she allowed to enter or speak to him. She took no tests, received no degrees of study or recognition of any kind. She was ridiculed by the men in his classes, laughed at, called an innumerable list of names no lady should hear. Some even told her bluntly she was surely headed straight to hell because it was blasphemous to want to be a man. That hurt her very deeply because Caroline has—has *always* had—an intrinsic belief in and love for God.''

The earl turned, stiffly, watching her closely.

She clutched her hands in her lap, sitting primly, staring him dead in the eye. ''But my brilliant sister persevered because breeding flowers was her passion. She took notes, read Markham's published works, and did what she could to emulate his experiments at home. And at last, about a year and a half ago, using only her mind and some of Markham's expertise that she'd noted over the years, Caroline discovered how to create the lavender roses with dark purple tips that had escaped every other noted botanist in the world. In essence, she and Sir Albert had created an extremely unusual and delicate breed before anyone else. With pride and elation, giving some but not all of the details, she wrote Markham and told him, requesting only to be allowed to meet him, work with him, privately if he preferred it, and to get due recognition for the creation.''

''I saw it . . .'' he whispered, frowning.

She blinked. ''You saw it? The rose?''

He nodded negligibly. ''She carried it with her the

afternoon we met." His lips turned up in smile. "I even criticized her for growing a flower so improperly that it came out two different colors of purple."

Jane stared at him, repressing a laugh as she imagined how Caroline must have reacted to such utterly arrogant words spoken in ignorance.

"Well, then," she maintained, "you had much in common with Sir Albert at the time, because instead of getting recognition and praise for doing something incredible in the botanical community, she received a letter from him, crushing her spirit by implying that a man had done her computations, and in the most condescending fashion suggesting she stay at home, raise babies, and grow flowers to impress her husband."

Jane clucked her tongue in disgust. "His response may seem ordinary, even expected, to you, but imagine for a moment how you would feel if you had a brilliant, gifted mind, had studied and worked for years for one purpose that you felt was your reason for living, and then suddenly and quite casually you're struck down by the very same person you admired and praised more than anyone else in the world, simply and only because you were born the wrong sex."

He slowly dropped his gaze to the floor.

Bravely she stood. "You above all people should realize how resilient Caroline is. She knew her experiments would be worth something to someone, but she'd also learned a very difficult lesson. When Markham wanted nothing to do with her, she wrote to Columbia University, only this time she presented herself as a man. Needless to say, she was accepted with open arms, applauded for her work, and practically begged to set sail immediately." She paused, then carefully articulated, "But she still had a huge complication standing in front of the only thing she'd wanted for nearly fifteen years."

"Your father," he quietly acknowledged.

"My father."

Folding her arms over her chest, she began to move toward him, dropping her voice to a fierce plea. "If there is one thing you need to realize, Lord Weymerth, it's that she never intended to hurt you. My father loves Caroline, but he's also an English baron who had a spinster daughter to protect and an impeccable reputation to uphold. There could have been significant disgrace to his good name if society learned that this same spinster daughter had sailed to America, all alone, with the intention of studying a man's science at a foreign university. Caroline knew this. And what would happen to his reputation if the American university turned her away after discovering her sex and she had to return home? Speculation about her conduct, even her virtue, could run wild among the *ton*. At least an annulment would be looked upon mildly in comparison, probably forgotten eventually in society at large. Neither you nor my father would be blamed for her brazen behavior. He found her a respectable husband in you; you had private reasons for annulling the marriage. The only reputation likely to be scarred would be hers, and that really didn't concern her.''

''But she never considered how I would feel,'' he said almost angrily, ''how I would react to her desire to leave.''

Jane snickered softly. ''You came along and provided her with the tremendous and timely opportunity of freeing my father's grasp without scandal. She never considered that any of her thoughts and plans would concern, much less hurt you. You were just another gentlemen, and not one gentleman in twenty-five years had ever paid her the least bit of attention. She was certain you'd allow her to do as she pleased, and would probably be overjoyed when she finally discussed an annulment—''

''If that's what she wanted from the beginning, then I don't understand why she never asked for one,'' he rebutted quickly, indignantly. ''I would have at least listened to her needs.''

Jane shook her head. ''Truthfully, Lord Weymerth, from what I know of you, you would no more annul your marriage than divorce your wife. You're far too loyal to her and the vows you spoke to ever consider it, and I think, after you were married, Caroline suspected this as well.''

She hesitated, then moved even closer to him. ''But the main reason she didn't bring the subject to your attention was because she found herself thoroughly confused by your attraction to each other. From the beginning of your marriage, she was drawn to you, growing to care very deeply for you as the days went by, and you, in return, seemed to want her as a woman, something I'm sure she found positively baffling. No man had ever desired her, so why would you? She was a spinster, she was unusual, she was old and unattractive—''

''I thought she was beautiful,'' he whispered.

His soft admission made her smile. ''She is beautiful, but she's as unique as her lavender rose. You love her inside, for who she is, and that is the only reason I'm here right now instead of helping her pack her bags for her trip to New York.''

She stood directly in front of him, two feet away, her side to the fire burning in the grate at her feet.

''I told you I came for two reasons, Lord Weymerth. One was to explain about my sister, the other is to tell you this.'' She calmly waited until he looked up to give her his full attention.

''Caroline is enormously determined, and for nearly all of her life she has dreamed of nothing but becoming a renowned botanist. She *never* would have gone to your bed if that wasn't precisely what she wanted, because when she became your wife physically, she was fully cognizant of the fact that she was ending that dream.''

He stared at her strangely, probably shocked by words from her that gently bred ladies did not utter to men they hardly knew, regardless of their relation. She, however, was sick to death of such conventions. Adult, married people had sex, and they all knew it. One should be able to discuss it without disclosing intimate details.

"Since you are not the type of man to force your wife," she boldly continued without the slightest trace of embarrassment, "my personal belief is that she became your wife the night of your dinner party nearly three months ago. Caroline hasn't told me this, but I witnessed for myself the adoration on your face and the look in your eyes, since, I might add, you couldn't take them off her for nearly four hours. Of course this is only conjecture, but it also coincides with another matter, which I will explain momentarily." She stopped, thinking, then added, "I realize this is none of my business, but I do have a point."

"I can't imagine that you wouldn't," he fairly drawled, suddenly amused.

She eyed him candidly. "My sister needs you and wants to be with you, but she is too proud ever to return here on her own after the insensitive way you tossed her out."

His eyes flashed in irritation, but she continued tenaciously. "I'm absolutely positive she will leave for America on Friday. Her intentions are clear, and she's made her decision. What you don't know is this, however. When she leaves for Columbia University she will leave with nothing. She has almost nothing in the way of notes for breeding her fragile roses, no complete records of her computations, and above it all, no proof whatsoever that she was the scientist to create them because"—she took a deep breath—"she sent everything she had to Oxford University last November."

Jane watched him closely. For a second he appeared confused; then, slowly, as the meaning of his wife's actions gradually sank in, the blood drained from his face, and he lowered his eyes to stare blankly at the floor.

"Whatever happened between you the night of your dinner party changed her forever," she cautiously, quietly confided. "The following day, she bundled years of paperwork together, keeping only the briefest notes so she would be able to breed the roses at Miramont for her personal gratification, then sent everything to Albert

Markham. Even after his rude treatment of her and her acceptance to a foreign university, she sent them to the man she's admired more than anyone in her life, because he is her mentor, he is English, and she wanted him and England to receive the praise for creating them.''

Her eyes never left his face as his expression quickly moved from shock to pride to sadness. That satisfied her as she had never felt before.

"Not only did she do this for you, Lord Weymerth," she added huskily, profoundly, "but I know you're aware of the fact that roses are named."

He looked back into her eyes.

"Caroline emphasized in the letter she sent with her notes to Sir Albert that by generously giving him the rose, the only thing she wanted in return was to have it named *Rosalyn*."

He stared at her starkly, unblinking, and at first, unfazed. Then, as her fierce, whispered words hit the target, intense pain sliced through his eyes, and he lowered them to the fire once more, slowly turning his body to fully face the hearth. He tightened his jaw forcibly, quite obviously shaken and deeply moved, blinking hard and quickly several times to contain the powerful emotions seizing him.

Jane refused to retreat or look away as she listened to his harsh, fast breathing over the pounding of her heart. Never in her life had she wanted to stress a point as she did now.

"I know about your mother, Weymerth," she gravely, cautiously revealed. "I know everything."

It took him a minute to fully grasp all she was implying, and then she knew he understood because his entire body stilled before her.

"Does Caroline?" he returned in a deep, throaty rasp.

She hugged herself tightly for confidence. "No, and I will never tell her. Not only would Caroline be as shocked as I was to learn the truth, but as things stand now, that truth would destroy her." Almost inaudibly, she bravely admonished, "Taking secrets to the marriage bed can have devastating consequences, Lord Weymerth. You know this now. But I think, so far, your lie has been the most grievous one of all.''

She waited for a response, but he said nothing, did nothing. He just stared into the glowing flames, as if mesmerized by the flickering patterns of congealing blue and yellow light and the comforts of their enveloping warmth. He'd heard her, understood the implications in her words, but except for a hard swallow and shallow breathing, he appeared otherwise unchanged by what she'd said.

So finally, decisively, she stepped away and walked back to the chair to retrieve her gloves. She'd done everything in her power, and the man couldn't be forced to surrender to a wife he felt had betrayed him, regardless of how logically misguided that feeling was. It was no longer in her control. His future with Caroline was now in his hands.

''You have three days,'' she gently warned. ''If you want her back, I think you know what you're going to have to do.'' She waited. Then without witnessing so much as a word in reply or a turn of his head, she dropped her chin in a gesture of defeat and moved silently to the door.

''Thank you for your time. I'll show myself out.''

With that final, gracious statement, he relented. Through the stilted silence she distinctly heard the faintest curse.

Sharply she turned at his muffled words, and just as quickly his demeanor changed completely. He stood upright, posture stiff and formal, hands clasped behind him, never looking away from the fire.

Quietly he said, ''I'd appreciate your help, Jane.''

Never had five words spoken so smoothly hit her so thoroughly with a rush of relief.

''What can I do?''

''I'll need tomorrow,'' he softly, thoughtfully replied, ''but can you get her to the greenhouse alone on Thursday?''

She grasped her gloves tightly and bit her lip to keep from smiling. She understood his intentions. "What time?"

"Three?"

"Most certainly." She paused, unsure. "Shall I tell her anything?"

"Tell her nothing," he grumbled quickly. Then he softened and looked to the floor. "Tell her whatever you must to get her there, but nothing else."

She could no longer help herself as her face broke out into a broad grin of raw pleasure. "I'll have Caroline at the greenhouse at three on Thursday."

He exhaled loudly, then reached up with both hands to roughly rake his fingers through his hair. "Since I've been married to your sister, I've learned two things." He turned to face her. "The first is never to underestimate the cleverness of any of Baron Sytheford's daughters."

"And the second?" she prodded, eyes twinkling.

He snorted and shook his head, one corner of his mouth turned up in light amusement. "That females, not the meek, shall inherit the earth. I've never been more certain of anything."

She laughed and nodded. "Good day to you, Lord Weymerth."

"Good day, madam."

Twenty-three

Cursing was not in her nature, and neither were such descriptive words part of her standard vocabulary. But of late, Caroline found herself contemplating a variety of fitting, colorful expressions she could use to describe her arrogant ass of a husband.

The afternoon had been cool and overcast, though not unpleasant for February. But during the last hour the sky had darkened to a dull, smoky gray, and the air had become almost unnaturally still.

The calm before the storm.

Caroline refused to go into the house, but traversing the grounds around the south wall was necessary to reach the greenhouse. With dignity, and wishing to God she could just become invisible for an hour, she gave her hand to one of her footmen, who didn't appear to even recognize her, stepped from the coach, and began her mile-long trek through the woods.

Caroline suspected that her husband had learned she was still in England from one of her sisters, but it didn't really matter, and she would probably never know for sure. What mattered was that, according to Jane, Brent was in London for the day, and in his absence he'd requested she return to retrieve old paperwork the idiot man had found in the greenhouse and wouldn't even bother sending her. Evidently time had not softened his heart.

Choking down the first sting of tears she'd felt in weeks, she dropped her chin and strode purposefully to the forest.

No longer could she allow herself to feel sorrow or anger. She needed to keep her spirits high, stay strong, as she was pregnant with his child and leaving tomorrow to another part of the world.

Thank God pregnancy made her irritable instead of sorrowful.

Already she loved her baby, and that surprised her a little. She'd never really wanted children, but now, with this one growing inside of her, a creation from her own heart, just the thought of Brent's ridiculous demands made her fume. Only God himself would be able to tear this child from her arms after his birth. Her estranged husband would have to slit her throat if he wanted his son without her involvement in his life, and sadly, knowing how the man felt about her now, she was almost afraid he'd consider it.

It annoyed her, too, that at the rate she was growing, she'd look like a whale in six months' time. Naturally being a small woman didn't help to hide her belly, but she was already showing, and she couldn't, even if she'd conceived on her wedding night, be more than thirteen weeks along, which meant she was probably carrying a litter.

That would serve the arrogant idiot right. Let him have a male puppy for an heir. Then maybe the great Earl of Weymerth would grace her with sole guardianship after the thing had the audacity to piddle on his shoes.

Nearly giggling from the thought, she spied the greenhouse through the trees. Sighing, she walked to the door, opening it silently. Although it wasn't quite three, it was fairly dark inside because of the gray afternoon, and she gave her eyes several seconds to adjust, inhaling deeply the fragrance of live green plants and flowers. Nothing remained of the French killer except the vivid memory of that horrifying day, and that would eventually fade to a distant recollection. Even now, alone in the dimness, she felt no lingering fear. Her greenhouse was her haven.

The first thing she noticed was how nothing had changed. Someone had been watering her plants while she'd been away, and that someone had to be her husband, because he now stood in the far corner, his back to her, his body outlined in shadows.

She stifled a gasp as her heart began pounding fast and hard with uncertainty.

"I—I thought you'd be gone," she blurted shakily, dryly, hoping she sounded less startled than she was.

Abruptly he turned. "Gone? I've only just arrived, Lady Caroline, and I'm transfixed already by your talent. Your woodbines and periwinkles are growing quite well with the density of soil you've chosen." He creased his dark brows, reaching over the back of the table to lightly touch a leaf. "And are you attempting to cross the runners here? Difficult job, really. These scarlets are remarkably healthy for this temperature."

Suddenly she was awash with numbness. She could positively feel her cheeks pale as she became paralyzed with shock and unable to breathe.

"I'd very much like to see your notes on your hydrangea variations as well. These don't appear to be at all sterile," he pleasantly added, apparently unconcerned with her silence and oblivious to her astonishment. He looked back to her face then, his eyes crinkling in a smile. "I was looking for a light to better view your work when you walked in. So far, I'm quite impressed. You evidently have as great an aptitude for growing vines as you do for breeding roses."

At that point she had to grab the desk to her left to keep from falling. She hadn't seen him in nearly five years, had never been this close to the man. But in the gray stillness of late afternoon, *in her greenhouse,* she stood ten yards away from Sir Albert Markham.

The room brightened as he lit one of the small lamps sitting atop the back table.

"Much better," he said agreeably. "Now let's have a look."

He turned to face her again, and immediately she recognized her initial mistake. From the back he was her husband—tall, formidable, same coloring save for his hair, which was slightly darker. But from the front, he was obviously years older and didn't resemble Brent as much as . . .

Revelation struck her like a searing streak of lightning. Albert Markham's features were masculine, but his face was a mirror image of her daughter's.

Caroline started shaking.

He looked like Rosalyn.

"Lady Caroline?"

He looked *exactly* like Rosalyn.

Suddenly, and almost too late, she realized she was going to faint. As quickly as she reached for the desk to catch herself before her knees buckled, the man was beside her.

"Good heavens, dear lady, you've gone gray," he expressed with immediate concern, placing his arm around her waist without second thought and helping her to one of the benches.

"I—I'm carrying," she mumbled, gulping for air, slowly lowering her body to the hard wooden surface.

His voice and alert expression quickly conveyed surprise. "Oh, my. Brent didn't inform me of that good news." He sat heavily beside her. "Well, just . . . relax. Catch your breath."

She didn't want to relax—she wanted to drown herself in a lake. Sir Albert was in her greenhouse, sitting next to her, holding her hand in a fatherly gesture, *speaking* to her, and in all the years she'd dreamed of having an intellectual conversation with this one man, the first words out of her mouth did nothing but remind him she was female.

She was so incredulous she'd been slapped with stupidity.

"I apologize, sir," she whispered, trying to regain some control, some dignity.

"Don't apologize to me, my dear," he reprimanded good-naturedly, patting her hand. "My nephew said you'd be surprised, and with that he should have informed me of your delicate condition."

"He doesn't—" She caught herself, her eyes shooting back to his face.

My nephew said you'd be surprised . . .

And then she knew. His eyes—expressive, dark, hazel—piercing hers with clarity and intelligence. Rosalyn's eyes. Brent's eyes . . .

"The Lady Maude was your sister," she whispered.

He seemed to grasp that she was concluding this now, for he blinked once then leaned back to eye her speculatively. "Brent didn't tell you about us, about Maude and me."

Caroline's lips thinned, her face flushed. "My husband, sir, has more secrets in his tiny, insignificant mind than the entire British War Department has had on file since its inception." She huffed with pure, disgusted outrage, lowering her gaze to the floor to murmur, "I'll kill him."

Sir Albert laughed, deeply and wholeheartedly, squeezing her hand affectionately.

"Don't be so hard on him, Lady Caroline. He's had a rather difficult life, and you must be the light of it or I wouldn't be here at all."

That both confused and warmed her. As she grew more composed and sure of herself in this great man's presence, the uncanny coincidences began to explode in her mind, and within seconds she was filled with questions. Before she could open her mouth to begin the inquisition, he started to answer them for her.

"This was my greenhouse," he disclosed softly, glancing around in remembrance.

That one fairly knocked the wind out of her. She'd

been working in Albert Markham's greenhouse for months without that knowledge. Brent wouldn't just die at her hands, he would die painfully.

"I haven't been inside it for nearly thirty years, though," he continued, releasing her hand and sitting back casually, "not since my falling out with Maude."

"I—Forgive me, sir." She turned her body to face him fully. "I'm not sure I understand any of this, why you're here, why I've been sent here today, why my husband never mentioned you were his uncle." She looked him squarely in the eye. "Truthfully, I'm quite stunned."

"You're stunned?" he exclaimed, smiling. "I was shocked to see Brent walk into my office at Oxford yesterday to speak to me for only the second time in as many decades. And imagine my amazement when he informed me his wife was the woman who had sent me years of extensive studies on the very same rose I've pulled my hair out trying to create."

"But I sent you a letter and copies of computations and growth conditions more than a year ago, and you weren't interested in my findings," she quickly rebutted.

He sighed loudly and waved his palm in annoyance. "Brent explained as much. I'm sorry, Lady Caroline, but my secretary answers all my correspondence through the university. He's an annoying individual but efficient, so I keep him in my employ. Unfortunately, because of his efficiency, I never received your first letter and I certainly never had the opportunity to look over your findings. If I had, I would have been intrigued and more than eager to discuss them."

"I see . . ." she murmured, dejected.

His voice and expression softened. "I know about your work, Lady Caroline, and quite frankly, I find it exceptional. You've made some remarkable discoveries, and your talent and knowledge are unsurpassed, from what I've observed today. Your garden is healthy and managed for this time of year, your breeding techniques are logical and convincing, and your crossings, some standard, some unusual, are challenging as well as productive. I also found myself utterly overwhelmed by the conclusive compilation of notes you sent last November. I've been a tutor for more than twenty years and never have I known a student more organized and, as it appears, more focused than you. I say this not because you are a woman or my nephew's wife, but because you are probably the most gifted botanist I've come across in years.''

Caroline beamed, dazed and, as the sincerity of his words seeped in, thoroughly touched. Clutching the folds of her pelisse in her hands, she attempted to remain composed. Sir Albert Markham was here, sitting beside her and telling her he thought she was gifted. This chance meeting was turning out to be more splendid and exciting than any botanical discovery. If she never worked as a scientist another day in her life, she would know that she had done something unique, respected among her peers, that her accomplishments were credible. *Please, God,* she prayed silently, *please don't let me start crying.*

''Did my husband tell you I've been studying your work for years?''

He smiled again, leaning toward her. ''Your husband is so proud of you I was certain he was nothing but a lovesick puppy embellishing fair success,'' he mischievously confided. ''That was, of course, until I realized he married the same woman who had sent me a bundle of notes she'd gathered regarding the now-famous lavender rose. The same woman who was one of the few to stand outside my classroom and listen to me lecture. Had I been allowed any liberties, madam, I would have gladly invited you and the other interested ladies to join us for our discussions inside the classroom, but alas, in our culture this is not permitted, and I must adhere to university rules.''

She blinked. ''You would have done that?''

He chuckled. ''My sister, if nothing else, forced me to look at life and women differently in my early years, but I should probably start at the beginning. If Brent hasn't told you anything, you're probably puzzled.''

"Puzzled doesn't begin to describe how I'm feeling at the moment," she disclosed. "Flabbergasted would be more accurate.''

He laughed again softly and leaned forward, elbows on knees, staring once again toward the other side of the room. So like her husband in stance, bearing, voice, and briefly she wondered why she had never recognized the similarities. Probably because she'd never been this close to him, hadn't seen him in years, but more likely, because it was all so coincidental. Too coincidental.

"My sister was only eleven months younger than I," he began quietly, "but much more aggressive, more mischievous as a child. She always felt cheated, threatened by me, partly because we were so close in age, but mostly because we were different sexes and treated as such. From the time I can remember, Maude took this personally, feeling neglected by our parents, believing thoroughly that I received more love from them, more . . . liberties and respect. With each passing year, she grew more bitter and resentful of her sex, her station, and of me.''

Slowly he stood and walked toward the oblong tables.

"I became interested in plants at a very early age. I was fascinated, not by the flowers and their appearance, but by how they grew, their varied patterns, the intricacies of their individual and unique structures. I found myself more engrossed in them as the years went by, and finally, around the time of my fifteenth birthday, I knew I wanted to make botany my lifelong work." He turned to her, resting his hip on the vines spilling over the thick slab of wood.

"What started all of this," he softly continued, gesturing to the room, "was Maude's insatiable desire to have what I had. She wanted to be a botanist because I wanted to be a botanist, and felt she'd make a better one than I if only given the opportunity to prove herself. But Maude would never be able to do such a thing because she was disorganized, acutely self-centered, and undisciplined to a fault.

"She was intelligent, but when it came to science, she was the kind of person who wanted answers given to her instead of working them out for herself. She had no original ideas, despised being told that she, God forbid, was wrong about anything, and had no patience when it came to learning something new. You and I both know that when it comes to botany, patience is not a virtue, it is a necessity. Absolutely essential to success."

Rain began to sprinkle atop the glass, creating a hollow, splattering noise, quenching the peacefulness inside.

Gently Caroline shook her head. "I don't understand how someone who wants something so badly wouldn't work for it. Even if I had no talent whatsoever, I'd find myself in my greenhouse every day because I love it."

Markham nodded and strode toward her, sitting once more on the bench. "Exactly, and that's why I worked at it myself. You were born with a gift, Lady Caroline, and the love of the challenge and the science. I wasn't born with the gift, but I, too, loved the challenge and the science. The only difference between you and me is that I must work harder at what comes naturally to you. This puts me at a slight disadvantage, but because I adore the work, I work harder for similar results. With all things in life, we each must accept and then deal with our own limitations."

He scoffed. "But my sister had neither the gift nor the desire to work. She fell into a fierce competition with me, only to lose because she never loved botany. She was not a scientist, was never born to be a scientist, but absurdly enough, she wanted to be a scientist because that was what I wanted for myself."

Caroline knew that the conflicts between siblings could be great. Indeed, she'd felt them herself over the years, especially with Mary Anne because of her gregarious nature, her exceptional beauty. But over time Caroline had grown away from the jealousies by finding the strengths in herself. Sadly, it appeared Lady Maude was never able to find herself because she was, ironically enough, so self-absorbed. Her jealousies became her enemy, the center of her hatred, only because she was too selfish to take an honest look at the qualities she alone possessed.

"But more than all of her problems combined," Markham stressed almost passionately, snapping her out of her contemplative thoughts by taking her hand once more, "my sister Maude despised the knowledge that she had no intrinsic *gift*. She had a green thumb, could make plants grow and gardens bloom when she took the time, but that was the extent of her ability, and it never came easily to her. Maude wanted everything in life to be easy."

"But inbred talents cannot be measured, Sir Albert," she reasoned quietly. "Many noted botanists sometimes have trouble growing flowers—"

"Exactly my point, dear lady," he cut in. "I am one of those noted botanists, and my reputation, as humbling as the thought is, exists worldwide. But Maude hated the fact that botany didn't come naturally to her, and she simply would not discipline herself enough to put forth the effort to learn and study as I did. She seethed with the knowledge that her achievements were strictly up to her and no one else, and she made me the cause of what eventually became her failures. She blamed me."

"As well as her children," Caroline said dejectedly.

"As well as her children," he softly concurred. "It's always easier to take out one's anger by abusing those who are small, dependent, and under one's complete control."

Caroline had no idea what to say to that sad truth.

Markham sighed and released her hand. "In any case, I left her and Miramont—which was rightfully mine— nearly thirty-five years ago because I could no longer stand her resentfulness. Maude was a manipulator, and if she was gifted with anything it was the ability to make a person feel guilt. My parents felt guilty, and that's why they had this greenhouse constructed for her. I was the one to use it, though, and she made me feel guilty because I did so. I was the botanist, but my father gave Maude the greenhouse.''

He snorted sarcastically, reminding her so quickly of her husband that she had trouble containing her sudden urge to laugh.

"Eventually," he continued, "realizing that my interests were not with marriage and family, but with teaching, I decided I didn't want the estate, this greenhouse, or anything else that had to do with a sister who had come to despise me. So, without regrets, I gave everything to her and her husband, the former Earl of Weymerth. He hadn't much in the way of property when they married thirty-six years ago, and truthfully, I think he suspected he'd one day inherit Miramont, since my life had moved in an entirely different direction by then. I also believe," he added simply, "it's the reason he wanted Maude for a wife. That, and the fact that she was physically beautiful and socially polished."

"And then you began tutoring at Oxford," Caroline mumbled.

"I didn't tutor at first," he corrected easily. "I studied on the Continent for a while, first in Paris, then Germany and Italy, eventually working my way to Northern Africa, where I stayed for three years before coming back to England. But I studied, Lady Caroline, and I worked hard. In 1799, I was knighted by King George for my accomplishments, having impressed those in the world-wide botanical community as well as His Majesty with my detailed analysis of breeding techniques—roses primarily—and my extensive fifteen-year study of—"

"Sterile vines . . ." she finished in a whisper, looking to the floor as she slowly stood. "I've also read most of your published works, sir, and have followed your studies very closely. I adore breeding roses because the flowers are so delicate and the colors so variable and lovely, but like you, I find great challenge in vines."

"They can be uniquely difficult," he acknowledged.

"Indeed they can," she agreed, walking to the table to gaze down at the healthy, plush hydrangea. "I seem to be drawn to all things difficult, which makes me again wonder exactly why you're here, Sir Albert." Quickly she hugged her belly over her pelisse and turned to face him. "I still don't understand what this has to do with my husband."

He regarded her closely for a long moment, then rubbed his jaw with his palm. "I think I'll just let him explain everything in detail. He's here, by the way, at the house."

Caroline felt her pulse escalate, her face flush. "Brent is here? At Miramont?"

He grinned devilishly. "I told him I'd send you along at my leisure, and I'm certain he's wearing a path in the rug just worrying about it. But again, don't be too hard on him. He's been through some rough times, and coming to me yesterday, inviting me back to my greenhouse, took courage. He and his sister are my only living relations, and I hear from Charlotte only once or twice a year."

She stared at him, her mind racing. Brent wanted her to come home, and going to Sir Albert, asking him to meet her, was his way of breaking the ice. And it was working, she had to admit, irritated at the weakness in herself. Her heart was melting.

"So why hasn't he spoken to you all these years?" Sarcastically she added, "I mean, my husband adores tossing people from his life; it nourishes his ego. But why you? Why for so long?"

Markham breathed deeply and became serious again. "Well, he resented me because he felt I was the cause of his mother's abhorrence of him. He didn't really toss me from his life, though, or pretend I didn't exist. He just didn't have any reason to contact me through the years—"

"But you're his uncle," she cut in, exasperated.

He nodded. "Yes, but I made him uncomfortable. I

reminded him of why his mother detested men, including him. You see, Maude wanted to be a botanist. I wouldn't take her on as a student or colleague because of her lack of talent, self-discipline, and desire for hard work. As a result, she became insanely jealous of my success. Brent understood this, especially as he matured and realized Maude was nothing but a selfish, conniving woman who used and manipulated people any way she could. But she was also his mother, and he's always felt, perhaps irrationally, that if I hadn't denied her what she believed was her right as my sister, she would have raised him with a warmer heart.''

He dropped his voice to a mere whisper above the sound of pelting rain against glass. ''Brent has always felt that Maude's love for botany was the reason she had no love for him, which would be natural for him to believe as a child because she all but told him as much. But what he's discovered by being married to you, Lady Caroline, is that his mother never loved botany. She never cared about working for anything, whether it was growing or breeding plants, maintaining a greenhouse, or raising children with love and respect, because she never loved anyone or anything but herself.''

Caroline considered his words carefully, thoughtfully, then felt her blood turn to ice. Brent had kept his mother's obsession and his parentage a secret from her, had never told her Albert Markham was his uncle, because he feared the science meant more to her than he did. Just as he'd always felt it did to his mother. Suddenly the answers she'd been looking for during the last few months were before her.

''I finally understand,'' she whispered, shaken with chilling realization. ''He didn't tell me you were his uncle . . .''

''Because, Lady Caroline, I believe he was dreadfully afraid he'd lose you to the science if he did. Discovering your intentions to study in America only inflamed that fear, as well as the resentment he's harbored toward botany itself for years. Asking you to leave the way he did was his way of shielding a very real and deep-seated pain of rejection.''

"If he had only allowed me to explain the situation, it would never have come to this," she maintained through a surge of aggravation. "And if you must know, Sir Albert, he didn't politely ask me to leave, he practically threw me out of the house on my tender behind."

He chuckled softly and slowly stood. "Well, as I said before, I think I'll let your husband explain his actions in detail, and I'm sure you're as anxious to hear them as he is to see you. In the meantime, if we're going to be working together, I would very much appreciate it if you would call me Uncle Albert."

She blinked quickly, her stomach churning, quite certain she hadn't heard him correctly. "Pardon me?"

He looked at her strangely. "Would you prefer to work separately, Lady Caroline, or are you just uncomfortable addressing each other informally?"

She swallowed, astonished. "You want to work with me?"

"Naturally," he replied, surprised. "You're industrious, organized, talented. I'd be stupid to forgo such an opportunity, and just between us, Lady Caroline, I wouldn't feel at all honorable taking full credit for creating the lavender rose."

He looked back at the ground, thinking, slowly walking toward her.

"My original idea was perhaps to have you start with the *Rosalyns*." Glancing up sharply, he added, "Naming them after my grandniece was a marvelous suggestion, by the way. A lovely name for a rose. I also have a series of experiments I'd like you to start with poisonous berries—English ivy, holly, and bittersweet primarily, as well as a crossing between two North African creepers. I've been meaning to work on these for months, but my time tends to get the best of me. If you're concerned about appearances or the birth of your child, don't be. You have the room in this greenhouse and you can work here at your discretion. I can visit once a month or so to compare notes and check your progress against mine, and after your baby is born, we can work out a schedule suited to you and your needs. I have a private greenhouse of my own not more than a three-hour ride from here, so perhaps we can split the time.''

He stopped directly in front of her and grasped his elbows with his palms. ''Unfortunately I won't be able to pay you for your labor or offer you a degree of study, and for that I'm truly sorry. But it's a prime opportunity for you to learn and associate with some of the finest botanists in England. I also promise that, to the best of my ability, you'll receive justified recognition for your work.''

He smiled down at her stunned face. ''Please say yes, Lady Caroline. You'd make an excellent colleague, and I desperately need the help from someone more interested in botany than in getting knighted for himself.''

Never in her life had she felt more honored. Or thrilled. And if she weren't so filled with disbelief at this odd turn of events, she'd certainly break down into a gushing river of joyful tears. The greatest dream she had ever envisioned was becoming a reality, given her by this one intelligent, celebrated botanist standing directly in front of her, treating her not as a woman, but as an equal. The most magnificent moment of her life as a scientist was happening now, and she would relish this memory forever.

Smiling with elation and choking down the quake of emotion in her voice, she held out her hand. ''I'd be delighted to work for you, sir. And please, call me Caroline.''

''Uncle Albert, remember?'' he corrected, smiling in return and taking her hand. He held it firmly for a moment, then patted her knuckles. ''Now, I think it's time for you to go and have a little chat with your husband. He was certainly a fool to toss out such a charming lady on her tender behind, and I hope you give him a devil of a time for it.'' He leaned toward her and grinned impishly. ''But please don't kill him.''

She laughed. "I'll try to restrain myself."

He turned and glanced around the room. "And while you're restraining yourself from murder, I think I'll look around here, take some notes of my own, then leave a list on your desk of things I'd like you to start working on. I'll return within a fortnight, and we can discuss them at length. Fair enough?"

She wanted to cry. "Thank you, Uncle Albert."

He smiled again, nodding toward the door. "The rain's letting up."

As unsure as she was of the prospect of facing her husband, she moved quickly to the entrance, took one look back for confidence, then raised the hood of her pelisse and strode out of the greenhouse.

Twenty-four

Perhaps because it was still sprinkling, perhaps only by chance, she kept her head down. Suddenly, not twenty feet from the door of the greenhouse, lying across the dirt path, she found the first rose.

It startled her, really, to see the striking peach flower on the brown forest floor, but she reached for it, intrigued, shaking it lightly to release the droplets of water from the bright, healthy petals. Before she considered her reasons for finding it there, she came upon another, exactly like the first, and then another, and another.

Her heart began to pound. The closer she moved to the house, the more anxious she became, and the more beautiful, long-stemmed peach roses she grasped tightly in her hand.

They were from him, she knew, and by the time she reached the back door of the house, she could hardly breathe from the desire to see him, from uncertainty at doing so after weeks of separation, and from hope. She wanted to be furious with him, but this action of his was, in itself, intended to soften the blow. It was working, too, for her heart was filled with nothing but tenderness, as her hands were filled with twenty-three roses, all perfect, all free of thorns, all peach.

Caroline drew a long breath, then stepped inside the kitchen. It was cold, clean, and completely empty save for the tiny trail on the dark, polished floor.

Peach rose petals.

Slowly she began to follow it, immediately warmed by the comforts of her home and the sweet scent of flowers. Led by her legs and heart instead of her mind, she finally found herself standing in front of her bedroom door, where the trail of rose petals seemed to end.

She grasped the handle and pushed it open.

Her room looked exactly the same. The bed was perfectly made, the furniture dusted and polished. The only discernable difference were the three plush, white rugs covering the floor where there had been none before. Something Brent had thought of while she'd been away.

The trail of petals lay in a straight line to the connecting door. Caroline stared at it for a long moment, stalling. Then, with resolution and a quick glance down her body to be certain her baby was hidden in the folds of her large pelisse, she held her chin high once more and swiftly walked to the door. With roses clutched in the left, she reached out with her trembling right hand, grasped the knob firmly, and opened the door.

She saw her husband first, sitting on the windowsill to her left, but her view of him was quickly distorted by the glorious vision surrounding him.

He'd filled the room with roses—pink, yellow, white, plum, burgundy, and more peach than she could count. There numbered twenty-five vases, all overflowing, sitting along the mantel, the two sills, the mahogany chest of drawers, on tables beside the settee, on both sides and at the foot of the bed. It even amused her to note how he'd drawn back the quilt and had covered the sheet with rose petals as well.

Rather presumptuous but, to his credit, horribly romantic.

From the corner of her eye, she saw him rise, and

with that she drew the courage to look at his face, masking her expression, attempting to keep her hands from shaking as she clutched the roses she held with both of them.

He stared at her, and although she couldn't tell at all what he was thinking, he exuded a nervousness she'd never seen in him before. Their eyes melded for several seconds, then she moved her gaze up and down the length of him, taking in his appearance, his strong, powerful physique, noticing how he looked so marvelously handsome in midnight-blue trousers and a white silk shirt pulled tautly across his chest.

And in his hand he held the twenty-fourth peach rose. A perfect two dozen.

She stood facing him, gracefully composed, eyes defiant and piercing his once again with blazing fire.

"I could kill you—"

"I love you, Caroline."

Her face went slack as she stilled completely. She never expected that, at least not right away, and although she'd known how he felt about her for so very long, nothing compared to finally hearing the words.

"I didn't know how much I loved you until you left," he continued huskily, "and I can't honestly tell you when I began to love you, although I think I realized I was going to the first night we had dinner alone together in the kitchen. You told me how my uncle had rejected your work, how you needed a greenhouse, and instead of giving it to you and telling you everything, I practically ripped off your clothes with the most urgent need I've ever felt as a grown man. I was jealous and selfish, and losing myself to you so quickly it scared me."

He inhaled sharply. "But I do know that I loved you so much the night you came to my bed and became my wife. I loved you then and I knew it then, without any doubts, but I was confused and afraid of the feeling, so I couldn't admit it to myself or to you. I've loved you for months, Caroline," he admitted brokenly, "and I'm so sorry I didn't tell you until now."

His voice trailed off, and the room became deathly silent as the rain lightened to a tiny sprinkle against the windows.

Caroline, heart racing and close to tears, refused to move, refused to alter her features the slightest bit for fear of breaking down. He was waiting for her to say she loved him, too, and she would. But he was the one who'd tossed her out on her tender behind, she had to remember, the one who'd kept incredible secrets from her, the one who'd driven a stake through their marriage. And he could just be the one to be unsure for a while.

He took a hesitant step toward her and stopped, looking increasingly unsettled as the silence surrounding them began to boom, thick and intense.

With all the strength she possessed, and utterly amazed that she could actually do it after what he'd just said to her, she turned away from him, closed the door softly behind her, and reached up to lower the hood of her pelisse.

On the nightstand to the right of the bed she noticed an empty vase. Quietly she walked to it, effectively ignoring his stare, and one by one, taking her time, she arranged each rose perfectly. That finished, she turned to him once more, still avoiding his gaze, and pulled her hair from its ribbon, shaking it loose and free of dampness with her hands.

Suddenly he exhaled loudly, irritably, and began tapping the rose against his thigh. "Have you nothing to say, madam?"

Caroline wanted to laugh as she looked into hazel eyes clouded by uncertainty. He was trying to be cross, intimidating, but he was failing horribly because his voice positively shook with confusion and worry.

She smoothed her hair so it draped over her left shoulder, casually dropping her arms to her sides. "Yes, I have something to say."

He waited. "Well?"

Glaring at him, she blurted, "I'll bury you alive if any of these roses came from my garden."

He blinked, then paled. "That's it?"

"For now," she purred.

"What does that mean?" he fairly barked.

She remained calm and self-assured. "I'm not sure what you want to hear from me, Brent. Do you want to hear how upset and lonely I've been for the last ten weeks? Do you want to hear how crushed I felt to be callously evicted from my home by my husband? Do you want to hear how desperately I've craved your arms around me and your lips on mine since the night you so gallantly saved my life from that French monster?

"Do you want to hear how much I've missed you and my daughter, how painful it was to spend Christmas alone without my family, how shocked and angry I am to learn that Albert Markham is my uncle by marriage and that you, my darling, kept that tiny bit of information from me?" Her eyes narrowed, lips thinned. "I am all of those things and more, sir, and yet I believe you want to hear something else."

Brent watched her in a daze, growing more tense and unnerved by the second. She wasn't acting as he'd thought she would, and what did he expect? Did he have the arrogance to assume she'd come running into his arms, forgiving him and begging to come home? If that thought had crossed his mind, it was laced with stupidity. Caroline would never do that. Not, at least, until she'd cut him down to size with her mouth. And did she even love him at all? He'd been so positive of it, but Jane hadn't said anything about her loving him, and there was always the possibility that even if she had, at one point during the last few weeks she'd lost the feeling altogether.

But the past didn't matter. She was here, in their bedroom, and just watching her now only a few feet away, he realized this wasn't the time for a battle of words, it was the time for him to back down and expose himself completely. He'd been unfair to her in so many ways since the day they'd married, and even if she returned to cut a venomous slash through his heart, he had to know the truth.

Perspiration broke out along his neck, and at that moment, as his heart began to beat hard and fast, he knew he'd never felt more frightened in his life.

"I need to hear that you love me, too, Caroline," he confessed in a deep whisper.

For what seemed like hours, she just stared into his eyes, unmoving. Then, sighing faintly, she lowered her lashes and began to unbutton her pelisse.

"I suppose, because you're a man, you've been closed to the love I've felt right from the beginning, pushing it away when it scared you and ignoring it when that suited your purpose. I forgive you for that because you can't help what and who you are, and men generally tend to be less open to love than women, especially when it slaps them in the face and they don't know at all what to do with it."

She shot him a quick glance, then slowly began to walk, staring at the floor. "Unlike you, I know exactly when I started loving you, Brent, and that was the day we married. You didn't know me at all and yet you were curious about my family, concerned about my feelings when I walked into a vacant house with nothing but a few trunks. You had a beautiful room waiting for me, the wife thrust upon you by her scheming father, and when I didn't want you physically, you didn't strike me, or demean me with words, or force yourself on me to take what was yours by law."

He'd expected a simple answer, but in her own sophisticated, intelligent way, she was exposing herself completely as well, telling him everything he should have already known. So like Caroline to notice the good in life, and to cherish the good in him.

She stopped in front of the window to his right, six feet away, facing him with strength and beauty.

"My love began to blossom only days later, when you gave me charge of your finances," she continued evenly. "You had known me for less than a week, whereas my father had known me for twenty-five years—yet you trusted me when he didn't. I think I realized then there was no turning back, because I had been blessed with an unusual, magnificent man.''

Her voice began to quaver, but she didn't move, didn't drop her gaze from his.

''I grew to love you more when I met your illegitimate daughter and realized you had taken this beautiful, deaf little girl into your home, disregarding the social complications and loving her when she would have been a disgrace to any other gentleman.

''I loved you even more deeply the day your sweet daughter began to communicate, because on that glorious afternoon I realized you were falling in love with me—the unattractive spinster you married with few qualities beyond the uncanny ability to grow plants and add numbers quickly.''

She inhaled deeply, hugging herself. ''And just like you, Brent, I knew I loved you absolutely the night you made love to me for the first time. You were gentle and patient, giving and passionate. You made me feel like a beautiful goddess, and I swear to you, sir, nothing had ever made me feel like that before.''

''Caroline . . .'' He took a step toward her and stopped, unsure.

She shook her head, straightening. ''You've had your say, and now it's my turn, Lord Weymerth. Don't even think about coming near me until I'm finished and give you permission to do so.''

The combination of irritation and gentleness in her voice melted him inside. He'd missed her sharp tongue almost as much as he'd missed her sweetness.

''Forgive me, madam,'' he said lightly, amused, ''but waiting to make love to you again is straining my nerves.''

She scoffed but she was quite shaken; he could see it in her expression, in the way she nervously toyed with the buttons on her pelisse.

"How awfully presumptuous of you to think I'd let you."

"You will," he insisted soothingly.

She gaped at him.

"Please continue," he urged. "I'm aching to hear the rest."

"You're as arrogant as usual."

"You missed it, though."

"I absolutely did not," she asserted.

He grinned. "You missed my arrogance almost as much as I missed your impudence, little one."

"That's absurd."

"I love you, Caroline," he softly, quickly replied, catching her off guard with such tenderness. "Move on before I decide I'm finished with this conversation, rip off your clothes, and show you how much."

Her eyes flashed, in annoyance or hunger he couldn't be certain, but she didn't falter. If anything she appeared more determined, more challenging in her stance.

"On the day we married, somewhere deep inside of me I knew I would never leave you," she maintained. "But I disguised and suppressed my feelings from the beginning because I'd wanted something else for so long, and no matter how hard I tried, I couldn't shake the desire I felt to be with you."

She shook her head and lowered her voice to an impassioned plea. "How could I not love a man who charmed me when he'd never been charming to another, who treated me with so much respect when no woman he'd ever known had respected him? How could I not love a man who saved my life so valiantly, who fit me, mind and spirit, as if we were born to be together, who had spent his life in loneliness just as I had, rejected as I had felt, craving to be loved and appreciated as I had always craved those things?"

He didn't utter a sound in response, and with that she averted her gaze and slowly began to remove her pelisse.

"Regarding your accusations the day you tossed me out, Brent, let me clarify it all by saying this."

After casually dropping it on the sill, she boldly looked back into his eyes.

"Since the moment we met, I've admired you, I've desired you, and above it all, I've honored you and will continue to do so for the remainder of my life. I have loved you for two hundred and four days, my beautiful, brave husband, and I swear to you now I will love you forever." Through a thick, sexy whisper, she added, "Is that what you wanted to hear?"

His throat closed tightly, inhibiting his ability to answer, which didn't really matter because he couldn't begin to find words to describe how he felt at that moment. Then he looked down the front of her gown and, through a staggered breath, his expression turned immediately to one of wonder.

"You're carrying my child, Caroline . . ." he said reverently, desperately attempting to control his suddenly failing aplomb.

With a defiant lift of her chin, she reached down and touched her slightly protruding abdomen. "I am carrying your son, my lord, and I know he's a boy because he's huge and he's giving me indigestion even now."

Brent felt the incredible urge to laugh and cry at the same time, but never got the chance to do either because in that instant, as if on cue, the sun broke through the clouds to shine through the window with brilliance, illuminating his wife like a vision.

She was exquisite to look at, surrounded by roses, standing gracefully and reminding him of a rare china doll with her luxuriant, dark hair falling over her shoulder, smooth ivory skin reflecting the rays of sunlight in striking contrast to the deep-purple silk of her gown. And her eyes, so extraordinarily gorgeous, like polished obsidian, starkly expressing the pureness of all that was good. She was stunning and elegant and regal, and more than all of it, she glowed with an inner radiance that took his breath away.

That's when he knew.

He knew why he'd lived through a miserable childhood, why he'd lived through the war, why he'd escaped the trench after living with disease and death for three horrifying days, why he'd been given a sweet, innocent daughter during a time of great tension and loneliness. And he knew finally, with absolute conviction, why such an incredible woman had become his wife.

"I believe in God, Caroline," he said softly.

She regarded him with uncertainty, then hugged herself tightly as she started to tremble.

Smiling, filled with sudden calm, he whispered, "Nothing but God could create something as beautiful as you."

She closed her eyes slowly, serenely, bringing her palm to her mouth as tears began to form on her lashes and roll down her cheeks.

"Caroline?"

As quickly as he reached out with his hand, she opened sparkling eyes to his, took the rose from his fingertips, and walked into his arms.

He pulled her against him forcefully, holding her firmly, feeling each contour of her body molding to his, the warmth of her skin, the steady beating of her heart.

"I'm so sorry I hurt you," he said shakily, burying his face in her hair.

"You should be," she scolded, sniffling.

He held her for a while, content in the peacefulness, the feel of her against him. Finally, bravely, he professed, "You are the greatest thing to happen to my life, Caroline. Please come home to me."

Slowly she lifted her head, placed her hand on his cheek, and looked fiercely into his eyes. "I'm home already."

In a sweeping gesture of truce and forgiveness, she lifted her mouth to meet his, kissing him with deep passion and love, wrapping her arms around his neck, pulling herself into him completely.

"I can feel the baby," he murmured against her mouth.

"You don't feel the baby, you feel my belly."

"You're so big already."

She ran her tongue along his lips, making him groan and come instantly alive with need.

"God, you feel good. You smell like rain and flowers." He gently cupped her breast, forcing a gasp from her when his thumb lightly caressed her nipple through the silk. "I missed you so much, Caroline."

She kissed his chin and jaw in quick feathery touches. "Where is everybody? Where's Rosalyn?"

He ran his fingers along her cleavage with one hand, and with the other he started to gently caress her bottom, pushing her hips against him deliberately. "I made everyone leave until Sunday. The servants are dismissed, and Nedda and Rosalyn are visiting the vicar and his wife for the weekend."

Without looking, she tossed the rose she still held onto the sill beside her pelisse, then quickly reached for the buttons on his shirt, working through them with swift expertise.

"We're alone," she said in a deep, sultry voice.

"For three days," he whispered in her ear. "It's a selfish attempt on my part to . . . seize the moment, indulging in my wife to make up for lost time."

She moved her hips, stroking him just enough for him to know she did it on purpose.

"I'm still furious with you," she murmured, kissing a line down his chest.

"Oh, God, please don't be furious," he choked out quickly. "Every female I know is furious with me. Rosalyn throws tantrums, and Charlotte hasn't spoken to me or written since you left." He moved his hands to unbutton her gown. "The morning I thought you'd sailed out of my life I started drinking and didn't stop until I'd finished two bottles. For three days I had a blistering headache, and Nedda couldn't for the life of her stop banging things." He groaned. "And I can't even begin to tell you about your sisters."

She laughed mildly, a lovely, melodic sound that filled his heart with joy. Cupping her face with his palms, he tilted her head, looking down into beautiful eyes of forgiveness and softness.

"I love you."

Gently she ran her knuckles along his cheek. "I know. I've always known. You are my dream, Brent, and my love. Never doubt that you alone are the center of my life."

He leaned over, brushing his lips back and forth against hers. "And you will always be the light and the hope of mine," he whispered, "my darling, Caroline . . ."

Epilogue

Brent knocked twice, then walked into Baron Sytheford's study, the same study where his life had begun nearly seventeen months before.

"Come in, my boy, come in," Sytheford directed good-naturedly, slowly lifting his sturdy frame from the chair behind his desk. "I was hoping you'd join me for a holiday toast. We haven't talked privately in months, and I'm certain you're getting tired of trying to be heard in a room full of ladies anyway."

Brent chuckled softly and closed the door behind him. "All the other husbands have conveniently disappeared, so I thought I'd do the same."

The baron walked to an oak cabinet, removed two glasses from the top shelf, and reached for a bottle. "Port?"

"Thank you."

Brent walked purposefully to one of the chairs and sat heavily, sinking into the soft leather without concern that he might wrinkle his formal attire. The day had been long, the Christmas dinner would be served shortly, and now seemed the perfect opportunity to have a much thought-out and private discussion with his father-in-law.

"Caroline tells me you're planning a trip to America," Sytheford said jovially, staring at the glasses as he poured.

"We're sailing in April," he replied, "to be gone most of the summer. I want to spend some time with my sister and her husband, meet my new nephew, perhaps see some of the countryside. I might take Caroline to Columbia University if she wants to go."

"Splendid opportunity," Sytheford offered, turning with both drinks in his hands and slowly walking in Brent's direction. "And how are the girls? I haven't seen them much today with all the ladies around."

Brent grinned with fatherly pride. "Rosalyn is learning with remarkable speed. I finally found and hired a governess from Wales who had a deaf child in her charge several years ago. Caroline took to Miss Darcy immediately, teaching her our finger alphabet and the gestures we use to communicate, and the woman is confident Rosalyn will actually start to read soon."

"Read? I would never imagine such a thing as a deaf child reading." Sytheford sat again in his chair, facing him from across the desk. "And how about my grand-babies?"

Brent took a full swallow of the warming, high-quality wine. "The Lady Margaret looks like Caroline, and the Lady Lily looks like me," he boasted, smiling smugly. "And I'm sure they'll be crawling by six months of age."

"Caroline did the same. Perhaps they'll be as gifted."

"I know they'll be as beautiful."

Sytheford softened his voice. "I'm truly glad you came to care for my daughter, Weymerth. You're a fortunate man."

"Indeed," he agreed mildly, grateful for an opening to finally discuss an issue that had been plaguing him for months.

Setting his glass on the desk, he leaned back casually,

eyeing the older man with speculation. "You planned the whole thing, didn't you, Charles?"

The baron lifted his brows almost imperceptibly. "No, I merely carried it through."

That confused him, but he refused to believe that he and Caroline had been thrust together strictly by chance. Caroline didn't believe in such chance happenings either, and as they'd discussed it over the last few weeks, they'd concluded that her father had to have been involved from the beginning. Most convincing was the simple fact that the odds of Caroline marrying Albert Markham's nephew by coincidence were far too incredible.

Sytheford, noticing his hesitation, suddenly grunted and smiled. "Your wife is not my only intelligent daughter, Weymerth." Quietly he revealed, "It was Stephanie's idea."

Brent just stared at him.

Baron Sytheford chuckled, straightening. "My daughters are my darlings, Weymerth, and they all have their different characteristics. Jane is headstrong and independent. Mary Anne is a socializing, heart-stopping enchantress. Caroline is the saucy-mouthed beauty with unsurpassed intelligence. Charlotte tends to be shy and sweet when she's not bringing home a hopeless, three-legged puppy. And Stephanie . . ." He grinned broadly and shook his head. "Stephanie is the schemer who hasn't yet learned to keep her mouth shut."

Brent rubbed his temple with his fingers. "Are you telling me a seventeen-year-old girl held my future in her hands, Charles?"

"She was sixteen at the time," he returned proudly.

"Jesus . . ."

His father-in-law watched him through narrowed eyes for a moment, then lowered his voice to a whisper.

"I'm going to tell you something, Weymerth, that I've never said to another human being. I also trust that it will never leave this room."

"I'm listening," Brent answered quietly.

"I love my daughters immeasurably, all of them, for who they are, but Caroline is and always has been my favorite. Her sisters, every one, took after their mother, a beautiful lady I adored for nearly twenty years. But Caroline was born in my image, different from the others and just like me in personality, appearance, opinions, and way of thinking."

He sat back abruptly and waved his palm. "Oh, I know parents aren't supposed to choose a favorite child, and believe me, it has nothing to do with her intelligence. I would never begin to assume she inherited her brilliant mind from me. But every time I look at her, speak to her, I'm overcome with pride and warmth because I see so much of myself in her."

Brent remained silent and reached for his glass, having no intention of interrupting such an interesting and forthcoming disclosure.

Sytheford sighed. "About two years ago, Stephanie came to me with the news that Caroline was planning to study in New York. Naturally I was infuriated because she'd arranged this without my knowledge or opinion, but I was also horribly upset. Not only would I not see my daughter again for perhaps years, and although she was twenty-five years old and self-sufficient, I was still her father, and my brain was instantly filled with all the horrifying things that could happen to a lady, sheltered for all of her life, when exposed to the realities of living on her own in a strange land where she knew nobody. I absolutely could not let her go, but neither did I know what to do to keep her here."

Suddenly he laughed. "Stephanie has this uncanny ability to know exactly what to say at precisely the right moment, and I'll never forget how she did it that day. She gave me about thirty seconds to absorb the news that my beloved daughter was leaving for America, then slyly, and in a quiet, sneaky voice, said, 'I think I have an idea, Papa.' Just like that. She'd already arranged everything, and I realized immediately that she wouldn't have brought Caroline's plans to my attention at all if she hadn't.''

He took a swallow of his port. "Stephanie began to consider ways to keep Caroline here, and truthfully, at her tender age, I don't believe she could think of anything besides marriage. Because my youngest daughter is quite a social butterfly, she began asking questions about eligible men as she attended various functions. She'd just made her debut, so appearing intrigued about marriageable bachelors was taken for nothing more than innocence. Eventually she learned, from someone or other, that Miss Pauline . . .'' He looked curiously at Brent. "What was her name?''

He swallowed hard to hide his choke of surprise. "Sinclair.''

"Right. Anyway, she learned that Miss Sinclair had recently snubbed''—he tossed him a quick glance—"snubbed is the word she used, Weymerth.''

"I've no doubt,'' he drawled.

Sytheford inhaled deeply. "Well, from this person or that, and very carefully, Stephanie learned that you, the quiet, reserved, former suitor of Miss Sinclair, also happened to be the son of a socially refined woman whose brother was a famous botanist. For a month or so after that, she attended the right parties to learn what she could of you, finding, to her joyful surprise, that not only were you unattached, financially stable, and respectably titled, you were also the nephew of Albert Markham.''

"I don't believe this happened,'' he slowly mumbled with a shake of his head.

Sytheford finished his port, then sat back and grinned in satisfaction. "That's when Stephanie came to me with her idea. At first I had reservations about attempting something that might only, at best, marry my daughter to a man who would never recognize her gifts and beauty, but my choices were, shall we say, quite limited. After days of careful consideration, my concern for Caroline overshadowed my conscience, which told me I should not attempt to manipulate your life, and I decided it couldn't hurt to at least look into the possibility of having you for a son-in-law.''

With a quickness that defied his age and bearing, Baron Sytheford stood and began to pace the room.

"My biggest concern from the start was your involvement in the war. I didn't know what that entailed, or if you'd even come home alive, although finally I had to assume the chances were better that you would return unharmed. At that point I decided to have you investigated—''

"You did what?" he interjected loudly, incredulously.

The man didn't look at him, just crossed his arms over his chest while he walked, head down, at least having the decency to appear embarrassed.

"I apologize, Weymerth, but it was the only way to learn about your character, your . . . personality and beliefs." Quickly he turned and stared at him directly. "Would you have had me learn of these things from a group of unmarried ladies who spend their afternoons gossiping about every unattached bachelor in England? If I didn't do something, Stephanie would have, and her resources were most certainly limited to what was spread around at parties. I think you would agree that I could not afford to give my daughter to an unscrupulous rake."

Brent wiped a palm across his face, and finding he, too, could no longer sit, quickly stood and walked around the desk to the window, placing both palms down on the sill as he stared out to the cold, dormant flower garden beyond.

"Once I knew how well you suited Caroline," Sytheford went on, "and learned you were honorable and educated and came from a respectable family, Stephanie's idea began to take shape in my mind, and I realized it was a good one indeed."

"Didn't my illegitimate daughter concern you?" he asked with underlying cynicism, turning to face the man. "Surely you learned about her in your extensive investigation."

Sytheford snorted. "Rosalyn was the least of my concerns. You aren't the first gentleman to father a child out of wedlock, and I knew such an indiscretion wouldn't faze Caroline in the least. Other ladies might faint from shock, but never her." He shook his head. "No, I was more concerned about you, when you would be home from the war, how to get the two of you to meet, how to arrange a marriage between a man absorbed in work and horses and a woman absorbed in plants."

He stopped in the center of the room, staring at the rugs beneath his feet.

"Finally, in May, two months before you returned, the opportunity I'd been waiting for sort of . . . fell into my lap. I learned from the man I had investigating you that your cousin was under the impression that you'd be coming home shortly and was trying to sell off some of your things. Naturally I was intrigued and arranged a meeting with him immediately."

Sytheford looked up, eyes shining. "I bought it all, Weymerth—furniture, paintings, china, crystal, and the horses. I then sold everything except the horses and deposited all the money anonymously into your bank accounts, which is why you had so much when you returned. You would have been suspicious if I'd purchased only your prized steeds, and in truth I thought redecorating a house might be a way for you and Caroline to have a go at each other from the day of your wedding. This arrangement worked out best for all of us anyway, since I'm certain your cousin would have just sold your belongings to someone else if given the opportunity. I paid him handsomely to lose himself in a crowd of men leaving the country, which he did, and I kept the horses, your most cherished possessions, to use as a bargaining tool for my daughter when you returned. Then I sat back and I waited."

Brent found himself incredibly shaken when Sytheford finished speaking, and not at all sure how he felt. He knew he should be enraged at his father-in-law's gall for purposely changing the course of his life, but he saw a certain wisdom in the man's actions as well. How would he react if one of his daughters were as decisive as Caroline and wanted to do something rash, something that could turn out to be questionable, even harmful?

The answer was very clear. If Caroline had been confronted by her father, she would have been more determined than ever to go through with her plans and wouldn't have stopped for anything or anyone. Brent knew this absolutely. What the baron did was turn the situation around to his, and ultimately Caroline's, advantage by finding her a respectable husband. That this respectable husband happened to be a relation of his daughter's mentor was simply sweet cream for the cobbler. He couldn't tell her because she'd then suspect his manipulation, but he knew she'd eventually learn the truth, and her dream would be in her hands.

No, what the baron did, he did for his daughter, not for himself, regardless of the risks involved and the fact that he'd wanted her to remain in England for selfish reasons. Baron Sytheford had spent an enormous amount of money, had taken a tremendous gamble, for the love and safety of Caroline. And that, Brent had to admit, as deceitful as it all was, was truly the most honorable action he had witnessed from a man in a long time.

"What if I hadn't come home at all?" he finally asked, subdued.

"I don't know," Sytheford admitted honestly. "I suppose I would have confronted Caroline."

"And if Caroline refused to marry me?"

The older man grunted again, walking with purpose to the oak cabinet. "If there was one thing I was absolutely certain of, Weymerth, it was that Caroline would agree to my conditions, planning to annul the marriage."

He blinked hard. "That actually crossed your mind?"

Sytheford turned back to him, smiling, the bottle of port in his hand. "Care for another?"

Brent nodded.

"To answer your question," Sytheford continued

smoothly, pouring two fresh glasses, "I knew Caroline would plan for an annulment because she is smart, can be a bit conniving in her own right, and is the daughter who is most like me. She thinks like I do, Weymerth, and I would have considered the same thing had I been in her position."

Sytheford brought him another half-filled glass, standing beside him as they both turned to look out the window.

"My greatest hope was that you and my daughter would grow to care for each other. But even if that didn't happen, I knew enough about you to know you'd respect her, and that the two of you would, at the very least, get along as well as any married couple of your station."

The baron exhaled loudly. "In the end, when I'd finally decided to force your marriage in such an underhanded fashion, I knew without question that Caroline's will to remain chaste would fail her. She's methodical, resourceful, and sometimes incredibly obstinate, Weymerth, but beneath the skin is a loving, giving woman who, when she met you, desperately needed the companionship of a man. I knew she would eventually succumb to you and honor the marriage vows if you pushed hard enough, and indeed she did because there's the proof."

Brent turned, and out of the garden walked his wife, side by side with Stephanie, one of his baby girls in her arms, the other in her sister's, and Rosalyn skipping along in front of them. They were bundled tightly against the crisp December air, but the sun was shining, and the view of their rosy cheeks and smiling faces was lovely and perfect from where he stood.

The baron dropped his gaze. "If you ever mention this to anyone, Weymerth, I'll deny I said it, but"—he lifted his glass and swallowed the contents—"I never needed a son to feel completely whole as a man, and truthfully I'm quite glad I never had one."

Brent glanced at his father-in-law, more than mildly

surprised to hear such an odd statement from a member of the nobility.

Smiling, Sytheford quietly lowered his voice in retrospection. "If I had sired a boy, I would have spent my life grooming him to be a baron and in many respects, I probably would have neglected my girls. This happens constantly in our class. And I'm certain, over the years, I've been the brunt of jokes and the pity of those men who are so ignorant they can't possibly understand or see the worthiness of the females in their lives."

Gazing back at his daughters, he warmly disclosed, "I can't bestow my title on any of them, but they've all received my support, my guidance, and my love, and I know there is no man alive with five sons and no daughters who could be any more proud of what his children have become."

Brent looked back at Caroline, his beautiful babies, his sweet daughter who'd been accepted into his wife's family as if she were one of them. When he'd married her, the only thing he'd wanted from the union was a son, and although there was merit to the fact that males alone inherited titles and property, he now understood the shallowness of the desire. His world was rich with happiness and completely fulfilling as it was right now, and if there was one thing he knew as absolute truth, it was the worthiness of the females in his life.

"Well said, Charles," he whispered. "Well said."

Author's Note

I took some liberty writing a story about a woman scholar in early nineteenth-century England. Caroline attempted to study at a university, but this really would never have been tolerated during her time, and certainly not at Oxford. It's true that some American universities, before the twentieth century, permitted a few brave women to stand outside classrooms and listen as Caroline did, but such allowances were extremely rare, even for the gifted.

A note of appreciation to Claudia Canady, Ph.D., for a wealth of information about speech-language development and the behavior of children with hearing impairments.